Darby Cox

A DAY OF BREATH

ANGRY ROBOT
An imprint of Watkins Media Ltd

Unit 11, Shepperton House
89-93 Shepperton Road
London N1 3DF
UK

angryrobotbooks.com
A deep exhale.

An Angry Robot paperback original, 2026

Edited by Desola Coker and Travis Tynan
Cover illustration by Morgaine Magloire
Cover design by Sarah O'Flaherty
Author photo © Veronica Lescallette
Set in Meridien

ISBN 978 1 8367 3002 6
Ebook ISBN 978 1 83673 003 3

Printed and bound in the United Kingdom by CPI Group (UK) Ltd, Croydon CR0 4YY

The manufacturer's authorised representative in the EU for product safety is eucomply OÜ - Pärnu mnt 139b-14, 11317 Tallinn, Estonia, hello@eucompliancepartner.com; www.eucompliancepartner.com

9 8 7 6 5 4 3 2 1

PROLOGUE

"On your knees, Champion."

The sibyl herself stands right in front of me, her voice floating through a mask of gold chainmail, the holes as small as the eyes of needles. I can only make out hints of her face – or it may be my imagination. I place where eyes should be, a nose, cheeks, a mouth, repeating her request.

But I can't move. I know what lowering to my knees means. Tears drip from my chin, landing on my chest. The throne room, with its towering ceiling and rows of arched windows revealing the late-night sky, begins to blur. Guards lining the walls wear polished silver and gold-plated armor, green and gold stitched tabards lain over their torsos. My parents are nearby, close enough to watch, but not close enough to dare equalize themselves with the sibyl, a servant of the almighty creator, Yuli-en. The sovereigns face me from their embellished thrones atop a dais, pride painted over their faces. Their twin heirs are silent beside them.

Heir Fallon glances between me and the sibyl, his expression frozen in awe at what is meant to be the most honored moment of my life, while Heir Abner stares intently at the sibyl, their mouth drawn in a tight line. When Heir Fallon's eyes catch mine, I quickly look away. Like most our age, I've always harbored a silly crush on him. God beyond, what if he has to watch me vomit all over the throne room's pristine runner? Trembling in my sleepwear, and one year shy of graduating from the Academy of the Guard, it's clear I'm the least powerful person in this room.

And yet, I'm the one the sibyl chose to drink the Blessing she holds in her hands. A mere speck of Yuli-en's power. I'll be given strength, speed, and healing abilities – the powers of the Champion. Then I'll be sent to the Edge, far from the city, to kill demons on my own.

There's no higher honor, yet all I want to do is run from the palace as far as my legs will take me. Where could I go? The academy won't accept a deserter. Mother and father won't allow me back home. They would hand me over to the guards themselves, horrified and ashamed, even if it meant a death sentence.

Mother and I lock eyes and I plead to her silently. *Please, please don't let this happen. Please.* She smiles back.

There's no life in me to scream. Even to glare. An unsettling sensation roams over my bones, like a humming. Anxiety churns my stomach and I swallow a mass of bile trying to claw its way up my throat.

"Do you deny this oath?" the sibyl asks. Her voice is smooth, almost melodic. I wish I could see her face, know what expression someone might wear as they grant godly power, but sibyls traditionally cloak their entire bodies.

I try to speak, to ask how Yuli-en could have chosen me. The academy ranked me middle of my class: a decent fighter but not a leader. Captains and generals don't need morning tablets to calm their rattling nerves. There must be someone stronger. This has to be a mistake.

"To your knees, Champion," the sibyl demands again. "Time is being wasted."

A guard, one of the two who escorted me from the academy dorms, lays a hand on my shoulder and presses down. My knees bend, feeble as a flower's stem. When they touch the pale gold runner I begin to sob uncontrollably. I couldn't be anymore shameful.

The sibyl bends down to me, holding out a bronze bowl. It's now close enough so I can see the burned etchings across the surface. Yuli-en and their shadow, the other god we don't speak of, Istral. While Yuli-en is pure goodness and light, Istral is the darkness. It's understood Yuli-en couldn't truly kill Istral, as light can only exist in opposition to darkness, so they banished Istral to their own realm with their monstrous demon abominations – countless eons before the world I know existed. But twenty years ago, a rift opened between our world and Istral's. And that's why I'm here.

"Please, don't," I whisper. Immediately, my muscles clench. Yuli-en doesn't make mistakes. Their sibyl doesn't make mistakes. I pray neither heard what fear has wrenched from me.

The second guard reaches down to grip my jaw and tilts my head up. His leather gloves are harsh against my skin, so I don't try to fight.

The sibyl rests the bowl's cold rim on my lip. Black liquid quivers inside, thick like stew, and reeks of something I can't describe. Against my will, I shudder. I flick my hot and weary eyes up at her. For a moment, I wonder if she'll smite me. She gives no reaction. A wave of movement travels through her veil like wind through a field of golden wheat as she tips the bowl. It presses against my lips, forcing me to open my mouth. Yuli-en's power slides over my tongue and drops down my throat in clumps. My throat tries to close, squeezing on the warm, bitter liquid, but I feel it travel into my stomach where it settles into a heavy, nauseating pool. When the bowl is finally empty, the sibyl straightens. She steps back as the two guards pull me to my feet.

I let my head hang for a moment, hoping the nausea will fade. Trails of the Blessing run down my lips and neck, staining the collar of my shirt black. Remembering where I am, I lift my head. All eyes in the throne room weigh on me, watching, as though they're waiting for something. I don't know what's supposed to happen next. Will my arms suddenly bulge with muscle? Should I feel like the sun itself is blazing inside of me? I scour my body in my mind, searching for some kind of change, but nothing comes. I'm still just a trembling girl on legs I'm scared won't be able to hold me much longer.

The sovereigns step down from their thrones and come to stand beside the sibyl. They smile warmly, with what feels like adoration. I know I should acknowledge them, but I look to my parents. Mother and father hold each other, their attention firmly on the sovereigns, tears collecting on their eyelashes. I inhale so sharply, my sternum feels as though it caves in, burying my heart beneath shards of bone. They're not crying because their only child is being sent to fight demons and may never return; they cry because of the prestige our family's name will hold for the rest of their lives.

"You have nothing to worry for, Champion. Your family will be well taken care of," Sovereign Adelaide says. She mistakes the way I stare at my parents as concern for their well-being.

"Oly Hoskins, on this night you have been granted the highest honor in Niawa's history," Sovereign Gerves says, his voice booming through the cavernous hall. "The Champion has fallen, and Yuli-en has chosen you to take his place. We honor you, and we thank you, for keeping our people safe."

"It's time, Champion. We wish you a safe journey. Our love is with you, always," the sibyl finishes.

Panic grips me. I throw my gaze toward anyone who might understand. *Please, will someone stop this?* Salutes of respect, smiles, and slight nods are what I get in return. The guards turn my body around, my feet stumbling, and guide me out of the throne room. Several more guards follow us out, bordering me like a cage, their spears and swords brandished high like a royal procession. I don't stop looking over my shoulder until we've gone through the palace's front doors and down the steps, into the late night.

They herd me past the stone wall surrounding the palace into an expansive, circular space paved in cobblestone. In this courtyard, I've seen grand carriages from visiting kingdoms, and large crowds gathered to celebrate Champions when they return home. Lively, loud, and colorful moments. Tonight, it's stark and nearly empty. Only two guards on horses and a lone cart wait in the center, making the circle seem as large as the sea. Metal encases the cart's body and wheels. Deep scratches carve along one side, resembling claw marks. An old woman sits on the driver's bench under the yellow glow of lanterns fastened to metal brackets. When we approach, she moves aside, making space for me.

My cage opens and the guards flow into two perfectly straight rows of silvered bodies, creating a path to the cart. Without the shuffle of their armor, it becomes eerily silent.

If I don't sit on that bench, the sovereigns will have me executed. If I do, demons will soon tear me to pieces. Though the choice has already been made for me, I falter.

"We must be on our way, dear," the old woman says.

With shaking breaths, I walk the path, catching envious looks through the eye vents of the guard's helmets, then climb onto the bench.

The old woman doesn't wait. She doesn't ask if I'm ready, or if I want to say any more goodbyes – not that it would matter. At the academy, I struggled to talk to the other trainees, much less make friends. Being the Champion may be the first time any of them learnt my name. First, the mounted guards ride on ahead, then the old woman steers her horses to face the main road cutting through the city, and we go – through the home I will never see again, beneath the portcullis, and out into Niawa's lands.

The Edge is many hours from the city, and now, there's no Champion to oppose the demons. I may even face one on the way there. My heart thunders at the possibility.

A black sky blankets above, both smothering and far too vast to bear. I can't help but search for the dark wings of a demon to appear and blot out the stars. Like most, I've only seen the creatures in drawings during lessons. Even on paper, they're terrifying and numerous in kind: Winged Hands, large demons with legs that look like thick fingers protruding from its body; Burrowers, toad-like monsters that keep low to the ground and have wide eyes that seem to ooze off their faces; Gargantuans, massive, scaly things with long, wispy wings that shockingly support their weight in flight; Yellow Biles, ones that make up for their smaller size by spitting acidic mucus that burns through skin in seconds. More of the recorded demons fill my mind, but I fight to push them out.

"Your weapons are in the back," the old woman yells over the pounding of the horses' hooves and the rocking cart. When I don't respond, she adds, "What's your name?"

I shake my head and wrap my arms around myself.

After a short time, she tries again. "Mine is Velma. We'll be seeing each other every month, so I thought we should introduce ourselves. I'm the courier, and the guards with us are my escorts. I'll be bringing your supplies." She winks at me.

"Oly," I reply reluctantly.

She nods and flicks the reins. The horses speed up. In the covered bed, I hear heavy items shift and rattle. *My* weapons, she said. Another honor that feels like it belongs to someone else.

"You're young for a Champion. I've sadly seen younger in my time, but not many. How old are you?" Velma asks.

"Sixteen."

Her head whips towards me. Sadness layers over her eyes in wrinkled folds. She opens her mouth to speak but seems to think better of it. We both know Yuli-en has their reasons for who is chosen, and they don't owe us mortals an explanation. Nothing can be done, so we watch the road ahead in silence.

Time takes no pity on me and before long, Edge Forest closes in on the road. Around a bend, the shroud of trees pulls back as abruptly as it appeared, revealing a wide field. Tall, dark cliffs rise at the far end. My eyes trail the rocky crag to the top where a dark, towering shape erupts from the cliffs as if it means to pierce the sky. It's too dark to make out, but I know that scars rake across the shape's face. The Rive. The portal allowing demons to slither into our world, aching to kill and destroy.

I'm suddenly consumed by a fantasy of throwing myself from the bench, hoping the fall will crack open my head. At least then I will have control over my death.

The cart and escorts finally stop, but Velma doesn't release the reins. She lays them across her lap with one hand. The other she uses to point past me. "Your cabin is over there."

A short walk away, into the tall grass, is another black shape, its edges traced by the moonlight's faint silver halo. This is where the Champions live out the rest of their lives.

The escorts descend from their saddles and walk to the back of the cart. I hear them open the doors. They come back around, both holding wooden crates, and continue carrying them towards the cabin.

"It's time, Oly," Velma says.

Her expression is stern, but she can't fix the worry in her eyes. I knit my eyebrows together, hoping she'll cave. Maybe I can convince her to take me somewhere else. Anywhere but here. She can just tell the sovereigns and my parents I died on the way from a heart attack. I'll promise to never return to Niawa. Velma shakes her head, her answer clear: This is where we part. Wordlessly, I slide from the bench to the ground. My ankles shake, threatening to buckle under my weight, so I hold tightly to the cart.

"Champion," the courier urges.

"Will you walk to the cabin with me?"

Her lips droop into a frown that is saturated with pity. "I can't, dear. My rolling chair wouldn't do well on the field." I crinkle my face in response, and Velma adds, "But I will see you in a couple days with more supplies, and every month after. Now, you need to hurry. Your armor and weapons are in the cabin, and you'll be needing those at any moment."

One by one, I release my fingers from the edge of a metal slat. Wringing my hands, I take a small step back. The humming surges, reminding me of something gravely important. "My tablets, for my nerves… Are they here? I need them," I ask in a small voice.

Velma nods. "Yes, the academy healer made sure of it."

It's a tiny comfort, but one I grasp onto as I follow the escort's path into the tall grass. A full moon hangs overhead, but it does little to illuminate my way, despite a well-trodden trail. Items litter the dirt, causing me to stumble. I can hardly tell what they are until I'm upon them: shields, armor, weapons, and bones. Some are clearly human – remnants of the bloody war from when the Rive first appeared – and the realization sends shivers up my spine. But I would rather focus on the horrors at my feet than the one over the cliffs.

When I reach the cabin, the escorts stand in the doorway, their backs to me. The wooden crates they brought sit on the ground. They look over their shoulders as I step into the light of two lanterns hanging over the door, casting an orange glow on their armor.

Peeking into the gap between them, my eyes land on a naked body. The Champion before me lays on the floor, a long blade protruding from his chest. Countless thin books are sprawled beneath him. Some lay open, dried blood browning the pages and already staining the floor. His open green eyes stare blankly at the ceiling.

I struggle to breathe. A tight pressure wraps around my head. If a demon didn't kill him, and there is no one else at the Edge, then he must have done this himself.

The escorts swoop upon the body. They first remove the blade, then pick him up by his arms and feet before carrying him out the door. At the last second, I break free from my stunned body and shift out of the way.

I don't watch them haul the former Champion away, though I know they'll take his body to the cart so his family can bury him – if they choose to. The shame they'll endure learning he abandoned his duty will be unimaginable.

A faint noise sounds from nearby, like a low squeak. I crank my back to see the Rive. It's still a silent, black tower. Everything is so dark here, except for the cabin's dimly lit interior. So I go into the light, making sure not to walk through the fresh blood that was hidden under the former Champion's body, or disturb the mess of books.

The cabin is even smaller than it looked from the outside. A bed against the wall occupies much of the left side, with a small table and chair beside it. They seem to be made of the same dark wood as the walls, ceiling, and floor. A large window faces the bed and table, taking up the entire wall to the right of the door. Through it, I clearly see the demon portal's shape against the sky. To the left of the door, two tapestries hang from the wall: one of Niawa's crest in green and gold, the other of the sibyl. Even woven in thread, her golden veil shines.

Though I turn away from the tapestries, I feel her presence linger on my back.

A few feet from the table, an iron hearth sits close to the right wall. Rows of hooks are fastened to the wall, holding plates of the Champion's armor and numerous weapons. Beside the hooks is a small room with only a bronze tub. I walk quietly to the room as though the former Champion still lives here and I'm disturbing his privacy. If I were to lay in this tub, another large window would allow the Rive to stare down at me.

This shelter was built to make sure the Champion can never escape it.

The escorts return, bringing more crates which are set beneath the iron hooks.

"Champion, we need to measure you," one says.

They beckon me from the washroom to stand in the middle of the cabin. One lifts my arms and runs a measuring spool across my shoulders. The other pulls a folded piece of paper and a charcoal pencil from a pouch on his belt. He scribbles quickly as the other calls out numbers.

"In two days, we'll return with armor fitted to you. For now, wear the armor here," the scribbling escort says, stuffing the paper and pencil back in his belt. Then they both begin to leave.

"Wait," I yell. The sound pings between the walls and I wince. "Wait, please," I whisper. "Can you bring me something when you come back?" They stop just outside the door. "In my room at the academy, there's a green bowl. I didn't have a chance to grab it."

"Whatever you wish," the escort with the measuring spool answers.

Long after they close the door, long after the sounds of hooves and spinning wheels vanish, I stand in the same spot, in the center of the cabin, watching the Rive through the window. Quiet wraps so thick around me not even my breath penetrates it.

Soon, demons will find the rift between our worlds, and they'll come after me. The Blessing doesn't only bestow strength and healing, but also the Trace: a magical pull that attracts the creatures. Tears rush fresh down my cheeks as I imagine myself running and hiding, knowing it doesn't matter where I go. There is no escape.

I look at the blood on the floor and the sharp blade that minutes ago protruded from the former Champion's chest.

Maybe there is a way out.

I rush to the wall of weapons and armor and the crates set beneath them. There are too many weapons to choose from. Swords of multiple lengths, scythes, axes, spears, and flails. A few of the crates are already popped open, revealing rows of glass orbs with colored powder inside. Special magic orbs that the sibyl herself creates for the Champion. I'm far too scared to touch those.

Desperation courses through my blood, pushing me towards the sharpest-looking weapon – a double-headed axe. The steel is thick, the blade impossibly keen, and the long staff is wide. It looks far too heavy, but it will kill me quickly.

The axe comes down from its hook like it weighs no more than a feather. Overcompensating for the weight I expected, I nearly throw it over my shoulder and stumble backwards.

"The Blessing," I gasp.

My fear, the humming, every thought of death gives way to a sudden surge of strength. It moves through every inch of me, like a storm that commands the awe of everyone in its path.

I grip the axe with fingers that had been trembling since the throne room. At the academy sparring grounds, I always chose the wooden staff because it was light and easy. The metal weapons made me too nervous. Slowly, I swing the weapon around, expecting my muscles to wither under its weight, but I control it with ease. In disbelief, I slash through the air with more urgency.

The blade swipes along the hearth, sending a violent vibration up my arms, but I don't let go. My grasp is strong and sure. I have never felt anything like this.

Eager to explore this power, I bring the sharp blade to the inside of my forearm and press it to my skin. As a line of blood runs along the metal, I hiss. New skin grows over the cut quick as a blink, the pain fleeing as if it never appeared.

Mother and father's faces drift into my mind. Always sullen, irritated, disappointed. It was my uncontrollable nerves that made them send me to the academy. By the time I was twelve, they had given up hope that I would grow to look people in the eyes and speak with confidence. To them, becoming a guard would forge them a stronger daughter.

Laughter bubbles in my chest, coming out of my throat in dry heaves as I imagine what they would think of me now. How their eyes would bug out of their heads as I walked up to them in the Champion's armor, towering and stronger than they could ever dream of. I drop the axe beneath the rows of hooks, my mind now on the armor plates. I pull down the closest one, a shin guard. Turning it over in my hands, I inspect the thick leather lining the underside of a nearly translucent white, quartz-like material. Demon teeth. One of the Champion's tasks is to collect the creature's fangs so they can be made into armor.

Eagerly, I strap the plate to my leg with its leather buckles. Then I take down another plate, and another – grieves, a breast plate, gauntlets, all similar to a guard's set that I was taught to assemble – and fasten them to my body. The finished suit is slightly too big, but I can still move freely.

The last piece is a helmet. It's shaped like an exaggerated skull with thin bars covering the mouth. The demon teeth weren't smoothed down like the armor, giving the helmet a crude, stone-like texture. I slip it over my head before returning the axe to my hands, already missing the feel of it.

The floorboards whine as I walk across the cabin and plant myself in front of the big window. At first, I look everywhere but at the Rive. I look to the rocky cliffs and pallid field beneath. To the night sky behind. Then I fix my eyes on it.

My breaths don't slow and my head grows fuzzy, tingling beneath the helmet.

For the first time since being dragged into the throne room, I'm curious to find out if I stand a chance.

CHAPTER 1

The cabin door gives way when I shove my shoulder against it, its hinges whistling into the silence. As it bangs against the wall, I hobble inside, dragging my bloody leg. In the dim light I forget about the caved-in plank of wood by the door and stagger over it.

"Gah." Pain shoots up my injured thigh. The doorframe barely breaks my fall, my fingers grappling at the wood.

Huffing, I flop my back against the door to shut it. The frame helps me on my way to the ground. Over my shoulder, the sibyl's woven tapestry watches in shame at her Champion crawling to a chair. I keep my gaze to the floor, pressing my sore hands and aching knees into the wood.

When I reach the chair, I look up with a groan. It may as well be a mountain's peak. The wood digs into days-old burns across my palms as I pull myself up, pushing air between my teeth. These are the same hands that once ripped the jaw of a Winged Hand clean from its thick neck.

"Can't even tear the tail off a Singed Fox now," I grunt, settling into the chair. My head throbs as I pull off my helmet and tug my fingers free of my gloves. They hit the ground with a splat, wet from demon blood and sweat. Blood pools around my gums from a cut in my cheek, which I spit onto the floor.

If I wasn't the Champion, if there wasn't an open portal to the demon's realm across the field, I'd let my limbs sigh and loosen, hanging like cooked noodles. For a small moment, I consider it.

Anger flares in my gut and I slam my boot into the floor, rattling the table behind me and the medical supplies strewn across the top of it.

"Do you want to die? Let these thoughts guide you to the cliffs and walk into the Rive, then. End it all now!" I shout at the ceiling.

Through the window, the Rive watches. Any moment it will tremble and pulse with red light, and more demons will spew from the long scars across its face. There's no time to waste. The portal won't wait for me to heal, to catch my breath.

My leg needs to be fixed. From the top of my thigh to a few inches above my knee, a gash splits my skin – and ruins a good pair of trousers. Fresh blood gurgles up, obscuring how deep the wound goes. I sink two fingers into the red puddle, slowly pressing until I reach bone. Sudden, blinding pain makes me jerk my fingers back out.

"Be more calculating if you can't be quicker."

I twist to grab a rag from the tabletop, then stuff it into the deep wound. Once the cloth's off-white color is taken completely by red, I replace it with another. Six bloody rags later, the bleeding lessens to a faint pink trickle. The last one is tossed over my shoulder with the rest. I watch as tendons and muscle slowly weave back together over my exposed bone. Far too slowly.

A year ago, the Blessing would have given me new skin in minutes. Often, I wouldn't even return to my cabin, just wait in the field for another creature, hungry for my next fight. But the healing has slowed, along with my strength. Yellow and violet bruises now flower across my skin, tender beneath my armor. My knees sting with every quick movement. My arms tire quickly from wielding heavy weapons that once felt like extensions of my limbs.

After ten years at the Edge, the Blessing is fading.

I glance at the Rive again. It's still, but my muscles don't relax. I don't know how long it'll take for this new wound to heal, the skin split open like a shallow ravine.

I'll admit, the Spiky Lizard tonight surprised me. While the barbs along its forearms demanded my concentration, its spiked tail thrashed at my head. My feet slipped along loose rocks causing me to land on my rear. That may have saved me from decapitation, but the demon still took hold of my shin and dragged me like a sack of waste. My tasset tore off, allowing a particularly sharp boulder to carve through my thigh.

From the table I grab a glass jar of starmoss and slather the pungent brown paste with small white specks over the gash. Then I wrap strips of linen tightly around my leg, allowing the paste to clot my blood quicker. Hopefully, I won't need needle and thread. Watching the Rive, my mind reels over all the sutures I've performed recently. The many jars of starmoss I've emptied. Yards of linen used to wrap wounds. The stink of infected flesh in my nostrils as the Blessing worked too slowly.

"Stop it," I snap. Champions don't whimper and dwell.

Nodding to myself, I focus on checking the armor and weapons on my body, making note of what I'll need to add to my list for Velma. "Missing a tasset. Straps on the shoulder plates are wearing thin. A crack on the left shin plate." I bring the axe strapped across my back to my eyeline. "Looks good, still sharp." I glance at an empty sheath on my hip. "But I left a short sword behind." A sour odor like spoiled milk wafts up from my leather neck guard, crinkling my nose. "Double the soaps and oils."

Still no movement from the Rive.

I tip my chin to the portal – a thanks for allowing me some time – then lay my axe on the floor and push off the chair to stand. The thigh wound pains like the sting of my mother's palm against my cheek. With careful steps, I test movement by pacing the short distance from one end of my cabin to the other. Then I sprint. Though I don't crash to the floor, my movements are jerky. "Right. I'll only run if I need too." I jump and land on a shaky ankle. "Let's go light on the jumping."

The portal is motionless, but anxiety still crawls up my back. To replace my missing and cracked plates, I have to turn away from it. My feet become stone, unable to move.

"You're wasting time!" I yell.

With great effort, I pull myself from the window and go to the wall of hooks. Buckling a tasset to my injured thigh makes me grimace, so I do it slower than I should. The other weakened or lost plates I fasten quicker to make up for lost time. My eyes catch moonlight flooding into my small washroom, bathing my tub in a heavenly glow. I've only taken a handful of proper baths at the Edge. The last time was a mistake that nearly cost my life when I couldn't pull my clothing on fast enough before a Gargantuan reached the cabin. I barely managed to kill the thing with half my armor on and no helmet. Washing has since become wiping eucalyptus oil-stained rags across my limbs, teeth, and between my legs, with as much clothing and armor on as I can.

Urgency grips me by the neck, and I finish outfitting myself. It's already been too long since I checked the Rive.

On my way back to the chair, I eye the stale corner of a stove-top loaf I made four days ago. I start to pass it, but my stomach rumbles. Quickly, I grab it from the stove and finish it off as I sit. The bread is hard and stabs into my gums. Swallowing is no easier.

"Shit." I forgot to grab a fresh pair of gloves. Leaving the window again feels impossible, so I slip on the blood-soaked pair from the floor before putting my helmet back on.

A shadow dashes across the sky.

I shoot to my feet. Warmth erupts from a sharp pinch in my lower back and spreads. Ignoring the twinge, along with the rest of the creaks, groans, and spasms throughout my body, I race to the door. The bones in my hand grind into the axe staff, the floorboards shake with the slamming of my boots. I fling the door open.

A small shape soars across the Rive's blackness as if it came from within. The bird spreads its wings and continues on its journey to the sea.

Panting, I return to the chair, leaving the door open. If I concentrate on the pounding in my temples, count them one by one, I won't think about the exhaustion plaguing my body. Sleep is hard to come by at the Edge. A few uninterrupted hours here and there is all I can be grateful for.

One… two… three…

My eyelids grow heavy. I slump over.

No. I have to stay alert.

Nine… ten–

A guttural screech tears me from a half-sleep.

"Wildberries for breakfast. Draw water. Organize items. Wildberries for breakfast. Draw water. Organize items."

Aches riddle my back from sitting in the chair. If I laid in bed, I would wake up too groggy and unfocused. I lift my hands to rub my hot, tired eyes, and knock them against my helmet. Images of the battle last night play in my mind, so I keep it on. Demon teeth wrapped around my head several times, the scraping still ringing in my ears. I favored one leg over the other. My hands shook from holding my axe too hard, fearing it would be knocked away. My footwork was sloppy from caution while the Yellow Bile flung its stinking, poisonous mucus.

"Wildberries for breakfast. Draw water. Organize items. Wildberries for breakfast. Draw water. Organize items."

Reciting my tasks for the day has become a tactic for staving off tiredness. It works less and less.

For hours, I've watched the sun grow from an orange haze outlining the cliffs to a brilliant golden chariot, pulling the deep blue sky behind it. Chores are best done in the full daylight, so I wait for the early afternoon when the sun hangs just above the Rive.

There was once a clock in my cabin. The Champion before me destroyed it in a fit of rage he dubbed "the cursing of his life." I read that in the journals he left behind. Some were still legible, even stained with his blood. For weeks I left them on the floor, occasionally skimming through the pages when I grew bored. He lasted three seasons. His mind slowly eroded until being the Champion became too much, and he wrote his goodbyes. One entry still revisits me. He damned the sibyl, Yuli-en, and the royal family. To him, being the Champion was nothing more than a human sacrifice.

He didn't understand. We are chosen above all others. Truly seen by Yuli-en and the sibyl as more than we are. More than meek, nerve-wracked children terrified of the world outside their bedroom.

After reading that entry, I stuffed the journals away into a chest beneath the floorboards that I had unearthed one night. The chest already contained knitting tools, painting supplies, books, and other distractions that must have aided in the deaths of the Champions before him.

I only asked for one thing to be brought to the Edge: my green bowl from the academy's dining pavilion. The dishes were either a muted gray that always made me feel heavy and melancholy, or a pale, gentle green. The color makes me think of waves breaking against the shore, just before they pull back into the tide. The bold, azure blue of the sea vanishing into the softest shade of jade. It feels like exhaling every time I look at it. And it reminds me of the rare times my parents took me to Niawa's eastern beach near the city. I loved sitting quietly in the sand beside them. There, under the open sky, it was okay for me not to speak. We just enjoyed the breeze and soft lulls of the ocean together.

The bowl now sits in plain view on the shelves beside the hearth. I don't want it here after I die. It will be buried with me. The next Champion won't think I lost my way like the others.

Yawning, I straighten myself.

"Wildberries for breakfast. Draw water. Organize items. Wildberries for breakfast. Draw water. Organize items."

Finally, the sun rests beside the Rive and I push off the chair to stand. Agony spreads from my thigh, bleeding into my hip, and I flop back onto the chair. I huff sharply, snot flecking my lips. It should be fully healed by now, nothing but a line of pale skin. Cold sweat breaks across my neck as I unbuckle my tasset with clumsy fingers. It drops to the floor with a clunk. After grabbing a small blade from my belt, I slice through the bandaging and hardened starmoss with jagged pulls.

A hard lump grows in my throat. Pink skin still shiny with fluid covers the wound. I press the edge of the knife to it with hardly any pressure. It tears like wet paper and blood bubbles out. My jaw pops as I grind my teeth against the pain.

"God, no."

Moisture slicks over my palms, pasting my gloves to my hands. My throat is dry and tight. Suddenly, I can't get a full breath. I grip my knees as hard as I can, hoping the strain in my forearms will bring me calm.

It isn't working.

The humming grows inside me, from the low crooning I have known all my life to a vibration that rakes against every nerve. I dig my fingers deeper, mirroring the tightness in my jaw.

It still isn't working.

Heaviness presses on my chest. I can't breathe. I gulp down air like a fish forced to the surface. The fight to stand nearly brings me back down again, my legs trembling. The humming fights to overpower my will. It throttles my brain until all I wish is to shrink, becoming as small as I possibly can.

I limp to the shelves by the hearth and sweep through my medical supplies. Glass bottles crash to the floor. Metal tins bounce against the wood and roll away.

"Where is it?" The shelves are nearly empty and my heart pounds mercilessly.

I scour the mess of vials, tins, and boxes on the floor. Tucked just behind the table leg is a small glass tube with a cork top. Tears swell in the corners of my eyes by the time I rip off the cork and swallow one of the compact cubes of green herbs and leaves inside. It'll be some time before the tablets can thwart the anxiety, and waves of nausea will accost me all morning from taking one without breakfast, but the familiar herbal taste on my tongue pulls me back from the edge.

I flatten my palms on the tabletop, clenching my eyes shut as a scream fills my skull. I won't let it reach my throat. I suck in air, then push it out until my lungs feel deflated. Over and over. Eventually, my heart starts to thump to a manageable rhythm, allowing me to open my eyes.

"Enough," I snarl to my tingling hands.

The Rive has gone unchecked far too long. Still, I linger, balling and loosening my fists, waiting for my anger to vanish. The demons may be stronger than me now, but I still have my wits. That is how I'll survive.

After ensuring the portal is still, I go to collect the tossed medical supplies, stacking them back onto the shelves in no particular order. I leave my tablets on the table.

"Wildberries for breakfast," I order myself.

My mouth immediately waters. Beside the hearth are the dishes and pantry food. I grab my green bowl, a jar of wine-colored berries, and a jar of dried beef. Back on the chair, I slide one of the salty meat strips between my teeth. As I chew, I pull numbing cream from the mess on the tabletop and apply a thick layer to the pink skin of my thigh. Before it dries, I bandage it again. Dull throbs persist, but the numbing cream hushes them. I've grown used to nagging discomfort and whispers of pain, so I will just keep applying numbing cream until it heals.

If it ever heals.

In all my lessons, I'd never heard of a fading Blessing. Perhaps after me, the instructors will speak of it. How the longest-living Champion survived without Yuli-en's power. Or how she died the moment it disappeared.

"Are we not meant to outlive it?" I direct my question to the sibyl's tapestry, then immediately feel guilt. She has already given the most incredible gift. I need to be grateful. What is supposed to come, will come.

And yet. Thoughts of my death – what it will look like, how it may feel, what demon will sink its teeth into my flesh for the last time, how I will be remembered – play in my head with each wrap of the linen until my thigh is fully covered. Little red spots seep through, but they don't meet.

"Wildberries for breakfast."

Inside the wildberry jar, a silver spoon coated in dark juices rests against the glass. I scoop heaps of the fruit into my bowl, then top the fruit with several strips of dried meat. The afternoon sun beams through the window as I spoon the berries into my mouth with the beef, my tongue twitching at the sweetness and saltiness. As I eat, the Rive doesn't move. Soon my bowl is empty, and my fingers are covered in juice. I lick them clean, leaving behind faint purple stains.

"Draw water."

Two buckets sit by the hearth, both holding brown, stagnant water. I bring them to the door and set them down. The well is outside, a short walk towards Edge Forest, where the vast northern river splits into a brook that winds into the Edge.

I'll need to replenish my magic weapons first. Lately, I've had to rely on them more than steel. Coming to my haunches, I examine the crates holding the glass orbs with colored powder. I glance down at the belt around my waist made to hold them. The battle last night cost me an ice bomb, two fire bombs, and a holy flare. Holy flares aren't as destructive as bursts of ice and fire, but they'll blind a demon with a flash of white light long enough to make an attack.

I reach for an orb containing violet powder, then pause to listen. A low whistle sounds from the door.

"Too windy for poison bombs," I say, remembering the day I had melted my skin when I crushed one too close to my face. The edge of the noxious cloud that erupted rode an errant breeze to whip against my cheek. Pus and boils covered the entire right side of my face, and I coughed clumps of bloody mucus for hours.

I pocket two holy flares instead.

After checking the Rive, I pull a clean helmet down from the hooks, one that doesn't reek of sweat. The well-broken leather inside sends tingles over my scalp as I slide it on; it's one reason I keep it shaved. The other is the time a Winged Hand took a chunk of my hair between its sharp teeth of and ripped the strands clean from my skin.

Satisfied, I secure my axe to my back, grab the buckets, and step outside.

The field between my cabin and the cliffs seem to stretch for miles, but I know I can run the length in short time. Before the Rive, I imagine the field was beautiful, an expanse of soft green fur. What surrounds me now is barren, scorched ground with pockets of wilted grass. Rusted shields and weapons, human and demon bones alike litter the landscape. The Edge is a graveyard from the War of Red River, waged against the portal when it first appeared twenty years ago. Gallons of blood were spilt, and the northern river ran pink with death for days.

The sky has never changed. Most days it's a perfect, cloudless blue. I look up, knowing in a few days, Yuli-en's Eye will be streaking across from the west. The comet appears on the day the almighty god left their mortal form to live in the god's realm. They return to see the world they created, then disappear at the day's end. No demons come through the portal as long as the god's eye is present. Niawa calls this brief moment of peace the Day of Breath and celebrates with a day of festivities. It's expected that the Champion returns to the city so they can be paraded around and showered with gifts.

I have never returned, and I never will. At the Edge, I don't have to prove my strength to anyone. The demons come and I send their souls back to their world. This is who I am now. There's no reason to endure my parents' probing eyes as they try to find their daughter beneath my armor. Even more, I fear they will find her. Especially now with the Blessing fading.

Beyond my cabin, a series of trodden paths wind out into the field in all directions. Many towards the Rive, others towards Edge Forest, and one towards the dirt road leading out of the Edge. I take one of the paths to the forest. The former Champions mapped it well, ensuring the Rive always stays in sight. There's not one movement I won't catch, even out of the corner of my eye.

I soon spot signs the well is near. Thick bushes with dark green leaves sprout from the ground, glistening with beads of wildberries. It's the middle of the warm season, and they are ripe and sweet, ready to be picked off the branch and popped into my mouth. A shallow brook runs between them and clusters of small white flowers. The well stands beside the brook, a column of stacked stone and wood.

Somehow, this small area was spared from the destruction of the war. As if the sibyl knew I was coming and protected it, so on the Day of Breath it could offer rare moments where I lie on my back and listen to the water trickle.

I come up to the well and set the pails on the lip. An iron hook on rope suspends from an arch over the top, which I hang the first pail on. I slacken the rope until the pail dips into the underground river.

Light breezes bring a tart scent across my nose and I suck in the air, savoring it. Lemon reeds. Tall, yellow stalks that seep juice when chewed on. There's a group of them nearby, nestled amongst the wildberry bushes.

"Draw water," I remind myself. Rest is a poison. It starts with meandering through the lemon reeds, and it ends with hesitating when a demon barrels down on me.

The rope sways, the pail pulling it to and fro in the current. I pull until it appears, filled with crystalline spring water, and set it back on the lip.

Something moves in my periphery. I twist around, knocking a pail back into the well. The Rive's face ripples like a stone dropped in a black pond. A demon pushes through.

I race across the field, getting as far from the wildberries and lemon reeds as possible, or the fight may spill onto my sanctuary. The portal swells, its surface trembling violently. A scream cracks the silence of the Edge. High pitched, yet gravelly. A Singed Fox. More screams layer atop the first. Singed Foxes. Smaller, weaker demons that resemble foxes if their fur was burnt off, exposing scaly, charcoal skin and black, veiny wings sprouted from their shoulders.

Sweat already drips down my back as I push myself. My throat shouldn't already be hoarse, my feet aching. I should be faster than this, but I am so *tired*.

The first creature emerges from a fissure. Two more follow it out. They hover above the cliff, flicking their heads and examining the new world they've stumbled upon. Their noses drink in the scents of rodents and hares scurrying to hide. In seconds, they will catch the magical pull of the Trace and come straight for me.

I dash across paths, cutting through the wild patches between, my axe in hand. The more stings of pain I feel, the harder I run, swinging my arms and pushing my knees up.

The demons crank their heads in my direction, the Trace beckoning. They shoot over the field like darts, their blurry shapes sharpening until I can see the red rings in their eyes. The Singed Foxes widen their jaws to intimidate me with rows of jagged white fangs.

Fangs I'll soon wear.

My first slice through the air rips across the narrow chest of one. Yellow-gray blood sprays over me, and the demon falls dead to the ground. Life essence rises from its body as red mist, taking the red rings in its eyes with it. The next Singed Fox catapults into my shoulder. The impact loosens my grip, leaving my axe caught in the dead demon's chest. Claws rake furiously across my armor. The creature screeches in frustration, rattling my eardrums. I force myself not to wince as I grab hold of its erratically flapping wing, digging my fingers into the webbing, and yank as hard as I can.

The Singed Fox jerks to the side, lifting its claws from my cuirass and helmet. I grab hold of the demon's neck and bring it down across my knee. Its spine cracks, and I let it fall. The last demon quickly wraps its claws around my neck from behind. To my shame, I flinch.

Wings beat around my head, blocking my vision. Teeth scrape against my helmet.

The scream I fought down earlier explodes from my throat, anger boiling my blood.

Reaching up, I wrap one hand around the demon's skull, getting between its fangs and my helmet. Teeth nail into my hand, puncturing my gloves. Blood trickles down my palms. My other hand squeezes the demon's claws, still clinging to my neck. Bones crack and snap in my grip. Its strength falters, and I take the chance to pull it overhead, slamming it onto the ground.

The squeak it emits may have been a brain-curdling screech if my boot were not already on its chest.

I lift my foot and bring it down.

I do it again.

And again.

Again.

Twisting my heel each time.

Bones splinter, muscle and fat molding into the sole. Blood paints my legs and torso. I slam my boot down one last time, grinding the Singed Fox's sternum into the dirt. Red mist rises.

I collapse to my knees in a pool of demon blood. My injured leg is fiery with pain, and I clutch my bitten hand to my chest. The glove is shredded, my skin wet and glistening beneath. Harsh breaths catch inside my helmet, warming my already hot skin.

I reach for my belt and pull out a short, thick knife, then place a small leather sack onto the ground. With both hands, I crank the crushed demon's jaw wide until it slackens. Blood surges from my torn hand as I stab the knife into the creature's gums. One by one, the fangs pop out, and I drop them into the sack.

Though there are more to collect, I force myself to stop. Pain erupts across my body. It's too heavy, too tired. I'm going to die. Maybe not today, but soon. I haven't seen my parents in ten years. I haven't stepped foot past the Edge's border since being brought here. No one will know the pitiful girl I used to be no longer exists.

And now, I will die as weak as they remember.

A roar pierces the air. This one is deep, booming like a cannon. I swallow the phlegm coating my throat, along with every glaring thought begging me to rest my quivering limbs in the dirt amongst the demons.

I yank my axe from the Singed Fox's chest and pull out two fire bombs just as the enormous shape of a Gargantuan emerges from the Rive.

CHAPTER 2

For weeks, Fallon watched the card players at the tavern from one table over, peeking beneath the thick lip of his hood. At first, he didn't see much other than hunched backs and blank expressions over fanned-out cards. Sometimes he caught irate, spittle-laced accusations after a losing hand. Those shouting were so sure they had been wronged, but Fallon could never understand why – until one day, he caught a flash of white sticking out of a careless man's sleeve. It disappeared in a blink, but that was enough for Fallon to understand the trick.

That night he practiced in his quarters until the crowning hours of the morning, slipping one card from his hand into his sleeve and pulling another out swiftly. Never one for patience, he returned to the tavern the next day with a pouch of silver coins he didn't expect to keep. To his shock, he left with all the winnings. It wasn't long until the card players groaned when he arrived, hood down, an heir's face on full display.

Today is an ordinary tournament at the tavern, but for Fallon, it's the day he pushes his trick, hoping to use it twice in the same hand. The card players grumble under their breaths as he flops down into the last empty chair at the table. Two winning cards jostle up his sleeve as he adds his bets to the center of the table. His pouch joins silver candlesticks, fine cutlery, and rolled up papers he assumes are rights to land or livestock.

Some of these folks really need to step away from the cards, he thinks.

His tutor stands among the surrounding audience wearing a deep scowl. Her expression reminds Fallon he's supposed to be reviewing accounting in preparation for a very important presentation in a couple of hours. *Card games are math-adjacent,* he assures himself. He flashes a smirk to a short, orange-haired young man tucked into the crowd. His friend Shavazme returns a conspiratorial grin.

Fallon brings his focus back to the game and the player sitting across from him. Ghade the Stone. A moniker earned by his uncrackable expression. Fallon was worried when he learned Ghade would be here today. But so far, the man has shown no demonstration of his namesake. Ghade glances left and right at the other players. His cards curl in his hands, nearing the point of creasing. Deep lines between his eyebrows persist as if they were carved.

The cards are dealt and Fallon fans out his hand. All low numbers and one mid-high. Nothing to worry over, he has the remedy up his sleeve to ensure he leaves the champion. The kingdom will speak at length of his unyielding calm; clink frothy beers together over the tale of Ghade losing his title to Fallon the Stone.

The final hand comes around and Fallon has barely managed to stay in the game. His tutor wrings her hands nervously while his friend inches closer to the table. Shavazme's large, blue eyes sweep over the other player's hands. He then scratches his nose with two freckled fingers – a signal that other players have high cards this round.

Fallon twitches his wrist to rustle the hidden cards, but they've become glued together against the clammy skin of his forearm. He jerks his whole arm. They don't separate. He rubs his arm against the edge of the table as if he has an itch. Finally, they do.

Fallon brings his hand up and fans the cards out just like he practiced, forcing his face to slacken. He needs to appear unbothered, almost bored.

Fan out, and bring in. Fan out, and bring in.

Fan out and drop the losing card into your empty sleeve.

Fan out, and bring in. Shimmy a winning card out of the other sleeve to join the hand as the cards come together.

And–

The losing card misses his sleeve entirely and drifts to the floor. *That's okay, just looks like an accident.* Fallon bends down to retrieve it.

Gasps rise from the audience. He follows their wide eyes to see his two winning cards have escaped his other sleeve and now lie on the floor. Fallon freezes, arched over, his hand hovering over them.

A shined boot comes down on top of the cards, nearly crushing his fingers. Fallon flicks his head up indignantly, ready to confront whoever dares to nearly step on the hand of an heir. Crass words melt on his tongue like ice as he meets the eyes of an old man in a verdant cloak, Niawa's insignia stitched across his chest.

"Heir Fallon, aren't you expected by the sovereigns in two hours?" Advisor Wilcon asks.

The advisor isn't a very tall man, nor broad in the shoulders. His chin and nose aren't sharp, and his balding head shines like the curve of a bowl. On any other person, those features would not strike a sense of fear. Yet, Fallon's veins run cold.

He is in fact expected at the palace this afternoon. Before his parents and their council, the Heads of the Regime, he must present the coming year's tax plan regarding farming, trade, production – god knows what else.

A feat he is not prepared for in the slightest.

"Yes, yes, of course. I'll finish here and be right with you," Fallon stammers. He timidly reaches for the cards beneath the advisor's boot and tugs at one. Wilcon makes a grunt in his throat then slightly lifts his shoe.

Fallon returns to the game, unsure which card he grabbed. When he slides it back into his hand, all hours of practicing his steely expression in the mirror are lost. He sighs at the same losing card he tried to get rid of. Fallon glances at the crowd for help, but Shavazme has vanished, leaving him to face the mercy of Wilcon and a losing game alone.

Reluctantly, Fallon lays his hand on the table. Ghade the Stone responds with his own, demolishing Fallon. Ghade should be elated, but he appears anything but. His eyes shift between Fallon and the advisor, fingers gripping the edge of the table, clearly holding back from scooping the purse into his arms and dashing to the bar to burn through a year's worth of libations in an evening.

Wilcon gives the man a curt nod, and Ghade rises to gather the pouches, silver, and scrolls. He quickly disappears into the crowd, heading towards the bar without a glance back. The spectators follow, emptying out the back half of the tavern. A small chandelier above swings from the mad rush, throwing flickering yellow light across the walls, the nervous tutor, and the advisor who looks down on Fallon with so little emotion Fallon would rather endure seething anger.

"Advisor Wilcon, I truly apologize," the tutor starts, "Heir Fallon *insisted* on coming here for his lessons; I didn't have a choice–"

Wilcon holds up his hand to silence her. "This is not your fault, Miss. Please return to the palace to collect your full pay for the day."

The woman bows to them both – Fallon notices she doesn't bend as low towards him – before escaping.

"Shall we?" Wilcon beckons.

Fallon anxiously runs his fingers through his short, dark curls as he stands. He follows Wilcon across the tavern, until the advisor suddenly veers towards the bar. His arm stretches between many bobbing, jovial heads to tap on Ghade's shoulder.

"Congratulations on your win. On behalf of the royal family, I must apologize for Heir Fallon's behavior. It can be a very stressful role, being an heir, and he only wished for a small bit of harmless fun, you understand," Wilcon says.

Before Ghade can respond, Wilcon turns swiftly on his heels and strides past Fallon towards the door. Fallon starts after him, wishing he could evaporate into thin air.

They exit into a wide street under a faded gray sky. Even so, the bright paint of the homes and shops around the tavern lose no liveliness. Fallon has always loved that even a somber sky can't dampen the vibrancy of Niawa. He focuses on the colors as Wilcon guides them through the city in complete silence. Yellows, blues, greens, pinks, reds, purples; even the white and tan-painted buildings add to the splendor, giving the eye a rest from the kaleidoscope. Bright flowers adorn steps and hang below windows, often clashing with the colors chosen for the brick or wooden exteriors. Not in a way that elicits a purse of the lips, but how sparklers and fireworks are only jarring until you inevitably find them beautiful.

As they walk, they are stopped by many citizens excited to greet an heir and the revered advisor who has served two generations of sovereigns. Fallon takes a moment to pause at every interaction and greet them warmly. Eventually, Wilcon has to remind him they are needed back at the palace, and Fallon is sad to cut the conversations short.

Soon, Fallon can spot patrolling guards rounding the balconies of the palace's back towers. He slows his pace, remembering his parents and the Heads are waiting for him. Wilcon slows too.

"Are you going to tell my parents about the tavern?" Fallon asks.

"I hide nothing from the sovereigns," Wilcon states.

Fallon scoffs. "I was only playing cards. There's no harm in that. And I didn't need you to apologize for me."

Wilcon's eyes point at Fallon like two sharpened arrows, notched, drawn, and ready to fly. "You *would* assume your actions have no consequences. You are wrong. An heir gambling is irritating. An heir cheating and taking advantage of his station is another thing entirely. At twenty-six, you should be far beyond this behavior."

"Taking advantage of my station? Absolutely not," Fallon argues. "Besides, most card players cheat."

"Perhaps. But when they are caught, there's punishment. For you, their heir, they turn a blind eye and lose their coin in return."

Fallon recalls the way Ghade the Stone was struck with nerves when Fallon came to the table, and his ears burn hot with embarrassment. He knows his skills at deception are not up to par with the seasoned players, but he truly believed he had become proficient in a short time. That he had found his calling. A spark of brilliance forever tied to his name. Fallon looks away from the advisor and begins to trace the grooves in the stone-paved road. His stomach pains with a hunger that no meal could ever satisfy.

You really thought it was because you were some gambling prodigy? Hands so slight the card players were too impressed by your skills to call you a cheat?

"I'll return everyone's coin." He hopes that will quiet the voice in his head, so insistent on adding to Wilcon's beratement.

"No need. I've known for a while about your trips to the tavern and guards have always been planted to watch over you. Your wins were returned every time."

Fallon's shoulders curl forward. "I'm sorry I disappointed you again. I only...What is the point of this charade with the presentation when we both know Abner will make a fool of me?"

"Heir Fallon, you will only be the fool if you don't try at all," the advisor responds, his voice a little softer. "Don't forget, you have just as much claim to the throne as your sibling." He pauses, then adds, "If you want it."

Now Fallon stops completely. "Of course I want it! It's the only thing I want. But it's clear Abner is the favorite and I'm an idiot for thinking it will ever be possible for me."

Wilcon cocks his head. "Do you know why the sovereigns seem to favor Heir Abner?"

Fallon clenches, but he doesn't speak. Much of him doesn't want to hear the reasoning. He doesn't need more confirmations of his inadequacy.

Wilcon continues. "It's because your parents don't know you anymore. They know you are charming and quick-witted, but they don't see the hunger in your eyes for the throne, for Niawa's bright future, that I have seen in you. While Heir Abner was having lunch with your parents in the afternoons, you were at the taverns. While Heir Abner and your father played chess in the gardens, you dined in the city and shopped. You need to *show them* you want it."

Fallon sighs. "Well, if the successor is being named on the Day of Breath, how do I do that now? It's only a few days away."

Wilcon tilts his head towards the palace and begins to walk. "This presentation, which we have practiced for, is a good start."

Fallon says nothing, the weight of his worries too heavy on his mind. He and Wilcon cross the city limits into the large circular courtyard before the palace. At the opposite end, the palace gates hang open as citizens flurry in and out.

With every step, Fallon resists the urge to slip amongst any gaggle of people and be swept away like driftwood in the sea.

Much to Fallon's chagrin, Wilcon escorts him to his quarters. The advisor may as well have put his hand on Fallon's head and steered him down the corridors and up the staircases like an errant child.

"Should I take a look at what you've come up with?" Wilcon asks as Fallon pulls the doors open.

Fallon shakes his head quickly, thinking of the blank sheet of paper on the desk of his study. "No. You've taught me enough already. I can take it from here."

The old man's thin lips curl upwards, lifting Fallon's spirits in kind. The reminder of Wilcon's faith in him makes the immediate future less daunting. Wilcon has assured him that no matter the outcome, support from his parents' most trusted counsel will hold more weight than any presentation.

"Do *not* be late." Wilcon gives Fallon a light pat on the shoulder, then leaves.

Fallon waits until the advisor's back turns the corner at the end of the hall before dashing through his quarters. His shoulder nearly crashes into the doorframe of his study when he reaches it. Inside the large room, a polished oak desk sits beneath a gold-paned window, rows of bookshelves and cabinets covering the walls. Wilcon handpicked the books and texts himself; horribly dull subjects ranging from economics to politics to history.

Fallon's eyes rove the shelves, his heart pounding. He pulls down two, three texts at a time, the titles entirely ignored. They're tossed onto the desk, causing the lone sheet of paper he hid from the advisor to flutter up and soar to the edge. Fallon catches it, crinkling a corner.

"Alright, let's see…" He lowers to the desk chair and lays out the paper. Licking his dry lips with an even dryer tongue, Fallon reaches for a fountain pen and bottle of ink. The pen hovers over the paper, black drops leaking off the tip to bleed into the parchment.

What have the Heads discussed during those boring assemblies my parents forced me to attend? Sheep? We have too many sheep? The sheep need more space to roam. The sheep are wandering off to the shore, drinking salt water, and dying at alarming rates. No, they return to the pastures covered in scales with large yellow fish eyes bugging out of their heads, and they eat the shepherds–

"Focus," Fallon snaps. His shout is smothered by the towering stacks of texts. They mock him with layers of dust coating their bindings, their spines uncracked. Fallon reaches for the thinnest book in the pile he dumped onto the desk and reads the cover: *Regional Planning and the Design of Living Sectors: Socio-political and Economic Challenges*. He drops it.

"Yuli-en, save me," Fallon cries into his hands.

It isn't until he hears the doors to his quarters slam, the sound echoing down the corridor, that he straightens. Footsteps trot down the hall. They sound deliberate, like a march. A wave of panic consumes Fallon and he returns to the empty page. He writes the first thought that comes to mind just before an arm reaches around him and rips it away, the pen leaving a faint trail of ink across.

"The sheep need more space, we should design their eating sectors more better..."

Fallon tears the paper back from his twin with a deep frown. Abner chuckles as they lean against the back of the chair.

"I hope this isn't what you're bringing to the meeting," they chide.

Fallon notices a heavily tabbed notebook stuffed with loose papers clutched to their hip. *Of course*. Abner has spent every waking moment for the past month researching and scribbling away in that thing.

"Uh, no. I decided after all my reading" – Fallon gestures at the dusty pile of books – "that my ideas would come across–"

"More better?"

"Would come across *better* if I speak from the heart." Fallon lays his hand on his chest. He immediately feels overdramatic and drops his hand to his lap.

Abner grins. "Yes, all the best taxation estimates have been supported by speeches from the heart. Numbers and patterns be damned."

Fallon launches to his feet, the chair and Abner stumbling backwards. When that doesn't wipe the smirk from his twin's face, he storms out of the study.

Wilcon was wrong when he assured Fallon could rise to this occasion alongside Abner. His sibling always makes a fool of him when it comes to these matters, and today will be no different. Fallon will bumble his way through a pathetic stash of knowledge, while Abner spouts statistics and historical examples. Fallon wouldn't be shocked if they pull out hand-drawn, detailed diagrams of Niawa from that notebook to discuss parade routes for the upcoming Day of Breath. Just for fun. After all, they'll have the time, since Fallon's presentation will last as long as a belch.

"Let's just get this over with," Fallon grumbles, yanking his quarter doors open. He realizes the lone sheet is still in his hand, crinkles it into a ball with a tight fist, then throws it at Abner.

His twin smoothly steps out of the ball's path, shakes their head, then follows Fallon out.

The two make their way through the palace's upper wings, only accessible to the royal family. Fallon hears the bustling of the public sector from the open windows. It houses the throne room, kitchens, medical wing, and offices for public matters. He wonders if the card players ever came to make formal complaints about him. He'd only been going to the tavern for a few weeks, and apparently, they were given their coin back. There's no reason Fallon should be grievously punished. A stern speech and extra lessons on civic responsibility seem more fitting.

Fallon glances at Abner out of the corner of his eye. They stand tall, shoulders back, wearing a dark-green, fitted jacket bearing Niawa's crest. Their cream-colored pants are creaseless, white heeled boots polished like glass. Abner struts down the hall with a surety that brews envy in Fallon. Though the two share the same dark brown skin and black, curly hair – Fallon keeps his shorter, while Abner's curls hang down by their ears and flick around their neck – the twins could not be more different.

Fallon has been labeled loud and rambunctious, but charming. He can speak to anyone, make people laugh, command a room by bringing it together with joy. On the other hand, Abner is very quiet, almost stern. They spend most of their time alone, and when they do speak, it's in a straightforward manner that makes the spine go rigid. Their eyes, a slightly lighter shade of brown than Fallon's, always carry distrust. But Fallon, Wilcon, and their parents, know Abner's tense nature comes from the anxiety they've battled since birth, and not a dislike of people.

Even still, Abner seemed born for the role of sovereign, and Fallon had long accepted he was meant to charm and entertain over wine. But over the years, Wilcon has convinced him otherwise. To the advisor, Fallon has all the traits of a great ruler – he just needs to prove it.

"I need a moment," Abner suddenly says. They abruptly stop in front of a set of stained-glass doors leading to a small balcony and abandon the corridor to step outside.

"Don't we have only minutes to spare?" Fallon can't believe he isn't the one chancing tardiness as he follows his sibling.

Abner responds by resting their arms on the columned stone railing. Birds dart in and out of the treetops below, tweets announcing their every whim. Fallon's eyes travel past the palace gardens beneath, over the multicolored buildings, and beyond the wall surrounding the city. Niawa's vibrant green land stretches out for miles until it vanishes behind clusters of a darker green he knows to be Edge Forest. A black smudge rises above the forest. Even a few hours ride away, the Rive still makes Fallon's skin prickle.

"What do you think the Champion is doing right now?" Abner asks, giving Fallon a look he's come to know as Abner struggling with their thoughts.

Fallon shrugs. "Locked in battle with a giant demon with blood-covered fangs and wings as long as the city's wall."

"On the brink of death, then? While we host parties and toast to our abundance of resources."

"Don't start with this," Fallon groans.

Abner keeps their gaze outward. "Out there is a woman alone, defending our riches and comforts when we have a servant of Yuli-en *and* a full army with new guards being trained every day." They shake their head. "It will never seem right to me."

"For someone who's always studying, you seem to forget it was sending an army to the Edge that attracted demons," Fallon says. "The sibyl only does Yuli-en's bidding, and this is what they want."

"Well… I question the sibyl."

Fallon grips the railing, pushing against it then bringing himself close. Abner doesn't even have the decency to look guilty at their blasphemy anymore. As though these dangerous thoughts wouldn't tarnish their reputation beyond repair.

"How many times must I beg you to keep that to yourself? The sibyl is the only reason this kingdom still stands. Not one demon has come to the city since the first Champion was Blessed. Thousands of lives have been saved."

Abner looks at Fallon in a way that makes him bring his forehead down to his folded arms on the railing. He knows what comes next.

"Don't you see what I see?" Abner asks.

Fallon doesn't, so he goes quiet. His sibling isn't stymied in the slightest.

"I think we need to look for the Veins of Istral."

"Who?" Fallon says into his sleeves.

"God above, Fallon. What happens during your lessons? The Veins of Istral are Istral's followers. Those who believe Yuli-en shouldn't have banished their shadow. The Veins' entire purpose was to liberate Istral from the demon realm, but they never succeeded. And haven't been heard from in generations–"

"Yes, I remember now. What does that have to do with us being late to the presentation?" Fallon straightens his back to lean on the railing with one hand, the other on his hip in an obvious show of exasperation.

Abner leans in. "Why did the Rive open in Niawa, and why now? Have the Veins been revived with new members? Did they finally succeed? Are they here in Niawa with us, eating at our restaurants and perusing through our market? Why isn't the sibyl looking for them? Why aren't we?"

"This is why I never invite you to the tavern. You think too much."

Abner scoffs. "Not one of those questions interests you? Makes your skin crawl with worry?"

"No. Please stop speaking in riddles."

"Fine." Abner returns to staring out over the railing and silently fuming.

"If that's all out of your system now, let's go."

"And the sibyl. She was sent from the Southern Temples to help us, but these Champions... they keep dying. There has to be a better way."

"You're a general now, too? Got battle tactics in that notebook?" Fallon smirks, but he doesn't know if he has another lighthearted joke in him to steer Abner out of their own way. The only thing that makes his skin crawl with worry is his twin's growing paranoia.

"Maybe the Champion could have a small army at her disposal that's stationed near the Edge, but not *at* the Edge, as support, so the world is not entirely on her shoulders," Abner pushes.

"If the Champion needed help, she would tell us."

"But she–"

"Has not returned in ten years and still lives, so I imagine she's just fine," Fallon interjects. He slaps his hand on Abner's shoulder. "We should go now."

Abner's lips mash together. They hold their notebook with both hands, rubbing it with their fingers like the nose of a pet hound. "Do you even know the Champion's name? Or the one before her?"

Fallon tilts his head back and sighs. He may be woefully unprepared for the presentation, but at least he doesn't question their god and the sibyl. "You have to see this obsession is not good. You don't even care we'll be late, and that isn't like you."

"It might not matter soon," Abner mutters.

Fallon grabs their shoulders, forcing them to face him. "Please tell me you haven't done something stupid."

His twin shakes their head curtly but looks away. "No. Of course not. I mean, I do have an idea I'm thinking of proposing."

"I'm going to regret asking, but what is it?" Fallon lets his arms fall back to his sides.

"Being born with a natural proclivity to magic is rare, so those who are become sibyls. But magic isn't impossible for everyone else, just harder to access. Somewhere in history, we decided only a special few deserve that kind of power. I think we should start teaching regular citizens how to practice. That way, they can better defend themselves should the sibyl or Champions fail against the Rive."

Fallon takes a deep inhale while pressing his fingers to his lips. "Practicing magic is forbidden. If anyone finds out about these thoughts, you'll be ruined, Abner. Maybe even banished."

Abner nods slowly. Their mind goes elsewhere for a moment, as if a memory has dragged them away. Their stern face falls, eyebrows tilting down, the wrinkles in their forehead disappear.

Fallon allows his twin a moment in their head. He knows they both understand the consequences of Abner's thoughts being shared openly. It would remove them from the race to the throne, a topic the two do not discuss. That one's succession means the other has been measured and found less than. Abner has tried to broach the subject before, and Fallon turns his heel on the conversation every time. He knows it frustrates Abner, whose empirical nature aches to address the decision that will change both of their lives – but Fallon feels nothing but hurt. He loves Abner. He has no desire to speak of this competition. He would prefer to pour the two of them wine, forget all this for a while, and just laugh over stories from their childhood.

He prays they still have moments like that after Wilcon helps him ascend the throne.

"Where were you this morning?" Abner asks, breaking the silence.

"As if you don't already know. Apparently, everyone does," Fallon grumbles. He will never return to that tavern as long as he lives.

"Yes, I heard. Judging by the ale stain," Abner points to a dark spill on the collar of Fallon's ivory shirt, "seems like you were having a great time."

"Thank Yuli-en for Wilcon. Otherwise I'd be at the bar drowning in ale with Shavazme by now."

Abner tenses. "How fortunate that he keeps such a close eye on you."

"It's not as wonderful as it sounds. He's like a fruit fly buzzing in my ear."

"I recall."

Another memory draws Abner away. Fallon is sure they now think of the day Wilcon ceased his private lessons with Abner and began showing greater interest in Fallon. Another topic the twins never breach.

"To the east rotunda?" Fallon tries again. To his relief, Abner nods. They take one last, lingering look towards the Edge before following Fallon to the corridor.

Fallon soon regrets rushing Abner off the balcony once the two enter a hall with a set of closed arched doors at the other end. Wilcon waits for them, alongside two guards. His eyes connect with Fallon's, and the advisor exhibits his skill for unloading a lifetime of scolds, lessons, and disappointment into one expression. Fallon's shoulders creep up to his ears with every step closer.

"Advisor Wilcon, I look forward to sharing my research with you. I remember you have a special interest in our trade with Kanan, so I think you'll find that part of my presentation interesting," Abner says when they reach him.

"You're late," Wilcon responds sharply.

Abner's nostrils flare. "We both are. Seems Fallon needed some extra time to prepare after his morning at the tavern. Lucky for him, he was brought back just in time."

"Of course. I would be a poor advisor if I didn't know where the heirs were and what they're doing."

A chill settles in the air. Fallon looks between the advisor and Abner, feeling the immense weight of their icy stares.

"Are you prepared, Heir Fallon?" Wilcon diverts his attention to Fallon, who immediately misses being ignored.

"Somewhat..." Fallon mumbles. The advisor's eyes narrow. "But, *but*, I remember our recent lesson on sheep very well, and I believe I've got some great ideas on... that."

"I wasn't aware you were offering private lessons for this presentation, Wilcon. Our parents asked that we work on them alone," Abner states.

The air chills even more, and Fallon briefly loses himself in a fantasy of sprinting down the hall and around the corner.

"I think we should begin." Wilcon smiles, showing a mouthful of gray-tinged teeth.

Abner opens their mouth to say something more, but when the guards pull the doors open at Wilcon's command, they fall deadly silent.

CHAPTER 3

Every face in the east rotunda turns towards the opening doors, their expressions like the blank paper that waited for Fallon on his desk, demanding he grace them with intelligent thoughts.

Wilcon sweeps into the room and stands beside two empty chairs at the near end of the table, opposite the sovereigns. He dips his chin to Fallon, so slight it's almost missed. A wordless reminder that the advisor is on his side.

"Can I confess something to you?" Fallon once asked Wilcon over a private lunch nearly a year ago.

"You can tell me anything," Wilcon responded, lowering a bowl of citrus and spiced pork broth from his lips.

Fallon stared at his hands, blinking the danger of tears away. "Sometimes… I struggle to understand why I want the throne. Why you and I have these lessons together, and why you have so much faith in me. I always assumed it would be Abner, and so did our parents."

"Niawa's throne is the most important in history. Our kingdom protects the entire continent from demons. We are the closest to Yuli-en because of that burden."

Fallon shook his head. "I know, I know. But why me? When I attend meetings with the Heads, or events in the throne room, it's hard to picture myself wearing one of the royal circlets.

Overseeing everything. It never even crossed my mind when I was younger."

"What else will you do then, Heir Fallon?"

Fallon heard the advisor's voice tighten. He inched away, preparing for more cutting words.

"I asked you a question," Wilcon said.

"I don't know."

"So, you would rather have an empty life while you watch Abner rise to power, when you had every right to that greatness? That is a pitiful waste of your birthright."

Hearing Wilcon's frustration so clearly, Fallon tried to bite his tongue, but he couldn't. "I just don't want to disappoint anyone."

Wilcon reached out and rested his hand on Fallon's, which were balled in his lap. When Fallon gathered the courage to look at the advisor, he found soft eyes staring back.

"That is doubt and fear talking, not your heart. I'm thrilled I saw the potential in you when I did. Together, we will find the great ruler within. I want you to start imagining yourself as a sovereign, every day, until you see what I see." Then the advisor smiled with a sincerity that unraveled the knots in Fallon's stomach.

"Alright, I'll try."

Fallon takes a deep breath through his nose, his chest swelling with hope remembering Wilcon's praise. He wraps his fingers around the advisor's words, gripping them like a lifeline. Despite spotting familiar looks that the Heads contrive just for him – ready to be entertained, void of respect – Fallon strides into the room and takes his seat first.

"Heir Abner," Wilcon quips.

Abner has yet to move from the doorway. Their face is awash with gray, their top lip puckering. Their restless thumbs leave pale streaks over the leather cover of their notebook.

Fallon cocks his head at the empty seat when Abner's traveling gaze reaches him. He sees the wheels turning in Abner's mind, can hear the voice inside demanding their nerves to relax. Public speaking is their mortal enemy. The tablets they've taken since their teen years have only managed to temper the anxiety, not eradicate it. So, Abner performs the act they have perfected over the years. It starts with a lift of their chin. Shoulders go back. Eyes steel over. All the while, their chest rises and falls in a slow pattern as they count backwards from ten in their head.

Color returns to Abner's skin. They bring a hand up to their chest and bow to the room. The Heads return the gesture from their chairs as Fallon berates himself silently for not remembering to greet the council as well.

Abner takes their seat and places their notebook on the table before opening it to a page filled with neatly written lines, the letters above never crossing the ones below. Though they made it into the room, their hands still grip the notebook so hard veins bulge from their skin.

Fallon nudges Abner with his elbow. "Don't worry, you're going to impress them like you always do," he whispers. Abner returns a smile and their grip relaxes.

"Let's begin," Wilcon states. He makes his way to the last empty chair beside the sovereigns. By the time he's seated, the guards have closed the doors, trapping Fallon inside.

The first Head stands. A short and petite woman clad in a thin wool vest over a long black dress, the hem dangling just above her ankles. As she launches into a report about rivers, Fallon wonders if she chose the long skirt to make herself appear taller. *It sort of works. Draws the eye up from the floor to the top of her head,* he muses.

Something jabs him in the ribs.

Fallon glances down to see it was the tip of Abner's pen. They quickly dip it back into an ink bottle they also brought along and bring it to hover over a fresh page, as if terrified to miss any notes regarding the importance of water.

"I'm paying attention," Fallon says under his breath.

"It's a muscle memory."

Fallon kicks Abner's boot under the table.

They kick back. Though Abner doesn't turn their head, they grin.

The petite woman's voice strains. Her arms rise, hands outspread. "...find it hard to believe the turbines will interfere with the northeast farmlands. I'm asking for a mere corner..."

"How have the new tablets been? Thought I caught a little shake from you in the doorway," Fallon asks under the protection of the woman's loud complaints.

Abner finishes writing a sentence, then leans towards Fallon. "Sleep is much easier, but I'm having more bouts of nervousness during the day."

At the same time, the twins catch their mother's glare from across the table. They snap away from each other immediately.

As the reports carry on, Fallon begins to trace the lines of every tapestry hanging in his eyeline. He starts on an emerald-colored one with a symmetrical design of whimsically curled, thorned vines. They come close but never touch Niawa's crest in the center. Next is a tapestry depicting Niawa from a distance, a white palace with its back to the sea and the city spreading before it. The artist captured the city's zest for color splendidly. Every small building seems to have been stitched with a hue not used for any other.

He pictures himself a tiny, woven figure, strolling through Niawa's colorful streets as the new sovereign. First, he would stop at the market and buy all the ingredients for a wondrous feast to be prepared for visiting royals from other lands. Over a long table of Niawa's greatest cuisine, he would listen intently as the Heads discuss the subjects they know best, while he charms the royals into agreeing with whatever trade or tax deal is in discussion. No one would be able to deny the savvy of the Heads and an enigmatic ruler who brings nations together. In fact, he would host a feast many nights of the week and invite as many citizens as he could.

"… Heir Fallon would agree, I think." A round of laughs follows.

All eyes are on Fallon. The Head of trade, he believes, is standing. Fallon smiles sheepishly, hoping that will suffice. When the Head clears his throat and continues, Fallon sends a prayer to the ceiling that he sinks into his chair. Becomes the chair itself. Chairs don't have to feign interest in reports.

"What'd I miss?" he mutters to Abner.

"We somehow ended up on the topic of how beautiful Princess Sonia is."

Fallon shrugs. "I don't know, she's kind of mean. Why are we talking about her beauty?"

"Because they think when she comes to rule in Kanan, she will be difficult to make trade agreements with. That's really important; you should pay attention."

"If they want her to be nice, we should just send you. I've seen the way you two sneak off whenever her family comes to visit."

Abner blushes. "We talk, that's all."

Fallon smirks. "Sure, sure. Anyway, I couldn't imagine being joined with her for life. She's vicious."

"She isn't vicious; everyone loves her." Abner tries to suppress a sudden burst of laughter, causing them to snort. "She's only mean to you."

The Head of trade finishes speaking and sits down, annoyance clear on his face at the heirs trying to collect themselves.

Advisor Wilcon stands next. "Thank you all for your reports. Sovereign Adelaide," he gestures to Fallon's mother, "and Sovereign Gerves," he gestures to Fallon's father, "will address your thoughts and concerns. But first, we have two more proposals to hear, from Heir Fallon and Heir Abner, on taxation."

Though no Head has received an ovation, Wilcon encourages a round of claps that quickly captures the table. He returns to his seat and the clapping fades. Sweat beads over Fallon's back and forehead as the expectant stares return. He struggles to hold onto the courage that guided him into the room.

"Fallon, why don't you go first?" Sovereign Adelaide says with a smile. Her voice is deep, but soft. Emeralds cut into numerous shapes encrust the gold circlet around her head. The largest is a teardrop stone that droops down the center of her forehead. Sovereign Gerves wears an identical one over his thick, dark curls, streaked with gray.

Fallon imagines wearing a circlet, the weight of the teardrop gem against his skin. In the reverie, he rises from the throne in a hall filled with adoring citizens, the gems sparkling from every angle.

He blinks. He's back in the east rotunda, the faint scent of ale wafting into his nostrils. Fallon clasps at the stain Abner had pointed out, then realizes that will certainly draw attention to it. Pivoting, he swipes at the spot with the back of his hand as if removing crumbs.

Though no thoughts form in his head, his mouth begins to speak. "Outside of Niawa, we are called 'The Demon's Lands,' as you know. And they are right. But without us, demons would run free as wild boar, tearing through every living being."

Confusion begins to ripple across the Head's expressions. Fallon continues regardless. He hopes that somewhere in the words leaping off his tongue, a point will emerge.

"Before Yuli-en's favor cured our lands, we experienced all the woes of the world: drought, floods, famine, war. Then, the Rive appeared. We sent thousands of guards to face the demons and banish them back to the hellish realm they came from. Many died until we discovered it was noise that attracted them in droves. Uh…for our sacrifice, Yuli-en sent us the sibyl and she blessed the first Champion, and our guards came home."

Please, mind. Give me something.

"As long as we continue to protect the continent, the sibyl's magic keeps our kingdom healthy. She gives us trees in Emerald Pine Forest that provide the strongest lumber, our plentiful… uh… strong sheep that give us wool and meat, among other things. And good, strong farm… soil. And what do we do with these resources?" Fallon hopes someone will provide an answer. He only receives perplexed faces. "We use these things… to create industry… which our people work in… which they make high income from because the kingdom does so well from the" – the right word is on the tip of his tongue, playfully dancing just outside of his reach until it trips and stumbles into his grasp – "demand! Yes, the demand is high for our good stuff. And if we trade well, we will be able to keep taxes low within the kingdom." Fallon clasps his hands together in triumph, bobbing his head.

At the very least, he said the word taxes.

Wilcon stares at Fallon, his lips slightly parted, before addressing the sovereigns. "I do agree that we will be able to keep the taxes low, Heir Fallon's enthusiastic reminder of our history aside."

Fallon drops to his seat when he catches his parents' disappointment. He stares down at his lap, curling his toes inside his boots until they hurt.

"Abner, if you please," Sovereign Adelaide says. There's a hint of excitement in her voice that makes Fallon cross his arms tightly.

Abner rises, their face void of emotion, all hard lines and flat surfaces. They have retreated into the stone shell they wear like armor. Abner opens their notebook and pulls out several sheets of paper. They hand the stack to the first Head on their left. The papers are passed around the table until Fallon is given the last one. Identical, hand-written notes with numbers.

Abner begins to speak, while Fallon struggles to stay upright in his chair. He's too warm, his toes still curl, his shirt now seems as if it reeks of ale. Curiosity reels him into Abner's words as quickly as jealousy thrusts him back out.

Eventually, his sibling comes to the same conclusion as his mindless rant, that the kingdom's internal taxes can remain low for the next year. However, they continue speaking, veering into Niawa's trade with other regions – and the tension created therein.

"The council has chosen to hike the cost on all our goods in the interest of protecting our rich resources. This has caused problems with many of our allies, particularly Kanan, who rely on our lumber. They have even made mild threats of invasion in the past, due to talk we may close our borders entirely, ending open trade." Their tone changes, almost nervous. Fallon perks up. "I'm aware that's not just talk. The council has been discussing, what some may call, hoarding our resources." They pause, looking around the room. The Heads listen intently. "I propose we don't go down that route and lower the taxes on lumber to Kanan. As Niawa will sustain wealth for generations to come, we can afford to be more generous."

For the first time, Fallon wishes he knew more about taxes to understand why Wilcon steeples his fingertips, his gaze sharpened to a needlepoint.

The advisor rises slowly. "Thank you, Heir Abner. Your comments on Kanan are noted, as they have been many times before. Kanan would never dare to declare war. We have the sibyl and Yuli-en on our side."

The Heads and sovereigns nod in agreement, but Abner doesn't. Though the advisor is a small man, his authority fills the room. Even Fallon feels the suffocation that brings Abner back to their seat.

"Now, let's turn our attention to the Day of Breath, only two days away," Wilcon says.

"Is there any chance the Champion will come?" Head Trevor asks.

"No, the courier has told us she declines again," Wilcon answers.

Murmurs of disappointment travel through the Heads, Fallon adding his own. He recalls the night she was brought to the throne room to receive the Blessing. She seemed to be the same age as him. Long, curly hair laid over her shoulders, as dark as her eyes. Small moles were scattered over her brown face and neck. He noticed she was pretty, even as she cried. When she drank the Blessing, she gagged as tremors coursed through her. Salutations were given, promises that her family would be well taken care of, then she was gone. He remembers feeling immensely sad for her, even though it was a momentous occasion. A small pang of guilt arises when he realizes Abner was right: he doesn't recall her name.

The discussion in the room turns lively, the Heads speaking out of turn. They talk of the parade on the morning of the Day of Breath, and a grand speech in the late afternoon, which the sibyl will attend. She hardly leaves her private tower, much less the palace. Fallon himself has only seen her at special events and the swearing in of Champions. He's always felt an immense swell of pride at living in the same palace as her.

All the while, Abner doesn't speak. Chatter of the festivities do nothing to pull them from their stupor.

This, Fallon thinks, *is where I may be able to save some dignity.* He leans into the table, resting his elbows on the surface, the way many of the Heads do now as they engage in the discussion. He nods, smiles, swallows their laughter and spews it back out. Once or twice, he nudges Abner's side, returning the favor. His sibling responds by sinking deeper into their gloom. Eventually, Fallon abandons his attempts and dedicates himself to plans for a commissioned tapestry depicting the Champion's likeness, to be split and hung on either side of the palace doors. The latest account from the courier a few months ago was the Champion has gotten a little taller and shaved her head. Artists in the city have been clamoring to create new portraits ever since.

Soon, Wilcon calls the meeting to an end and invites the Heads to a late lunch in the southwest garden. They all rise from the table, collecting their handouts from Abner along with their own notebooks. Fallon and Abner wait until the room empties, as is customary, leaving the twins with the sovereigns and the advisor.

"Your presentations today were very informative," Sovereign Adelaide starts. She glances at Fallon, "...and creative. You gave us a lot to think about when it comes to the future of Niawa."

Abner lights up. Their racing heart is given away by shallow, rapid breaths.

Are they going to announce the successor now? Fallon too can hardly sit still.

Wilcon bows his head to Fallon, a gesture that Abner notices. They inhale sharply, and the air doesn't come back out.

"Fallon, would you please attend the lunch and entertain the Heads until we arrive? Your excitement for the Day of Breath was inspiring. I'm sure they'll want to continue discussions with you," Sovereign Gerves says.

"Abner, stay behind for a moment," Sovereign Adelaide adds.

Fallon's building anticipation shatters. He stands, his gaze flicking to Wilcon. The advisor is a statue. He doesn't smile or nod, only stares as Fallon backs away from the table, facing them all. If he turns around, there will only be darkness behind him. A bleak tunnel leading to the existence of a forgotten man. His name only a small stitch added to his family tree on a low-hanging branch.

Fallon finally turns when he reaches the hall outside. The doors to the east rotunda begin to close. Unable to bear hearing them shut, he starts down the hall in a daze. The soft whine of metal hinges cuts short. Fallon glances over his shoulder to see Wilcon gliding towards him as he orders the guards to shut the door.

"What just happened?" Fallon's shaking voice is unrecognizable to his ears.

Wilcon guides him away without a word. When they have turned a corner, they stop. He grasps both of Fallon's shoulders, looking intently into his eyes. "The sovereigns have chosen Abner as the successor."

The world becomes a splotch of muddled colors blending together like melting wax. "But you told me–"

"I did. And I still believe *you* are the right choice. You believe in the traditions that keep our people safe. You honor our history and Yuli-en. Abner will drive us to ruin. They think only of their own ambitions. Even today, they've shown no care for guarding our precious resources."

Fallon sputters, his tongue unable to work. It seems the advisor's support isn't enough after all. The praises he has stuffed into Fallon's head for years feel meaningless now.

"None of that matters," Fallon shouts, ripping his shoulders from Wilcon's grasp.

The advisor sneers and Fallon immediately quiets.

"*Collect yourself.* It's not over until the Day of Breath, when the sovereigns make their announcement to the city. I suggest you join the Heads for lunch and be your charming self. I will see to this."

With that, Wilcon returns to the rotunda. Fallon stays just around the corner, unable to move long after the doors close.

CHAPTER 4

Fallon paces the length of his bedroom, crossing between the door he flung open and his private bar in the corner. Every time he nears the rainbow of glass bottles and decanters, he chides a growing desire to reach for one.

That's the last thing he needs. Discovered by his parents or Wilcon – or worse, Abner – drunk and ranting on the floor. Especially as he abandoned direct orders to join the Heads for lunch.

Fallon gouges his fingers into his scalp, grasping at the short, tight curls. He pours over every lesson with Wilcon, every assurance of his path to the throne. The advisor always spoke as if Fallon was the sole heir, and Abner a distant cousin who posed no threat. What will he do now? Abner is far too pragmatic to name Fallon as their advisor.

His resolve breaks, thin as an eggshell. In seconds, he's filling a crystal glass with the spirit from a ruby-red decanter. Fallon takes a hearty gulp, savoring the sting as it washes down. His parents must be able to see that Abner can barely smile in the face of company, let alone nurture relationships with other regions. *And their blasphemous thoughts! They would sooner have the sibyl shipped back to the Southern Temples. Demons will be ripping limbs from bodies by the first snowfall.*

Fallon tosses back the last of his glass then leaves it on

the bar. He charges towards the door, fueled by a sudden determination. He will *not* let bloodshed come to his people. He will tell his parents how Abner truly feels.

Something jerks him backwards. The door's long, curled handle is caught in the pocket of his trousers. A cold sensation takes the opportunity to wash over him, snuffing out the determination. Fallon cups his mouth and exhales into his palms. Could he really condemn his own twin? No, he couldn't. Groaning, he makes several attempts to lift the handle from his pocket before it comes free. Then he returns to the bar, refills his glass, and brings it to the window across the room.

In the garden below, palace staff mill about tending to tall lily stalks, pruning and clipping. Sweat coats their foreheads, dirt smeared across their skin like brush strokes. They laugh and speak happily to one another, exchanging looks of pride as they inspect their work.

Fallon sips his drink with soft, uncalloused hands. The sovereigns have always admired hard work. They speak so highly of the farmers, the laborers, the bakers, the gardeners, the trainees at the Academy of the Guard. Fallon recalls many visits to the academy where he watched future guards train and spar. He always longed to wear the forest-green uniform and slip into the fray, testing out his own strength and agility.

No one would ever equate him with brawny strength. Or Abner. The heirs were raised to oversee, not get into the dirt. A chortle escapes Fallon at the image of Abner slashing through the air with a halberd in their imported, pristine clothing and perfectly kept hair.

Then again, the guards themselves have only fought at the academy. Niawa hasn't experienced a war, even a threat, since the Rive opened. No kingdom wants the burden of facing demons, nor would any dare oppose a sibyl. The only true warrior is the Champion. Beloved by all, yet a complete mystery. She refuses to return no matter what gifts are sent, no matter how pleading the letters from the sovereigns. It would take a miracle, or a very persuasive person, to lure her home.

Fallon gasps – and chokes a bit on his drink. Wilcon has told him countless times his greatest strengths are charisma and charm. What Abner lacks the most.

Taking long swigs from his glass, a hazy plan forms in Fallon's mind. He pictures himself marching into a throne room filled with citizens. His parents, Wilcon, and Abner stand by the thrones. When they see him, everyone cheers. Because the Champion walks by his side, returning from the Edge for the first time in a decade. Joy bursts among the people, so loud the windows rattle. What better way for Fallon to prove how much he cares about Niawa? This will certainly be more exciting than taxes and equations and estimates – whatever Abner presented today. Wilcon will be so proud.

Smiling from ear to ear, Fallon returns to the bar to fill his cup a final time. He empties it in one gulp then slams it onto the bar. Glasses shake and clink, as if applauding. He marches into his large closet, his skin tingling with exhilaration. Trousers, tunics, shirts, and cloaks hang from the walls, smelling strongly of florals. Fallon takes a moment to consider, fingering the fine silks of some and pondering the detailed stitching of others. He settles on a loose-fitting black shirt with buttons up to the collar, eggshell trousers, and a burgundy waistcoat. He inspects his choice in a tall mirror and his reflection grins back. This is what he should have worn to the east rotunda.

No matter. After Fallon returns from the Edge, the sovereigns will forget about the ale stains on his shirt and the card tournaments. With the Champion as his ally, he'll take back the throne.

Fallon doesn't bother calling on Shavazme at his home. He knows exactly where the general's son will be on a warm, clear day like today – and a rainy, gloomy day. Lightning splitting the sky couldn't keep Shavazme from Gilded Hall.

The establishment stands out like a gray block would, surrounded by buildings painted in bright yellows, greens, and blues. Even Gilded Hall's windows are a flat gray, the shutters tightly closed. There is no sign to tell patrons they have arrived at their destination, but other indications could not be clearer: from the top of the door, a thick gold line runs down its center, splitting into two thinner strands like symmetrical waves forming two bulbous shapes, the second wider than the first, until the two unite again in a sharp point. To Fallon, the design always looked like the soft curves of a body. Outside the door, a large man with broad shoulders like an ox stands with his arms crossed over an equally wide chest. One half of his face is painted gold.

The door swings open and two women stumble out, kissing furiously while attempting to walk. As they hobble past Fallon, clinging to each other like two octopi, gold flakes flit off their clothing and fall to the ground, where the remnants of their dalliance join all the other gold specks littering the street. He smiles at them, wishing he could join their fun; but there are more important tasks at hand.

Fallon strides up to the door. The ox man twitches in a strange way that appears to be a bow before ushering Fallon inside. Fallon walks onto a high platform with one set of stairs leading to a massive space below. Elaborate chandeliers cast butter-yellow light on neat rows of wooden tables, all packed with patrons. They howl and laugh, argue and babble. Ale flies from their lips and dribbles into their bosoms. On a large stage, a quartet manages to strum two mandolins, tap on the keys of a harpsichord, and pluck reverberating notes on a bass with wonderful harmony, despite the racket.

Fallon starts slowly down the stairs, the spirits beginning to play with his coordination. A man eagerly greets him at the bottom, his torso bare and covered in gold flakes, giving the illusion of gilded skin. He's a handsome sort, the kind who is keenly aware, with a mischievous expression plastered over his face – one Fallon knows will entice him into a private room if he's not careful.

"Heir Fallon, how wonderful to have you visit today. Much earlier than your usual time," the man teases. He holds out his hand whimsically as if balancing an invisible platter.

"I'm not here for the usual activities, Thistle," Fallon replies.

Thistle pouts. "Are you sure? I could have Floria meet us. She's only got a few tables to mind."

"No, no. Here for one reason only. Could you point me to Shavazme?"

Thistle gives in with a shrug and a wink, then motions for Fallon to follow. They round the edge of the hall where the chandelier's light only makes hints of faces and bodies. Along the far wall, several doors lead to private rooms, which Fallon knows contains plush velvet couches, and small bars stocked with expensive imported drinks. Behind those gold-painted doors are wealthy business owners, members of the council and their closest friends, and high-ranking members of the guard – and in Shavazme's case, their offspring with too much time on their hands.

Thistle comes to a stop outside one of those doors. When he goes to knock, Fallon shakes his head and taps his pointer finger to his lips. The tavern server smirks, then backs away before turning swiftly on his heel to disappear into the crowd.

With the liquor cheering him on, Fallon thrusts the door open. "In the afternoon, no less!"

Yelps fill the smoky room. A soft pillow flies over Fallon's head.

"Always making an entrance," Shavazme drawls from a couch. Two women with gilded skin sit on either side of him, their legs curled over his lap, and over each other's. When they realize who has disturbed their time with the general's son, they quickly preen themselves, tucking wayward strands of hair behind their ears as they sit up straight, drawing their shoulders back to bring attention to their chests. The straw-haired one, Fallon recognizes as an entertainer named Ramini who he has spent time with before. The other girl is new. She glances at Ramini, looking for direction.

"Are you going to sit, or stand in the doorway and let all the smoke out?" Shavazme leans back, spreading out his arms. The women snuggle into him like magnets.

"Actually, I need to speak to you. Alone." Fallon emphasizes the last word as he sits in a lone armchair across from the couch.

The women hastily untangle themselves, then shuffle out the room without argument. As they go, Shavazme gives Fallon a rude hand gesture, which Fallon ignores. He gestures to the table between them laden with steins, liquor bottles, and a tray of pipes and herbs.

Shavazme shrugs, still brandishing his irritation.

"Sorry for ruining your afternoon," Fallon says, packing one of the pipes with herbs that smell strongly of licorice root. He hopes even one puff of this will muddle the last of his apprehensions. After striking a match and holding it to the pipe, he takes a long pull.

Through the thick cloud of smoke Fallon expels, Shavazme leans forward to prop his elbows on widespread knees and clasps his hands together. If it weren't for his very youthful face, the pose would be as intimidating as Shavazme aims for. He was always trying to bolden himself to counteract his oval blue eyes, round cheeks, and the smattering of freckles across his skin that match his bright orange hair.

"How did the rest of the tournament go?" Shavazme asks.

"It was wonderful! The best card players in the city watched Wilcon scold me after my trick failed spectacularly. Too bad you had to leave early."

Shavazme smiles. "Well, we had a good run. Maybe we can take a trip to Kanan and try our luck at the taverns there?"

Fallon shakes his head with a laugh. Shavazme may be crass and impulsive, but he was also fearless to the point of disrespectful. Fallon needs that boldness to rub off on him today.

"What do you want, Fallon? Must be important enough for you to send the girls away, so out with it. I have another two hours in this room."

"It is," Fallon asserts. The herbs meld well with his alcohol haze and he relaxes into the chair. "In a short time, the courier will leave for the Edge to bring monthly supplies to the Champion. I plan to be on that cart, and you should come with me. When we get to the Edge, I will convince the Champion to return for the Day of Breath."

Shavazme is silent for what feels like an eternity. He stares at Fallon, head slightly cocked, creases in his face appearing, smoothing, then returning deeper. "Pardon?" he finally says.

"Do I need to repeat myself?"

The general's son holds out his hand for the pipe. Thinking nothing of it other than Shavazme's matching affection for smoking, Fallon obliges. Shavazme first dumps the charred herbs onto the tray, then lets the pipe fall from his fingers in a dramatic fashion.

"I think we should let the smoke clear from your head, then order you some coffee from the bar."

Fallon balks. Shavazme has never once missed an opportunity to involve Fallon in mischief. It was Shavazme that brought Fallon to his first card tournament at the tavern, and Shavazme who perfected the art of sneaking liquor bottles from the palace kitchen. Fallon enacting a plan of this magnitude without his friend at his side seemed absurd.

"It must seem like an odd thing to say –" Fallon begins.

"An asinine thing to say. There are *demons* at the Edge. You've heard the lessons, they're attracted to our blood, our flesh." The seriousness layered in Shavazme's voice breeds anxiety in Fallon. This is not going well at all.

"That's why we have the Champion. She'll protect us if anything goes wrong. I have complete faith in her, don't you?"

"Of course I do! Bless the Champion." Shavazme waves his hand irritably. "But why can't you send guards instead?"

Fallon needs to choose his response carefully. Shavazme is his oldest friend, but he's still the son of the general. One slip of the tongue to his father that Fallon is attempting to steal the throne from Abner, and their familial problems become council discussions and kingdom whispers.

Like Wilcon said, his parents don't believe he wants the throne. That must be the reason Abner was chosen over him. He has to show them they're wrong.

"Our longest-living Champion has yet to be properly honored. We don't know why she refuses to return, but I intend to find out face-to-face, rather than send a letter as we always do. She deserves to know how grateful we are for her protection."

Shavazme's gaze travels around the room, landing on the door several times. It's obvious he aches to call the women back in so he can continue drinking and trifling.

Fallon pushes on. "The courier and escorts have never been grievously attacked – to my knowledge. There's been reports of demon sightings, but they've always said the Champion protected them. Imagine seeing one slain before your own eyes!"

Shavazme shoots Fallon an incredulous look, and Fallon realizes the promise of danger is not the route to take.

"You'll have full access to any liquor in my family's collection," he adds. That piques Shavazme's interest. "And I will pay for your private rooms at Gilded Hall for the next three months."

Shavazme re-packs the pipe with fresh herbs, sprinkling red flakes from a small bowl on top. He takes a hard pull then blows a thick cloud towards the ceiling. Fallon stirs uncomfortably in his seat, but he doesn't jump up and demand an answer like he wishes to. He waits patiently for Shavazme to finish the theatrics.

"For the next year," his friend states. "Both the liquor *and* the rooms."

Every clench in Fallon's body releases. "You've got a deal."

Shavazme lets out a wild howl. "This is the wildest and dumbest thing we'll ever do." He fills two short glasses with a dark amber liquid and hands one to Fallon. "To traveling to the Edge and living to tell the tale."

They clink their glasses together and drink.

When Fallon stands, he nearly falls back into the chair when a rush of blood, smoke, and liquor coalesce in his head.

"We need to catch the courier at the portcullis, then?" Shavazme asks, rising to his feet with the same shakiness.

Fallon nods as he leans against the chair's tall back, waiting for his head to stop swimming.

The two share a hearty laugh before heading for the door. In the hall outside, the entertainers stand feet from the room, waiting to be invited back in. When Fallon and Shavazme exit instead, Ramini huffs before guiding the new girl away.

"Never worry, beautiful girls! I will return soon, and often," Shavazme calls after them as Fallon throws his arm around Shavazme's shoulders – partly to keep himself steady – and begins to steer him to the street above.

Outside, it takes Fallon a few long blinks to adjust to the mid-afternoon sun. He still squints as he and Shavazme exit the side street and enter a wider, busier road. Citizens flow in one direction towards the city center, where the afternoon market will be in full swing. Fallon pulls Shavazme into the steady stream of people and lets it take them willingly. It will be faster to cut straight through the marketplace, than go around it. In a short while, Fallon and Shavazme walk, sometimes stumble, briskly through excited shoppers. Some sling over-flowing sacks over their shoulders, others pull small carts behind them on wheels. Children run circles around each other before their parents snatch them by the arm. The stalls tempt Fallon to peruse their offerings, while buskers croon ballads of love and adventure. He wonders if they'll write songs of his spontaneous and daring journey to the Edge one day.

Beside him, Shavazme tucks his hands into his trouser pockets, looking straight ahead. He's never cared for the fussiness of the market. Too many people, too many sounds, too many scents, Shavazme always complained. This was more Fallon and Abner's affair. The twins have spent endless hours enjoying the people, sounds, and scents before returning to the palace with bulging bags. Fallon's were always filled with treats from traveling merchants bringing flavors of faraway lands, Abner's with fresh floral bouquets for their quarters and countless articles of clothing.

Fallon smiles at the memories until guilt wrings his stomach. He pushes Abner from his mind. Instead, he indulges in his fantasy of returning with the Champion at his side – this time, the reaction is louder, especially from his parents, who break into tears at his bravery–

"Now what?" Shavazme says.

Fallon snaps back to the present. They've reached the portcullis. The city's entrance gate is bordered by two stone towers, tall as ancient trees. Guards pace the walkway above the portcullis that continues along the city's bordering stone wall. Fallon tucks his chin, hoping the crown of his head isn't noticeable from the wall's height. He's sure every guard reports as much information to Wilcon as the general himself, if not more. And the advisor would *not* approve of this endeavor.

"We need to find the courier's cart; it's not hard to miss," Fallon says.

He scans the spacious area before the portcullis, mostly packed with parked carts and workers tending to horses at the large stables to his right. It hardly takes a minute to spot the cart meant for more dangerous roads. It sits alone in an open space as if the others give it a wide berth. Scuffed metal covers much of the wood, the sides and top heavily armored; the wheels are entirely metal. Two of the largest horses Fallon has ever seen wait patiently with it, harnessed and hitched to a wooden pole sticking out of the ground. They flick their heads, tousling thick braids of chestnut hair.

The driver's bench is empty. Fallon finds himself both relieved and nervous he didn't miss the trip. He runs his hands through his curls, then adjusts his collar and sleeves several times. Gold flakes pepper the ground around his feet.

"We can't convince the escorts and courier of our passage covered in gilded flakes and smelling like liquor and herbs," he gripes.

Shavazme looks down at his clothing, much more gold-dusted than Fallon's, and bursts into laughter.

The ground begins to shake, and Fallon jerks his head towards the portcullis. The gate rises as the courier and her escorts come around the stables and head towards the armored cart. She moves herself in a chair made of metal and wood, with two metal wheels fastened to the sides. The escorts lead two more large horses by the reins.

Fallon swipes at his shirt and pants, trying in vain to remove every bit of the Gilded Hall's evidence. When he notices Shavazme only brushing lightly at his clothing, Fallon abandons himself to smack at his friend.

"Alright, alright," Shavazme dances out of Fallon's range. "We both know a good wash is the only thing that gets these flakes off. We'll just demand they keep their opinions to themselves."

Fallon nods, though he isn't convinced. "I wish there was something we could do about the smell, at least."

"Ah!" Shavazme pulls a small perfume bottle of midnight-blue glass from his pocket. He untwists the top, then sprinkles several yellow drops onto his wrists before handing it over.

Fallon gags. It reeks of a too-sweet syrup drizzled over wet, muddy leaves.

"It's *imported,*" Shavazme snaps.

The courier reaches the driver's bench, which sits lower than most carts and carriages Fallon has seen. She reaches for a metal ring nailed into a wooden bracket on the side of the bench and uses it to haul her body from her chair. Once settled, she slips on a pair of black gloves from a pocket in her baggy brown cloak, then reaches to slip the horses' reins from the wooden pole. One of the escorts attends to the courier's chair – popping the wheels off, folding the contraption in various ways until it resembles an odd stack of wood and metal, then slides all the parts into a large compartment beneath the cart.

"All supplies and gifts accounted for? Especially the tablets?" the courier calls out.

Both escorts confirm with nods.

It's now or never. Fallon douses his wrists and neck with the perfume. "Onward." His nostrils sting from the pungent scent as he and Shavazme stride up to the cart. The escorts immediately pause from saddling their steeds and turn towards their heir, standing shoulder-to-shoulder.

"Heir Fallon, Master Shavazme," one greets with a bow. The other does the same. "Is there a problem?"

"No problem at all." Fallon looks the speaking escort in her eyes, like someone would if they weren't drunk and about to do something reckless. "We'll be accompanying you to the Edge today."

The courier's head swivels around from her seat, shock stretching the lines of her aged face. Had the escorts not undergone strict etiquette training at the academy, Fallon imagines they would look much the same.

"We didn't receive word from the general or the sovereigns of this." The speaking escort chews on her next words before saying, "This has never happened before."

It dawns on Fallon that if the results of this day are not received well, or, god forbid, he and Shavazme are injured, the punishment will fall on the escorts. *When I'm on the throne, I'll adorn them with praise and increase their rank. They'll be seen as heroes. They'll thank me.*

"You are correct, Escort..."

"Denya, my heir. And Escort Burkhard." She motions to the other guard.

"Escort Denya and Escort Burkhard, I thank you, deeply, for your service. I have always admired what you do." *Laying it on too thick.* "The sovereigns are worried Shavazme and I are too sheltered in our knowledge of Niawa's strife with demons. They send us with you, in your care, to bring back experience and insightfulness." *A little self-deprecation, a little sense of duty. Just right.*

The escorts share a look of unease. If they send for confirmation from the palace, they'll insult an heir, the general's son, and possibly the sovereigns in the process. They'll also waste precious time with the sun in the sky.

Shavazme doesn't wait for a reaction. "For heaven's sake! We're climbing aboard this metal crate on wheels and we'll all take a merry trip to the Edge. End of discussion." He brushes past the stunned escorts to the driver's bench, where the courier gives him a knowing look. There's clearly not space for all three of them. Eyes rolling, Shavazme stalks to the back of the cart.

"Looks like we're stowing away in the bed like vagabonds," he remarks loudly.

"I apologize for Shavazme's behavior; he shouldn't speak to you like that," Fallon says to the escorts. He begins to sway on his feet from the liquor and smoke, and Escort Denya's eyes narrow. Her suspicion pushes Fallon to follow Shavazme. The cart doors splay open and Shavazme pulls himself into the covered bed, half-full with wooden crates. Fallon's hands and knees scrape against the rough flooring as he climbs in after.

The escorts come around to stare at the scene of two high-ranking members of the kingdom tucked away in the back of a cart, helpless to stop it.

Fallon fears they'll rise above their loyalties and wise up, so he regretfully takes a page from Shavazme's brusque book. "I want to leave *now*. Tell the courier – please, and thank you – that we are ready."

The escorts only hesitate for one more second before each taking a door in their hands. As sunlight flees from the bed, Fallon's legs begin to jitter. The door latch falls into place with a loud thud, shrouding them in darkness.

Had the escorts waited even a breath longer, he would have escaped with the light.

CHAPTER 5

"I can't see a damn thing and it's sweltering in here," Shavazme whines.

Fallon leans against a crate that smells strongly of salt and rests his arm on another. He tucks his knees into his chest, as there isn't much room to spread his long legs.

"Would you settle down? It'll be hours, and we only just started."

He isn't sure how far they've traveled, but his back and rear already ache from jostling against hard surfaces.

"Thought I'd at least get to see the countryside on our way to hell," Shavazme says. Fallon hears him rustle around, then a soft thud tells Fallon he has finally sat down. "Why are we *really* doing this?"

"I told you. To convince the Champion to return. Think of how we'll be the talk of the city. People will be begging us to describe the particular shade of a demon's eyes, to reenact the fearsome roars that rattled our ears, to tell them how it feels to touch the bristling fur on the creature's backs–"

"Oh, we're petting the demons too?"

"No, I only meant–"

"Also, they don't have fur. It's all rough skin the color of charcoal."

"Really?"

Shavazme snorts. "Do any words that aren't about drinking stick inside that head of yours?"

Fallon's retort dies a quick death. The darkness shields him from exposing how true Shavazme's comment strikes. He tries to remind himself that the Champion's return will wipe such jabs from everyone's minds. Fallon leans forward to his hands and knees – squeezing his eyes against a dizzying spell – then crawls towards the front of the bed where Shavazme sits.

"What are you doing?" his friend asks.

Fallon rises on his knees to rap his knuckles against the wall above them. A thick shaft of light bursts into the bed when a slat opens. The courier peeks over her shoulder through the small window. She must only be a decade older than his parents, but a deep frown adds years onto her face. He realizes he's never even spoken to the woman burdened with this harrowing task for longer than he's been alive.

Fallon searches his foggy brain for her name, determined to show her the respect she's earned. "Valerie –"

"Velma, my heir," she interjects.

"Sorry. Velma, would you mind leaving this open so we can have some light and air?"

She only nods, then turns back to the road.

Through the open slat, Fallon sees tall hills of green roll out under a cloudless sky. In the far distance, dark shapes jut out between the slopes and rises. Edge Forest, maybe. He rubs the back of his neck roughly. It's far too late to turn back now.

"Let me see!" Shavazme suddenly yanks him back to fit his boyish face into the window. "How'd you know this was here?"

"Just something I recall my family's travel carriage having, and I wondered if this cart did as well." Fallon shrugs, though he feels a little vindication after not knowing whether demons have scales or fur.

They take turns peeking out for a long while. Eventually, Fallon tires of crouching and leaves Shavazme to call out anything interesting. A large bird with a long neck. Wild stallions. What he thinks is the Rive but turns out to be a long-abandoned watch tower. Fallon busies himself with poking around the crates. Many of the lids are not nailed down but are too heavy to lift. Others would take a tool to open. Two are even strapped to the cart wall. Fallon tries in vain to glimpse into those, but all he gathers are neatly placed rows of glass objects. Long crates at the bottom of the stacks are clearly stocked with weapons – given away by glints of metal that he catches between wooden slats. The crates Fallon can easily thumb through carry clothes, piles of cloth strips, salted meats and jars of various foods, and medical supplies.

He spots something familiar amongst the medical supplies and pulls it out; a glass bottle with square cubes of compact herbs – like Abner's tablets. *Huh. The Champion has frazzled nerves.* Fallon carefully wraps it back in a layer of cloth and nestles it enough that he's sure it won't shift around.

The lid on the last crate pops open with little force, the crack resounding in the bed. Fallon shrouds the noise with a giggle. Intrigued by the sound, Shavazme abandons the open slat and crawls over to see.

"Thank Yuli-en," Fallon breathes. He picks through bottles of wines, spirits, ale, candies, and food – ignoring random trinkets and letters. He'll need more liquid courage once they reach the Edge.

While Shavazme grabs a tin of chocolates and a bottle of wine, Fallon samples an unlabeled brown flask. The liquor is remarkably strong and tastes homemade. He makes a mental note to hand pick wine from his family's private cellars to replace what he and Shavazme drink for the courier's next trip. Before long, the two go through a wine bottle, half the unlabeled flask, and several small boxes of treats. Fallon hardly notices the time fly by until Velma yells out, "Prepare yourselves."

He wipes dusted sugar from his lips as he and Shavazme scramble to the small window. They attempt to look out at the same time, their temples rubbing together. The dark, distant shapes have swelled into a forest of broad, towering trees with rich brown trunks and leaves of a hue that put the green of Niawa's crest to shame.

"Are we here?" Fallon asks.

"Almost. This is Edge Forest."

Fallon's body threatens a mutiny, his legs weakening as he tries to stay on his knees. He doesn't want to see the Edge anymore. The voice in his head – so confident before, so determined to get onto this cart – now cowers in the back of his mind.

Shavazme gasps and clutches Fallon's arm. "Is that what I think it is?"

Past the courier's grayed head an unfathomably large, black rock rises into the sky. As the cart pushes on, the cliffs at the base of the Rive come into view. Fallon shrivels into himself as Shavazme brightens with each turn of the wheels. He bombards Velma with questions about all she has seen: What is the Champion like? Will they see a demon breathe fire like a mythical dragon? Can the creatures speak?

"Leave her alone. We'll find out soon enough." Fallon forces a smile. He hopes it hides the way his neck strains from clenching his teeth.

The trees soon pull back, revealing a destitute world. Weather-beaten bones protrude from the dirt, curling over rocks or shooting straight up like blades. Long skulls with eye sockets Fallon could put his whole leg through are buried throughout the terrain as if slumbering. Rusted shields and bits of armor are half-submerged like tombstones. These sights steal even Shavazme's glee.

The cart begins to slow, pulling Fallon deeper into his horror, even as the wine and spirits make his head swim. He spots the Champion's cabin a short distance away, tucked away at the edge of a vast field. It's surprisingly small, and quaint, like a farmer's shed.

Before he's ready, the courier pulls on the reins and they come to a complete stop.

A woman waits for them.

Fallon has seen many drawings and paintings of the longest-living Champion, even dolls and figurines. But no artist has ever truly captured her. The Champion's hair is a dark shadow over her scalp. A yellowish-gray liquid splashes over her demon-teeth armor and flecks across her face. From under her neck guard, a scar travels up behind her ear. Another few faint lines cross her cheeks and the bridge of her nose. Her pretty face is exactly how Fallon remembers, yet, that crying girl is nowhere to be found.

This faraway land that's only existed in Fallon's lessons, more terrible than his imagination could ever dream, is clearly hers to rule.

For the first time, he feels like a stranger in his own kingdom.

CHAPTER 6

Velma and her escorts come around the bend. The guards raise their swords, signaling to me as their horses slow down. As soon as they dismount, they begin the process of lugging my supplies to the cabin without a word. They change from time to time, so I don't bother remembering their names or faces.

I glance at the Rive – no movement – then go to greet Velma.

"Hello, dear," she says brightly.

"Pleasant journey?" I respond, stroking the soft muzzle of one of the horses. I hold out my hands to them both, strips of dried meat on my palms. The stallions lap them up vigorously.

Velma glances over her shoulder. "A bit louder than usual."

Embarrassment warms my neck, but I still ask the question I always do when she visits. "Any letters from my parents?"

"I wish there were. Even sent a missive myself to ask them to write. They didn't respond."

I avert her pitying eyes and fasten mine to the horses. "That's alright."

My parents have only sent seven letters in my ten years here. When they did come, I read about the dinners my parents had been invited to, the gifts left on their doorstep in my honor. I shouldn't be surprised anymore, the last one coming two years ago.

"I'll keep trying." Velma gives me a wink. "There may not be a letter in my satchel, but I did bring a surprise. I'd wipe that blood off your face if I were you."

I'm hardly given a second to manage my confusion before a tall man and a boy hobble from the back of the cart. The boy looks at the surrounding landscape with a crooked sneer, his hair as orange as tangerines, while the man immediately sees to the wrinkles in his clothing and unruly curls. He's strikingly familiar, but I can't quite put my finger on how I know him. As he walks towards me, trying not to trip over loose rocks and fix a freed button on his blouse, recognition hits me like a Spiky Lizard's tail to the head. I'm taken back to the throne room where I lowered to my knees before the sibyl and the royal family. I've long since made peace with that day and how little I understood my calling as the Champion, but sometimes, it feels like my body can't let go of the terror.

Seeing Heir Fallon again – he looks older than that day, a more carved jaw, longer nose, but the same lively eyes – the humming storms through me.

He stops a few feet away, looking me over with open curiosity. I attempt to greet him verbally, but my throat is shut tight while my mind battles my body for control. For so long, I've only spoken with myself, and Velma, and it took me a long while to give her more than one-word answers.

"Wow, Champion, the artists do not do you justice. You are the picture of glory, and I'm truly honored to see you again after all these years," Heir Fallon greets me, his words slightly slurred. He and the orange-haired boy reek of alcohol, and they have strange gold flecks spattered across their clothing.

"Mm," I manage to get out, with a curt nod. Which is disrespectful. He is an heir to the throne, not an escort. I have to show him the girl he remembers is long gone. "Lift your chin," I mutter to myself.

"Excuse me?" the boy says.

I think of the Gargantuan I forced to eat three fire bombs and watch burn from the inside out just hours ago. That helps. "Thank you, Heir Fallon." Now what do I say? The royal family has never visited the Edge since the Rive opened. If an heir is here, there must be news so important it couldn't be sent in a letter. "Why are you here?"

The boy quirks an eyebrow as if I've said something odd. I decide to ignore him; he's most likely the heir's assistant.

Heir Fallon takes a step closer. He clasps his fingers together over his stomach and turns his lips inward. Is he nervous? The news must be bad. My eyes widen. There's something wrong with my parents.

"How long have they been dead?" I blurt out, my heart beginning to race.

The heir tilts his head. "Who's dead?"

"How did it happen? Is it a sickness? How long have my parents been dead?" The humming swells even more. This is why they haven't written. They were both ill and didn't know how to tell me. Didn't want to distract me from my mission.

"No, no, Champion, please, calm yourself. Your parents are alive." Heir Fallon's hands are outstretched, as if he's placating me.

I realize I've taken two steps closer to him and my hands grip the blade hilts sticking out from my waist. I quickly walk those steps back. "I'm sorry, I thought – I'm sorry."

"Almighty above, this place must make you insane," the boy comments.

Heir Fallon rounds on him. "*Shavazme*." To my surprise, the boy rolls his eyes in the heir's face before dipping his chin to me as an apology. I don't like him at all. Heir Fallon turns back to me. "No need to apologize. Now, to answer your question..." His nervousness returns in a flash. "I came to ask you something. Uhm, I hope you'll say yes. Actually, before we get into that, please remind me of your name, my brain is a little murky right now."

I know the answer, of course. It's my name. But my tongue is dormant. I try to remember the last time I spoke it, until it returns like a faded ghost: "Oly. Hoskins."

"Lovely." He smiles widely.

I suddenly feel a burning need to run to my cabin. Or for a demon to come. I look at the Rive and feel disappointed it doesn't glow and tremble. That would surely send them back down the road. "It isn't safe for them here," I say.

"Who are you talking to?" the boy asks with a tone that makes me whip my head back around.

"I'll get on with it, then," Heir Fallon interjects. "Champion, I came to personally invite you to the Day of Breath. I understand you've already denied our invitation, but as this year will swear in a new sovereign, it's especially important. You are a beacon of hope for Niawa, and having you at the side of the newly crowned sovereign will be a treasured moment for years to come."

"No," I answer the moment he stops speaking.

The boy screeches like a long-necked scavenger bird. He doubles over in a fit of laughter, holding his belly while the heir's cheeks redden.

"Would you please reconsider? Think of the parade! The entire city gathering to praise you. You haven't seen your family in years, they'll be happy to –"

"No," I repeat.

Heir Fallon chews his lip. He seems frustrated. "What will it take for you to say yes? I'll have anything you desire sent on the next courier trip." He reaches out to touch my upper arm.

I jerk my shoulder back as if his hand is a demon's claw. The quick movement tweaks an injury from months ago. Pain sprints into my right shoulder and I grunt.

"Are you okay?" Heir Fallon closes the gap between us to inches. His hand drapes over my shoulder, concern twisting his face. I freeze entirely. The smell of him is overwhelming, the scent mixing with demon blood as if a carcass has been adorned with fruit syrup and moss – then dunked in a tub of liquor. It's a terribly strange smell that inspires a fluttering in my stomach. I don't dare meet his eyes, his face so close to mine. Our breaths crash together, creating a cloud of mist between us. I fear inhaling, breathing a part of him in. He's so close. What must I look like right now – what must I *smell* like? I haven't bathed in days. How long has it been since someone was this close to me? I think of hugs. My parents wrapping their arms around me, back when my head only came up to their thighs. Tears threaten to sting my eyes as a powerful yearning to lay my head on his shoulder fights to breach the surface. The heir's mouth moves out of the corner of my vision, but I can't hear him through the humming, as if cotton has been stuffed into my ears, muffling everything.

"Oly, dear!" Velma says just under a yell.

A demon is coming. Instinct takes over, returning me to clarity. I aim to check the Rive, but my eyes catch on bright orange bobbing in the field.

Heir Fallon must catch the same sight as he darts past me, waving his hands about and shouting with full lungs. "Shavazme! What the hell are you doing?"

I come up behind him and clasp my hand over his mouth. "Do *not* make loud noises. The Rive can hear you," I hiss. At first, he tries to buck me away, but my warning subdues him.

The boy cuts from a footpath into the field. He hasn't gone far, but he moves quickly. I take off after Shavazme – thanking Velma with a glance for bringing me back to my senses – and Heir Fallon follows. Behind me, I hear him bump into every rusted weapon and chunk of armor, kicking several things with a low curse.

The boy doesn't acknowledge our presence when we reach him. He searches the ground with a determined face.

"What in Yuli-en's name are you doing?" the heir demands.

"Looking for a souvenir, like a skull or something," Shavazme answers.

"We shouldn't be running through the Edge."

"Seeing as your plan spectacularly failed, might as well bring something back to remember this ridiculous voyage." Shavazme picks up a chunk of white stone, inspects it, then tosses it aside. His face is even more flushed than Heir Fallon's, eyes cloudy like dirty glass.

I can no longer ignore my suspicions. They're drunk. Protecting myself from demons is already a challenge, especially with my waning strength, but having to mind an heir with a liquor-logged brain and his rude and equally sloppy assistant is a distraction I can't afford. My only solace is if they survive an attack, they may be too drunk to remember details of my slow movements and the grunts and wheezes I expel as I swing my weapons. Either way, it's time for them to leave.

"You need to go, Heir Fallon. It's too dangerous here. Especially in your condition," I say with my eyes on the Rive, in case it has a sense of humor today and wants to give a demonstration.

"Condition?" he responds.

I mull over my response. It's been a long time since I've been in the presence of royalty, but I still know accusing an heir of being drunk wouldn't be favorable. "I only worry about... your ability to run, if necessary."

Hair Fallon lowers his chin, his eyes trailing over the ground. I tense, wondering if I insulted him.

"I'm embarrassed you noticed. You deserve me at my best, Champion." He looks back at Shavazme. "She's right, we should get back to the cart."

I hadn't realized the tightness in my shoulders until I lower them now. Hearing an heir speak as if he could possibly shame himself on my account makes the weakness in my body dissipate, if only for a moment.

"You're the one who dragged me here. Help me find something good, or scary – scary is better – then we'll go." Shavazme's tone drips with disrespect. He talks to Heir Fallon in a way that would beg a guard's swift blade at his neck. But the heir just joins the boy to rifle over the ground, nudging rocks and rusted armor around with his boot.

I trail behind them as they move further into the plain, powerless to deny the heir's wish to explore his own land. Watching the two, hearing Shavazme hurl more disrespect about how I denied Heir Fallon's request to return for the Day of Breath, and the heir only chuckling in response, I drift back to the pink house I grew up in. My parents' open anger at my nerves, my fits of short breath and lightheadedness when I struggled to find words – I, too, couldn't find it in myself to ask for understanding. For relief.

After a while, Heir Fallon leaves Shavazme to scour the ground – the boy peppering his search with comments on disgust at the state of the Edge – and comes to walk beside me. Quite close, so I take a short step to the side, recalling that immobilizing need for a hug.

"I remember the day you received the Blessing," he says, rubbing dirt off his palms. "You're very different now."

"I should hope so," I respond.

He stares at me with curiosity as if waiting for more. Did I not answer him? God, I hope they find a suitable souvenir soon.

"How do you entertain yourself out here?" he continues.

I don't entertain myself, my duties are plenty occupying. The heir continues to study me, his eyes twinkling like stars in their glassy haze. I look back at my cabin, wishing I was sitting on my chair watching the Rive right now, with only the sibyl's tapestry watching me. At least I can't *see* her roaming gaze.

"Is it comfortable in there?" Heir Fallon notices where I look. "I really hope" – he angles himself in front of my vision – "that it is. For all you do, you should at least be comfortable."

"It's fine."

"That's great to hear." He then proceeds to make awkward swings with his arms. "Do you have a favorite animal?"

"Why?" His questions seem determined to strip my armor away, layer by layer. Is his true goal to discover if I'm not honoring my calling? Does he know about my weakening strength? "Is my favorite animal some kind of test?" I wonder aloud.

He laughs softly. "Just wondering."

I release my bottom lip, having chewed it quite thoroughly, and decide that a favorite animal is not a test. "Elephants."

"That makes sense. Strong, impressive, beautiful. Like you."

I'd put on my helmet, which is fastened to my hip, if it didn't feel the most obvious way to hide. Though, perhaps, I should understand he doesn't shower praises on Oly Hoskins, mid-ranked guard trainee who could barely look anyone in the eye; he offers them to the prestige of the Champion. And that's who will accept these compliments.

"Thank you, Heir Fallon." I pause to bow to him. My back is tight as ropes, so I don't bend far.

"No, thank you. I meant what I said. Being here with you both excites and humbles me. In the cart, I saw all the gifts and letters sent from the city. It must be nice to hear from your friends and family and know how respected you are." His voice trails off at the end, leaving behind a silence tangled with more thoughts he doesn't express.

"The gifts are from strangers I've never spoken to before," I respond.

Heir Fallon stops. I take a couple steps before stopping with him.

"You don't hear from your friends?".

"I don't have any. Well, maybe Velma."

The heir's face cracks into a sorrowful expression that makes me look away. I haven't thought about my time at the academy in a long while. Struggling to connect with the other trainees, the nights I spent alone watching them relax in the courtyard from my dormitory window. A longing feeling hollowing out my stomach.

"Do you only have her to talk to when she visits once a month?" he presses.

I don't want to answer any more of these questions. Or remember. I keep my gaze to the Rive as I start walking again. Gratefully, the heir joins Shavazme again. But, every few minutes, he looks back at me with determination in his eyes.

In a short time, we veer towards Edge Forest, nearing an area where, a few days prior, a Burrower led me on a tiring chase. The demon's unearthed path has yet to be swept away by winds or patted down by rain, and its charcoal body still lays half-submerged, its wide, flat head hidden inside a hole of its own making. At the end of our battle, it tried to wriggle back underground, but I'd already thrown a poison bomb inside. To be sure it was dead, I hacked the stubby legs from its body and tossed them about.

Heir Fallon comes upon one of the severed legs, as long as his own arm. His entire body reacts with shock. He clasps his cheeks with his hands, angling himself away as though the leg will suddenly come to life. With wide eyes, he inspects the flat foot with its thick, sharp claws, and the pale muscle and fat hanging from exposed bone.

Shavazme stands beside the Burrower's body, its spine coming up to the boy's waist. His smarmy, boisterous air dampens as he reaches out to touch the carcass but flinches back every time his fingers get close. The heir notices Shavazme standing over the gray mound and joins the boy to gawk.

I know exactly what will satisfy their search and get them to leave. "Burrowers have a bone shaped like a butterfly between their neck and head. It's kind of pretty. Would that be a good souvenir?"

"Sounds perfect," Heir Fallon answers. Shavazme just shrugs.

I walk behind the demon's body and grab onto the spinal disc protruding from its back while digging my arm beneath its belly. When I pull, the heir and Shavazme nearly trip over their own feet to move out of the way. The Burrower is heavy, and God, does my back ache from the strain, but I'm able to drag it from the hole and lay it down a few feet away.

Heir Fallon and Shavazme inch closer. They are flushed of color and their fingers ball into fists. I'm not surprised. Burrowers are by far the ugliest demon I've encountered. Their bodies are as wide as their flat heads, with black eyes that seem to ooze over the sides. Two thin slits make up their small nose, and its wide mouth houses several rows of tiny but numerous sharp teeth. With four short legs and long, curved appendages protruding from its neck for the sole purpose of digging, the thing has roused a shiver or two up *my* spine.

I can't help but glance to make sure Heir Fallon is watching before I pull my axe from its straps. In the same movement, I bring the sharp blade down into the Burrower's neck. Bone splinters with a dull snap, barely drowning out the shouts of horror from my audience. I shoot them a look they've come to know as my reminder for lowered voices.

My axe makes quick work of removing the head. A few more swings breaks the spine and slices through muscle and sinew. When the head is freed, I drop my axe and reach into the bloody hole, feeling for the butterfly bone. I find it, wrench it free from its ligaments, then hold it out for the heir to inspect.

He doesn't move. Yellow-gray demon blood splotches over his waistcoat and the blouse beneath. More blood splashes up his neck and dots his face like freckles. Shavazme is equally stained and looks very angry.

"Oh." I dig into my belt, pull out a rag, then toss it to Heir Fallon. It lands on the ground and Shavazme grabs it first. He breaks into a stream of obscenities as he runs the cloth over every inch of exposed skin. The words 'barbaric' and 'horrifying' are thrown around more than once.

"How did the boy expect me to get a bone nestled inside a demon's head?" I muse.

Shavazme glares at me as he wipes his hands. Once he's done, he tosses the blood-covered rag to Heir Fallon. The heir wipes himself down in silence while his assistant continues to rant. I open my mouth to remind Shavazme of his volume, but I'm beat to it.

"Don't shout and stomp around in the Champion's face after she's done exactly what we asked for." Heir Fallon's voice holds depth, and edge, even if it wavers a bit.

Shavazme slows like the last bits of life from a wind-up toy, looking bewildered. He keeps his disapproval known by crossing his arms tightly, but his mouth snaps shut.

The heir takes small steps towards the butterfly bone I again hold out to him. He retches, throws his fingers over his mouth, then takes a moment to gather himself. "Thank you, Champion. It's as beautiful as you said."

I nod. And strangely, smile. Though his face is locked in a grimace, the corners of his lips also turn up.

"Hearing about your power and seeing it are very different things," he says, taking the bone from my hand.

I'm glad someone of importance can witness my strength before it disappears entirely. I hope he speaks of it often, and this is how I'll be remembered.

"Looks like the escorts are done and it's time to go," Shavazme drawls.

I turn in the direction of the cart to see what he means.

One escort stands beside the cart, the other is on their way towards us. They wave their arms wildly. Velma also waves hers. But no one makes a sound.

I snap my head to the Rive. Its face ripples furiously, surge after surge of disturbing movement. A Winged Hand emerges from the scar, rising into the sky. Another demon I don't recognize follows it, crawling down the cliff face like an insect.

The Winged Hand unleashes an anguished scream. The Trace will ignite, calling them to me, and the heir.

I pull my helmet on and grab my axe. “Run as fast as you can.”

CHAPTER 7

The Winged Hand spots me first and soars over the field with its bat-like wings. Long, thick appendages like fingers unfurl from around its short, scaly body as it nears the ground. The finger-legs twitch with anticipation until they pound into the dirt several yards away. It scuttles furiously in my direction as the wings fold into its back. Between harrowing screeches, its long black tongue flicks out over rows of sharp teeth.

The other demon I don't recognize stalls in the field, as if it can't decide where to go. It's eerily human-like, if a human's torso, legs, and arms were stretched like taffy over the bone. A large, bald head is held up by a thin neck, making me think of a balloon. The creature's skin isn't charcoal like every demon I've seen so far, but pale and tinged with pink. It stands on all fours, rising tall above the field, shifting its large, oval, red-ringed eyes between me and the two figures racing towards the cart.

The heir and the assistant, Shavazme, move slower than I would like as they keep looking back. One of the escorts rushes to meet them. I stay by the Burrower, using the short time I have to calm my mind. The Winged Hand will need to die first, and quickly, before the new demon reaches me.

Clouds of dirt erupt in the Winged Hand's path as it rushes closer. Spit froths on the creases of its tongue.

I arm myself with a holy flare and tighten my fingers around my axe.

It's feet away now.

I take a step back, and my foot slips.

My legs fly out, dropping me on my back against a hard and jagged surface. And wet. The putrid scent of demon blood tells me it's the Burrower. The impact vibrates up my back, even through my armor. When I try to jump to my feet, my spine refuses to bend.

The Winged Hand rises above me, finger-legs fanning outwards. Its jaw widens, tongue flicking excitedly to taste the side of my face. I can see down its throat, where my head may soon be.

I shut my eyes and clench my hand, praying there's still a glass orb in it. The holy flare fractures and the demon roars. Its tongue leaves my face, along with the heat from its body. After a few seconds, when the flare's light has faded, I open my eyes and try to push myself to my feet. My back still refuses. Anxiety strangles every nerve as I lay limp over the Burrower. Yuli-en above, am I paralyzed?

The Winged Hand writhes around nearby, sending tremors through the ground from the jerking and lashing of its mass. Its wings spread open and close as it struggles to make sense of losing its sight. It rolls away from me, but not far enough that one lucky move won't scoop my legs into its gaping mouth.

As if it heard my thoughts, the demon charges forward clumsily and collides with my body. I'm flipped onto my stomach – but I haven't let go of my axe. The Winged Hand goes still, but I hear its finger-legs tap anxiously on the ground. Though it can smell me, it can also smell the dead Burrower. Our scents mingle, and it doesn't know which is which.

The blinding magic will fade. I need to move. Now.

Holding my breath so it won't hear me, I wriggle one shoulder, then the other. Then I shake my arms. So far so good. The demon's wings flap over my body and I go rigid as thin membrane brushes over my helmet.

I need to breathe. Screams fill my head, my lungs pleading for air. The wing shakes but doesn't lift. Shivers wrack my skin. My heart pounds in sync with a pulse in my temples. Unable to hold it any longer, I inhale deeply, tasting air soggy with dirt and blood. The wing rises, and the demon's head swivels around, red-ringed eyes finding me. It propels forward, deciding the sound it heard is exactly where the meat is.

I have no choice but to act as if my back is mine to command again. I throw my body, rolling down the carcass and sending myself out of its range. The Winged Hand's teeth spear into the Burrower's back, where my head had just laid. I crawl away quickly, feeling control of my muscles return. The Blessing hasn't completely abandoned me yet.

The Winged Hand walks through the carcass, smashing what is left of the Burrower into the dirt. It senses me. I allow it. The demon screams and rushes in my direction. It's still partially blind, so I move easily out of its path, dodging its head by a hair. I drag my axe along one side of its thick torso, hot blood spraying from the tear. Wetness trickles beneath my armor and soaks into my trousers.

Another axe swing separates a finger-leg entirely.

The demon spins around, slumping to one side. Its hot breath billows into my helmet's openings. I know the skull is hard, there's no point in driving my blade there. Eyes are always soft, however.

I flip my axe around and grab it by the blades with both hands, then ram the butt of the weapon into one glistening eye. The haft of my axe disappears halfway before the Winged Hand roars and jerks backwards, taking my weapon with it.

The short swords at my hips replace my axe immediately.

As the Winged Hand thrashes in pain, I look past it towards the Rive. The new demon is close, maybe a minute away. But it can't seem to keep moving forward, as if an invisible wall thwarts it from getting to me. Or, like it's being tugged on, but it fights against the pull.

The Winged Hand swipes with a claw tipping its wing and I catch it in the chest. It knocks me backwards, but I manage not to fall. Finger-legs sweep out from below. I jump just in time to stay upright and make a wild slash with my swords. One blade leaves a deep gash across the demon's face. The other collides with my axe, knocking it out of the gory eye socket.

Furious, the demon flicks its tongue out, trying to curl the thing around me. I dodge left and right, all the while looking for a way to get to its other eye. It rears onto two back finger-legs and spreads its wings out wide.

In the same breath I yell my frustration, a way to kill the demon reveals itself. A bulge travels from its stomach up through its neck. Mucus that won't eat through my armor but could sizzle any exposed skin like grease in a pan. I don't wait for the bulge to reach the creature's tongue. I drive both swords deep into its neck and rip the blades downwards until bone stops me from going further. Then I let go of the hilts. As the Winged Hand shrieks, wavering on its hind limbs like a transfixed serpent, I jump and kick out both legs, lodging the blades down to the hilt. Once again, I land on my back with a thud, my flexibility not what it used to be.

The demon lunges weakly as I roll up to stand. We both heave, doubling over, staring at each other. One by one, the remaining finger-legs curl around its torso in a sad, defeated caress. I limp to my axe at its feet and pick it up with no fear of an attack. Its last red ring watches my every move.

"Oly!" Someone screams. I look to the other demon.

It heads straight for the cart, moving with odd jerks, as if every other step fights to go in the other direction. What I feared is true. The Trace calls it, but the demon brawls with the magic's pull, and it's winning.

I run into the field, leaving my swords to finish off the Winged Hand.

Heir Fallon stands with the escorts beside the cart while Shavazme is nowhere to be seen. I assume he's inside the wagon, cowering. The guards brandish broadswords and stand in front of the heir. In the driver's bench, Velma pulls the reins to steady the horses, even as they beat their hooves anxiously.

I know why she doesn't run.

They can't leave the Edge with a demon on their trail. It may follow them to Niawa. This is one of the rules the courier and the escorts are held to. If the Champion falls, then they're the last line of defense until a new Champion arrives. Even with an heir in their midst.

CHAPTER 8

Nothing could have prepared Fallon for seeing a living demon. He thought it would be like the traveling circus, bringing bears as large as merchant carts for performances. They are large, they are fearsome, they have rows of sharp teeth. But the bears never snatched his breath away. They don't send tremors through his body so violently tears shake from his eyes.

The demon comes for him, moving as quickly as it can, even though its limbs seem to disagree. If Fallon survives, the true battle will be to not bash his own brains in to rid himself of the memory.

He looks to the courier, pleading silently.

Velma shakes her head, knowing the desperate question in his eyes. Shavazme begs the same plea through the open slat. But she won't budge, and neither will the escorts.

The guard's horses have already taken off, spooked by the demon the moment it started heading their way. He wishes he was on one now, riding to safety, able to scream until his voice is hoarse.

"Maybe it'll turn around," Escort Denya says. She stands in front of him, her sword angled towards the oncoming demon. She damns her own optimism by taking a small step back.

"Haven't you fought one before?" Fallon asks.

Escort Denya shakes her head. "We've only been escorts for a short time. But don't worry, Heir Fallon, we're trained for this."

Fallon has so far bit his tongue, knowing he shouldn't shout, but he notes the way the guard's arms rattle, their feet unable to still. "*Oly*!" he yells with every whisp of air in his lungs.

The escorts react with horror, and the courier hisses over his shoulder.

In the distance, the Champion spins around and sprints towards the cart. Behind her, the large dark form of the other demon crumples. A small bit of hope lights in Fallon. If she defeated one on her own, this one will be killed just as easily. His hope is short-lived when he notices the Champion runs in an odd way, as if a limp drags her down.

The demon will reach him first.

"My heir, get in the cart," Escort Denya orders.

Fallon nods erratically, but he can't seem to move his legs. He can see every detail of the skeletal creature now. Bone pushing against thin skin. Massive black eyes that take up much of its pale, bald head. Red rings hovering in the black depths of its large eyes, somehow both blank and hungering.

There isn't time to run to the back of the cart and not call attention to himself now. Fallon glances at an extra sword hanging from Escort Burkhard's waist. Before his brain can argue, he frees it from the sheath and points the sharp tip towards the demon. Fallon has never felt sillier.

It reaches them.

A collective inhale sucks all the air from the world. Fallon's heart ceases to pound. Everything goes quiet. His tongue still holds the faint taste of the only life he knew before coming to the Edge: wine and pungent, sticky herbs for smoking. Then, the sun disappears, blotted out by the demon's round head. Fallon cranks his neck back to behold its full horror. It's tall as a house, and though it seems to be made only of skin and bone, its wrists are the width of his thigh. The demon's lip-less mouth hangs open, revealing crowded rows of teeth, all different sizes – all brutally sharp. The red rings in its eyes drift over them all, seeming to float in the massive black pools.

Escort Denya moves first. She dashes between its front arms and thrusts her broadsword up at the demon's protruding chest. Only the tip reaches its ribs, but she manages to run a tear between two bones. Yellow-gray blood rains down on the guard before she can move from beneath it. Fallon gags from the putrid, indescribable smell. Like sulfur and raw meat. The demon releases a deep, elongated moan that makes Fallon jump, then bats one arm at them all, barely missing the cart with its long, bony fingers peaked with flesh-colored claws. The escort's training affords her the good sense to duck, but Fallon doesn't. He lands several feet away on his stomach, hacking dirt out of his mouth.

The demon leans back onto its haunches as it reaches out towards Escort Burkhard. To the guard's luck, the demon's movements are slow, as if its in no particular rush to devour anyone. Escort Burkhard slides out of the clawed hands path while slashing out with his sword, leaving a gash across the demon's palm. It moans again with an expressionless face, somehow thrusting Fallon into deeper terror.

The demon seems to decide the people with the swords are too much trouble and abandons Escort Burkhard to lean forward and reach for the courier with its injured hand.

"Watch out!" Fallon shouts. He finally jumps to his feet and races to the cart bench, dragging the heavy sword awkwardly along. He can't believe he's running *towards* the demon.

Velma's face is steely, unmoving as if she studies a painting. With one hand, she pulls back on the horse's reigns, steadying their growing anxiety. With the other, she reaches down behind her and whips out a fearsome-looking spear with several large spikes running from the blade and halfway down the pole. She jabs the weapon straight through the demon's wrist, just as its fingers hover over her head. Fallon stops in his tracks, his sword still touching the dirt. The demon yanks its hand away, taking the spear with it.

"I want that back!" Velma barks at the escorts. Then to Fallon, she yells, "Get in the cart!"

Fallon decides to listen this time. He couldn't even bring himself to lift the sword. All he's managed to do is serve as a distraction for the real warriors – including an elderly woman. He drops the blade and starts towards the cart bed, but a scream of alarm has him twisting back around.

The demon slowly lifts Escort Burkhard off the ground, both hands wrapped tightly around his torso and arms. Demon blood flows down the guard's legs from its lacerated hand as he struggles to push against the demon's fingers. His sword lies on the ground beneath his flailing feet. Sounds of bending metal scar the air, each creak followed by Escort Burkhard's breathless exhales. Escort Denya slices at the demon's legs, hips, anywhere she can, but it pays no mind to her. She wails as the creaking grows louder. Blood spurts from the corners of Escort Burkhard's lips, thick and dark. Escort Denya cries out, her litany of swipes becoming more erratic as she watches her companion go from wriggling to twitching.

The demon's mouth widens, and it brings Escort Burkhard up to the gaping void, as black as its eyes.

An explosion of fire ignites against the demon's back. It releases the escort, and his body drops to the ground like a sack of potatoes. Its head slowly swings around to see the Champion holding a glass orb with swirling red powder.

She hurls it directly at the demon's face, causing another explosion. The fire contracts into itself as quickly as it appeared, but leaves behind large swathes of charred skin crackling with embers. Strips of blackened flesh peel off the demon's bone where the blasts struck. Its back is even more skeletal, a paper-white spine halfway exposed. The black, burnt skin around its eyes makes it seem as though the dark pools around the red rings has spread. Fallon throws his forearm over the lower half of his face against the overwhelming stench of demon blood and smoldering flesh.

Somehow, the demon still has the strength to thrash its arms at the Champion, who darts over and under. She swings her axe in turn, cutting clean fingers and more strips of skin. When one of the demon's arms comes low to the ground, the Champion jumps with both feet to land her boots down on it. Bone snaps so loudly Fallon winces.

The demon emits a low, almost melancholy, wail. It brings the broken arm into its chest and curls over it, becoming a grotesque ball of exposed bone and crackled skin. The Champion wastes no time in sliding her axe into the straps across her back, then climbing onto the demon's sloped spine. She drags herself up to its thin neck until her legs dangle on either side of its shoulders. The demon starts to shift, attempting to buck her off, but the Champion is quick to free her axe. In a quick succession of movements, she lets the staff slide through her fingers until she holds it right beneath the double-headed blades. Then she slams one side of the sharp metal against the back of the demon's neck. Fallon loses count of the furious strikes, his mind staining with the sight of bone splintering, skin slicing, and deep moans, until the demon's head plops to the ground.

The Champion rides a now headless body down, then hops off into the pool of yellow-gray blood below. She looks at the Rive before leaning onto her knees to take long, haggard breaths.

Fallon also doubles over, expelling the full contents of his stomach until only sour bile coats the inside of his mouth. He didn't think he'd witness one demon beheading today, let alone two.

Escort Denya sobs loudly from beside the cart, breaking a brief, eerie silence. She holds Escort Burkhard to her chest, his helmet removed, her face buried into his hair. His eyes stare ahead through a dull sheen, the only color on his gaunt face is drying blood.

"*Quiet,*" the Champion urges.

At first, Escort Denya is affronted. Rage twists her mouth, and she looks ready to fight, but the demon's body draws her gaze. She trembles, folding further into her dead companion to stifle her sobs.

Fallon's stomach twists as he watches the escorts. How many of them have died at the Edge? Is this normal when they bring the Champion's supplies? He was stupid for thinking he could just stroll into this world wearing his nicest blouse and shined shoes and leave unscathed. He failed, as Shavazme said. Someone as ignorant as him may not deserve the throne after all.

"I think it's time you leave," the Champion tells him plainly. Her face is emotionless – stoic, even, though she still pants.

Fallon nods, unable to speak, and walks somberly to the back of the cart. Every sound echoes in his head as if they're far away – his feet against the rocks on the ground, the butterfly bone falling from his pocket, the snap of the cart doors opening, Shavazme's freckled face launching into his, spewing words.

"–ridiculous, foolish, horror-show. Deranged Champion talking to herself! How could I let myself be dragged into this? I'll sooner chew off my own hand than ever join you on one of these flights of idiocy again!" Shavazme shrieks.

"*Quiet,*" Fallon whispers harshly. The idea of any more demons escaping the Rive chills him to the bone.

"Don't tell me what to do! This is your fault!" Shavazme pushes past Fallon, a wild look in his eyes. He rounds the cart and makes a beeline towards the demon's severed head. Fallon follows, begging for Shavazme to get back inside, but his plea falls on deaf ears. "Help me get this on the cart, Fallon! It'll be a much better souvenir than a butterfly bone. I can't wait for you to parade it around the palace. Proof of your well-known intelligence and bravery."

Shavazme's skin is blotchy with adrenaline and unrelenting fear. He drives a fierce kick into the demon's sunken cheek with a maniacal laugh.

Even dead, the red rings in its eyes feel like they're watching Fallon, and he stops feet away. All he wants is to go home. He doesn't want a trophy. He wants to be in his quarters, where the Rive is only a black smudge on the distant horizon. He'll never speak of this again. His parents, Wilcon, Abner, they will never know. No one will. He will order – bribe, if he must – the escort and courier to bury this day. And he'll let Abner become sovereign. Clearly, he can't do anything right.

The demon's head suddenly lurches up. Fallon only has time to gasp before its teeth sink into Shavazme's calf.

Shavazme falls to his knees, then flops to his stomach. His pant leg has been torn away, revealing pink muscle and blinding white bone in the deep punctures left behind.

The Champion launches into action, bringing her axe into the back of the demon's head. Its skull dents, and the creature snaps its jaws, trying to flop away. The Champion keeps swinging until her axe makes a crater and the head finally goes still, chunks of Shavazme's calf sticking to its sharp teeth.

Red mist rises in a thick stream as the rings in its eyes fade.

CHAPTER 9

It seems strength isn't the only thing leaving – my good sense is following close behind. How could I miss the rings in the demon's eyes? Beheadings have always been the most certain way to kill them.

Dropping my axe beside the severed head, I rush to the boy, along with the heir and the living escort.

"Move back." Hands grasping at his seemingly lifeless body pull back quickly. I fish in my belt, searching for the small tin of starmoss I always keep on me.

"Is he d-dead? Oh, God, is... is he dead?" Heir Fallon stutters.

The answer isn't immediately clear. I find the tin and pop it open. Starmoss fills every corner of it, some of the stuff erupting from the lip. It should be enough to clog the wounds.

"What are you doing?" The heir asks as I slather the paste over Shavazme's torn calf. Thank Yuli-en the boy is small. The starmoss fills most of the punctures, and the rest I cover with clean rags from my belt.

"This should keep him alive for a short while, but he needs proper healers," I say. No one moves. "Did you hear me? He might live if you get him to a healer as soon as possible. Continue to plug the wound with clean rags – is there a medical kit on the cart?" The escort nods. "Yes? When these rags soak through – and they will – douse new ones with any cleansing oils you have and replace them. Keep him hydrated too, and awake."

The escort goes to grab Shavazme first, which shakes Heir Fallon out of his stupor. Together, they delicately haul the boy up, then shuffle to the back of the cart. As they do, I go to Velma.

"Tell the sovereigns there's a new demon. It has pale skin like a human, a large head, long, thin limbs, very tall, and can still hold life after a beheading. I'll need more long-range weaponry." Velma nods, but she's clearly shaken. "Will you remember the description?"

"Dear, I have seen many demons in my time as the courier, but that thing… I'll never forget it."

I glance at the Rive. It's dormant. Next, I find the dead escort, who slumps against the cart's front wheel as if taking a nap. I pull his body over my shoulders and carry him to the back. When the living escort sees me, she is openly stunned, then begins to express her gratitude.

I don't respond. She thinks I retrieved the body as a gesture of kindness. I don't tell her I dislike the idea of a freshly dead human laying around. She helps me place the body in the bed, beside Shavazme's small form, and the heir.

Just then, I notice something on the ground. The butterfly bone. I pick it up and hold it out to Heir Fallon.

His face deforms with disgust. "I never want to see that again."

To my surprise, sadness creeps into my chest. I flip over my palm and let the bone return to the dirt. The heir says nothing more, so I begin to close the metal-covered doors. They don't move easily. In fact, I have to slightly exert myself to move one at a time. The Blessing is practically leaking from my body now. Those demons were killed with magic and luck – and it seems the Rive has more to show me. I pause closing the doors to tilt my head towards the sky. Yuli-en's Eye hasn't arrived, but its faint outline grows clearer. In one day, the Day of Breath will be come.

I've never been more sure it'll be the last one I see. Unless I ask – beg – the sibyl to return my power.

"I have to go back," I say.

Heir Fallon's hand shoots out, pressing against one half-closed door. "What did you say?"

I look at him. "I've decided to return."

His eyebrows rise, lips parting but no words come out. That look burns into my eyes as I shut the doors and drop the latch in place. My declaration repeats in my head as I come back around to the driver's side of the cart, hardly believing I spoke it.

Velma waits for the living escort to climb onto the bench. She takes a short moment to place a comforting hand on the guard's knee. "Hold on back there. It'll be a much bumpier ride home." With a click of her tongue and a shake of the reins, the horses take off with a gallop.

I struggle not to chase after the cart and take back my promise as they both thunder away, but my weakening legs would never catch it.

It's done. Tomorrow, I break my deepest vow and go home.

CHAPTER 10

Fallon has never been so relieved to hear the horn of the portcullis guards, signaling he is nearly home. The gate lifts, metal grinding against metal, as the horses race towards it. Shavazme rustles against his chest and Fallon tightens his arm around his friend's torso. He presses his feet against the wall, keeping them both steady as best he can. The liquor and smoke had long been scared from his head, leaving the stark clarity of demons, blood, and screams.

Escort Burkhard's body rolls across the cart bed, stopping against Fallon's leg. His blood stains the wood and it glistens in the dim moonlight shining through the open slat. Fallon tries to ignore the guard's pressure and focus on Shavazme, whose breathing has become dangerously shallow. Fallon gently taps Shavazme's sweat-smeared forehead until he hears a small moan. Exhaling deeply, he presses the back of his head against the wall.

"Clear the path to the palace, clear the path!" the courier shouts.

The cart slows briefly before the horses are once again urged into a gallop. Fallon pictures them speeding down the city's main road, citizens rushing out of the way.

"Move!" she yells again.

Even as a dead body jostles against his leg and Shavazme's

blood soaks into his pants, Fallon can't stop picturing the pale demon. Its unrelenting bloodlust. Those red-ringed eyes staring deep into his soul. The Champion faces those abominations every day, by herself. How many times have chunks of muscle and skin been torn from her body but she continued fighting?

Abner already knew. On the balcony this morning, they'd proposed a small battalion of guards nearby. *Maybe at the abandoned watchtower along the way to the Edge,* Fallon remembers. Somehow, he'll find a way to give her aid. He has to.

The courier's shouts to clear the road continue until the cart suddenly stops, its wheels sliding along what sounds like stone. They've reached the circle courtyard in front of the palace. Fallon squeezes Shavazme tighter to his chest, searching for a heartbeat. A faint thump pulses against his fingertips.

"I'm so sorry," Fallon whispers, wiping stray tears from the corner of his eyes.

The latch lifts. Escort Denya appears in the opening first. She pulls herself into the bed and immediately reaches for Escort Burkhard's body. A grave look darkens her face and she stops. Then, she takes hold of Shavazme's legs. As she lifts, Fallon adjusts to an uncomfortable crouch so he can slip his arms under Shavazme's. He and the escort carry his friend's limp body out of the cart and into the fray outside.

A growing crowd spills onto the edge of the circle, undoubtably brought by the loud, recognizable cart speeding through the city. Guards stream down the palace stairs, bursting into action when they see the heir carrying the bloody and flaccid body of the general's son. Some voice their intention to summon the general to the palace before rushing off. Others dash back through the palace's open doors, calling for healers.

The stairs soon flood with pale-gold tunics. Healers clutch

brown leather bags and lanterns in their hands as they come. Two carry a metal gurney, lifting the wheels over the steps until they reach ground level.

The first to reach Shavazme take him gently from Escort Denya and Fallon's arms. At first, Fallon resists, not able to bear letting go.

"We'll take care of him, Heir Fallon. Don't worry," a healer says.

Fallon's grip tightens one last time, then he forces himself to slacken his arms. Shavazme makes a pitiful noise as his body is laid atop the gurney's cushioned bed.

"He was bit in the leg by a demon," Escort Denya tells the healers. Those who hear, freeze, their mouths gasping, eyes deeply questioning. "The Champion put starmoss in the wound to slow the bleeding," she adds.

The stunned healers snap back into the present. Half of them begin carrying Shavazme up the stairs. Those who stay behind swarm around Fallon and Escort Denya, dropping their bags on the ground and splitting them open. Eyes look Fallon over, hands reach for his legs.

"It's not my blood," Fallon explains, his mind both alarmingly clear and muddled at the same time.

"We'd still like to inspect you, my heir," one healer says. He gives a quick bow, then gestures for Fallon to follow him into the palace.

Fallon trails slowly in the healer's path. Behind him, the guards begin to question the courier and Escort Denya. They demand explanations only Fallon can give. Why were the heir and the general's son at the Edge? Why didn't the Champion protect them? He quickens up the steps, silently promising that he will fix any repercussions the courier and escort face when everything calms.

As Fallon walks into the entryway, his heel skids against something wet. Glancing down, he finds a trail of red beads rapidly growing into small puddles. The path of blood veers towards the left corridor, in the direction of the medical wing, and Shavazme's stopped gurney. Healers crowd around it, their fists full of linens. Fallon runs to them. He tries to see between shifting gold shoulders, but all he can gather is red. So much red.

Finally, two healers break away. Shavazme is covered in strips of linen and bottles of ointments. Healers fight each other to replace the soaked strips and wipe the wound clean at the same time.

"He's losing too much blood," a healer murmurs as they douse a rag with water and dot Shavazme's sweat-soaked forehead.

Fallon clutches at his shirt, suddenly too tight against his skin. He was so sure Shavazme would survive – or, he hadn't let himself accept otherwise. Fallon closes his eyes, welcoming the darkness beneath his eyelids. Will the sovereigns blame him? Will the general blame him? He wants to believe he wouldn't run away, escaping into his quarters to avoid witnessing Shavazme's last breath – or steal a horse from the stables and tear into the night, heading as far away from Niawa as he can. But his legs tingle with desperation to run.

When he forces himself to open his eyes, Wilcon, Abner, and his parents rush into the entryway from the opposite corridor.

"Fallon, oh, my son, are you okay?" Sovereign Adelaide's arms are outspread, ready to pull Fallon into her embrace. Her eyes find the blood on his pants and the streaks across his hands he hadn't noticed until now, and she instead presses her hands to Fallon's unblemished face. "Whose blood is this?"

"Shavazme's. I'm not injured," he utters.

"What in Yuli-en's name happened?" Advisor Wilcon probes.

Fallon's throat closes. He has no idea where to begin.

A flurry of whispers breaks out among the healers. Many stop squabbling over Shavazme's wound, their red hands frozen in mid-air. Fallon follows the direction of their turned heads towards the low-lit hall ahead.

The sibyl glides from the shadows between the sconces, adorned in layers of intricately draped fabric. Some silks, some woven cloth, all verdant shades, from the deep evergreen of Niawa's crest to the poisonous scales of spring vipers to the softness of jade. Green leather encloses her neck, matching the gloves that grip her tall white staff. Her gold metal veil ripples as she moves.

She flicks her wrist at the healers, who clamber from the gurney. At Shavazme's side, the sibyl brings her staff level over his still body. The tall pole is clear like glass, and hollow. Within, small bursts of soft yellow lights dance lazily like snowflakes.

Whispers drift from the veil as she waves the staff in circles over Shavazme. Her words are unintelligible, only sighs and hisses to Fallon's ears. Yuli-en's Tongue, he has been told. The language of conjuring magic that only sibyls are allowed to speak.

A ball of light appears parallel to the blunt tip of the staff, hovering in place. Cloud-white lines emerge from the ball, ebbing outwards then coming back to the staff, where they sink into it. The light spills down the pole like molten liquid, filling the space between the sunny bursts. She moves the staff in a pattern of wide circles then smaller circles, over and over, the staff flashing brighter with each wave.

The light abruptly changes direction, surging back up to the staff's head. It absorbs into the floating orb, swelling it to a larger size. The orb detaches from the staff and floats down to

Shavazme like a leaf falling from a branch. When it lays upon his leg, it decomposes into a fog. Her voice deepens and the fog grows thicker until it shrouds Shavazme entirely.

He coughs from beneath it. Murmurs of excitement fill the entryway. The sibyl only ever performs magic in her tower, where she creates weapons for the Champion and draws from Yuli-en to keep Niawa's lands healthy. Every soul witnessing this moment will never be closer to the god than they are now.

A red hue glows within the fog for a few seconds, then vanishes. Fallon is helplessly brought back to watching the red mist rise from the pale demon's severed head.

The sibyl makes a sound like a sharp inhale and the fog funnels back into the head of her staff. She calmly steps back from Shavazme, the click of her boots on the marble echoing off the walls.

"Shavazme!" General Jaits hurls in from an adjoining hall, flanked by several guards. He reaches the gurney just as his son's eyes flutter open.

Fallon snaps out of his awe of the sibyl, and he steps up to the gurney's other side. Slowly, Shavazme's blue eyes open, filling Fallon with the sweetest, most desperate relief. He grabs his friend's warming hand, remembering how cold it felt in the cart.

"Yuli-en bless you, sibyl," Fallon chokes out.

"Son, are you with us?" General Jaits asks, his voice shaking.

Shavazme's head lolls around as if it's too heavy to lift. He tries to arch his back and see his leg, but barely rises a few inches off the gurney. Fallon glances at the wound for him. Where several gaping holes once were, there's only reddened skin.

"Demons. Beheaded demons," Shavazme wheezes. "Red eyes and human."

General Jaits leans closer to his son. "What are you saying? What happened? Why did you go to the Edge?"

Fallon tenses. He won't dare peek over his shoulder for his family and Wilcon's reaction. The story of his excursion must have already spread like wildfire. By midnight, the entire city will know. What conclusions will form on their own if he doesn't confess the real reason he went to the Edge? Would they be worse than the weak excuse he gave Shavazme – that the Champion deserved an in-person invite? Is that enough to paint him in a good light, or did he just further prove how unfit for the throne he is?

"We should take Master Shavazme to the medical wing for rest and to be monitored," a healer chimes in.

"Yes, yes, of course," General Jaits responds. He directs the nearest healers to take hold of the gurney.

"One moment." The sibyl's voice stops everyone in their tracks. Despite nearly losing his son, the general immediately forfeits his spot next to the gurney. "What did you see at the Edge?" she asks Shavazme.

"Demon," Shavazme answers hoarsely.

"What kind of demon?"

Shavazme's head rolls off to the side. Gurgled noises seep from his lips instead of words.

"Answer me." The sibyl grips Shavazme's chin to turn his head upwards again. He only whimpers.

"It was a human-skinned demon that attacked us," Fallon interjects. The sibyl's veil turns towards him and his heart leaps. Fallon quickly collects himself and continues. "The most evil thing I've ever laid eyes on. It towered over us on long, thin arms and legs. The Champion killed it, but even after she cut off its head, it bit Shavazme."

"Was anyone else bitten?"

"An escort died. We brought his body back, to be honored by his family and friends." Fallon can't believe he is conversing with the sibyl in front of all these people. The urge to look around for their reactions is overwhelming, but he keeps his eyes on her.

The sibyl's head tilts up, as if she stares at something behind Fallon. He allows himself a curious glance, but only his family and Wilcon are there.

"I'm returning to my tower. The boy will live," she states before turning her back on Fallon and sweeping from the entryway, layers of green fabric rippling around her feet.

When the tap of her boots dissipates, healers launch back into action, cleaning up their rags, tinctures, and leather bags, then pushing the gurney towards the west corridor. General Jaits walks along Shavazme, clutching his son's hand. He whispers, "Bless the Champion. Bless the sibyl," over and over.

The entryway clears out much quicker than Fallon likes, leaving him with his family, Wilcon, and a handful of guards who stand watch from a few feet away. As he turns to face them, he wonders if he would prefer a demon attack right now. "I know I have a lot to explain."

"Leave," Wilcon orders. The guards know this declaration is for them and they are gone in a burst of clinking armor.

"What could have possessed you and Shavazme to go to the Edge? We'll be given a full report by the courier, Fallon; do not *think* of lying," Sovereign Adelaide starts, on the brink of shouting.

"Well, I–" Fallon wraps his arms around his waist. He tries not to meet Wilcon's eyes, knowing the advisor's disappointment will undo him.

"Are you okay?" Abner asks.

Fallon nods, but he isn't sure if that's the truth. Not when he feels cursed by what he endured. He decides that if his half-truth was good enough to convince Shavazme, it's good enough for his family. "I wanted to bring the Champion back for the Day of Breath. I thought if I went myself, with Shavazme tagging along, she would say yes."

Sovereign Gerves clasps his hands together and brings them to his chin. "We send missives with the courier for a reason. It's too dangerous."

Fallon nearly huffs. He knows far too well how dangerous it is now. Even for the Champion. He has to help her. "I'm truly regretful for my stupid decision. But if I hadn't gone, I wouldn't have learned something. The Edge is an unspeakable place, Father. I thought I knew, but I had no idea. I think," he steals a look at Abner, "we should reconsider giving aid to the Champion. Station a handful of guards nearby, or something."

Abner cocks their head but doesn't say a word. They look at their parents and Wilcon with a brazen curiosity. Fallon imagines they've mentioned this before and were only met with resistance.

"Quiet is paramount to demons not finding the Rive, Heir Fallon," Wilcon responds cooly.

"But she's entirely alone. If even just to give her some kind of companionship –"

"Wilcon is right. Yuli-en and the sibyl know what they're doing. We have to trust in them," Sovereign Adelaide says.

Fallon watches Abner's curiosity dim. His twin looks dejected as if they were the one making the request.

"Of course," Fallon says, feeling the same dismay. He wants to push harder, thinking of Oly alone in the field with only her weapons, but his faith in Yuli-en rears a stronger head.

Without them and the sibyl, Niawa would be in ruins. Wilcon is right. He has to believe in their plan and be grateful for the gifts they've already given.

Still, guilt brews inside him.

"You're lucky Shavazme lived. *And* you will personally apologize to the family of the fallen escort," Sovereign Adelaide demands. She turns to her husband. "How do we control the city's knowledge of this?"

Wilcon answers. "I think Heir Fallon's reasoning was sound, albeit misguided. In an attempt to invite the Champion himself, demons attacked. The citizens know how dangerous the Edge is. We can present it as an unfortunate accident."

"It *was* an accident!" Fallon insists.

Wilcon shoots him a pointed look, then continues. "Though the Champion still denied the invitation, Fallon has seen her bravery with his own eyes. Few have been able to. I'll write a speech for him to recite during the Day of Breath's ceremony."

Fallon's eyes widen. A surge of life crackles through him, straightening his back and dropping his arms from around his waist. Even amid the chaos of Shavazme's near death and the sibyl's appearance, he can't believe he forgot. "She's coming home."

Wilcon's eyebrows raise. The Sovereigns gasp. Abner's hands fly to their hips.

"The Champion agreed to return?" Sovereign Gerves asks.

Fallon nods. "She told me just before we left."

"How did you possibly convince her?"

Wilcon unleashes a very rare expression: he laughs. "Because our Heir Fallon has a charm like nobody else."

Like rays of sunlight breaking through a ceiling of stormy, gray clouds, smiles break out across the sovereign's faces.

"God above, Fallon, that's miraculous. She's been adamant about never coming back. Adelaide, imagine, the longest-living Champion by our side as we announce our successor." Sovereign Gerves wraps his arm around his wife, beaming from the inside out.

Fallon catches that Abner is not directly named. He looks to Wilcon, wondering if the advisor also noticed and finds the old man staring intently back, his direction clear as day: keep going.

"Yes, it will be a glorious moment for Niawa. I wanted to show you both how deeply I care for the kingdom and its future. Which I do. Care." His eyes flick back to Wilcon one more time. "More than you realize."

Wilcon appears pleased, so Fallon releases an anxious breath. The sovereigns look at each other contemplatively. Fallon doesn't have a clue what words pass between their eyes, but he wrings his hands together so fiercely his skin becomes dry.

"I'll admit, I'm surprised you would go so far, Fallon. Despite what occurred, it's a welcome sight to see your dedication," his mother finally says. "It's getting late, and we need to call for the Heads early in the morning and adjust plans for the Day of Breath. It's been a stressful evening, and I think we all need to sleep." She looks at both of her children. "We'll expect both of you to attend the morning meeting."

Fallon nods erratically, his stomach in knots. He cautions himself not to seek more from the words his mother spoke, but he can't help hoping something has changed. "I'll be there. First, I'm going to visit Shavazme in the medical wing, then right to bed."

His father sighs and rubs his cheeks with both hands. "While I'm grateful the Champion is returning, and I commend you for your bravery son, do I need to warn you not to do something so brash again?"

"No, father." Fallon smiles.

The sovereigns embrace him and Abner, then turn to leave.

"I'll escort you to your quarters, there's some thoughts I want to share," Wilcon says. He gives Fallon one last knowing look, then walks with the sovereigns down the opposite side of the entryway. They make sure to give Shavazme's pools of blood a wide berth.

Abner stays behind. They don't say a word, just stare at Fallon, reading him up and down. Fallon knows this means Abner is sorting through several thoughts at once, placing them in order from least to most important. Do they believe Fallon's excuse? Or do they suspect there was more to the plan? Fallon tries to hold his ground, not let Abner's scrutiny get under his skin, but with every passing second, his chin lowers and his shoulders tighten.

"Not my finest hour," Fallon jokes to cut the tension.

"Seems it went exactly how you wanted."

Fallon's entire body clenches. Abner knows. Of course they do. "How could you say that? I didn't want anyone to get hurt."

"That's not what I mean. I assumed Wilcon told you what mother and father decided after the presentation. So then you concocted this plan."

"I don't want to talk about that." Fallon turns abruptly, ready to walk away.

Abner shocks him by grabbing his bicep, stopping his escape. "Are you really going to pretend I don't know what you're trying to do? Or do you have that little respect for me?"

Fallon twists out of Abner's surprisingly strong grip. He faces his sibling but can't seem to get himself to keep eye contact. Because Abner is right. Wilcon has convinced him he deserves to be sovereign, but Fallon has never outright expressed that to Abner. He'd gone along with the lessons, the trials, the conversations with their parents about Niawa's future, but never looked in his twin's eyes with matched determination. Fallon had let everything be assumed for far too long, because he feared how Abner would react. That they would laugh. Or roll their eyes. Going to the Edge was no longer about proving his worth to the sovereigns, but to Abner as well.

"Are you even going to congratulate me?" Abner says. "I worked hard for this; you know I have."

Fallon crosses his arms. "And I haven't? I went to the Edge today. I tried to get the Champion aid." He swallows a lump in his throat. "I deserve to be sovereign as much as you do."

"I never thought you didn't, Fallon. But had you been chosen, I would've stood by your side, no matter my feelings." Abner lowers their voice, even though the two are still alone. "I wouldn't try to steal it from you."

"Well I… I was just trying to play to my strengths. You've been doing the same since our parents told us they want to step down."

"It's *decided,* Fallon. You almost got yourself and Shavazme killed for nothing."

Fallon senses the shift. The moment he and Abner had been careening towards like ships helplessly thrashed about in an unruly sea. They were no longer siblings, but two hungry animals snarling over a sole piece of meat. No one thought he had the teeth, not even him. That was, until he faced a demon and convinced the Champion to come home. He straightens his cowering spine, exhibiting every bit of the two inches of height he has on Abner.

"I wouldn't be so sure."

Abner takes a quick step closer. "You've never cared about listening to the Heads or learning how the city is managed. Not until Wilcon started taking you under his wing. Did he make you do this?"

The hairs on the back of Fallon's neck stand. "Oh, is that why you're so angry? Because you're still jealous Wilcon saw something in me and stopped mentoring you? That was years ago, Abner, when are you going to let it go?"

"You have no idea what you're talking about. As usual. He's getting between us, and you can't see it." Abner's fists ball and loosen, their arms shaking. Fallon sees the nervous fit rising to the surface, threatening to breach.

Fallon is about to respond when three palace workers drift in from the closest hall, talking animatedly and holding bowls. They must have been in the kitchens for a late-night snack. As they pass the heirs, they pause to bow, their wide smiles dropping when they feel the frost in the air. They quickly rush off, whispering and peeking over their shoulders.

Abner waits until they're gone to say, "You thinking that going to the Edge proves you can be the Sovereign is exactly why you aren't. It was reckless and stupid–"

"*Stupid*? You think I'm stupid?" Fallon doesn't care if anyone hears them now.

"That's not what I said! You don't listen, for heaven's sake. You really can't see how bad this plan was? You still have Shavazme's blood all over you."

"Just admit it, Abner." Fallon starts pacing back and forth, anger fueling his legs. "You enjoy having a sibling that makes you look even smarter than you already are. And *I'm* the one our parents think has an ego."

Abner throws their hands up in frustration. "You're impossible to talk to. What I don't understand is why you even went to the Edge."

Fallon stops abruptly. Abner's eyes suddenly find the marble pillars behind Fallon very interesting.

"Say it," Fallon pushes.

"Say what?"

"Don't be all coy now; it's unbecoming. I'm not a weak little boy, so stop treating me like one."

"Fine." Abner folds their hands behind their back. "I don't understand why you even want to be sovereign. You didn't care until Wilcon started mentoring you. I think this is all about him."

"That's not true," Fallon says too hastily. It makes Abner purse his lips in a way that suggests they've won. "You don't think I can be sovereign, do you?"

Abner closes their eyes. They've started the countdown in their heads, a wave of nerves about to crest.

Fallon scoffs, his usual patience nowhere to be found. But he doesn't have to wait long. A second later, Abner opens their eyes.

"I don't. And neither do you."

The ground feels like it bows under Fallon's feet, ready to swallow him whole. He had always worried Abner didn't believe in him like their parents. But hearing it, spoken so plainly, is a knife to the gut he isn't prepared for. Fallon locks eyes with his twin and takes a sharp step towards them. "Wilcon was right; you can't see past your own ambition. You're selfish and cold. Under your rule, Niawa will become a godless kingdom overrun with demons. You're a heretic, and I'm done protecting you."

Abner recoils as if Fallon had slapped them across the face. "If that's what you really think of me, then we have nothing else to talk about." They go silent, lingering for a response, but Fallon doesn't budge. He won't lose this war of resolve, not this time.

He turns and marches stiff-legged out of the entryway, nausea ebbing and flowing through him, bringing in shame and washing it back out, leaving a hollow emptiness. Abner has only ever looked at Wilcon with that much malice, and Fallon made it clear who he trusted more. He sets his mind on visiting Shavazme, desperate to leave the fight behind. Desperate to push down the gnawing feeling he did something wrong.

Fallon arrives at the medical wing and is immediately directed to one of the private suites. He finds Shavazme propped up in a large bed, a tray of fresh fruit, cubes of cheese, and herb-crusted crackers on his lap. A healer checks the sturdiness of a stilt propping up his leg before pressing two fingers to his wrist.

"It's so good to see you sitting up," Fallon says, seating himself in a chair beside the bed.

"Leave," Shavazme mutters to the healer through soft cheese strung between his teeth. The woman bows to Fallon, then hurries out, shutting the door behind her. "I'm surprised you came. Thought you'd be wallowing in your failure." Shavazme tries to look smug, but he's betrayed by beads of sweat across his brow and a purple hue under his eyes.

Fallon thinks on whether now is the time to prove Shavazme wrong. His friend looks weak and tired, strings of red cracking across the whites of his eyes like lightning. He decides he'd like to know if something good came from nearly dying. "Actually, the Champion agreed to return. You were out of it by then, so you didn't hear, but... we did it." Fallon adds the last bit, hoping to lift Shavazme's spirits.

Shavazme quickly swallows a bite of melon to gape at Fallon, all smugness wiped from his face. Then he smirks. "That's right.

We did. You wouldn't have gone without me. Cheers to us, then."

"You're right. Thanks for supporting me." Fallon smiles and squeezes Shavazme's shoulder. His relationship with Abner may be wounded, but at least his oldest friend doesn't think so little of him.

Shavazme suddenly lurches forward to cough. Blood spatters over the tray of food. Fallon whips the tray away, placing it on a side table next to the bed. He stands to help Shavazme lay back on the large pillows set against the headboard.

Shavazme waves his arm irritably. "I'm fine, stop fussing; you're like my father. Just a scratchy throat."

Fallon stops fluffing the pillows, but he doesn't return to his seat. Shavazme has already grown paler, a sheen of moisture plastering hair to his forehead. "I should maybe get a healer."

Shavazme tips his head back and lets out an anguished groan. "No, I just need to sleep. And father will be back soon, he's off fetching my silk pajamas and food that doesn't taste like dirt." He tugs at the neckline of the white tunic given to patients. "I'm sure he'll also bring a fresh lecture on the dangers of ignoring rules and whatever. Not that it matters, I'll never visit that hellscape ever again."

Fallon makes a noise of agreement. "I don't even want to hear the word 'demon' again."

Shavazme cinches his face, then reaches to scratch at the bandage covering his calf. "Ouch!" When he raises his hand, blood coats his fingertips and there are red chunks stuck beneath his nails. Fallon blanches. Shavazme yelps, yanking at the linen to expose a mess of red smears. Crimson lines run up his calf, skin peeling away from the edges like curled paper.

"Healer!" Shavazme screams at the door.

The healer enters with a rolling cart of supplies. When her eyes lay on Shavazme's leg, she gasps and grabs a tin container and a spool of linen. "Some ointment to soothe the skin should help," she says in a calming lilt.

"You already put that on, and it didn't work," Shavazme snaps. "It itches unbearably!" He keeps scratching, tearing more skin and gouging into the red lines.

"Shavazme, stop, stop!" Fallon yells from the nearby wall he hadn't realized he backed into.

The healer tries to wrestle Shavazme's arms away, but he fights her with every bit of strength he has. "I need assistance!" she shouts.

More healers flood into the room to pin Shavazme's arms down. He howls in pain, kicking his legs. "It *burns!*"

"I've got a long day ahead of me tomorrow. I'd better go," Fallon stutters as he inches towards the door, his eyes glued to the scarred leg. Blood gushes from the wounds, and Fallon thinks he catches a hint of pink muscle.

Shavazme pays him no attention. Though the healers lather a generous amount of ointment on the scratches, he wriggles an arm loose to slap the wounds with his palm between layers. Ointment splashes across his torso and the sheets.

"Please refrain," a healer pleads, smearing on a new layer.

"I'll come see you soon," Fallon mumbles before ducking out the open door. Behind him, Shavazme's yelps deepen into low whines.

Down the sconce-lit halls on the way to his quarters, Fallon releases a deep, guttural exhale. When he rubs his eyes, images of the human-like demon bombard him in the flashes of black. He's sure sleep will be an elusive herd of sheep tonight.

CHAPTER 11

The cool lip of the tub feels nice against my bare skin. It's been a while since I didn't need to wear most of my armor while washing myself. A year to the day. I rub a rag soggy with ginger oil and water over my hip in slow circles, taking my time. On the Day of Breath, there's no need to rush. Still, I can't bring myself to strip fully naked. My brown pants scrunch around my ankles, and I barely lowered my undergarments to free my thighs. The long sleeves of my linen shirt are soaked.

When the skin over my hip grows irritated from rubbing, I drop the rag into a bucket of water in the tub. The Rive may sleep until midnight, but I've always felt like it keeps one eye open. It watches me from the washroom window, and I return the stare. Above it, a white streak, as large as the tip of my thumb when I hold it to the sky, hangs suspended against the early morning star-speckled canvas. Yuli-en's Eye will travel from one end of the sky to the other as the day goes on. When it disappears, I'll be back here, feeling strength course through me like the night I first stepped into this cabin.

I stand, pull up my pants, and head for the chair facing the other window. The thigh wound has healed enough that I don't feel a stab of pain every step, but I worry it could tear again at any moment. As I pass the tapestries hanging on the wall, I pause.

"Will you say yes?" I ask the sibyl's portrait. Fear grips my organs in its unforgiving claws, squeezing them tightly. She has to. There's no other option. "If you don't bless me, I'll slit my own throat."

I run my oiled palms over my scalp as I wonder how I'll do it, and where. At the academy? In my childhood bedroom with my parents watching, their faces blank and unmoving? No, I'll return to the Edge, and I'll walk into the field. I'll wait for a demon to take me – as it should be. The next Champion won't find my body crumpled on the floor. Won't have to scrub my blood from the wood.

Velma should be here any minute to take me to Niawa. I remember the Champion always arrived early in the morning, just when the sky was firmly sapphire. Hot blood pumps through my veins at the thought, urging me to get moving. I go to the shelves of clothing beside my bed. More brown pants, long-sleeved shirts, undergarments, and thick socks lay in sloppy piles. When my parents see me for the first time in ten years, what will they think of this clothing? Will I even look like the child they knew who used to enjoy wearing dresses? I was always fond of the ones with simple stitching on the hems and wide straps buttoned at the shoulders. Once, in Niawa's summer market, I gathered the courage to ask mother for some fabric. School was starting soon, and I wanted something different. I wanted to feel new.

"Fine. Go get it," mother said in an annoyed tone. She was haggling with a jeweler and losing.

I held out my hand. Eleven-year-olds needed coins. She huffed through her nose, then dropped three bronze pieces on my palm. I turned around to face the fabric cart and froze. People surrounded it, all talking at once. The clothier bounced between several conversations at once, running their hands animatedly over a strip of silver silk, then pointing at other fabrics hanging from a wooden rod.

"Mother..." I started to sniffle. She didn't hear me. I pulled timidly on her sleeve.

"*What*?" she said.

It was impossible to find the words to describe the feeling – but I was petrified. Too many voices and bodies and conversations at the clothier's cart. The humming would eat me from the inside out.

So I whispered, with tears in my eyes, "Could you go?"

"God above. I don't know which one you want."

I looked back at the crowd, somehow triple in size, and shook my head.

Her hand struck out like a whip, fingers curling around my wrist. With her other hand, she pried my fist open to reveal the bronze coins. Her eyes grew more and more fiery as she plucked the coins away. "Such a simple thing you can't do," she seethed through her teeth.

My wrist ached as she yanked me towards the clothier cart. By the time she and the merchant were bargaining for a soft, cream-colored fabric with satin lavender trimming, the skin on my wrist burned, but I was too afraid to ask her to let go. Mother finally released me to thrust the fabric into my arms. Without a word, she marched back to the jeweler. I stayed out of her way until we returned home and I could escape into my room. Through the walls, father agreed with all her complaints about how hopeless I was. Though I'd already suspected, that was the day I realized my parents would never understand me. They didn't even like me.

Pants and a shirt won't be good enough. I need to wear the most impressive thing I own.

Ignoring the scuffed and worn plates scattered around the chair, I go to the wall of armor. A fresh suit will capture the sun's rays, making the demon teeth's cloudy, quartz-like material glow. After I'm fully armored, I consider my weapons. It's silly to bring them, but my hand already reaches for a freshly sharpened double-headed axe with a long staff. I wrap leather straps around my chest to secure it across my back. The armor is imposing, the axe fearsome, but I still feel incomplete. My belt is on the floor, emptied of magic orbs and supplies. I strap it to my waist before filling it with two of each orb, rags, a tin of starmoss, and numbing cream.

"I think I'm ready," I announce to the cabin.

With only waiting left to do, I sit in the chair facing the big window.

In the stillness, other thoughts I've chastised myself for entertaining creep in. Syrup-y, muddy scents and Heir Fallon's dark brown eyes so close to mine. Warm breath tinged with alcohol. The unbearable desire to be embraced.

"Shush," I say to the pitter patter in my chest.

A faint rumbling in the distance pricks the silence. Wagon wheels. The humming surges like a geyser in my stomach. I've already taken my tablet, I can't take another one. Desperate for something to grasp onto as the wheels grow louder, I look for my green bowl. It's behind me on the table, my breakfast of oats and berries crusted around the inside. I bring it to my chest and hold tightly, stroking the smooth sides with my thumb. Soon I can hear the horses snorting.

The rumbling stops.

I breathe as though a stone lodges in my throat. All I can bring myself to do is clutch my bowl and stare at the Rive. Maybe, hopefully, it will defy Yuli-en's presence and tremor with activity.

"Oly, dear!" Velma shouts.

It startles me. My bowl slides along my fingers and falls to the floor. In a panic, I jump to my feet, needing it back in my hands, and take a clumsy stomp forward. My boot lands on the bowl, shattering it.

A small sound comes from my throat, like a strangled rodent. My bowl is scattered in large chunks around my feet. I drop to my hands and knees and grab at the pieces. Small ceramic flakes drift to the floor as I try to press them together.

"Oly!" Velma shouts again.

The bowl won't hold together no matter how hard I try. I know the pieces won't stick, but I need them too. The shards are jagged at the edges and cut my fingertips. I grab the gloves I've worn for days from the tabletop, still damp with sweat, and pull them on. "No, no, no." Cold then hot then cold flashes race over my skin as I try to slam two large pieces together with all my might. They explode in my hands. Green and white dust coats my gloves, jagged slivers like glass slip through my fingers. Panting, I give up and plant my hands among the soft green ruins and hang my head.

"Get up," I whisper. *"Get up."*

My blood feels thick as I haul myself to my feet. I'm careful not to step on the shattered bowl, not even the tiny green specks, as I walk slowly to the door and open it.

I pause at the opening to look back at the carnage. Is this an omen? Is Yuli-en telling me I'm going to die soon, that I won't get another Blessing?

"Maybe this is a test." Yuli-en and the sibyl are stripping me bare, pushing me to fight for my strength when I have nothing left. I'll return to the academy and get another bowl, and I'll convince the sibyl I'm worthy of getting my power back.

"Don't worry," I say to the shards, then I step through and shut the door.

Velma waits on the driver's bench, smiling as she always does. She laughs when I approach.

"You won't be needing all that." Her hand bobs in the air at my armor. "Especially not that," she points to the head of the axe peeking out over my shoulder. I respond by silently joining her on the cart.

"Are you alright?" she asks.

"Broke my bowl," I respond. The sound of crushed ceramic in my ears almost makes me flinch.

"Oh, dear. I'm sincerely sorry. Can you get another one?"

I can tell she's sorry by the worry in her voice. It soothes the humming enough for me to nod absentmindedly. "Yes."

"Good. Something to look forward to." Velma flicks the reins, and her horses toss their large heads before pulling the cart around to face the road. The lanterns hanging over our heads cast so little light, the deep, royal blue of the sky is still noticeable. After a while, she looks upwards. "I find it's never *truly* dark. Always some kind of purple or blue tint. You have to look in the space around the stars."

We watch the sky together as the Edge fades to black behind us.

CHAPTER 12

Some time back, the sun arrived to paint a soft morning gold across the hills between Niawa and the Edge. Then, Niawa's city was just a mirage. A faint sketch of a kingdom on paper. Now the soaring stone wall rises ahead in absolute daylight. It threatens me. All shadows and depths, sharp angles and bevels. Rising from the ground like a colossal dungeon. I press my back against the cart wall, hearing my armor scratch the metal casing as a faint but familiar wish to throw myself from the bench creeps into my head.

The portcullis lifts and Velma's gaze darts to me several times. She must hear my heart pounding in my chest. I don't doubt she's seen the many times I've stroked the blade of my axe.

"Ten years is a long time," she says.

I nod in agreement. It's a lifetime.

The gate rumbles one last time before the iron bars are pointed ends hanging above our heads as we pass beneath. I barely have a second to prepare myself before sounds bombard me like a volley of magic spheres exploding in all directions. People rush to the cart from every angle, all hurling words at once. I don't know where to look, to assess the danger. Too many faces crowd around us, their eyes spearing into me. A cannon goes off a little way ahead at the start of the main road. Two more follow. Confetti rains down. Beyond the curtain of green and gold paper, the road is lined with countless, cheering people. They wave their arms in my direction while they scream. My ears are throbbing. Guards appear from within the crowd to grab the reins from Velma. Some pull the horses towards the stables, while others push the crowd back.

"Give them space! Return to the parade," they order.

The citizens scowl, their arms filled with gifts. Young children on their shoulders burst into tears as they're turned away.

As the space around me grows, the darkness that had started to crawl into the edges of my vision evaporates. I can breathe again.

Why am I doing this? I should be at the Edge by the wildberry bushes, watching the sun rise over the cliffs. The tall grass would be like velvet against my exposed skin as I pulled up scraggly white roots from the moist dirt and squeezed them in my palm. The air would smell strongly of the berries and the tang of lemon reeds. I would bring a cupped handful of the brook's cold water to my lips. When my eyes tired from the sun, I would fend off sleep for a little longer by collecting rocks and pebbles. I would pick them up one by one and examine them closely, noting every small detail in the different graining.

The cart rocks a bit, yanking me from my sanctuary. Guards pull a stack of metal and wood and two wheels from the bottom of the cart and place them on the ground beside Velma. They unfold the stack into a chair, then pop the wheels onto the sides.

"Dear," Velma says. She leans in and tries to lay her hand on my forearm but I move it away. "My house is on Wellswood Road, the one with yellow wooden ducks on the door. I'll leave it unlocked." She smiles, then uses her arms to descend from the bench into the wheeled chair.

Needles of fear stab at my stomach as I watch her push the wheels towards the stables. I want to beg her to come back, but I swallow the words. There are too many eyes on me and Champions don't beg. Instead, I bring my axe to lay across my lap, but the little comfort it brings drowns in the surrounding noise.

No one speaks to me or gives any direction. The guards just stand around, their backs to me. I should just run. Use the last of my Blessing to get back to the Edge as quickly as possible. None of the guards would be able to stop me. This noise is too much, and it keeps getting louder.

From my angle at the stables, I can only see the start of the main road until houses obscure it, but I can tell something is coming. All the faces glued to me turn in a rippling wave. The guards shape up, stiffening their necks. I wring the axe staff.

"Calm down. It's the Day of Breath," I say. There aren't any demons here. Even so, my heart won't stop thundering.

From the edge of a row of houses comes two snow-white horses, their black manes braided with gold beads. They haul a large, topless emerald carriage at a glacial pace. I spot Heir Fallon first. He waves to me from the bed in a pearl-colored blouse and dark green vest. His twin, Heir Abner, is beside him in a bright-gold jacket that shimmers with every movement. They give me a nod with their hand splayed across their chest. Behind the heirs, the sovereigns stand in gowns made of green silk and velvet. The emeralds in their circlets sparkle as the carriage draws closer. I recognize the look in the sovereigns' eyes: pride and joy. They once showered me with those sentiments as I blubbered on my knees in front of the sibyl.

I can't let them see that girl again. If the sovereigns don't think I'm worthy of the Blessing, then the sibyl will feel the same.

"Go away," I hiss to the humming and thick ropes of anxiety coiling around my ribs.

The carriage sweeps the perimeter of the large space, dazzling the crowd, until it stops at the stables, feet from me. Sovereign Adelaide and Gerves wait for a guard to open the carriage door, then descend first. Advisor Wilcon is also in their procession. He doesn't beam with pride like the sovereigns or wear the cheek-bubbling smile Heir Fallon does. He only stares, raking over my armor as though looking for a dent. I glance down quickly, wondering if I accidentally wore a dirty plate. No, this suit is immaculate. I made sure of it.

Heir Fallon rushes ahead of his family to reach me first. "So good to see you again, Champion."

God above, my face feels hot. I avoid his eyes, worried he can tell my body refuses to move and my lips are too heavy to open. *Get off the cart. Show them you are strong.*

"You probably won't need that." Heir Fallon points to the axe in my lap with a grin.

I squeeze the weapon one last time, then convince my arms to slip it back into its straps.

The royal family and the advisor join him. Staring. All staring.

Get off the cart.

A guard comes to my side of the bench. She holds out her hand. "May I escort you, Champion?"

My skin feels clammy.

She says something else, but I can't discern it. Twists appear in my gut like a cyclone, threatening to bring my lungs into the storm. I double over to gouge my knees with my elbows. My head hangs, filling with liquid, so heavy it can't bear its own weight anymore. I throw myself upright again. White stars pop across my vision.

"Champion?" Heir Fallon's voice comes from above the surface, too far to grasp.

Bile shoots up my throat. My tongue burns with it, the taste acrid and sour. I twist away from facing my lap, knowing what's coming. The vibrant red and violet of wildberries spurt from my mouth and splash over the guard's helmet. She yelps and jumps backwards, vomit sliding down the metal to plop onto her tabard.

While I scuffle with my belt, trying to retrieve a rag, I hear her launch into a chorus of retches. As I wipe my chin, the nausea pulls away like the sea calling back the tide. I glare ahead at the main road, the cheering crowd packed along the edges, the colorful buildings expanding in every direction. Niawa has won the first battle to drag me back into my younger body, but I won't let it win another. Mother would get so angry when my nerves drove me to feeling ill. The other trainees at the academy would scream and run away, or laugh. I killed this urge at the Edge in the first year when fighting waves of sickness meant taking my eyes off the Rive for too long. I can do it again.

"Get off the cart," I demand.

I stuff the pink-stained rag back into my belt and swing my legs around on the bench. Facing the royal family – and the guard who picks berry chunks from her helmet – I harden my face. The sovereigns wear half smiles, but their necks clearly strain. Heir Abner looks concerned. Heir Fallon's hands cup his lips, but the edges of his eyes wrinkle. Only the advisor shows his disgust openly.

"The road is bumpy," I express, hopping down from the cart. It's the first excuse I can think of. "Sorry," I say to the guard's back, who is being moved away and replaced with another.

"Yes. Yes. Of course, Champion," Sovereign Gerves says after clearing his throat. "We can't convey our delight and gratitude enough at having you here with us today. We hope you enjoy the festivities prepared on this Day of Breath."

Though my nerves still spark beneath my skin, my cheeks now taste of wildberries, albeit spoiled, and it makes me smile. The Sovereigns and Heir Fallon smile back.

"Shall we go?" Sovereign Adelaide chirps.

It truly begins now. The parade. The grand celebrations. If I can get through this, I'll prove I'm worthy of another Blessing.

"I suppose," I respond. She looks affronted, then quickly adjusts her face back into a half smile before looping her arm into her husband's and gliding to the carriage.

Heir Abner and the advisor follow closely behind, while Heir Fallon stalls. He lets a few feet grow between him and his family before motioning for me to walk alongside him. He says nothing, only matches my slow stride, his hands tucked into his trouser pockets. I chance one look at his face to catch a bright smile. Even without liquor, his eyes still manage to sparkle.

I notice someone is missing from the procession, and I wonder if the boy that came with Heir Fallon to the Edge survived the journey back. "Where is your assistant?"

He looks confused. "Who do you mean?"

"The orange-haired boy, Shavazme."

"Oh!" The heir laughs heartily. "He's the general's son, and he's in the medical wing, healing. I can't wait to tell him you thought he was my assistant, though."

"Glad to hear he's okay," I respond. "Though he was very rude to you. It bothered me."

Heir Fallon's eyes widen. I suddenly worry my observation insulted him and make a note that I should talk as little as possible. Then, he says: "I… yes, he can be abrasive, to say the least. You're not the first to point that out. Abner has mentioned it a number of times. We've just been friends for so long, I don't know. But… thank you for caring."

"Okay," I say, immensely uncomfortable with his soft tone.

As we approach the carriage, and the parade beyond, the cheering heightens. My legs lock up.

Heir Fallon stops too. He looks at the rabble of excited faces and waving arms, then back at me. "It must be strange to be here after so long. If you need anything, please tell me. No matter what it is."

Damn all this noise and celebrating. I need to put on a more formidable show. The Champions before me stood proudly by the sovereigns, shook their hands during the public speeches. I need to do the same.

"Everything is perfect, Heir Fallon. Let's greet the citizens," I say, puffing my chest out. Then I march the rest of the way to the carriage, grinding my heels into the cobblestone with every step.

The sovereigns, Heir Abner, and Advisor Wilcon are already in the topless bed. I pause at a set of short metal steps painted white.

"Climb the steps," I urge. With each bend of my knee, my ears start to ring. Not even a Gargantuan's roar could drown out this racket. I reach for my belt, grasping for my helmet.

It doesn't hang from my hip. I left it at the cabin.

Gritting my teeth, but making sure my company can't see, I shuffle into a corner across from the sovereigns and the advisor, and beside Heir Abner. There are seats, but everyone else stands, so I do as well. Heir Fallon practically leaps into the carriage. He takes the empty spot on my other side.

The carriage driver flicks the reins, and the white horses slowly turn to face the main road. Impossibly, the crowd explodes into an even louder uproar.

I immediately cover my ears with my hands and flop down onto a seat, fighting not to tuck my head between my knees. The royal family stays standing, unphased by the noise as we break into the parade. The sovereigns gesture at the crowd with elegant turns of their wrists. Heir Abner's waves are much less enthused, but they do it all the same. Heir Fallon adds his own flair with blown kisses. Advisor Wilcon just wears a lazy smile and folds his hands within his long sleeves.

Several concerned and quizzical looks are cast my way. They expect me to join them. I would rather be caught in a Burrower's hole, but I imagine the sibyl hearing how I cowered. My legs shaking, I come to stand, keeping my ears covered. The carriage moves at a snail's pace, the palace still a good distance away. We'll be trudging down this road for far too long. The crowd's cheers feel like oncoming attacks that will never end. When one section tires, another fills the lull, giving no time for me to adjust to the blow before it. Every face my eyes land on blurs into the next, their features melting into dark smudges. Black, soulless eye sockets and gaping mouths that croon unintelligible noises.

From my periphery, Sovereign Adelaide mouths something at me. I squint, trying to make out her words. She points at her waving hand with her other hand. I politely decline with a shake of my head. This is the best I can do. She looks disappointed, and the advisor looks cross.

Something tugs on my wrist. Heir Fallon pulls gently, asking to be let beneath my hands. I hesitate, remembering the odd sensations I felt last time he was this close to me. He tugs again, and reluctantly, I tip my palm away just enough to hear the raucous noise along with the words leaving his lips.

"Is it too loud?"

I nod. The heir presses my hands back over my ears, then he goes to lean over the side of the carriage. He gets the attention of one of the guards stationed between the crowd and us. The guard comes up to the carriage, walking alongside it. Heir Fallon reaches down and pulls the helmet right off the man's head. The guard is bewildered for a moment but quickly collects himself and performs a low bow. He returns to his station, helmetless. The heir turns to me, holding one of the most ridiculous pieces of armor I have ever seen. Gold feather plumage spews along the top like the hackles of a scared dog. More gold embellishments resembling vines, curl around the eye holes and across the cheeks, which would effectively obscure vision in a battle. I would never wear this.

"A demon would snatch that plumage with their teeth, and by the time you see past the flashy gold parts you're already spraying blood over the families below," I say.

"What did you say?" Heir Fallon leans in closer. When I don't respond, he shakes his head with a smirk, then plops the helmet onto my head. I whip my hands away from my ears just in time.

The world becomes muted. Still louder than I prefer, but now my own thoughts don't need to compete. The metal is moist and warm against my skin, and I close my eyes to enclose myself in the shroud. I'm back at my cabin, the endless quiet wrapped around my shoulders. When I open my eyes, Heir Fallon's dark ones meet mine. I nod, thanking him. He pats my forearm then resumes entertaining the crowd.

Beneath my shelter, the parade slows. The surrounding faces and bodies pressed against each other becoming clearer – sparks igniting my memory. Classmates from the academy. A baker my mother sent me to for fresh bread. The carriage passes by a particular street breaking from the main road. My heart leaps into my throat as I trace ghostly steps past the clustered houses on each side. It leads to a round end. A bright pink house is on the left side of the curve. Mother cooks in the kitchen, her back to the window. Father reads in the sitting room. Orange drapes obscure the window on the second floor, where a child's room is.

I look away from the street and scan the crowd. If my parents are here, they're watching confetti rain down over me, the shimmery strips of green and gold paper catching in the crevices of my armor. They watch Niawa rejoice over my presence. When they see me – taller, stronger, my axe peeking over my shoulder – their eyes will fill with wonder. How had I changed so much? Was this warrior inside me all along? The humming radiates through me, though I can't discern whether it's nerves or excitement.

I never stop looking for them as the parade carries on, down the main road until the carriage enters the courtyard circle in front of the palace. To my relief, guards bar the crowd from entering the circle. The palace's pristine white walls rise above, and awe fills my chest as if I'm seeing it for the first time. My gaze is drawn upwards to the emerald-green tiles covering the tower spires. One dwarfs the others, even though it rises from the back. The sibyl's tower.

The sovereigns, Heir Abner, and the advisor have already descended from the carriage. With caution, I lift the absurd helmet from my head.

"What do you think?" Heir Fallon says.

"It was far too much. I didn't even enjoy the parades when I was a child," I say.

"Hm? No, I mean the artwork." The heir points to the palace's tall front doors.

I startle. "Oh…"

My face, or a likeness of it, has been woven into a long tapestry, split down the middle on each side. In the threads, my hair is still long and curls neatly around my cheeks. No scars mar my skin. The lips are set straight across, a fire burning in my almond-shaped eyes. This is how Niawa sees me. Fierce and commanding. Their protector. But it isn't true – not anymore.

"Your hair is a little darker than the artists captured, and they didn't get the shape of your nose quite right, but it's magnificent," Heir Fallon says.

"It's…big, Heir Fallon," I utter as my giant eyes stare me down.

"Sure is. The artists worked on it for months." The heir seems to contemplate for a moment, then says, "You can just call me Fallon. I'd like to call you Oly, if that's alright."

"Alright. F-Fallon." I stutter without the title, and he chuckles.

We step down from the carriage and follow the sovereigns up the palace steps. The doors open as we near, splitting my face apart.

Just before the gap is wide enough, Fallon leans in close.

"By the way, we've arranged a surprise for you. Your parents are joining us for breakfast."

I see them. Standing in the center of the vast entryway, the throne doors wide open behind them. Light from the arched glass windows exposes every crease and wrinkle on their aged faces. There's no hollering from the parade anymore, and the whine of the palace door hinges fades into nothing. The world becomes smaller, bare. We're entirely alone. Me and these two people who share my brown eyes and skin, round cheeks, and straight nose.

Starting from the tips of my fingers and toes, the humming explodes along my nerves, sending violent ripples through my limbs. My bones shake as I take a step forward. Each tap against the black marble floor pounds like a hammer in my head. Mother smiles and I drop my gaze – a long-forgotten instinct.

My shoulders bow in with every closing inch and I can't stop it from happening. Their hazy reflections sneak into the black marble and I nearly jump.

Mother launches forward to wrap her arms around me. That does make me jump, but her hold is tight enough to hide it. She still smells like lemons and olive oil. As it coats my nostrils, dread settles into my stomach, making me think of the Rive.

Behind me, the royal family claps excitedly. I forgot they were here.

"My darling, it's so wonderful to see you. You're very... tall," mother exclaims.

"We can't wait to hear all your stories of the Edge." Father smiles widely and reaches for my hand.

My gloves are only leather. I don't want to feel his fingers constrict around mine, so I yank them out of his reach. Shock runs through my parents' expressions, a flicker of anger follows, cracking the masks of kindness. Their eyes travel over my body, lingering on the axe.

"We've missed you," mother says tentatively.

On Velma's cart, only hearing the wheels crunching against the road, I thought of this moment obsessively. No matter how hard I tried to picture myself in the throne room or the city square, the reverie always placed me in my childhood bedroom. My parents stood in the doorway, their arms crossed protectively. I felt far too large for that room, my essence filling it wall to wall. There was no room for them to enter, not anymore. And I told them. Ten years, only seven missives. They didn't deserve to stand in my presence. I'm the Champion, and *they* should be begging to receive word from *me*. Mother and father didn't know what to say, or how to apologize. They felt my power and knew every word needed to be carefully chosen. The humming under their skin like an undisturbed field of crickets in the early morning.

I said so much. They listened.

I can't remember any of it now. My lips are sewn together. I can't un-ball my fists.

Mother sighs in disappointment, which she shares with father through a long glance.

"Speak," I plead to my frozen body.

"I said we missed you," mother repeats, her tone already sharpening.

"No, not you," I push out. Pressure builds in my throat and behind my eyes. With horror, I realize I'm in danger of crying. Like a frustrated child.

Mother's hands go to her hips, her frustration mounting too. She peeks around me at what can only be the royal family. Her face twists with confusion as if to ask them 'Why have you brought home the same daughter that left ten years ago?'

As I focus on breathing to expel some of the air making my head swim, footsteps tap over with an urgency. Fallon pops into the space between my parents and I, facing us. His eyes flick back and forth, lingering on me far longer than them, but they finally rest on my mother.

"Thank you from the bottom of my heart for coming. I think" – he lightly places his hand on the back of my bicep and I'm too immobilized to stop him – "we'll need to have a private breakfast. The Champion has a lot to report. You're still welcome at this evening's ball, of course."

My parents look as if they've been slapped in the face. Even in the presence of an heir, they're unable to hide their affront.

"Heir Fallon, please, we haven't seen our Hush in ten years. We've been looking forward to this since we heard of her return." Mother softens like warm butter, her hard eyes widening, eyebrows cinching together. "The family of the Champion has always dined with the royal family following the parade."

Fallon looks at me for a response. I breathe in and out, squeeze my fingers into my palms tighter. The tension traveling from the base of my skull to my shoulders starts to sting. He nods in understanding.

With a lazy shrug, he says, "Ellen and Kyel, another time?"

Mother's nostrils flare and she opens her mouth.

Father grabs her shoulders with both hands, stopping the tirade. He glares at me before smiling politely at Fallon. "We'll go, as Heir Fallon wishes." He then steers her around me, starting with a forceful push.

I don't watch them leave, but I hear mother say, "I'm deeply sorry, my sovereigns, but I'm not feeling well. I should be in much better shape by the evening."

Their footsteps trail off for what feels like hours. I'm still frozen to the marble, my muscles locked. Fallon does watch them go, however. When he finally turns his head back to me, I decide to trust his eyes and not the echoing steps in my ears.

"What do I say?" I wonder. The heir tilts his head, curious how I'll explain my behavior. All he's seen of the Champion is nerves, vomiting, hiding. Now, my parents. But I don't understand myself what happened. I was petrified.

The sovereigns, advisor, and Heir Abner, appear like a sudden falling branch, the loud crack sending my heart into my throat. My ice-cold blood thaws too quickly, a bead of sweat rolling down my spine. I can't think of anything to do but smile crookedly.

"Reuniting the Champion with their loved ones has always been so lovely to witness. It's a shame your mother wasn't feeling well. Oh…" Sovereign Gerves' cheer plummets as he looks me over.

"It was *very* moving," Fallon responds. His hand is still on the back of my bicep. Three light taps vibrate through the plates. "After you, father." He extends his free hand toward the open throne room where a long table is being set in the very center. Palace servants flit around it, filling chalices with wine and placing them among more food than I have seen in my life.

The sovereigns take Fallon's suggestion and glide away, the advisor and Heir Abner following. Heir Abner casts a few blank looks over their shoulder at Fallon, who stays behind.

Fallon drops his hand from my arm. "That seemed uncomfortable," he says sheepishly.

The movement encourages me to search my body for life. My shoulders slowly drop as I unfurl my fingers. Tension still holds in my core, but my arms and legs are free from the humming's shackles. My heart finally slows its pace.

"Yes," I respond.

He goes quiet like he did at the Edge, his torso leaning slightly forward, waiting for me to say more. This time, he doesn't wait as long. "Family can be complicated, to say the least. I understand."

I nod with a stiff neck, then remember something he said to them. "My parent's names are Eloise and Keane. Not Ellen and Kyel."

"I'm aware." Fallon smirks.

My chest involuntarily twitches with the start of a laugh. I stop it in time but remain confused by an heir insulting my parents on purpose. Even if I find it strangely amusing. Fallon's widening grin tells me he still caught the reaction.

He motions towards the throne room and we continue across the entryway.

As we walk, Fallon launches into details about the oncoming meal, but my mind is elsewhere, following the path my parents will take to get home. They'd usually avoid the busy main road, especially today. But they need excited voices chirping in their ears. Hands grasping theirs in gratitude. They're the Champion's family, after all. When mother kept glancing over my shoulder at the royal family, it was clear. I could have returned to Niawa in pieces. As long as she and Father still dined with the sovereigns, they'd be satisfied and happy.

It made me feel sick, and the gut curdling hasn't gone away.

I didn't show them who I am. I could barely speak. Somehow, they knew my power was fading away. They could sense it. Mother even called me by the nickname I hated. 'Hush' was a punishment for returning weak, as it was a punishment in my childhood for letting my nerves force me into silence.

I need to get my Blessing before the evening ball. Next time I see my parents, they'll never call me Hush again.

CHAPTER 13

No one reaches into the topography of dishes, even after every seat at the table has been filled and many overzealous compliments of the food have been exchanged. I don't understand what I'm supposed to wait for. My empty plate leers up at me, mirroring the empty, bottomless pit in my stomach. A growl sounds from the depths and I reach for a nearby plate topped with cubes of yellow and white-blotted cheese. Fallon, who sits to my right, subtly shakes his head.

I frown and flop my back against the chair, eyeing the thinning steam from a pile of fatty ham slices. It's been so long since I've eaten meat that wasn't kept in salt boxes. Four large bowls of fruit sing to me, their contents so shiny they seem to have been polished. I long for the breadbasket, inches away, overflowing with golden brown rolls, cracked to reveal herbs toasted into the bake. And dairy. Sweet, thick dairy. Decadent porridge topped with raspberries and blueberries, walnuts mixed into pale yellow pudding, and caramel-coated flan that dances whenever a new dish is set down.

"I'm eating," I declare as I reach for a plate of thick bacon slices and scoop several onto mine.

The servants pick up the pace, racing to set down more pitchers on the edges of the feast and fill the spaces between dishes with tiny bowls of salt and pepper. A bowl of what I hope is some kind of custard catches my eye, but it's too far away.

"Would you?" I ask an amused-looking Fallon.

"I don't think whipped butter would go well on your bacon." He grabs a different dish of light-blue stuff and plops one large scoop onto my plate. "Try this blueberry custard; it's fantastic."

When I don't grab my spoon immediately, he giggles and gives me another helping. I dive right into the custard, already overtaking my bacon like a mudslide. My eyes flutter closed as the flavors coat my tongue. Heavens, this is good. Fallon sets the bowl beside me rather than bringing it back to its carefully chosen place. It takes only minutes to clear my plate. I wash down the last of the bacon with a glass of fresh milk garnished with rose petals.

"Don't really care for flowers in my drink," I muse between gulps, but I empty the glass anyway.

I pull a rag from my belt to wipe my face when Fallon points to a bird sculpture next to my plate. It's made of a red fabric with printed blue flowers and white birds. I assumed it was frivolous decoration, not a napkin. I drop my rag to the floor – a servant scurries to retrieve it, I put my foot on it before she can – and unravel the bird. The material is much too smooth to sop up moisture, so I set it back down.

No one else at the table, including Fallon, has yet to start eating. They watch me, instead, each face a different expression ranging from blank to baffled.

"Is all this food for me?" I wonder.

"Are you speaking to us, Champion?" Advisor Wilcon says from the other end of the table. "I can hardly tell sometimes." He flashes a smile, giving away teeth as yellow as urine, some with dark spots like ants on butter. I'm now re-thinking a helping of eggs.

"He is *quite* old. Like death itself," I say, also noticing the brown spots and purple veins on the advisor's hands.

The sovereigns both release little gasps, and Advisor Wilcon's smile sinks into a puckered line.

"We should eat now," Sovereign Adelaide announces sharply. A flurry of movement follows as servants ask what the royal family wishes to try and prepares their plates.

Fallon leans towards me. "Can I ask you a question?"

I nod with a mouth full of bread roll.

"Do you know that you speak, what I assume are your private thoughts, out loud?"

I think for a moment. "I suppose I talk to myself at the Edge to combat the silence."

"I see." He sounds sad. Perhaps even a little guilty. But I'm not a prisoner. Being the Champion is a divine right. I was *chosen*. In fact, all I wish now is to see the sibyl, ask for my Blessing, then return to my duties.

"That's an invasive question, Fallon," Heir Abner, who sits on my other side, chimes in.

Fallon leans his head farther out to glare at the other heir. His twin returns it. Strange. I'd always heard they were very close.

"Anyway," Fallon drawls as he leans back, "I think it's great." His voice raises a bit. "Honesty is a rare quality these days."

Heir Abner huffs as they cut their ham slice into thinner strips.

Feeling uncomfortable, I dive back into the food. Conversations between the royal family and advisor buzz around me like flies in the dead of summer. Occasionally, one of the sovereigns asks me about my life at the Edge. Though it pains me to lay my silverware down, I pause to look them in the eye and answer. Opportunities to atone for my behavior so far can't be wasted. Though, when I begin to describe battles with demons in great detail – the yellow-gray blood, the stench of rotting meat, finding strips of scaly skin and bone shards stuck to my armor – Sovereign Adelaide drops her fork with a grimace and her husband politely asks me to stop. Despite their reactions, I'm satisfied I've showed them how well I use my power.

Halfway through a fourth plate, my stomach begins to bulge against my cuirass. The leaden feeling is grounding, and I decide now is the time.

After wiping my face, hands, and chest clean of smudges and food debris, I interrupt Advisor Wilcon's conversation with Fallon about something. "I would like to request an audience with the sibyl," I announce to the sovereigns.

The advisor answers. "What business do you have?"

I should have thought of an answer to that question. No Champion has ever gotten a second Blessing. I can't possibly tell them the truth. What will the royal family do with a fading Champion? Will they allow me to become a guard – soft-bellied and delicate without Yuli-en's strength? Will they force me to stay in the city and banish me from the Edge? I scrape my tongue along my teeth until the dull pressure stings and my mind sharpens.

"To thank her. For honoring me with my title," I say.

"That's a lovely sentiment, Champion. We have a grand ball planned for tonight, which the sibyl will attend. You can express your gratitude there," Sovereign Gerves says.

I nod, even as I squeeze my hands together in my lap. A private audience would have been more ideal. I don't want the royal family – especially Fallon – or my parents, to witness me beg.

"Champion, as we said before, we are thrilled to have you here for this Day of Breath. Today is bounteous with celebrations and events!" Sovereign Adelaide beams around the table, capturing every returned smile. "Abner, would you please tell her the day's schedule?"

Heir Abner folds their napkin neatly in their lap then turns towards me, their torso rigid as a plank of wood. I see the physical similarities between them and Fallon, but their demeanors are night and day. Fallon's eyes are bright, sparkling. Heir Abner's also shine, but with intensity. Fallon looks at me curiously with a smile while Heir Abner's stare reminds me of the advisor's: searching. I succumb to a sudden urge to straighten in my chair and square my shoulders.

"Following breakfast, my family will accompany you on a tour of the academy, alongside General Jaits. While you're there, we hope you'll impart some inspiring words to the class soon to graduate. In the late afternoon, there will be a gathering in the palace circle, during which the sovereigns will make an important announcement." Heir Abner flicks their gaze towards Fallon, and Fallon's eyes narrow. "After the gathering, there's time in the day for you to do as you like. In the evening, the grand ball will be here in the throne room. Finally, the courier will take you back to the Edge before midnight."

That sounds awful. My ears stabbed with noise. People invading every inch of my space, until Yuli-en's Eye completes its trek across the sky. My only solace is the academy visit. The green bowls are there. I'll need one to get through this day.

"I'm ready for the tour now," I state.

Advisor Wilcon laughs softly. "Let's finish eating first. Please, Champion, enjoy this day. It's all for you." He raises his chalice, and the royal family follows suit. Do I toast to myself? I decide not and take a sip of ice water.

Several sips later, they're all still dining and talking about parades and speeches and decorating the throne room with silk streamers. My anxiety heightens, thinking about the vast stretch of time between now and seeing the sibyl. I wish I had the power to move the sun across the sky, collapsing the hours around me. But I sit here wasting time, picking at the crumbs of bread on my plate. Every once in a while, I glance up from my lap to check the state of the sovereigns' slowly vanishing food and catch both heirs staring. Fallon winks or smiles – then I look away quickly – while Heir Abner always darts their gaze elsewhere as if I caught them doing something bad.

After far too long, palace servants close in on the table, stacking half-empty plates against their forearms. A woman sweeps into the throne room flanked by several people. They all wear matching green tunics buttoned up to their necks, the royal family's insignia stitched into pockets on their chests. The woman tunic is lined with gold thread, separating her from the rest. She comes to stand between the sovereigns and Advisor Wilcon, her smile reaching both ears. Her subordinates gather behind her, giving ample space. They, too, look proud.

"How was the meal, my sovereigns?" the woman asks.

"Morea, it was superb, as usual. You've outdone yourself. We're all properly full," Sovereign Adelaide responds. She taps her palms together in a soundless clap, which is mimicked around the table.

We must finally be finished if the cook has come out to receive praise. I sigh with relief and stuff my food-soiled rag back into my belt pouch.

"Champion," Morea says with a shaky voice, "I, and my staff, are honored beyond words. Did you enjoy your breakfast?"

I stand from my chair and her smile spreads even further.

"Is it time for the tour?"

As every cook's expression drops, Fallon buries his face in his hands, his shoulders twitching. When he emerges, he wipes tears from the corners of his eyes as he also stands.

"Thank you, Morea. We have a tight schedule today and the Champion is anxious to visit the academy that trained her to be so great." He looks at me. "Isn't that right?"

"Yes." I limit my response. Judging by the sovereigns' and the advisor's cross faces, I'm not saying the right things.

The sovereigns take a little more time to slather the cooks with compliments as they rise from their chairs. Fallon waits by my side for the pleasantries to end before the rulers give a final goodbye and announce we can now leave for the academy.

I picture myself breaking into a run, sprinting through the city, getting closer to a bowl, but my feet move at a slow pace, allowing the sovereigns and advisor ahead of me out of the throne room. Heir Abner trails behind them, and Fallon and I are the last to leave the hall, now drenched in sunlight. As the sovereigns and advisor stride across the marble entryway, a procession of guards fall into a practiced step around us all. Four on each side, one in front, and two behind. A cage. Leading me down the front steps in the dead of night to Velma's cart, vomit thrashing around in my throat ready to be released, my young body trembling with fear, the sky violently dark. But when I look up now, all is blue, the sun too bright to challenge. Yulien's eye is no longer a faint streak, but a powder-white stamp of an impossibly large rock. It appears suspended, motionless.

"I never get tired of seeing it," Fallon says.

He brings me back to the bottom of the stairs, where the royal carriage waits for us just outside the black iron gates between the palace entrance and the large circle. He suddenly stops. I take a few steps before stopping as well. The guards behind us follow suit, but Fallon asks them to continue on.

He turns to me, his sparkling eyes blinking with uncertainty as he runs a hand through his short curls.

"Champion – Oly– I wanted to take a moment to thank you."

"For what?" I ask.

"For returning. It means more than you know. To my family, and Niawa." The way he clears his throat and lowers his eyelids inspires a rush of nerves up my back. "And especially to me."

"It's my duty," I respond hastily. Too quickly. He nods in understanding but seems unsatisfied with my answer. I should show more appreciation. "I'm thrilled to be home."

Fallon's mouth opens but nothing comes out. I'm just about to keep going when he says, "Are you okay? I mean, are you safe at the Edge? Are you happy being the Champion? I remember when you were called. You were so scared."

My body reacts against my will – eyes widening and arms crossing tightly. Does he think I'm ungrateful?

"No, I only meant – not that you aren't capable. I saw with my own eyes why you're the longest-living Champion. I suppose it wasn't until I saw you that I remembered you're also a woman. Like me – not like me; I'm a man. You're a person, like us all." He sighs with exasperation. "None of this is coming out right."

I think of the gash in my leg that took far too long to heal. The Singed Fox that punctured my neck guard. The Burrower's bone that shocked my back into incapacity. I've feared for my life – no, I've feared feeling weak again – every day for the past year. But even if I knew this would come, I would still drink from the bowl. I'm *not* just any person shopping at the market, too scared to talk to the merchants, my mother forced to speak for me, her grip wringing heat into my wrist. "Everything is fine."

Fallon raises his hands in an appeasing gesture. "Of course. My sincerest apologies for insinuating you can't handle your duty. That wasn't my intention. To be even more frank, knowing you even for this short time, I've already grown fond of you, Oly. It'd make me very sad to hear of your passing, that's all."

"You won't. I'm not going to die," I say with determination. No doubt, my answers to this obvious test will be passed to the sovereigns and the sibyl.

Fallon looks at me the way Velma did when I didn't want to get off the cart my first night at the Edge: pitying. Even so, he nods. I gave acceptable responses.

I glance behind me to see Fallon walking slowly, rubbing the back of his neck with a vengeance and shaking his head. If he means to disarm me, I won't let it happen.

The sovereigns, Heir Abner, and the advisor already wait in the carriage when I haul myself into the bed and flop down on a corner seat. I only need to endure a few seconds of stale silence before Fallon bounds up the small stairs and takes the seat next to me.

"What did you and the Champion need to speak privately about?" Heir Abner asks at the same time Advisor Wilcon tells the carriage driver we're ready to go.

"I wanted to know what gifts Oly–" he emphasizes my name like it's something important "–would like to return with. She seemed to really enjoy the bread rolls," Fallon responds.

"Such good friends already?"

Fallon's face darkens. "That happens when you experience something horrible together."

"Horrible for you. She lives at the Edge every day."

"Enough!" Advisor Wilcon snaps.

The heirs both cross their arms and angle away from each other immediately. I can't fathom why they bicker so much, but as long as it doesn't distract from getting my Blessing, it's not my concern. As the carriage rolls across the circle courtyard and towards the city, I get comfortable in the tense silence – the only kind I know. On this carriage ride, I don't need a ridiculous helmet. The parade has dispersed into people in small groups on the side of the road, drinking openly and talking with their mouths full of cakes and candies. They shout and wave when we trail by, but the royal family only returns polite nods of the head and smiles. If they don't feel the need to be attentive, neither will I. Without the noise bashing my head around, I can really focus on the city.

Every brightly painted building feels both familiar and remote, as if I travel through a kingdom in a storybook. Did I walk through this narrow alley to reach the marketplace quicker or was that another little girl? Is that my handkerchief stuffed beneath a set of wooden stairs, soaked from my tears because mother yelled at me, or is it just a rag fallen from someone's pocket? By the time the city pulls away, houses replaced by stretches of bright grass, well-manicured trees, a widening road, I've stopped trying to place myself in the story of Niawa. I don't belong here anymore.

The first sign of the Academy of the Guard are two white pillars on either side of the road. My back to the oncoming grounds, I eagerly twist my torso as we pass between, not wanting to miss them. Following the pillars, placed evenly apart, tall statues of black stone shocked with gray and white lines watch the carriage with clear purpose chiseled into their eyes.

The Champions before me. Each wields a different weapon, their smooth hands gripping the hilt of a sword, an axe, a gleaming mace, a stocked crossbow. In the brief time they surround us, I feel protected. They know who I am. I crack a smile at the final row of statues, even as I lock eyes with the

Champion who took his own life. Niawa still honored him.

Then there's space. To my right and left, square stone bases are set where statues will one day be. Where I will stand encased in black rock after I die. I know that day will come, it's inevitable, but I still twist back around. The humming rattles my hands, and I grip them together in my lap, trying to ignore the dread spreading in my chest.

I can feel Fallon's eyes on me, so I keep mine lowered. They stay there until we go beneath a metal arch braided with ivy and the carriage finally slows to a stop. I wait for the royal family and advisor to descend first, taking those few seconds to collect myself. Once my bowl is back in my hands, everything will feel right again.

The moment my feet are firm on the ground, I take in the home of my teenage years. We're only in the entrance courtyard, steel double doors between me and the training grounds. The tan rock wall extending from either side of the arch, and marking the perimeter of the many academy buildings, seemed much taller before. It felt suffocating as I cried into the nook of my free arm, the other yanked by mother. Father just followed silently as he always did. I hadn't stopped crying since they told me a week prior that I was being sent to the academy. It was my twelfth birthday, the day trainees are of age to be enrolled. I'd barely even had a bite of breakfast.

I follow the phantom bodies of my parents and my smaller form to the double doors. When my fingers wrap around the handles, someone calls out my title. Bodies surround me as if they appeared from thin air. The guards who accompanied us from the palace. I forgot they were here. One steps around me and extends her arm, asking me to step back.

"I can open my own doors," I grumble, but I move out of the way.

She and another guard pull the doors open, then stand alert on either side. The royal family and advisor walk through with me into the training grounds beyond.

The royal family pauses on the edge of the first training plot to watch the sparring sessions, much to my annoyance. Unfortunately, this group are the younger trainees. Not even allowed metal weapons yet, just wooden sticks and shields. This will get boring quickly.

Groups of trainees stand off to the side of the plot in dark green uniforms as two spar before their audience. The session is overseen by an older trainee, whose collar is lined with gold stitching. Metal bars are clasped to his chest in angled rows. He is high-ranking and top of his class. If he were chosen as the next Champion, no one would bat an eye. But status is not how Yuli-en chooses their warrior. No one but the sibyl knows. Champions have always been tapped from the academy or the guard, but rank doesn't seem to matter. Yuli-en only seeks a will to fight. I didn't know that existed in me until I felt the Blessing.

The sparring suddenly stops and all heads turn our way. The wave catches on to the next two plots behind the young trainees. Even the high-ranking trainee can't control the shock in his eyes. He bows far too deeply to me first, then gives more appropriate bows to the royal family.

I look past him to a dormitory building that is hollowed out in the center with a short, curved tunnel leading to another section of the academy. My bowl is on the other side.

"Carry on! The Champion will be speaking to the classes during our next break. You may ogle then," the high-ranking trainee bellows. He immediately barks another order when the young trainees remain stunned. They jump back into their sessions, though many still sneak glances from the corners of their eyes.

I'm ready to move on, so I head towards the tunnel first. The royal family follows. As we skirt the plots, the echoes of wood whacking together bouncing off the surrounding walls, I take note of the resolute faces dodging wild swings as they consider their next move. Whereas I was so petrified I couldn't distinguish the humming from the whistling of blades through the air.

One day, a teaching captain pulled me aside after I lost every spar in a session. I knew her expression all too well. Frustration. Disappointment. Not at my lagging behind in combat training, but at the way I struggled to meet her eyes. The way I nervously rubbed my forearms over and over, the skin growing hot and dry from my palms. I already knew her reaction before she sighed slowly with her eyes clenched shut. That was defeat.

"What do we do with you…?" I recite the captain's words aloud.

I expected to be sent to my room, where I would wait for a letter of expulsion. My eyes watered at the thought of my parents coming to retrieve me. It had only been a year. They would be furious. But instead, the captain sent me to the infirmary, where I was prescribed my tablets.

Fallon comes up to my side. "Has it changed much?"

I turn my head sharply. It's Heir Abner, not Fallon.

"Not really," I answer honestly.

"Change can be good, though. I think the guards can certainly be tougher. Have more weapons at their disposal."

I nearly scoff, then remember who I'm speaking to. As long as the Rive exists, no kingdom would dare invade Niawa. And guards are not strong enough to face demons. They might as well be issued the wooden sticks after graduation.

Heir Abner continues. "I've always wondered about magic aids for the guards. Maybe then, they'd be strong enough to assist you at the Edge." I notice their voice quickens, then goes abruptly silent – just as Fallon comes up to my other side.

"Discussing something interesting like trade routes and farming?" he asks.

I don't respond, my head swirling. Heir Abner also thinks I need help with my duty. Fallon saw with his own eyes how slowly I moved, and he must have told his sibling. That means the sovereigns know too.

"Absolutely. I wouldn't be able to talk to you about anything like that," Heir Abner snaps.

"This isn't a meeting, Abner; let Oly enjoy her one day of freedom."

"Freedom is a *very* interesting word to use," Heir Abner says.

I quicken my pace, aching to find my bowl. If the royal family believes I can't handle my calling, I need a calm, clear head to convince them otherwise.

The tunnel opens into another large, open space, this one bordered by dormitories and the dining hall. The center is bare except for a handful of trees, stretches of contained grass, and benches. A resting place for trainees between sparring and classes. I avoided this area like a sickness. Idle conversation was never my strongest trait.

To my right, the chancery is tucked against the perimeter wall. Bright vines roam over its rust-colored walls and green-tiled roof. A window by the door displays the high desk inside, where my parents signed forms and attempted to explain away my timid demeanor. Standing by the door, hands stacked over the hilt of his sword, is General Jaits. An intricately patterned tabard lays in large folds around his neck, leading to a long gold cape that kisses the heels of his boots. Nonsense clothing for a warrior. He has the same, orange-colored hair as Shavazme, as well as the same round cheeks and sky-blue eyes.

As soon as the royal family spots the general, they make a beeline for him. I look longingly at the dining hall, only strides away. One quick introduction, then I'll cut away to get my bowl.

With heavy feet, I go to the chancery. The general immediately claps his gloved hand on my shoulder. I tried to move out of the way, but my slowing reflexes decide now is the time to worsen. "Champion, it is an honor to meet you. You saved my son's life. I thank you from the bottom of my soul. May Yuli-en's light shine upon you always."

I tilt my eyes up to the sky. The god's comet is exactly overhead, marking the late afternoon. Half the day is already gone.

"Champion? Did you hear me?"

"Yes, he's a fine boy. Could we begin the tour now?" I say impatiently.

General Jaits jerks his head back at the same time he frees my shoulder from his large hand. He begins to speak again, but Fallon rushes in.

"We're all eager to start the tour. The Champion's time is very limited today."

"Of course. We'll get started then," General Jaits responds, though he looks at me with confusion. "I'm sure you sense the excitement at your arrival. The graduating class is thrilled to hear from the longest-living Champion and drink in your words of encouragement."

I'd forgotten about the damn speech. As a trainee, I'd seen six Champions impart their tales of the Edge. Now that I've stepped into their shoes, they certainly left out many of the gory details. A lot of imagery about quiet mornings and feelings of triumph for keeping Niawa safe. I'll be more honest. The next chosen one should know what they're up against. But first: "I'd like to start with the dining hall."

General Jaits chuckles. "The dining hall is the least interesting building. I promise, you'll be thrilled to see the expansion of the training grounds in the east sector."

I huff with impatience as I glance at the dining hall again. It's right there. I can't wait another minute. "There's something I need to get first. I'll be right back." Worried I'll be pulled away again, I leave before the general can rebut.

It isn't until I'm nearly at the open doorway that I hear boots clopping on the cobblestone behind me. Fallon jogs up to my side. He doesn't look upset or confused and doesn't ask me to stop, so we enter the long, gable-roofed building together.

Nothing here has changed. Large skylights bleed the morning sun upon long rows of metal tables with wooden stools. On the far side is another set of doors, leading to the kitchen. The hall is empty, as breakfast has recently ended and the cooks now prepare for lunch. They shout at each other through the walls, barking orders then laughing in the same breath. I head straight for the kitchen, shoving the swinging doors open with my shoulder.

A volley of yelps rings out. The cooks demand for us to leave or explain ourselves – until they get a good look at the intruders. They remove their caps and head scarves, pressing them to their chests.

"Where are the dishes?" I ask. "The bowls, to be exact."

One cook points to a closed door in the far corner. I waste no more time and walk the perimeter of the kitchen, around metal tables laden with meat, vegetables, pots, and pans. One last door remains in my way. A simple metal one with one round handle. I pull it open, filled to the brim with excitement, and step into a pantry.

Cold washes through me, freezing into little pricks on my skin. The shelves should be stacked with pale-green dishes. But I'm surrounded by towers of gray.

Gray plates.

Gray cups.

Gray bowls.

"This isn't right."

Fallon steps into the pantry. He looks around, trying to find what I'm searching for.

"Where are the green bowls?" My voice quivers and I can't stop it.

"Uh, I'll go ask," he says before slipping back into the kitchen.

I hear him speaking to the cooks. They say the academy switched entirely to the cheaper gray dishes years ago. The green ones were sold in the market. I refuse to believe that. The shelf to my right is all plates, but I scour through them anyhow, yearning for the calming jade. I spin to check the shelves on the other side and the head of my axe swipes along the plates. Several crash to the floor.

Dishes breaking. Like my bowl in the cabin. It slipped from my careless, weak, nerve-wracked fingers and then I crushed it.

My axe is in my hands. I swing it at another row.

I hate this gray. It shouldn't be here. I can't see it a second longer.

Ceramics smash into the walls and floor. Sparks fly when my axe collides with the metal wall beneath the off-white paint.

"There has to be more!" I slam my boot through a bottom row of cups, cracking the shelf in half. Pain flies through my hip. I use the other leg instead to break the row above it. The entire shelf wobbles forward. I jump out of the way before gray can bury me.

"Where are they?" I scream. This can't be happening. To not have the bowl anymore, to return to the Edge without it…

My throat closes to a pinhole. Gray shards cover the floor. My bowl is in shards on the cabin floor. I ready my axe for another swing, bringing it over my head–

A flash of green catches my eye and I stop my blade midair.

Fallon is next to me, his breath audibly catching. He lifts up a green bowl in his hands.

I drop my axe and snatch at the bowl. It's cool against my fingers. The ocean's soft waves breaking against peach sand fill my head. I breathe with the waves easing in and out of the shore as I stumble out of the closet, dish shards sticking to the soles of my boots. They scrape against the floor as I bring the bowl to the nearest table and lay my elbows on the surface.

The cooks peek at me from the opposite end of the kitchen, some through a sliver between the swinging doors. They grip cooking utensils like weapons. As calm slowly returns, so does shame. I look at the trail of gray leading from the pantry, then to Fallon's open concern.

Before citizens, and an heir, I've shown my declining strength in a way I'm more ashamed of than if I hadn't been able to lift my weapon. A Champion screaming, smashing dishes like an unruly child. I bow my head.

"You are the Champion. The strongest of them all," I whisper into the table, condensation marking my words on the metal.

One inch of my spine at a time, I straighten. "Where did you find it?" I ask Fallon.

"There happened to be a set of old dishes in one of the cabinets. We checked them all."

That's when I notice the kitchen is in complete disarray. Every cabinet door hangs open, kitchenware and cutlery is tossed about on the tabletops and counters.

"Did you find everything you need?" Fallon asks, taking a small step towards me.

I nod.

"Good." He sounds genuine, and a splinter of my shame falls away. "We should get back to the chancery."

Avoiding the cook's stares, I return to the pantry, bringing the bowl with me. One-handed, I try to slide my axe back into the straps – with difficulty. When I raise it overhead, my arm shakes in a new way. Not from bruises or exhaustion. It's becoming heavy. I check the doorway for Fallon, worried he saw, but he isn't in my eyeline. Reluctantly, I part with the bowl to use both arms and secure my axe. Scooping the bowl back into my embrace, I leave the pantry, wondering if the Blessing will even last the day.

Distant sounds drift into the kitchen. They're faint, and many, layered and frantic. Screams.

The cooks quiet their complaints about the state of the room to listen.

Some screams separate from the rest, sharpening into familiarity.

A word forms.

"Demon! Demon! Demon!"

CHAPTER 14

Trainees move in frenzied mobs into the dormitories while instructors and captains bellow orders over clanging bells in their hands. After the third, wild-eyed child crashes into me, I start pushing through their uncoordinated bodies, while also making sure Fallon doesn't get lost in the swarm. We break through to the chancery where General Jaits convenes with several captains and the royal family. Every one of them looks scared. Even the advisor's stern face darts left and right, and up to the sky, searching.

"Did you hear? Are there demons?" An instructor steps into our path. Behind him, a group of young trainees, likely in their first year, huddle together.

"No," I answer definitively. Of course not. That would be impossible.

I reach behind for Fallon's sleeve and pull him with me around the instructor and trembling kids.

General Jaits and the captains break from their conversation when they see me.

"Do you know anything, Champion?" the general asks. He can't hide the fear in his eyes.

I shake my head. "I don't, but I will find out."

"As will I." He turns towards the royal family, and Fallon, who is attempting to calm his parents. "The Champion and I will report back to the palace as soon as possible. These captains will escort you back to the carriage. Wait!"

General Jaits calls after me, but I've already started towards the tunnel. "Go with the royal family. I won't need your help," I yell over my shoulder.

There are no demons. But if there are, he would only get in the way. As I fly towards the academy entrance, I look to the sky for proof and find Yuli-en's Eye exactly where it should be. The Rive still sleeps.

The screams lead me back into the city's streets and down a road of homes. A group of citizens race towards me from the opposite end. I flatten against a soft blue wall to let them pass. As they do, I assess their faces, listen to what they say. Terror. Confusion. Swearing they've seen a demon, but they don't describe what kind it is. I refuse to believe them. These people have only been caught in a frenzy of their deepest nightmare.

One man notices me. "The Champion!" He stumbles to stop, more citizens bunching up behind him like a snagged thread pulled in fabric. He points at me, and there's blood on his hand.

"Which way?" I shout over an eruption of prayers to Yuli-en that the Champion is here to save them.

The man aims his red finger back the way they came, towards the farmlands. Without hesitation, I push through the crowd and run as best I can down the street. More people stampede in the opposite direction. Beneath their feet, I catch smears of human blood.

Screams now sound from all directions, making it difficult to determine the right way to go. Looking ahead, the smears continue down the street and disappear around a turn. I let them guide me.

"Several rabid boars not ready for slaughter have escaped a pen," I assure myself, even as I pass two women slumped together against a tree; one's face is carved from ear to chin, thin strips of skin peeling away as her companion struggles to hold her up.

"An angry, belligerent man is on a rampage."

My foot lands on a chunk of something slippery. When I lift it, a ragged strip of fatty, human flesh falls from my heel.

Soon I'm no longer following smears of blood, but more slabs of discarded, mushy flesh. Some chunks appear to have been torn off with claws, others rest on the ground in smooth peels as if they slipped off the bone. Nausea brews in my stomach. I've sewn my own skin together, soaked many rags with my blood, smelled my own pus-mottled wounds as the Blessing fought against infection, but I've never seen so much carnage of other humans. I nearly trip trying to avoid stepping on a brown ear laying over a wiggling lump of yellow fat.

"Focus," I pant.

The gory trail leads me to a short lane ending in a small park. I stop abruptly on the park's cobblestone border, trying to make sense of what I see. "Almighty Yuli-en..."

Four demons are in the middle of the park. At a glance, someone may not know it. Because they wear humans like ill-fitting suits.

Three stand on two legs and wear human clothes, but the clothes are torn and stretched to make way for unnaturally curved spines and elongated arms ending in long, thin fingers. Pale skin tinged with pink shows from beneath tears across their exposed shoulders and backs. The human skin barely clinging to the creature's bodies curls at the edges of the tears. A slab of deep brown forearm skin slides off one demon and slops to the ground. It doesn't react to the decay of its former body.

The fourth one uses its long arms as another set of legs like an animal. It's larger than the others, the last of its clothing hanging in frayed strips. Dark brown patches of hair sprout from an abnormally large and nearly bald head.

It looks at me, and I jolt.

One eye is still human. A wide, blue iris. The other is a large, black oblong, half covered by a drooping forehead. A red ring hangs in the center.

I've seen this creature before. The human-like demon that appeared the day Fallon came to the Edge.

My chest heaves up and down and I take a large step back. The humming makes my fingers numb, but I still clutch my bowl to my chest. There was nothing in my lessons at the academy or in the former Champion's journals about this demon. How did it get here? How did it survive a beheading and a crushed skull? I saw its essence escape, I *saw it.*

"What are you?" I exhale.

The fourth opens its mouth wide and the human skin on the right side of its face splits up to its temples. Several blunt teeth tumble out as it bares crowded rows of human teeth and needlepoint-sharp fangs.

From an adjoining street, a group of people dash into the small park. They see me across the way and hope brightens their faces. The path they take in my direction takes them right past the demons.

"Get away!" I shout, but it's too late. The creatures charge.

"There's more!" a man yells. He scrambles to get away, pulling several in his group with him. His warning is useless to one young woman who moves the slowest.

The fourth wraps its fingers around her leg and pulls. Her head slams into the cobblestone before her wriggling body is dragged within the circle of demons.

"Help me!" she cries out. Her screams violently break me out of shock. I tuck the bowl beneath a row of short shrubs to my right, then sprint towards the demons, my axe raised as high as I can manage.

"Run!" I command the others. They listen.

Distracted by the unlucky woman, the demons don't notice me until I embed my axe into the back of a two-legged one, aiming for where I hope a heart is. To my surprise, the blade carves through its body. My axe completes its arc with no resistance, and I have to exert myself to stop it from slamming into my own shins. It crumples to the ground. I'm glad to see this abomination dies like the rest of them. The red mist that rises is a thin stream, like a sprinkle of sand.

Another two-legged to my right carves through the air with its clawed hand. Like the one at the Edge, its movements are slow. Sharp fingers scrape across my armor at the same time I land my boot into its concaved chest. Ribs snap easily from the blow and the creature drops onto its back. The low moan it releases still faintly resembles a man's voice.

The demon to my left chooses to fight with its wide mouth of jumbled teeth. I thrust out my elbow, allowing it to chomp down on my armor. As it tries to gnaw through the plates, I swing my axe into its neck from below.

The blade cuts clean through, leaving the head still clamped on my elbow as the body falls. Thank Yuli-en these are easy to kill, my arms are painfully tired.

I turn quickly. The demon I kicked is back on its feet and opens its jaw to take a bite. I spin my torso, and it gets a mouthful of its kin's severed head. The creature pulls back, ripping the head from my arm. I duck down, both dodging the fourth's swinging arms and taking the chance to send my axe through the other demon's legs. It crumples again, gagging against the head lodged in its mouth. It doesn't get back up.

A blow lands across my face, knocking me off my feet.

White stars dance across my eyes, only fading to leave me in a world of blurred edges. Not knowing where the fourth is coming from, I clamber backwards until my back hits the wall of a building. I squeeze my eyes shut and open them wide over and over, hoping my vision will sharpen.

This fourth is much stronger than the others.

A pale shape comes into view above me, and I swing my axe wildly. The fourth doesn't immediately try to attack, only waves side to side in a trance-like motion. I must have made myself something to be wary of.

I shake my head. The movement stings horribly, but the pain clears away the rest of the shroud – just in time to catch the fourth's hand wrapping around my ankle. I raise my other leg up and drop it with force on the demon's wrist. Its arm doesn't break, but it's enough to loosen the creature's fingers. I'm on my feet a split second later, one side of my head hot and pounding.

The demon stares, but I only feel its pointed gaze from the red-ringed eye. The human eye is dead, disconnected, hanging on its face against olive-tinged human skin that jars against the demon's paleness.

I know this man.

"Escort Burkhard?"

There isn't even a glimmer of the guard who was seemingly killed at the Edge. I laid his limp body on the bed of the courier's cart myself.

"You're not a man anymore," I accept.

As if the creature agrees, it lets out a guttural moan and hurls forward. At the last moment, I dodge to the side and it crashes into the wall behind me. The moment it turns back around, I jab the butt of my axe into the side of its head with all my strength, happy to return the headache. Then I bring my weapon down and across its chest.

Yellow-gray blood gushes out, slathering my face and torso. I blink through it and slash again. My shoulders ache, but I keep slashing until I feel bone break. The demon stops trying to grasp at me as blood floods the cracks between the cobblestone.

It sinks lower and lower to the ground, the ringed eye never leaving me. A thicker fog of red mist rises from the creature's head, leaving its demon eye black and hollow. Its ravaged chest exposes a bizarre tangle of human bones pushed aside and weighed down with new bone growth. This isn't the time for inspection, even if my curiosity is piqued to know more.

I march back to the other three and survey the still bodies. There is one thing I won't forget from my first battle with this creature. I slam my boot down on one severed head, crushing whatever kind of brain grows inside. It won't be coming back to life this time. The other two heads meet the same end. Without any fangs or claws trying to tear through my flesh, I lower to my haunches and get a closer look. Straw-colored hair flows from one skull; a freckled cheek falls off another. Maybe even as recently as this morning, these were people. They stood in the parade throwing confetti and cheering. This demon found its way beneath their skin and grew like a stalwart weed. The pieces of flesh and smears of blood I followed to get here now make sense. It's some kind of parasite, and it's spreading through the city. I need to find out how before I meet the same fate.

In a panic, I look over my body, though I'm confident the demons didn't get past my armor.

A whimper sneaks out from beneath the demon bodies. I toss one aside to find the unlucky woman. Her hip is torn open, flesh and muscle eviscerated. She tries to raise one violently shaking arm. The stone ground has marred her face, her cheek scraped up and raw.

I watch for a few seconds, a theory forming in my mind, but she remains a terrified woman. Then, one of her green eyes sinks into her skull, a puddle of black leaking over. A red ring slowly flickers to life. The woman's arm suddenly finds new strength as she plants her clawed hand against the ground and pushes her torso up.

I bring her back down with a quick slice through the neck and a boot to her head. As the red mist rises, my theory firms. Bites and scratches must carry the parasite, or else they would have eaten her.

"Champion?"

My neck spasms from turning so fast.

Leaning against a wall in an alleyway nearby is Escort Denya, wearing a very dirty nightgown. She holds two long swords in her hands, fresh red and yellow-gray blood caking the silver blades. The tongues of her boots flap over the hastily tied laces. Her black, straight hair is plastered to her temples with sweat.

The escort lowers to the ground as I approach. When she raises her bowed head, she holds an expression of unfathomable despair. Her breathing is ragged and red circles her eyes, from tears or tiredness – or something else.

"Have you been bitten?" I ask sharply, pointing my axe.

She rolls her head against the wall side-to-side. "No… we have to… get to the sibyl. She will know… how to stop this." Escort Denya coughs. "I'm so sorry. I couldn't do what needed to be done." Her gaze looks past me, towards the demon that was once Escort Burkhard. Tears rim her eyes, followed by heaving sobs as she lets the two long swords clatter to the ground.

I drop to one knee, laying my axe across the other and hanging my arms over the staff. "What do you know?"

Denya's face droops. She's about to bury herself into her knees but I grab her shoulder to keep it pressed against the wall.

"Talk," I demand.

She shuts her eyes, wringing out fresh tears. "When we returned to Niawa after Liam – Escort Burkhard – was killed, I laid him to rest at the edge of my property alone that night. He had no family, no real friends. Truly, he only had me. I tried to sleep after I buried him, I was so distraught, but I couldn't. In the early morning, I visited his grave." She clutches the gown's linen at her chest. "My heart ached so deeply I thought I would die. And then, I heard him. Beneath the soil. I thought I was plummeting into insanity until his hand shot out from the dirt. I screamed and ran – but I didn't get far. I had to know if he was alive. So, I dug him out."

Escort Denya looks at her fingers, brown dirt still crusted around her nails. "He was alive and breathing. Before I buried him, I wrapped a scarf around his neck to keep his head attached, but he didn't need it. His neck was healed; a new patch of pale skin covered the bite. But he couldn't speak, only groaned. I should have seen it then, but I was blinded by joy. My love returned to me. I brought him to my villa and just watched him. All morning. But all he did was moan and twitch and stare. When the parade started, he began to change. First, it was his arms and legs. They stretched, becoming thin and bony. One of his eyes blackened and a – a red ring, like a demon's, appeared. Then he attacked me.

"I managed to evade him, knocking over damn near everything in the room. Luckily, I'm a collector of blades, and two were mounted to the wall. I grabbed them to defend myself, but it wasn't me who needed defending. One of my live-in house servants, Nina, flew into the room to see about the commotion. I didn't have a chance to warn her before Liam tore her arm clean off her body. At first, I froze, then Nina cried for me and I fought Liam away so I could bring her to safety. We went into the kitchen and I locked the door behind us. My cook tried to help me stop the bleeding, but Nina died in my arms. Or so I thought. I had laid her down and gone to listen at the door for Liam. He moaned and scratched at the wood, then he left. At first I was relieved, until I remembered the other help. My gardener, other servants, the cook's nephew. I heard them arriving for the day's work. Then I heard screaming. So much screaming. I ran from the kitchen into a massacre. Liam had bitten and torn into them all. Blood covered the walls and furniture. He came at me again, but I couldn't kill him."

"Hurry this along," I urge.

Denya nods erratically as she pushes her torso up against the wall. "Liam kept changing in front of my eyes. I was so focused on him I wasn't paying attention. Nina nearly tore into my shoulder from behind. And the cook almost had his claws in my back. I ran then. Through the house to my armory – for its heavy door. I shut myself inside."

"Why didn't you leave your villa and warn the city?" I retort.

She looks away shamefully. "Liam isn't my husband. I would've had to explain why I buried him. And why he was at my house at night. My husband, who is away visiting family, already suspected."

A flash of anger launches me to my feet. "You're a coward. I could've had time to prepare. The parasites must be in every corner of the city by now. If it took Liam hours to change and minutes for your help, then the infestation is getting faster with every kill." How many demons could there be now? Hundreds? I won't be able to stop them without the Blessing.

I gasp. The general's son. Fallon said he was healing in the medical wing inside the palace. The royal family doesn't know. My throat goes dry at gruesome images of demons roaming the palace corridors, ripping into guards and servants. One creature wearing Fallon's sparkling eyes above fangs as long as fingers.

"I swear to you, I've found my courage," Escort Denya sputters. "Eventually, they left the villa. I followed them towards the city and managed to kill three on my own, but Liam was much stronger. When I realized I needed help, I started to warn every person I saw."

I'd be impressed with a guard killing three demons if their lingering humanity didn't make the task easier. But, as shown by Escort Burkhard and the persistent pounding in my head, the longer the demon grows, the stronger it gets. It's been at least an hour since the villa demons tore through the farmers and reached the city.

I want to collapse. Hide in the armory with Denya. In the safety of my thoughts, I admit, that I don't want to fight today.

"That's not an option," I state.

The academy may train guards in weaponry, monitor their steps as they learn to dodge attacks, but they don't prepare them for demons. If I don't get my strength back, I'm as useless – and dead – as everyone else.

"I need to get to the palace," I say. The sibyl won't be able to deny my request now.

"Wait, don't leave me here," Denya cries.

She'll only get in the way, so I ignore her plea and find the shrubs where my bowl safely waits. Looking down at my axe in both hands, I sneer at the weapon for the strain in my biceps and weight on my shoulders. I certainly can't hold it and carry the bowl at the same time.

"Damn it all." I sacrifice one arm to hold my axe so the other can extend the bowl in Escort Denya's direction. "You're coming with me, but only to protect this."

She pushes herself upright as if she weren't just panting and sobbing, and rushes to me with new wind beneath her wings. "Thank you, Champion. For giving me a chance to redeem myself." Her basil-green eyes blink a few times at the bowl, but she sheaths one of her two swords before taking it.

"Can you kill them? Even if it's someone you recognize?" Escort Burkhard wouldn't have gotten so strong if emotions hadn't clouded her judgement.

Denya nods. "I won't make the same mistake again."

She presses the tip of her sword into the ground and taps my bowl to her head.

"No time for that." I cut off the Guard's Oath and leave the park. The escort follows without another word.

CHAPTER 15

Fallon sits idly in the royal carriage with his family and the advisor as a stream of citizens push their way beneath the arch and through the academy doors. Guards form a tight circle around the carriage, weapons rising when someone veers too close.

Academy instructors and General Jaits try their best to bring order, but the people are screaming, crying, begging for answers. The royal family has none, and Advisor Wilcon strongly urged the sovereigns to delegate their request for patience and calm to the guards.

"We need to do something," Abner says. They have yet to sit down. Their eyes are glued to the chaos, arms crossed tightly over their chest.

"Nothing can be done until we know what we're dealing with. Jaits will give a full report as soon as he can. Now sit, please." Sovereign Adelaide grabs her child's hand and coaxes Abner down to their seat.

They shoot back up a second later. Someone in the crowd shrieks. Then another person. Fallon stands next, his heart thumping in his chest. Bodies fall near the carriage, limbs flying out. He can't discern anything from the tangle of arms and legs until a spurt of blood soils the pristine white flanks of the carriage horses. A balding man rises from the heap, red streaming down his chin. People shove to clear away from him, causing a ripple of falling and scrambling. In the small clearing remaining, the balding man stands over another man whose stomach bubbles with dark blood. The man on the ground whimpers as the balding man looks at the surrounding crowd as though he's choosing a next victim. After what feels like far too long of a pause, a guard steps forward and places her blade under the balding man's chin.

"Get on your knees!" she demands.

He moans, his head rolling from shoulder to shoulder.

"Arrest him, now," Sovereign Gerves orders. Fallon's family is bunched together on the far edge of the carriage. He's the only one at the lip, transfixed by the bloody scene.

More guards leap into action, seizing the balding man by his arms. The man on the ground, who had been forgotten in the havoc, lurches his torso up. Blood gushes from his stomach wound as he grabs at a guard's leg and bites into the metal shin plate. The guard yelps in shock and stabs their spear downward, straight through the man's shoulder.

He's pinned to the ground, but his neck strains upwards, jaws still snapping.

"Behind you!" Abner yells.

A woman with one black eye jumps onto another guard's back, knocking his helmet clean off. In the same motion, she sinks her teeth into his neck. Fallon feels himself being pulled away from the edge of the carriage into his family's arms. But he already saw it. A red ring flashing in the woman's eye.

"Demons," he chokes out.

The carriage driver doesn't wait for orders from the royal family. Reins are snapped, the horses whinny and rear their front hooves, then they bolt forward.

Fallon throws his arms over the carriage lip, holding on as tight as he can. He's no engineer, but it's easy to tell this carriage wasn't designed for speed. The gold-painted wheels bump and slide against the road as the driver attempts to maneuver through hordes of citizens without flipping them all over. Halfway through the Champion statues, General Jaits and four of the eight guards who had escorted them to the academy gallop ahead and take over clearing the way. A chill runs through Fallon as he wonders if the other four are dead.

Fallon meets the eyes of his parents, Abner, and the advisor. Wordlessly, they all accept the truth. What they had denied to the terrified instructors and even more terrified trainees, and to each other. Demons. In Niawa. On the Day of Breath.

But what kind of demon, Fallon can't comprehend. He watched a man bleed to death on the ground and then rise with teeth like a row of knives. What kind of demon grows inside a human? Was the man always a demon, hiding among the citizens?

Fallon nearly retches from the weight of the possibilities, and the cart's erratic rocking. They burst back into the city streets, more packed with citizens than the road to the academy. The escorting guards waste no time in clearing a path for the carriage. As they fly towards the palace, the tall white towers growing in size, relief spreads through Fallon. They'll be safe there. While Oly finds every wolf in sheep's clothing, they'll be safe.

Fallon looks away from the palace's turrets and catches the blunt end of a guard's spear slam into a woman's chest. She seemed to be grappling for the guard's saddle, blood pouring from her temple. A small crowd gathers to help pull her to her feet. Fallon watches as long as he can, waiting for a black eye to appear. But the woman just sobs as someone holds a rag to her head. Then the crowd disappears around a turn.

Fallon presses his fingers to his mouth and curls into himself, unable to look outside the carriage any longer. How will the guards know who is a demon? How will anyone? He clutches at his chest, a sudden fever beading sweat over his clavicle. Fallon can't endure what happened at the Edge again. He can't.

A gold arm drapes around his shoulder. Fallon peeks up at Abner's face, the bones in their jaw rippling to keep themselves stoic. But Fallon knows his twin is succumbing to the same panic. He scoots closer to Abner's side and wraps his arm around their waist. There Fallon stays, his head on Abner's shoulder, holding onto the pillar of their torso as the carriage jerks, side to side, a small boat in an angry ocean. The surrounding screams that pelted him now land softer.

They just need to get to the palace.

"Nearly there," Abner assures.

Fallon doesn't know how long he curled into his sibling, but when he straightens himself, the carriage is just entering the large circular courtyard. More citizens block their path, attempting to funnel through the gate and into the palace. General Jaits demands the bodies part with a booming shout that carries over the chaos. Slowly, a lane widens enough for the royal family to make it to the gate. Guards rush to the carriage, holding out their hands to the sovereigns. They usher their heirs ahead of them. Silver bodies enclose around Fallon, his family, and the advisor, and they move with the guards' shuffling feet. Up the front stairs, across the entryway's marble floor, and beneath the throne room's tall doors. They are not set free until Fallon sees the end of the golden runner leading up to the dais.

Late-afternoon sunlight bursts into Fallon's eyes as the guards change from a tight border to a perimeter around the dais, separating the royal family from the citizens that rush into the palace and throne room. Through gaps in the guards, the people cry and limp, wailing at any guard who will listen. But the guards appear just as confused. The lower ranking look to their superiors, who look to theirs for answers. Not even General Jaits and his four captains break their stride to provide answers as they head towards the guard perimeter.

Advisor Wilcon steps out in front of the sovereigns. "This is a catastrophe, why are you not keeping better order?"

General Jaits' orange moustache twitches. "My focus was getting the royal family to safety. The Guard was not prepared for a mass rush of citizens through the city. Some were still tasked with clearing the roads from the parade."

"Then what is your report?"

The general shares an ominous look with his captains before saying, "Sightings of demons. I didn't believe it until I saw the carnage at the academy. All the descriptions brought to me have been the same. Black eyes with red rings. Long arms and legs. Pale skin growing from beneath." He pauses. Fallon is shaken by a such a large, formidable man cowed by his own words. "From *within* humans. It seems the creature is... infectious."

Sovereign Adelaide breaks from her husband's arms. "God above, Wilcon. How could this happen today?"

"I... have no answer, my sovereign," the advisor replies.

That shakes Fallon even more.

General Jaits steps closer to the royal family and lowers his chin. "My son was bitten at the Edge. By the same demon? I don't know. But I need to go see him and make sure."

Fallon pushes his fingers into his hairline. He'd forgotten about Shavazme. No escort or Champion that was killed by demons and brought home to be buried ever launched a parasitic nightmare. The thing growing inside his people has to be the human-like one. His friend is infected now. And it's Fallon's fault. He begged Shavazme to come to the Edge.

Advisor Wilcon reads Fallon's mind as he has always done and lays an assuring hand on his shoulder. "Shavazme will be fine. The sibyl not only healed his leg but extracted any of the demon's essence from his body. But to assure you all, I'll visit with the sibyl."

The General sighs with relief. "Thank you, Advisor Wilcon."

Fallon retreats further into himself. Shavazme was saved, but Escort Burkhard was not. The infection must be rooted with him. Protecting the heir and general's son was a sure distraction that cost the guard his life.

"Before you go Wilcon, what do we do?" Sovereign Adelaide asks. Her cheeks are soaked with tears, one hand gripping her husband's wrist, the other wrapped around her neck.

The advisor looks towards the entryway, blocked by the wall of guards. But the sounds of distress and people stampeding into the palace on the other side know no boundary. "Fortify the palace and check everyone inside. Anyone bitten or scratched will be dealt with."

Fallon's eyes widen. He feels an argument climbing up his throat, but it's Abner who actually speaks their mind.

"Then we condemn every citizen left outside. We can't do that."

Wilcon twists to face Abner and the sovereigns, leaving the general and his captains outside of the conversation. This is now a decision between the royal family.

"What other choice do we have? Niawa isn't prepared for this. We can protect the people here while I consult the sibyl," Wilcon responds.

"Or, we set up guards at the palace doors to inspect everyone before they enter," Abner pushes back.

Two monotone voices brimming with ire. Fallon would almost prefer they shout.

"And if a demon somehow slips through and infects another? In turn, they infect more? One becomes fifty before we realize, and the only secure place in the city is overrun."

"Abner, quiet." Sovereign Gerves interjects. "Wilcon is right."

Had it been the advisor who told Abner to be quiet, the icy war would have continued. But Abner shakes their head in defeat and clasps their hands together behind their back. Then they look at Fallon, a plead in their dark eyes. Asking for support.

Wilcon catches it. "Fallon understands as well. He knows this is the right strategy. Protect who we can and trust in the sibyl. She'll tell us what to do. Do you agree?"

The advisor motions at Fallon like he's on display. All eyes are on him, even the general's. At first, Fallon is angry at Wilcon for putting him in this position. But he realizes: his mentor has seized an opportunity to align Fallon with his parents. Judging by Abner's unabashed glare at Wilcon, they've come to the same conclusion.

This is not for the throne. This is the right thing to do, Fallon's head states firmly at the same time he says, "Yes, I do."

"You have your orders, Jaits," Sovereign Gerves says.

The general bows. "My captains will handle fortifying the palace. Once I return from visiting Shavazme in the medical wing, I'll take charge."

With that, he heads back into the crowd, the captains following close behind.

Fallon stares at his shoes for a long, drawn-out time before he can bring himself to look at Abner. When he's brave enough to lift his gaze, Abner has curiously moved to the wall of guards and peers into the gaps. They say something to two of the guards. One shakes their head, and the other points into the crowd.

"That was immensely brave, Heir Fallon," Wilcon leans in to say.

"It didn't feel brave," Fallon admits.

"The sovereigns were impressed. I could tell."

Wilcon's praise doesn't send fireworks off in Fallon's head as it used to. Instead, it's a sickly drip down his spine. Oly is out there still. Though he has no doubt she'll be okay, he can't keep her terrified face from his mind when she returns to shut doors. And the lovely young girl who runs his favorite fruit stand by the fountain. And Thimble at Guilded Hall. Ghade the Stone. All panicked faces in a frantic mob.

A faint clang sounds from outside the throne room. Fallon can't see from here, but he recognizes the closing of the black gate. It's begun. He darts to peek through the wall of guards. It doesn't take long for people to understand. A mad rush erupts towards the front doors, already being released from the mechanisms that hold them open.

A slew of guards have been tasked to hold back the crowd, and they leap into action, using the long staffs of their spears and threats of their blades. Fallon wants to turn away, but he forces himself to endure the consequences of his words. He can hear the citizens who are not allowed in, screaming from outside. A consistent whine threads between the anger and sadness like a violinist's final note.

The music stops with a series of bangs. The doors shut. A metal bar slides through the handles.

It's done.

Wilcon calls Fallon and Abner back from the perimeter, and the heirs join him and the sovereigns by the dais. "Now that we're all safe, I will visit the sibyl and return with a plan," the advisor says. He bows to the sovereigns, smiles at Fallon, then glides towards the nearest guard and orders they escort him out of the throne room.

Fallon couldn't possibly feel sicker, so he turns towards Abner, ready to accept whatever punishment his twin deems fitting. Abner only has eyes for the direction of the entryway.

They wait until Wilcon is gone before mumbling, "I need something from my quarters."

"Abner! For heaven's sake, now is not the time to wander around," Sovereign Adelaide begins, but it falls on deaf ears. Abner is already heading towards the wall and pushes through without an escort.

Worry, but moreso curiosity, sends Fallon down his sibling's trail, against his parent's objections. Ahead, Abner tears through the mess of people, hardly paying attention when several attempt to stop them, expressions sopping with desperation. Fallon skirts around the same weeping couple on the floor, hops over the same spilling sack of household items, food, and children's toys, and waves away the same guards who try to intervene. When he pops out of the throne room and into an even more packed entryway, he almost loses sight of Abner – but a fringed gold jacket is hardly inconspicuous. His sibling is two small groupings of people away, the gaps in their bodies allowing him to make out Abner speaking to one of the royal family's private messengers. Fallon recognizes the older man from his many interruptions of family meals to deliver some important note from another kingdom. Though, he has never looked so disheveled. He must count himself lucky to return to Niawa just in time for a parasitic demon to tear through the streets. The messenger hands Abner a parcel. Then he bows, and Abner jets off toward an adjoining hall where a line of guards stands wall-to-wall – likely to keep people from roaming the palace.

Fallon maneuvers slowly through the crowd, hoping no one shouts his name or title. Some do, but Abner is not deterred. The guard wall splits for them, then immediately tightens again, just as Fallon finds the end of the horde.

He marches to the guards. "Excuse me!"

On the other side, Abner is halfway down the corridor. The last hours of sun bathe the tiled floor and stone walls in amber. Palace servants will be out shortly to light the sconces along the wall. Fallon doesn't care anymore if Abner knows they're being followed. He lets the heavy landing of his boots ricochet off the walls, but Abner never reacts. They lead Fallon out of the east wing into the cusp of the south. All staircases and shorter halls, servant quarters and armories.

"Where are we going?" Fallon eventually yells out when Abner passes an empty sitting room.

They reach a dead end and stop. Ten or so feet up a rugged, gray stone wall, two towering stained-glass windows reflect colored honeycombs over the ground. The other two walls are bare. Fallon walks into the small pocket of the palace, hands on his hips. He can't recall ever stopping here, though he knows he's passed it many times.

"Could use a bench or something. Why is this even here?"

Abner finally faces him, the parcel held delicately. "I come here to think sometimes. It's quiet and tucked away. Pretty windows."

"Right. What'd you come to think about now?" Fallon begins to feel nervous.

"Let's find out."

They pull open the parcel flap carefully. Inside are sheets of paper. Fallon can see lines of words, like a letter, and possibly a drawing, but he can't make out detail.

Abner pulls out one paper filled with writing. As their eyes snap left to right over the page, Fallon's irritation grows. They should both be in the throne room helping, or at least not being another worry for their parents. Abner must have known Fallon was following them the entire time. This was deliberate, and Fallon can't wait any longer to know why.

"Well?" he asks.

Abner's face is grim as they hold out the paper. "Believe me when I say, I am sorry. Part of me wanted to be wrong."

Fallon swipes it from the air and walks a few steps away before reading.

Heir Abner,

I reached the sibyls' Southern Temples. They're all dead. Every one of them. At first, I thought the temples had just been abandoned. Dust and dirt covered every surface, but nothing was destroyed. Then I entered one of the sleeping quarters. Bodies decayed in beds, on the floor. I went to the next room. More death. Another large room was entirely black from fire. A library, I gathered, by the charred shelves and remnants of books scattered everywhere.

Then I went deeper into the cathedrals, hoping to find some sign of life. I found a prayer room with a statue of Yuli-en. Laid across the god's arms was a sibyl with a spear through their chest. And in the center of the floor, a symbol was burnt into the ground. It has faded, but I drew as much as I could for you.

I fled after that. Evil has taken over the temples and I couldn't let it corrupt me. Do what you want with this knowledge, but I believe a massacre occurred. Your sibyl may be the only one that survived.

As we agreed, I'll take my payment of five notes and disappear. My name will change, and I'll move to a new region. You will never hear from me again.

Fallon looks up from the letter to find Abner inspecting another paper, one with a drawing. Before he can stop himself, Fallon storms towards his twin and rips the drawing away. He didn't know he could feel this much anguish, outrage, and sorrow at once. Five notes is a large sum of money, but not enough to pay a royal messenger loyal to the sovereigns to travel to sacred grounds, desecrate them with his unworthy presence, and return with information. No, the messenger was in between. Abner paid some godless miscreant.

"What have you done?" Fallon seethes.

If Abner is at all ashamed, they hide it well. Emotionless, they say, "I'm going to liberate Niawa."

Fallon can't find his words. He gapes, the papers crinkling in his hand. Now Abner reacts as they eye the spreading creases.

"Give those back. I'll explain everything, but that's my only proof."

"Of *what?*"

"You don't recognize that drawing, do you?"

Huffing, Fallon holds it up to his eyes. Intersecting lines form to make triangles with no closed ends around a thick line that split into two curls at both tips. He wracks his mind, but nothing emerges.

"It's the symbol of the Veins of Istral," Abner says.

At first, Fallon shakes his head. Not much of his lessons managed to stick, but the ones that did would call Abner a liar. The cult is gone. Disappeared. Thwarted by sibyls in their attempt to open the Rive and never heard from again. But another voice chimes in, one that sounds far too much like his twin. The Rive did open. And demons are here. Everything that shouldn't be happening, has happened. Maybe, in this secluded, private space, he will entertain one of Abner's wild theories. If only for a minute. "You think the cult has returned?"

"Yes and no. The ones who tried to open the Rive before have been dead for a generation. I think our sibyl is acting alone."

A dry laugh erupts from Fallon's chest. This is what he gets for letting Abner into his head. "You almost had me. Now you think the sibyl is a worshipper of the demon god? An imposter? Would it be too far-fetched to assume you think she murdered the other sibyls, too?"

Abner's stony face answers the question Fallon hoped was rhetorical. He shakes the now crushed papers inches from his twin's face, desperation coursing through his blood.

"Please, please stop. You have to stop. Demons are killing our people, Abner, you can't... just, please, stop."

Calmly, Abner pushes Fallon's hand down and plucks the papers from his grip. "Just listen. If I'm right, and I believe with my entire soul that I am, the sibyl will burn Niawa to the ground tonight."

Fallon is struck into silence. Abner may be a lot of things, but stupid is not one of them. They have thought this through, meticulously, obsessively. If there was ever a moment to truly open his ears, this is it. Fallon exhales long and deep, fingers steepled against his lips. "Make it quick."

Abner nods. They turn on their heels, starting to pace slowly towards the stained-glass windows.

"That isn't the first letter I've received. I've been hiring an unnamed man to find information for two years now. I grew tired of telling my theories to a wall; I had to know if I was right. First, I had him search for information about the Veins of Istral. Who they were as people. What did they believe about Istral that our teachings failed to tell us? I thought if I knew more about them, I could help close the Rive for good. My hire found nothing. He visited several libraries in kingdoms as far as the Agni Desert. Even private libraries of historians I had to send extra funds to use as bribes. All writings about the cult seemed to have vanished. But they had to exist somewhere. I realized there was only one corner of the world that could hide our history's darkest shadow: the Southern Temples. The sibyls must have kept every journal, item, study, spellbook, and scroll ever associated with the Veins." Abner pauses on their third pace back from the window and looks at Fallon intently. "Imagine you're one of the most powerful beings, and now you have access to even more power."

It takes a second, but Fallon understands what Abner is hinting at. "Sibyls are pure. That's why they're chosen, not just for magic. They would never touch that darkness," Fallon says.

"*Pure* is an interesting word to describe them. I also paid my hire to learn more about the sibyls. Their rituals and practices. All I heard were rumors. Ones even I struggled to believe up until I read this letter and saw this symbol.

Fallon, the sibyls don't cover their faces because of modesty; they are marked. When children are brought to the temples, elder sibyls carve into their skin, their faces, to keep them from the outside world. Take away their choice. They are coerced with torture into a life of servitude."

"Shut up," Fallon snaps. He has heard enough.

"No," Abner says defiantly. "You can't silence me like Wilcon did. Our sibyl is an angry child who lost herself in the hidden keepsakes of the Veins and was consumed with what the cult promised. Freedom and power from those who oppressed her."

Fallon leaves the dead end and moves quickly down the next corridor. His ears burn. His vision blurs. None of this is true. It can't be.

Abner catches up and grabs his arm. "She killed the sibyls, Fallon. She burnt the library to hide the Veins' secrets. She came to Niawa and opened the Rive to finish what the cult started – returning Istral to this world."

"Let me go," he snarls.

"You believe me. That's why you're running away."

"No, I don't!" Fallon knows that's a lie. He doesn't want to believe. "Why hasn't it worked? The Rive has existed for twenty years."

"Exactly." Abner releases him. Fallon inwardly curses his curiosity for rooting him to the spot. "She's only one person. What better way to search for Istral and keep a rift between our realm and the demon's open than to anoint a Champion to fight the demons that find their way through. While Niawa is distracted with celebrating Blessings, she is given more time."

Exhaustion brings Fallon to the nearest wall. He collapses against it and digs his fingers through his hair. "Why Niawa?"

Abner joins him against the wall. "We were too young to remember Niawa before the sibyl, but we were a poor kingdom with dry lands and sick livestock. The sibyl's promise to fix our earth with Yuli-en's favor was too enticing to question. She protects us from the demons and secures a rich future, so we never question her."

"Smart," Fallon admits in a small voice.

"Yes."

"Do you think she did this? The infestation."

Abner shrugs. "I don't know."

"This is too much, Abner. I can't."

They push off the wall and angle themselves towards Fallon. "Say you believe me. I need to hear it. I need to know you won't do what Wilcon did."

"What do you mean?"

"This is why he hates me. I had already started questioning, wondering. I thought I could trust my mentor with my curiosity, but he only tried to snuff it out. He started showing interest in you not a day later."

Fallon flinches from the return of an old fear. Abner was devastated when Wilcon suddenly stopped their private lessons, so Fallon hid how joyful he felt. But a part of him never fully understood or trusted why the advisor pivoted his focus. How could he – the dumber twin, the one who never remembers their studies, goes to the taverns, but can tell a good joke – be chosen over Abner? Over the years, Wilcon's praise became louder than Fallon's doubt, but never defeated it.

"Everything is clear now. I'm every bit the idiot everyone thinks I am," Fallon says bitterly.

"You can't be serious. Now is not the time for a silly fight." Abner holds up the papers. "I need your help."

"To do what? Kill the sibyl?" Fallon's laugh dies quickly when he realizes that's exactly what Abner wants.

"This has to end. One way or another."

CHAPTER 16

Niawa used to smell like baked bread, flowers, and trees from Emerald Pine. Now it reeks of blood, the metallic air clogging my nose. Denya and I tread lightly through the streets. I ascertained most mobs of frightened people were heading to the academy or the palace, so we moved off the main roads leading both ways. Crowds will hinder me with their wriggling, pushing bodies, but also with the possibility that demons grow within them.

It's difficult to not inspect every injured person I see and end their lives before the parasite takes hold. If I engage in every battle, I may not make it back in time. While three of the creatures in the park were easy kills with their soft human flesh, the fourth was a grave warning of what's to come. My jaw is still tender from the blow it dealt.

"You couldn't have waited until we're evenly matched?" I turn my head in the direction of the Rive, far across the lands. The portal doesn't answer, but I know it enjoys stealing my one restful day.

Ahead, I spot another road-blocking crowd, so we cut down the first side street. To my annoyance, we come upon another crowd. Between a small temple and a brick wall covered in crawling ivy, the citizens block the road completely. I stop to examine them from a safe distance. No bloody wounds, slumped bodies, or blackened eyes that I can see. Still, the risk is too high. I look around for alleyways to the next street.

A cry breaks out. The center of the crowd concaves like a sinkhole as several people drop to the ground. Denya rushes past me, alarm in her eyes. When I don't follow, she looks back.

I can't let anything distract me from getting to the sibyl. Once I'm stronger, I'll be the Champion they need – and expect. Shamefully, I half-turn towards the road behind me.

"Champion, where are you going?" Denya says. I glare at her, a pebble in my boot since the park. "They need our help."

"God above," I groan, rubbing my forearm across my brow.

I hear my title murmured ahead. There's no slipping away now. I shoot the escort another glare before striding towards the crowd and pushing my way through. At first gentle, as people seem lost in confusion, then roughly, as they aren't able to collect themselves quickly enough. At the center, a man lays on his side. He moans, curling into himself, then tosses his legs out and splays onto his back. Something jagged was slashed across his stomach, cutting his clothing and the dark skin beneath. The wound is shallow, yet he wriggles on the ground as if his organs may slide right out.

"Isaac! Isaac, what's wrong?" a woman shouts. A newborn baby cries into her chest, secured by thick strips of bright purple fabric. When she sees me, recognition smooths the distress across her face. "Champion, please, help my husband!"

If Isaac's wound were normal – which I greatly doubt – linen, soap, rags, needle and thread, and medicine would be all it takes to help him. I drop to my haunches to get a closer look. Pain flares through my hip, sending me to both of my knees. I aim my grimace at the ground before lifting my head.

Isaac rolls towards me, letting out a low moan. His teeth are still blunted, arms the correct length, dark skin still covering his body.

"Do you have the black eyes?" I wonder at his tightly shut eyelids.

I hold my axe to Isaac's neck, just in case. His wife starts to yell but cuts herself off when I only press my fingers to her husband's right eye, then slide the lid up. A deep brown iris surrounded by white. Good. I check the other eye.

Blackness floods the white like ink in cream. The skin around his eye bulges and stretches as the black pool swells. From within, a red ring glows into life.

I jump up into a wall of bodies I hadn't noticed had crept closer.

"He's turning," I say to his wife.

She holds her baby closer. "I don't understand."

Isaac rolls onto his stomach, hiding his deforming face. One of his arms strike out, clawed fingers raking into the stone, leaving fine lines of red blood. His arm already stretches, becoming too long for his tunic.

The crowd breaks into hysteria. Some run across the opening, trying not to step near the demon, causing them to crash into others. Bodies fall beneath chaotic feet.

"Quiet!" I shout with the full power of my lungs.

Whimpering quiet falls over the crowd as Isaac's humanity bleeds away at my feet. I count the seconds in my head. By the fifteenth, both of his eyes are black, and his mouth is full of sharp teeth. Including the time it took for me to get to him, the demon bloomed inside Isaac in half a minute. Somewhere, the demon that infected him has already taken others. This spread is beyond control. Even for a Champion. I'll do my part, but Niawa's people may have to join the fight, starting right now.

"The demons spread through bites, and possibly scratches," I shout. "New ones are weaker. As soon as someone is tainted, you have to kill them." The demon tries to rise, but I slam my boot into its chest as hard as I can. Then I do the same to his knees. I need him still for this demonstration. "To be sure of death, destroy the heart, or cut off the head." I get to work. It takes two swings to hack through the demon's neck. The entire time, his wife screams and begs for me to stop. People in the crowd turn away dramatically. It may be hard to watch, but they'll soon understand. "Most importantly, after cutting off the head, you must crush the brain." I step on the skull, feeling it crack down the center. When the red mist rises, I point to it. "This is how you know it's done."

Disgust warps the faces of those who were close enough to watch. The wife bawls into her baby's crown.

"You killed my husband," she sobs.

"I killed a demon," I respond.

"He was my *husband,* Champion. Why didn't you save him?"

The crowd packs in around us, filling any gaps with furious faces.

My skin quickly warms. "I don't know how to stop the infection yet, so you need to know how to protect yourselves."

"*You* are meant to protect us!" someone behind me spits out.

I don't understand. I did protect them. This demon would have tore through the crowd like wet parchment.

"We will *not* fight any demons; that's what you are called to do! To save us!"

I shake my head. "I can't save you all."

"Yuli-en smite you, Champion," another voice yells.

More faces close in and I push against them. People fall backwards, shouting and damning me from what feels like all directions. Force from behind knocks me forward. I look, expecting another demon, but its more citizens brimming with anger. Panicking, I grab my axe and raise it high, even as my arms tremble from the weight.

"She's going to hurt us!" the wife exclaims.

"No, I won't, I need space." I aimed to yell, but my voice comes out meek.

Another force pushes me and I nearly fall.

Denya elbows her way to me and links her arm around mine.

"Move, or there'll be hell to pay!" Denya shouts. She points her sword ahead of us. Those who don't want to be skewered hastily part. She continues to pull me through until I can see the street again.

Clarity rushes in as the humming comes to a simmer, but I still feel it crawling over my bones.

"That took a turn," Denya says.

"I only tried to help," I explain. I shouldn't care what a guard thinks of my methods, but I find myself wanting Denya to understand what the citizens couldn't.

The escort nods. "Chaos makes people dumber, Champion. I should know."

My bowl still in her care, she continues with me up a street quickly filling with more people. We all seem to share the same idea of getting to the palace. By the time I'm close enough to see the late afternoon's sun shining in the turret's green tiles, Denya and I are forced to rub shoulders with every person who rushes past.

In a short time, the street opens to a large intersection where many others branch out in wild directions. Citizens flood into the intersection, all funneling towards the palace. We have no choice but to join the growing, slow-moving mass.

Beads of sweat drip from my nose as I adjust my hands around the axe staff. Even my grip is weakening. I try to tighten my fingers, but one loosens against my will. The rest follow, as if finally given the permission they needed. My axe falls to the ground with a *thunk*. I try to pick it up quickly, nearly cleaving through two nearby women.

"Let me help," Denya says.

"Don't touch it." For ten years, I haven't needed a guard's assistance, and I don't need it now.

She doesn't listen. The escort sets my bowl between my feet, then grabs the axe still in my hands and helps me lift it up and over my head. Eventually, I have to let go. Though she grunts from the weight, she straps it correctly to my back.

Denya goes to scoop my bowl up, but I grab it first. I start walking again, letting the crowd push me along.

Above the sea of bobbing heads, I see the palace walls and the black, spired tips of the front gate.

It's a miracle we made it without–

A cluster of demons stagger our direction, too many to count. Near-human faces burst from connecting streets, sending people scurrying the other way. There, they meet more demons who have shed much of their humanity and come on all fours. On instinct, I reach for the magic bombs in my belt. No. There are too many people around to control the blasts of magic.

A demon grabs at a woman whose skin is peppered in gold flakes and yanks her out of eyesight. The man with her holds on too tightly. She screams out the name Thistle as he looks down in horror at the severed arm left in his hands.

More people are dragged away, starting at the edges of the crowd and quickly moving inward.

My hands and knees slam into the ground. The man who knocked me over doesn't even look back. He keeps running. Everyone is running and shoving and screaming.

Denya wraps her arms around my waist and hoists me up. She yells something.

Everything is muffled. The words are buried beneath low moans and screams that rattle my eardrums. I stare blankly at her.

My legs move slowly at first, then I'm running as best I can, adrenaline pumping into my heart.

We make it to the palace circle, filled to the curved edges with scared people. Demons gain on our backs. We're lucky they're slow and awkward on their limbs, but the gap closes quickly.

Denya lugs us through the crowd until we are stopped by a wall of still backs. She stands on her toes. What she sees scares the blood from her face. "The gate is locked and the palace doors are closed."

Fear attacks me like a crack of lightning. Every breath I take coats my mouth with the rising panic of the crowd. The royal family has left their people to die. In seconds, this circle will be a massacre. Thousands of demons will come to life where people now cry and shove and beg Yuli-en's Eye for help.

"I'm going to die," I whisper, the truth dawning on me. "I'm going to die."

With every last shred of my strength, I thrust into the backs in front of me, forcing a path through. Denya shouts after me, but her voice fades into the chaos. Hands grab at me, pulling on the plates of my armor, my shoulders, my hands. I ignore them. If I can get to the gate, tell the guards behind it the Champion is here, call for Fallon, they'll open it. They *will*.

My bones groan, suffocating beneath inflamed muscles. I won't stop trying.

People take to climbing on each other to get closer to the palace. A boot kicks at my head. I rip it away from me. A woman falls to the ground and I step over her.

Finally, I reach the congested, furious head of the crowd. Bodies press on the black iron, arms flailing through the gaps between the posts. Guards armed with tall halberds and swords face us from the safe side. They lower their weapons at the crowd. A few step forward and jab the sharp ends.

"Back! Get back!" they warn.

A thin man beside me grinds his face against the posts to reach farther. He manages to grab the end of a spear and thrusts it back towards the guard. Perhaps taken by surprise, the guard loses his grip on the staff and finds the butt of it slammed into his chest. He staggers back, anger contorting his mouth. He rips the spear from the thin man's hands, spraying blood over the ground, then stabs it forward. Pinned against the gate by the crowd, the man has nowhere to go when the spear's head embeds into his chest. He slumps forward, kept on his feet by the pressure.

The guard's eyes blink frantically as they rove over the red-soaked tip.

Anger explodes from those who witnessed the death. They throw items through the posts, which encourages more of the crowd to toss items over the gate. The guards retreat a few feet, dodging pots and pans and shoes.

"Open the gate," I yell. I try to shake the metal poles, but they don't budge. Dread mounts inside me, growing like the parasite. My teeth grind together. Pins and needles poke at my feet. "Please, open the gate!" The crowd shoves me against the metal. "Fallon!" I scream over and over.

The palace doors begin to creep open behind the guards. I see the marble of the entrance floor and the row of chandeliers in the throne room beyond.

"Fallon! Please. God, please." My voice becomes foreign to me, sounding like a frightened little girl. The gate grinds into my cheeks. Smells of metal and sweat and blood. "It's Oly! It's Oly! I'm the Champion! Open the gates!"

Darkness peeks at the edge of my vision and rapidly closes in. Funneling the guards, the palace doors, the marble floor, to a pin's head. I only see feet and legs packed together, and stone. I tuck my bowl into my stomach and curl into myself.

"Open the gates." I close my eyes, the tunnel of darkness sending me into a dizzying spiral.

I thought death would be more violent. This is slow, like pulling a blanket over my head, hoping in the morning when I emerge from the wool, the world is different.

CHAPTER 17

"We need to consult Wilcon," Fallon parrots himself. He'd said it after Abner declared their intent to kill a holy woman, a voice of Yuli-en, the very reason Niawa isn't destitute – and it bears repeating.

Abner's stern face intensifies. "He can't be a part of this. I don't trust him."

"Mother and father would never agree to killing the sibyl without his input, and you know that. Think about the havoc her death would leave behind! We only have one Champion. Oly can't kill what may be thousands of demons by now. And the Rive still exists. At midnight, it will wake up."

"I know that. Before we kill her, we force her to close the Rive. Demons can't exist in this world without the connection to their own. The parasites should, theoretically, die."

Fallon can't recall if that's true, but he doesn't want to give away a gap in his knowledge. He wishes more than ever he'd paid attention. "What about the lands?"

"Every other kingdom in our world functions without the sibyl. We can too."

"Seems like you've planned Niawa's future entirely on your own. Without anyone else's help or permission."

"I don't need permission now. I'm the next sovereign."

"Not yet, you aren't," Fallon mumbles under his breath.

Abner had trailed to the other side of the corridor. They whip back around. "What would you do then, Fallon? Enlighten me with your plan."

It's Fallon's turn to pace. He intertwines his fingers around the back of his neck and rubs his thumbs over the tense muscle. Abner may be resolute in their vision of Niawa without the sibyl, but he can't see it. Twenty years they have relied on her, on her connection with Yuli-en.

Could she be reasoned with? Niawa's continued protection from demons in exchange for worshipping the god she believes in? Would Istral's presence be any different from Yuli-en's, or just another comet in the sky one day a year? He shudders at the thought of worshipping the human-like demon he encountered at the Edge.

What scares Fallon the most is Abner's surety the sibyl can be killed. He questions if Oly could even win that fight – as tired as she's looked. Niawa's Guard hasn't seen battle since the War of Red River, and most have only patrolled and held back crowds during parades.

Abner can't see through their own ambition, Wilcon's voice reminds Fallon. He nods to himself. There has to be another way, and Fallon will find it. But he needs guidance.

He walks to Abner, who has waited patiently in the middle of the hall.

"I believe you," he says. Abner smiles, which promptly breeds guilt. Fallon pushes past it, knowing more than just his life is at stake. "And I'll tell Wilcon the same, when we talk to him."

His sibling chews on the inside of their cheek. In their mind, countless anxieties connect to other anxieties in a tangled spider's web. Eventually they nod in agreement. "To the sibyl's tower, then."

* * *

Fallon and Abner turn into the short hall leading to the sibyl's tower. When they stop, their last footsteps linger in the air.

Fallon has never entered the sibyl's quarters, only stared at the large black door at the base. From outside the palace, the tower is the same white stone as every wall, its tiled roof the same emerald green. The halls leading to the tower are not distinguished. The same stone floral designs in most corridors hang overhead, curving with the arched ceiling.

But the aura is different. It feels unnerving, like even the dust crackles with power.

The heirs look at each other. Abner holds the parcel, and Fallon's damp hands burrow into his pockets. Wordlessly, they seem to both decide there's no turning back and walk towards the door together.

"Do we knock?" Fallon asks.

Before Abner can answer, a familiar voice drifts from behind the door. The twins freeze halfway down the hall. Wilcon is clearly irate. The advisor doesn't shout, but his tone is cutting. Demanding.

"Kill that thing immediately," Wilcon says. "Should it escape your spell –"

"You'll blame the bloodshed on me?" the sibyl responds coolly. "Even as you reap the benefits?"

"I do not reap any benefits from this. You've become far too impatient and greedy, Leizus. I can't possibly explain away that monstrosity," Wilcon stresses.

"This was always the deal. It would have taken me countless more years to connect with them."

"Have I not given you everything you need?"

"You have. But I couldn't ignore this opportunity. It's fate this particular demon has found its way out of the Rive. A *primordial.* One that lives so deeply in the demon realm, they are closer to Istral. Extracting essence from a Rive so far away has been fruitless for twenty years. Now, they will finally hear me, but I need a few more hours."

"These demons are parasites. They've already spread through the city. What can be done about that while you tinker with one? The sovereigns expect your protection."

The sibyl doesn't respond. A loud bang on the door follows. Fallon grabs Abner's hand out of instinct.

"After all I've done, you'll leave me a ravaged kingdom overrun with demons?" Wilcon shouts.

"Demons that will bend their will to me. To Istral. When I have their power, I can stop the infestation."

Wilcon laughs in a way that chills Fallon to his bones.

"I see. Your greed and sloppiness is clear now. You want to enslave your own god."

"I want to *become* my god. Give my body and soul to them. Istral has been asleep for eons. My memories and history will help them understand this new world."

"Not to mention unfathomable power for you–"

"And for you," the sibyl interrupts. "I'll give you Niawa, and immortality, as promised."

Abner squeezes Fallon's hand so tightly it hurts.

"Say you fail. Yuli-en's Eye will disappear, and the Rive will awaken. More demons will come and one Champion won't be enough. Then we all die."

"I'll only fail if you continue to stall me. Two more hours, Wilcon. Say what you must to keep the guards from my tower," the sibyl says.

"As you wish," Wilcon finishes, his voice saturated with venom.

The handle on the black door turns.

Fallon and Abner sprint down the hall. Fallon holds his breath for fear Wilcon, who has focused on him for so long, will recognize it.

He runs until his feet ache, Abner keeping pace even in the heeled lavender boots they chose for the day. When Fallon's ears pick up on the throne room's noise, he veers into a wall space between two sconces. He pounds the side of his fist into the stone. Again and again. With each sting something builds in his chest. It rises into his throat and Fallon sets it free. He screams towards the floor, emptying his lungs.

Abner's hand rests on his back. With a sigh, Fallon faces his sibling. They appear unperturbed. Abner already despised Wilcon and distrusted the sibyl. While Fallon's world has toppled over, Abner's has been righted.

Jealousy roars in Fallon's head. Always a hundred steps behind. Not brave enough to see through the smoke.

He finally understands.

"Wilcon didn't just abandon you because you were too smart. He chose me because I'm perfectly stupid," Fallon says.

"That's not true," Abner insists.

"Yes, it is! He couldn't manipulate you. But I have a brain like dough. Easy for him to fold and warp into any shape he likes. I never ask questions because I can barely comprehend."

"Fallon… Fallon!" Abner grabs Fallon's shoulders, holding him still. "Keep it together. Niawa needs us. Our parents need us. We have to tell them everything before Wilcon gets back. Are you with me?"

Fallon can't bring himself to say it, so he nods. He and Abner start towards the throne room, towing an insurmountable burden that Fallon wishes he had never learned.

The heirs make it to the edge of the entryway just as the day's light fades into sheer beams of moonlight. Somehow, the palace servants were able to light the crystal chandeliers despite every inch of the space being packed with bodies. The bordering wall of guards make a small space for the twins to slip through. Citizens have formed small plots for themselves, bundling together in families or groups on the ground. In the time they were gone, the guards had done their job of bringing a semblance of calm. Yet, Fallon quickly gets the feeling the royal family is the subject of many terse conversations they pass by.

One man stands quickly as they approach, mouth parting beneath bloodshot eyes. A nearby guard intervenes with the threat of her halberd.

"No, it's okay," Fallon says hastily. The guard backs down. "Any more reports from outside?"

"We only have our vantage point through the door. There's still a very large crowd outside the gate." She tries to even her tone, but Fallon can hear the tremble of shame.

"Maybe they're demons. Or becoming demons," he says, trying to be helpful.

"They seem to be human. For now."

Fallon glances at Abner, who has started to trail towards the throne room. They're anxious to speak with their parents. Fallon isn't quite as eager to dismantle the fabric of Niawa's society.

"I'd like to see," he says to the guard.

Behind him, Abner makes a grunt of disapproval, but Fallon already follows the guard to the doors. Much like the courier's cart, a slat was built into the thick wood. Fallon grabs the cold metal handle at one end and slides it over, revealing a window as long as his forearm and a third as tall. He slightly bends his knees to see. Fallon's ears make sense long before his eyes do.

His people scream for help. For mercy. They push against the gate, smothering those against the metal poles. A handful of guards face them, weapons angled outwards.

Fallon gasps. A man reached for a spear and was stabbed through the chest. He hangs against the poles, blood leaking from the corner of his mouth. He died a man, not a demon.

"Who is that guard?" Fallon demands. He immediately realizes only he can see through the window. "I want the names of all guards stationed outside."

Something catches his eye in the crowd. Between the pulses of torsos and limbs: demon teeth. Oly is slammed into the poles, the skin of her face pulling with the sway of the crowd.

She screams his name.

Fallon tears himself from the window. "Open the door."

The guard almost looks affronted. Her head swivels around, probably searching for a captain.

"I'm giving the order. Open the door *now*."

She gives an awkward bow then dashes to the nearest guard, who runs to grab another. In a short time, six guards are at the door while another three usher away citizens who will be in the way.

In the disorder Fallon caused, Abner is barred from getting to the door. They glower when Fallon meets their eyes, but he brushes it off. After the heavy wooden latch is lifted, the six guards split to each door and begin to pry them apart.

"That's enough!" Fallon yells when the doors are wide enough.

He races down the steps, ignoring every request for his next order. Oly has collapsed to the ground. She's curled into herself. People step over her and on her. One boot collides with the side of her head just as Fallon shoves through the stunned outside guards to reach the gate.

"The keys," he commands. The same guard that stabbed the man holds out a ring of metal keys by a particular one.

Fallon will deal with him later. He struggles to free the lock as his gaze keeps darting to Oly. With a satisfying click, the key turns. Fallon lets the lock and key fall to the ground and he yanks the gate open.

People flood past him, neither noticing or caring who he is. He throws up his arm against the stampede, fighting his way across. Oly isn't moving when Fallon reaches her. He drops to his knees and lowers his face to hers. The green bowl is tucked safely within her body.

A mother and child trip over her, nearly knocking Fallon back. The mother barely utters an apology before picking up her son and continuing.

"Oly? Wake up." Fallon shakes her. She doesn't even twitch. The Champion is out cold.

He looks back at the guards for help, but they are overwhelmed. Fallon tries to lift her himself. She barely rises a foot. He can't imagine being able to remove her armor plates or weapons.

"Help!" Fallon shouts to anyone who will listen.

His distress is heard. Two men who had just flown by spin back around. A vaguely familiar woman wearing a dirtied nightgown with two swords attached to her belt also stops. They all slip their arms beneath Oly's body, and lift her up. Fallon notices the woman makes sure to grab the bowl. He makes a note to thank her later, remembering how important it is to Oly.

"Thank you," Fallon exhales as they adjust her body between them. Slowly, they climb the stairs, struggling to keep hold as people bump and push against them. Fallon hears the guards shouting below with the familiar sound of the gate swinging shut. He can't think of those who didn't make it right now.

As soon as Fallon is safely in the entryway, the guards move to close the palace doors. Abner appears at his side and finds a place to help carry Oly's body.

"Into the throne room," Fallon says. The helpers oblige.

Whispers of the Champion's state follow them all the way down the runner, where a path has been cleared to the perimeter around the dais. The wall of guards parts to let them in, then the hole is immediately closed.

Carefully, they lay Oly down. Fallon stands over her motionless body, panting.

Their strongest warrior. Destined to kill every demon.

Fallon is sure more than ever if Abner wages war against the sibyl, Niawa will lose. He has to propose a deal.

CHAPTER 18

"Is she breathing?"

"Check for movement in her chest."

"I can barely tell under the armor."

"Should we remove it?"

I feel small tugs in several places. One at the lip of my cuirass against my collarbones. Another at my left grieve. Another at the fingertips of my right glove. Warmth cups my face, turning it right and left. Light shines through my eyelids, fading in and out between passing shadows. I don't recognize the voices hovering over my head, and the chatter beyond them is so loud it reminds me of the parade. But I'm not being hauled to my feet and told to run for my life. I must be somewhere safe.

So, I won't open my eyes yet.

I want to be heavy, an unmovable boulder. If Yuli-en is not disgusted with me and hears my prayers, they will let me to sink through the hard surface at my back to join the earth far below. Roots will crawl over me, dirt will pack my lungs, trapping me in a state I have no will to leave. I'll finally be left alone, in profound silence.

Like being at my cabin.

I miss the hush over the fields, stars that don't compete with lanterns and chandeliers to sparkle – only the Rive asking me to prove myself. It understands who I am, and I understand it.

"She's awake. Champion, you need to sit up and drink." Fingers dig under my scalp and lift, but I stay leaden. The hand lays me back down.

"Remove her axe first, so she can lay more comfortably."

I open my eyes. "Don't touch that."

"Oh!" Healers back away, only to return and lean in even closer. A pair of eyes are so close I see flecks of green and gold in the hazel irises.

"Give me room," I say through a dry and throbbing throat.

I push myself to sit up, blinking away the sudden brightness from crystal chandeliers above. Then I notice the throne chairs to my right. To my left, a wall of guards facing outwards, creating a small area containing myself, the royal family, the advisor, and healers. It looks like a barrier. Whatever lies on the other side is loud and messy.

"May I?" Another healer bends to bring a small bottle to my nostrils. Citrus and mint oils, for alerting the senses. And a very strong concoction. My sluggish senses wind up like oiled gears grinding into motion. Lucidity brings me back to the palace gates, where I begged for my life. How I shoved through citizens, scared beyond reason, ignoring every plea for help.

Hush possessed me. She dragged me through that crowd, drunk on delirious terror.

The healers part, revealing Fallon walking briskly towards me, holding my bowl. Across the small space, the sovereigns look cross. They must know what I did. That I failed.

I point my gaze to the floor between my splayed-out legs and allow my shoulders to slump.

Fallon's outstretched hand comes into view.

"If I take it, they'll know I can't do it myself," I mumble.

"Don't be so proud," Fallon whispers back.

I gingerly place my palm in his. We immediately discover his strength is not enough when I nearly pull both of us to the ground. Guards come to assist until I'm standing on painfully tired legs.

"Thought that'd be easier if you were awake," he chuckles. "Here. Figured you'd want this the second you woke up." He returns my bowl, and I curl one arm around it.

Fallon looks down at my hand he still holds, his thumb rubbing over the glove's braided stitching. Is he struggling to reprimand me? Will the sovereigns strip me of my title and take my axe – my breath hitches. I take back my hand.

"How did I get here?" I ask.

"You called for me. Happened to be in the right place at the right time. Let's call that fate." Fallon smiles widely.

I avoid his sparkling eyes and that warm smile, feeling undeserving. "Thank you. I may owe you my life."

He shrugs. "I've owed you mine for ten years."

"How long was I out?" I change the subject.

"An hour."

Too many demons have spread in that time. "I need to see the sibyl. Before it gets worse."

Fallon scrunches his face like he's in pain. He glances back at Heir Abner, who is in discussion with the sovereigns. "We can't go to the sibyl, Oly. I don't know how to begin explaining, but she can't help. She won't."

That can't be true. Perhaps I need to be clearer. It's time for me to tell him, if he doesn't already know. "My strength is failing. It has been for a year now. The Blessing is proving not to last forever, and if I don't get another, I won't be able to fight."

The humming is relentless, but I steel the parts of me Fallon can see.

"Oh." Fallon looks distressed. He grips his mouth, eyes scanning over me. "I thought you seemed tired. I remember you limping at the Edge."

"Am I... Are you still denying my request? Please, don't. I'll –" I bite my own tongue. The heir doesn't need to hear anymore begging. I couldn't prove I'm worthy of Yuli-en's power. Though I could scream, I nod in false understanding.

"None of that matters anymore, Oly. There's something you need to hear. Abner and I waited until you woke up because we need your support. *I* need it."

"But I just told you –"

"You're still the Champion. That means everything. People will listen to you."

He motions to follow him towards Heir Abner and the sovereigns, and I go, sorely, my face rapidly warming. He doesn't understand. If I was going to die powerless and weak, I would have chosen the Edge as my final place. Not here.

Fallon guides me to stand beside him and Heir Abner in a line, facing the sovereigns and the advisor. The heirs look determined, but nervous in their own ways. Fallon keeps flexing his fingers and his twin grips a parcel in their hands so tightly they leave permanent creases.

"Is it time to hear what's in the mysterious package?" Advisor Wilcon starts.

Fallon's hands ball into fists. "Yes. You'll want to pay attention, especially."

The advisor tenses as he eyes the parcel.

Heir Abner takes a deep breath before pulling out two sheets of paper. They hand them to the sovereigns, even though the advisor reaches out. "One is a letter from a man I hired to investigate the sibyl. The other is a drawing of what he found at the Southern Temples."

Sovereign Adelaide looks up from the letter. "Investigate the sibyl? What the hell do you mean?"

"Exactly as I've been warning you, my sovereigns," Advisor Wilcon cuts in. "Heir Abner has become obsessed with undermining our sibyl. They've gone so far as to research the Veins of Istral outside of the approved lessons. I've been concerned for years that Heir Abner is far too interested in demon worship."

The sovereigns look worryingly at Heir Abner, the papers already forgotten.

"Don't listen to him, he's a liar and he conspires with the sibyl!" Fallon nearly shouts. His neck is taut with anger. Much more than the heir who is being accused of demon worship. Heir Abner looks surprisingly calm – even amused as they stare down the advisor.

"*I* am a demon worshipper? You're the one who has sacrificed countless Champions to keep the Rive open for your own gains. Immortality, I believe Leizus said."

"Who is Leizus?" Sovereign Gerves asks.

"The sibyl's name," Fallon answers. "Abner and I overheard Wilcon speaking with her at the tower. When he was supposed to find a way to stop the parasites, he was securing his power. Mother, Father, he's been helping her, for twenty years."

"Helping with what? Children, I don't understand, and I'm growing more concerned," Sovereign Adelaide lays a hand on her chest. The letter dangles from her other.

It seems the answers lie there. Champions are being sacrificed. The sibyl opened the Rive. I need to know what this means without this tangled arguing. Abner jumps in again, explaining something about a library housing information about the Veins of Istral. While they babble on, I grab the letter from the sovereign. She gasps.

With my back turned to them all, I read. Every word is a knife to my gut. The sibyls are all dead, except one. What the heirs have already said plasters to my brain, sinking in against every ounce of my will. I remember the journals under the floorboards at my cabin. The Champion before me also called our calling a sacrifice.

No. The heirs are wrong. Yuli-en speaks to the sibyl. And she chose me.

"I am not a sacrifice," I say aloud.

I turn back around, which silences them all. Heir Abner is inches from the advisor's face while Fallon holds his parent's hands, grief in his eyes.

"This isn't real. I have the Blessing, that is Yuli-en's power. Our god wouldn't damn us." I point to Heir Abner. "Are you a demon worshipper?"

"Oly, stop." Fallon abandons his parents to push down my shaking arm. He also grabs my other from rising towards my axe. "I believe Abner, so believe me. The sibyl has been corrupted."

I hear guards shuffling behind me. Fallon orders them to back away.

"Then what is the Blessing?" I ask.

Heir Abner answers. "I'm unsure. But Leizus has been siphoning magic from the Rive to search for Istral, I imagine she uses the same power for the Blessing."

"Demon essence?" I whisper, running my hands across my chest and neck feverishly. "Inside me?" I want to vomit, purge every bit of the red mist out. The air feels too thick, shivers roll up and down my back. I don't know what else to do but drop to my bottom and cradle the bowl in my lap, leaving the letter on the floor.

"You're scaring her, Abner," Fallon warns.

"Good! We should all be scared. While we bicker, the sibyl calls for Istral in her tower. Two hours is what she asked Wilcon for." They look at the grand clock hanging above the throne room doors. "We have forty minutes left." Heir Abner grabs the letter, eyeing me nervously, as if I'll cut them where they stand. They return it to their mother, along with the other paper.

"This is ridiculous, don't entertain –" Advisor Wilcon attempts to grab the sheets, but is stopped by a knife to his throat, which Heir Abner whipped out with surprising speed from inside their gold jacket.

"Enough out of you, traitor," they sneer.

"You don't know what you're doing," Advisor Wilcon growls.

Guards swarm us, some brandishing their weapons, others glancing left and right for an explanation. But none take action.

"God above, Abner!" the sovereigns bluster. Fallon looks even more surprised.

"Read the letter and look at the drawing," Heir Abner demands their parents as though they're common folk. The sovereigns eyes flick between the advisor and their child several times before sticking to the letter.

"Oly?" Fallon lowers to his haunches beside me. I can't look at him. "No matter what happens, you won't be sacrificed. You'll live, I promise."

"How?" I ask. Without the sibyl, I'm only Hush. I don't want that life.

"I have a plan," he answers. "Don't lose hope."

I nearly laugh at the sentiment as he rises. The sovereigns have finished reading the letter and stare blankly at their heirs.

"Everything we're saying is true. I know you've always trusted Wilcon – as I have – but there isn't any more time to question. We need to get to the sibyl's tower and confront her." Fallon stalls. "And make a deal."

"Fallon, what are you doing?" Abner exclaims.

He ignores them and keeps his focus on the sovereigns. "Abner wants to kill the sibyl, but I don't. Niawa can't survive without her, we've grown too dependent. If we fight her, we fight with a fraction of our guards and no training against magic. She will destroy us. There has to be a way Niawa stays protected from the parasites, the Rive, and Istral."

"You want to allow the demon god back? That is blasphemous and an affront to Yuli-en," Sovereign Gerves argues.

I wonder if I should say something, having lived among demons for ten years. Fallon said the Champion still matters, even without power. But none of them ask for my thoughts. I may as well be one of the floor tiles. Or one of the surrounding guards who now stand idly by, gaping and wheezing after every word from the heirs. I decide to keep my mouth closed.

"We don't have a choice, father. The sibyl is too powerful to stop. We need to protect ourselves," Fallon explains.

"If you agree to this, you're all cowards," Abner says. "We must fight. Take back Niawa. Force her to close the Rive for good, which will kill the parasites, too. This can all end tonight."

The sovereigns are stunned into silence, looking like helpless sheep surrounded by wolves. Their eyes shift to the advisor over and over. It's clear he would have made this decision for them, were he not under suspicion.

"If my council still means anything under these baseless accusations, I propose you follow Heir Fallon's lead. Visit the sibyl's tower and speak to her yourself," Advisor Wilcon says. "In good faith, I will go along as a prisoner if that assuages the heirs' worries."

"No one is falling for any more of your lies." Heir Abner presses on the knife, cutting off the advisor's voice into a grimace.

Sovereign Gerves angles towards his wife. "Niawa is already falling. Without the sibyl, we may not exist by the morning."

She closes her eyes for a moment, then nods in agreement. "I don't understand what's happening, but we must believe in Yuli-en now more than ever. General Jaits, the Champion, and his captains will take Advisor Wilcon to the sibyl's tower and bring back answers. If any of this is true, we will secure Niawa's future before the Rive wakes. Abner, release Wilcon into the custody of the guards."

A small smile cracks Fallon's face, but he quickly hides it. Heir Abner huffs through their nose as they remove their knife and slip it back inside their jacket.

With a puffed out chest, Fallon turns to the nearest guards. "Arrest Advisor Wilcon."

The guards hesitate at first but then swoop in to tie the advisor's hands behind his back. The old man doesn't petition for his freedom, only looks upon the heirs with a pointed scowl.

For a brief second, our eyes meet. He holds nothing for me. I'm not an important pawn in this game. Not anymore.

Sovereign Gerves calls over a captain from the border of guards. "Find General Jaits and gather your best for a visit to the sibyl's tower. You have ten minutes."

The captain bows then leaves.

"This is a mistake," Heir Abner protests.

"This is being the sovereign. You may not understand now,

but you will when Niawa still stands and you become its next leader," Sovereign Gerves responds sharply. Despite his words, his fear and uncertainty is palpable.

Heir Abner deigns to glare at their father. "I don't know if I can rule a kingdom under a demon god and the corrupt sorceress we cowed to."

"I can," Fallon interjects. He looks taken aback by his own outburst.

The expression on Heir Abner's face makes me wonder if the knife will make another appearance. Fallon endures the vexed look for a few seconds before looking away. I know deep shame when I see it.

"No decisions will be made until the guards return from the tower. In the meantime, we will continue to pray and tend to the citizens. Abner, this will be good practice for you in assuring your people," Sovereign Adelaide says.

"I'll be going to the tower," Heir Abner says. "To make sure nothing goes wrong." They march to a nearby guard and pull a thin sword right from its sheath. The guard watches in confusion as the heir returns to the sovereigns, elegantly spinning the sword as though they've sparred at the academy. "I've been training on my own for years now in anticipation of this day. I don't believe the sibyl will humor any kind of negotiation, and we should be prepared."

"And I faced a demon at the Edge. The very one that started this infestation. I'll be going too. This is my plan, after all," Fallon announces with his arms crossed.

"No. You will both stay here. If the sibyl is corrupt, it will be too dangerous," their father responds.

"I love you both. But I'm not asking permission." Heir Abner turns away from their parents and walks across the confined space.

"I – me as well," Fallon says with a speck of the conviction his sibling held. He leaves the sovereigns to blubber back and forth about insubordination and follows Heir Abner.

I'm left on the floor in the midst of a beehive. Guards march back and forth, called into groups by captains. Some of them openly weep, their minds shattered. They won't be chosen to go to the tower. Neither of the heirs have any idea what they're up against. If what they said, and the letter, is true, the sibyl has garnered so much power she convinced an entire kingdom it came from Yuli-en. She is unstoppable. The demon god will come, and every creature from the Rive will look like a kitten in comparison. Istral can't be reasoned with, no matter how hard Fallon believes otherwise. Niawa will crumble by morning. We'll all be demons, or dead, if lucky.

I look over my shoulder to watch Fallon speaking tersely with Heir Abner. He expects me to be a show of force against the sibyl. Her own chosen warrior turned against her. I feel like a traitor, even imagining it. Even with her deception, her corruption, the demon essence she forced me to drink – I am nothing without her.

"Protect our children, Champion." I hear Sovereign Adelaide remark before the blubbering moves away.

She worries for them, even after their blatant disrespect. In the end, the heirs will run into their parents' arms and die with love. I'll die alone. My parents would sooner use my body as a shield.

Oh.

Anxiety surges up my back, bringing a realization. My parents are not in the palace. If they were, they would have forced their way into this barred off area using their notoriety. I doubt they even left the pink house – if they're still alive at all. I push clumsily to my feet, still gripping the bowl.

There isn't a part of me that doesn't ache. New bruises bloom over my ribs and legs that I can blame on being trampled at the gate. Fragments of the Blessing still cling on, but they flicker like a dying flame.

I wanted so badly to show mother and father who I am now. I dreamt about it countless times at the Edge, knowing I'd never return. This is my last chance. What good is a dying flame if it can't cast light on its final day? Before the Blessing completely abandons me, I'll get them to the palace, where they can live out the last minutes of their lives with the royal family. Then they'll finally see.

The clock across the throne room lets me know I have four hours until the new day. I could slip away now, no one would notice. No one but Fallon. He saved me at the gates, the least I can do is tell him I won't be coming to the tower.

I walk over to the heirs' small corner of the space. They don't even notice me when I come to stand behind them.

"I'm not going to apologize for doing what I think is best," Fallon is saying.

"You've now betrayed me twice. If I wasn't so disgusted I'd be impressed. Never seen you have so much vigor," Heir Abner responds.

Fallon's eyes narrow. "I'm not trying to hurt you."

"I don't care about me, Fallon. I care about Niawa. Whatever is in that tower, you better be ready, because I am."

Fallon says nothing back, so I take the chance to interrupt. His sour face gleams when he sees it's me who taps him on the shoulder.

"How are you feeling?" he asks.

"Fine. I'm going back into the city. My parents may still be at their house, and I need to get them to safety."

Fallon looks stricken. "No, Oly, you can't do that. We need you at the tower; you're the Champion."

I look down at the demon-teeth armor. It's strange knowing I'll be the last to wear it. "I can't help, not with my power barely hanging on. Once it's gone, I'll be too tired, too broken to fight. This is something I *can* do. I need to."

"Maybe we can convince the sibyl to give you another Blessing in the deal. Give me a chance."

"Then she can do so when I return," I lie. He needs to think that I believe Niawa will be left standing tomorrow.

Behind him, Heir Abner angles themselves away as if to give us privacy, but I can tell they're still listening.

Fallon also notices and lowers his voice. "What if… if it comes to it… we have to kill her. What do we do?"

My stomach twists. I don't want to have a hand in killing the sibyl. He stares, waiting for an answer, like I did to the sibyl's tapestry in my cabin. I talked to her so often, my words seeping into the golden thread of her veil. She never answered, but I felt her presence all the same. It makes me nauseous to imagine my last hours alive without that tether. Then I'd be truly, utterly, alone.

Fallon's brows pinch together. He needs to hear something. Anything.

"With magic," I say, not knowing if this is true or not. But it won't matter in the end.

He grows more visibly nervous but says, "Thank you." He grips at his collar with distress. "Is there nothing I can do to stop you?"

"No."

"Thought so. Not that I'd try; you can still beat me into a pulp." He smiles.

"Of course," I reply, strangely smiling back. The reaction

is so genuine, doubt sneaks in, and I'm suddenly aware of my bowl and long for its calm. Bringing it to my eyeline, I see the scratches around the edges, a small chip along the rim. It can't come with me. Parting with it again makes me deeply sad, but I'm grateful it returned to me at all. I hold it out to Fallon and he takes it without question.

"I look forward to returning this to you," he says. His cheery demeanor vanishes. We both know I will most likely die.

Fallon gently touches my elbow. I don't move away. Even through my armor, I feel the sensation of his fingers slowly sliding up the back of my arm. He closes the distance between us and I stop breathing. The memory of his odd scent at the Edge clouds my head, making me dizzy.

"I'd like to give you something too. It's small. But given the circumstances, it feels important. If you'll accept it," he says softly. Then he taps his own cheek with his finger.

It takes me a humiliating number of seconds to understand. When I do, my throat tightens. But I whisper, "Okay."

Fallon leans in and briefly presses his lips to the curve of my cheekbone.

Wings beat mercilessly in my stomach and I'm painfully aware of every person and sound in the room. Heir Abner looks suspiciously over their shoulder towards the dais as if studying the throne chairs. I still see the smile they try to hide.

The small flame inside me burns a little fiercer. I can't fathom how to express that, so I say, "Thank you for your kindness."

And I leave.

"Where is the Champion going?" I hear Sovereign Gerves say, but I've already broken through the wall of guards.

The throne room reminds me of the courtyard circle, bodies packed into every inch. At least they don't push against each other, fighting and clawing for safety. I start to move through. As they did before, people call out my title, asking me to find a loved one who didn't make it to the palace. I keep my eyes on the entryway. All the citizens can do now is nurture their false hope. I envy them for not knowing what I do.

The palace doors are shut again. I'll need to find another exit. Looking right, then left at the connecting corridors, I choose to go left. Another wall of guards blocks my way.

They barely hear my request to get through before creating a gap. My title still means something in their ignorance.

Before I came to, sunlight still ruled the sky. Now, the deep, twinkling violet of night shows through the windows. The tail of Yuli-en's Eye is visible, even more bright now. I question if the god truly is watching. And why they don't intervene.

Boots pound behind me, beneath the shifting of metal plates.

"I'm coming with you, Champion," a familiar voice calls out. Denya jogs down the corridor in full armor, a green and gold tabard over her chest. Her two swords hang from her hips in polished scabbards. It seems she made a visit to the armory. I hardly recognize her as the crying woman in a blood-stained nightgown. She must have spotted me leaving the throne room.

"I'm glad to see you survived," I say truthfully.

"Where are we going?"

"*We* aren't going anywhere. This is my burden," I respond. There's too great a chance I won't even make it to the pink house. The escort shouldn't walk into that fate with me. For helping me in the city, I'll thank her by ignoring her brazen fortitude.

"Oddly enough, I need to run some errands. If we happen to walk in the same direction, then so be it."

It's obvious she'll trail in my footsteps no matter what I say. Once again, she's determined to be a pebble in my boot.

"There may be thousands of demons now. I need to be quick and quiet. You'll draw attention," I push.

"Forgive me, but I'm not the one limping. Or wearing the teeth of my enemies. Let me help you."

I glower at the escort, but she only lifts her chin higher.

"The royal family needs you more than I do. You don't understand what's happening."

"Yes, I heard. You didn't recognize me, but I was one of the guards nearby. The sibyl is corrupt and the heirs plan to make a deal. Or kill her."

"Fine, then you know. Go help Fallon." I walk away, done with this distraction.

Denya follows. Though I try to walk fast, she is already beside me. I stop in frustration.

"I'm going to find my parents. They live across the city. I doubt I'll even survive. If you come with, you absolutely won't."

"So, I die fighting the sibyl, or I die fighting with the Champion. If this is the end, my choice is easy."

I sigh in defeat. I need to conserve my power for demons, not keeping this nuisance away. Suppose I could have worse company. Guards may not be prepared for fighting demons, but Denya is an escort. She has seen the creatures and fought one.

"The Trace may still be alive. Demons will come right to us." I give her a final warning.

"Thank you, Champion. I swear to carry out your mission to the best of my ability." She unleashes one of her swords and holds it with one hand by the handle at the center of her chest, blade pointed downward. Her other hand touches her helmet over her forehead, then her stomach, then lays on her heart. The Guard's Oath.

"Where do you suggest we leave the palace?" I ask halfway through the pledge

Denya sheathes her blade. "Follow me."

CHAPTER 19

As Denya leads me through the palace, the city outside grows louder. Low moans follow us from the windows, breaching the wall surrounding the palace. If the demons could climb the stone barricade, they would be in the gardens, scratching at the glass. I keep my gaze ahead, but the escort turns at every sound.

"How many do you think have spawned?" she asks as we pass an empty kitchen, its doors flung wide open.

"Maybe half the city, if people haven't learned to defend themselves," I answer bitterly, remembering Isaac and the angry crowd.

"We may not be a kingdom of seasoned warriors, Champion, but I'd wager everyone down to the florists may find their will to fight tonight."

It's a good sentiment, but one I scoff at.

"Do you think the heirs will succeed?" Denya asks.

"I don't know."

"I can't imagine fighting the sibyl. She was always an uncomfortable topic with my husband. If I can speak freely now, I feel oddly vindicated knowing what she's done."

Though I was on the verge of strongly suggesting that she stop talking, my interest is piqued. "How so?"

"When I became an escort, wishing to stand out from my peers, I'd never thought I could feel such sympathy for you.

Alone at the Edge, in that small cabin, facing the Rive. My stomach would be in knots as we rode away after delivering your supplies. Like I saw something I shouldn't. Felt things I shouldn't. Sometimes, I'd lie awake at night imagining what it would have been like if I was chosen, and I'd feel sick. As a guard, I could have been. Any of us could."

You're wrong, I nearly shout. An hour ago, I would have. When I believed Yuli-en chose their Champion through a rare, divine connection. It was the sibyl that chose me. And now I don't know why or how.

It's too much right now. I push the thought aside.

Denya rambles on, "I realized, I wouldn't want to be chosen and I wouldn't wish it on anyone else. Learning the sibyl has sacrificed so many under the guise of protecting the kingdom, and we have willingly allowed her to, even worshipped her for it, makes me even more ill." Denya seems to be finished, but then she adds, "She's made Niawa weaker than we could ever imagine."

I don't respond, hoping Denya hears my unspoken wish for the talking to end. To my relief, she does. We move in silence until reaching a set of metal doors where two guards stand watch. They face the door, holding shining, untested weapons, waiting for their nightmare to crash through the metal. When our footsteps reach their ears, they flinch, heads jerking in our direction.

"We've been given permission by the sovereigns to leave the palace," Denya states. She flicks her wrist at them when they don't break from their stances.

"Why would you go out there?" one guard asks in horror.

"That's between the Champion and the royal family," Denya says. She reaches between them for two brass handles. As she pulls the doors open, the guards rush to the other end of the hall, angling the sharp points of their weapons outwards.

A light breeze drifts through the opening, trickling over my exposed scalp. I sigh and turn back to the guards. To my luck, only one wears the ludicrous plumed helmet; the other's is like Denya's, plain steel with Niawa's crest etched over the forehead. It isn't demon teeth, but it's better than nothing.

"I need your helm," I say.

The guard I address backs further into the wall.

"Give the Champion your helm," Denya orders.

Slowly, the guard lifts it from her head and hands it to me. I slide it on, missing the worn leather of the Champion's helmets.

"And the gate keys," Denya says. The same guard unhooks a ring of keys from her belt and tosses it to Denya.

The escort and I step through the doors.

Beyond is a well-kept garden between the palace and the surrounding wall. Denya gives me a look and I read her unspoken message: now is the time to turn around.

My first step into the garden is heavy-footed. The next is surer, landing lighter on a winding stone path. Tall lily stalks whiter than the hanging moon bend over the path's edge. Thick bushes line the wall, their leaves gleaming as if dipped in wax, soft pink roses nestled among them. Trees with thin branches curl and wave with intricacy. It's a bit busy. I prefer the wildberry bushes and lemon reeds. The path splits towards a smaller version of the black iron gate. Half-human faces push against the poles and long, pale arms swipe lazily through the gaps.

I hear Denya free one of her blades.

"Take this one; it's my favorite." She holds up the sword, eyeing my hand reaching for my axe.

She remembers that I struggled to lift it on my own. The sword is thin but sharp, a lighter one meant to be paired with another. I huff but grab the hilt. My arm doesn't strain to hold it, so I accept this will be my weapon.

"Destroy the heart or destroy the brain. If you cut off a head, crush it," I say, readying the blade.

"I recall." Denya raises her sword and slashes it across two clawing arms. They flop to the ground and the demons pull back. "The more human they are, the easier the kill."

She bends to shove each key from the ring into the lock. More demons replace the ones with no arms. I jab the sword into the chests of as many as I can, aiming for the heart. The lock clicks and falls. Denya gives me a nod, then fastens the key ring to her belt.

"This is the way we'll return." She kicks at the gate. Demons fall over the ones I have killed, and we rush out.

"Cover me," she says quickly.

I drive the blade across the chest of a creature hobbling my way. When it slumps to its knees, I turn to hack at a rising pile of bodies. My sword slices through arms, legs, stomachs, and necks as Denya locks the gate. I keep slashing, demon blood splashing over my boots.

The moans stop, and the only sound is my blade grinding against the stone ground under a pile of severed body parts.

Denya's fingers wrap around my bicep. "I think they're dead."

I stop, panting. There's demon blood across her shins and viscera caked over her boots. The creature that fell to its knees lies still, its head stomped in.

"Took me a few tries without your strength," she explains.

The adrenaline dissipates, returning me to my battered body. I'll need to conserve my energy better.

The side lane we stand on curves around the palace to meet the courtyard circle ahead. From here, I see shapes moving in the darkness. More demons.

"I propose we only fight when necessary. If we have to run, then we run," Denya says.

"Agreed."

We head down the lane, clearing the path of demons until reaching the edge of the circle. All the people I had ignored, pushed past for my own safety, are gone. Creatures roam unopposed, wearing bodies as young as toddlers. Most crowd by the black gates, drawn to the beating hearts inside the palace.

Denya jerks her head towards a row of tall trees bordering the circle. The thick trunks and shadows between provide ample cover as we dash through. My boots nearly catch several roots as I fight not to watch the circle. The Trace hasn't called to the demons yet, but I'm not convinced it won't.

"This way," Denya whispers. She points ahead to an alleyway on the far side, then breaks into a sprint. I follow, at half the speed.

The alleyway is even darker, the sole light source a window on the second floor of a house. I look up at a street lantern that would have normally been lit by this time of night. We can use the dark streets and alleyways to our advantage.

I step ahead of Denya, motioning for her to follow, and we slip into the murk.

Another advantage soon makes itself known: the cloak of screams and crashes of terror. As we rush down more alleyways, cutting across wide streets to keep between buildings, I witness what's become of the once colorful streets. Citizens have either shut themselves into their homes, their windows boarded up with furniture and wood, or are hastily packing carts and horses in the street. Demons stop them from escaping, coming from every direction to tear a screaming child from their parent's arms or drag a person to the ground as they attempt to run away.

Denya struggles not to stop. She wavers on the attacks, grimacing beneath her helmet. Several times I have to push or yank her along.

Breaking from a dead-end alley, we find ourselves in a large, open space with a tiled fountain in the center. Clear water spurts from the top, doing its best to cleanse the bloodied reservoir in the basin. A man's limp body hangs halfway in the pool. His arms twitch as we pass by. A window on the first floor of a house breaks to our right. We crane our necks to watch another man fall with the shattered glass. He lands on his head with a sickening crunch. What was once a young boy clambers down after him. The demon pays no mind to the window shards carving into its stomach and arms. It sinks its fangs into the fallen man's back, and I look away. Tears run the curve of Denya's exposed chin. We keep moving.

There are no shadowed alleys unravelling from the fountain space, so we take a narrow lane ahead. A cart pulled by two horses thunders our way, nearly flattening us with its wheels. It disappears past the fountain, leaving us with an empty street, lit only by the light of a tall fire several streets over.

A twinge in my lower back spreads, pushing sharp pain through my left leg. I'm forced to a slow walk, and Denya matches my gait.

"I'm fine," I snap when she gives me a look of concern.

"Let's find a place to rest. For two seconds," she suggests in a meek voice.

I glare, making my answer clear, then look ahead. If my memory of Niawa is correct, we're halfway to the pink house. Another hour, at least. The humming bristles with agitation. It's already accepted I won't make it to my parents.

The lane is bordered on both sides by houses; all with secured windows and closed doors. We near a window clotted by a couch and chest of drawers. I almost miss a pair of eyes peering through a gap. They vanish, only for several more to blink into other spaces between the furniture.

The front door of the house opens, and a man's head pokes out. He looks up and down, left and right, before opening the door wider.

"Champion," he whispers. "Thank the god you are here. Our street is nearly deserted. Many of our neighbors ran for the palace." He grips the door frame. "Some were attacked and changed right before our eyes. What should we do?"

Denya starts to veer towards him, but then she goes rigid, her eyes fixed on the end of the lane. Small red lights flicker into being where there was only darkness seconds ago. They hang in mid-air, quickly forming into circles, as if an invisible hand draws with red ink.

"Where do we go, Champion?" the man calls out, louder. He hasn't seen the creature yet. A child appears in the doorway and presses his cheek into his father's leg. The man rubs the child's head delicately. "The Champion and the guard will protect us. We'll soon be safe."

"Quiet," I hiss. The man looks cross, as if I'm being rude.

Denya rushes to him and the child. "Get back inside and don't say a word." She points to the red rings.

"Denya, we need to go," I urge.

The little boy bursts into tears so loud that Denya hastens to calm him.

The red rings brighten and grow in size until I can see the demon clearly. Stringy blonde hair sprouts from the back of its head and down its neck. The head of the woman it stole hangs down its back like a cloak's hood, empty of blood and bone. The creature is tall. All of its limbs have elongated, and its entirely naked body is a patchwork quilt of peach and pale skin.

Denya pushes the family back through their door and shuts it. "You could try and be a little more tactful," she says, returning to the street.

"Those are problems for calmer skies."

The demon's jaw lengthens, as if the muscle is only held by tissue. It ambles towards us, moaning and rolling its large head from side to side. Its knuckles dig into the ground with each step, coming up bloody and torn. The loose head slips from the demon's back and dangles by its legs like a traveling sack, fouling its stride.

"That's its weak spot." I point at the hanging head. "Be cautious; this one is strong."

Denya lifts the bottom of her helmet and retches onto the street. Vomit sticks to her chin, but she slides the covering back down. Then she runs, her sword pointed at its target. I can't help but feel proud, watching her race towards the demon, nearly colliding with it, but spinning to its right side at the last moment with a slash.

Yellow-gray blood sprays up the creature's sternum. The loose head is freed, landing on the ground with a sound like a pile of wet linen. Denya's humanity fails her then. She can't help but glance down at the stolen woman's face, her empty eye sockets staring back.

The demon lowers its head and barrels into Denya's chest. She flies backwards, landing atop several flowerpots outside a house. Dirt and clay unfurl beneath her like wings.

A perfect opening for me.

By the time the creature's slow movements have it facing me again, I've already rammed my fist into its cheek. Bone cracks beneath its pale skin. The demon and I both wail from the impact.

That was stupid. I'm not strong enough to trade blows. The demon shakes off the strike, and I scan it rapidly. Its skin is paper thin, stretched tight over protruding ribs.

It raises up, leaning onto its back legs to swipe at me with both arms. I duck and position myself, waiting for the arms to swing back around and embrace me to its chest, my sword leveled sideways, blade facing the ribs. The arms drag me closer, allowing the sword to slice between the bones as I push.

I feel its hands clutch my waist, claws raking across my back. The strain in my leg deepens and my knee nearly buckles. I lean back into the demon's hands to hold my body up, praying its claws don't sneak beneath my plates.

Then I reach into the cut and squeeze my fingers around its beating heart. The demon topples like the mass of bones and blood it truly is. Red mist rises from its body in a plume.

I step back from the creature, panting.

Denya comes to my side, her shoulders and helmet covered in soil. She holds her hand to a large dent in her breastplate. "I wasn't expecting it to be as strong as the one from the Edge. It's half the size."

"It wasn't." I flick my hand, throwing off chunks of gray and pink heart. "But left alone, it would have become that thing."

"Yuli-en, save us," Denya exhales.

I thought Denya's words an empty cry to the heavens. I wasn't looking at her when she spoke them. When I do, her eyes flicker between the lane ahead and behind us. Ahead are four demons in varying stages. Behind, six or seven more.

If they were the running kind, we would be torn to pieces already.

"Denya," I say curtly. She trembles, twisting back and forth. I dip my chin towards my belt. "Take out two fire bombs." I look around the street. It's too narrow, and the houses are decorated with moss, vines, hanging planters. Highly flammable things. "Better yet, two poison bombs. They're violet. It won't outright kill the demons, but they'll die eventually."

She pulls two purple-clouded spheres from their pouches, and holds them gingerly in one hand, clearly terrified they'll break. Good. I prefer her to be more wary than overzealous.

"If we're too close when they explode, we'll die too," I whisper as if the demons can hear me planning. They're closer now, two houses away.

Denya rears her arm back and pelts one bomb in both directions.

Purple smoke erupts in thick clouds, completely obscuring the creatures. Their moans heighten to low-pitched screams. I hear them scramble amidst the smoke. Some manage to crawl through, coming out feet from us. Boils grow from their skin, larger ones already popping a ghastly mixture of demon blood and black sludge.

Denya charges forward, cleaving into the nearest demon. She severs its still-human arm from its body with ease.

"Wait!" I yell. The cloud has dissipated, and Denya now faces three poisoned creatures – and the four behind them that escaped the bomb.

A demon with one elongated leg and one that hasn't quite stretched yet trips over the fallen body in front of it. As it goes down, it grabs the escort's leg. She slams to the ground.

I'm torn between turning my back on the demons coming up the rear and helping Denya. My thoughts shout she needs to fight for herself, as I will be forced to do the same. Yet, I can't pull my eyes from her.

Denya kicks at the demon that keeps her down with wild abandonment. She completely forgets her blade. Panic drives her as more of them close in, and she can't break the demon's grip.

I ram into the wall of demons around her without another thought. A few topple over, and I nearly trample over Denya, my balance hindered by my injured leg. That split-second decision surprises the demon holding onto her, and it lets go. I pull her to her feet, and we scurry backwards until colliding with a wall.

The demons surround us, snapping their jaws. Human skin slops off their bodies, changing more before our eyes. Their feet crunch over the human teeth falling from their mouths.

All we can do is slash with our blades. Mine are shallow, barely clearing the shrinking space between us and them. Denya screams, extending her sword as far as she can. She manages to cut through a hand, lob off a few fingers; one demon's stomach flesh opens like a book, leaking blood and organs. It staggers but stays upright.

The creatures are only held back by our erratic cuts through the air, which slow with every passing second. My arm grows so tired, I squeeze tears from the corners of my eyes to keep it moving. Denya's breaths are heavy and labored.

"I can't –" she gasps.

My heart beats so violently it may explode in my chest.

Denya's sword drops for the briefest moment. It's enough for the demons to strike. They leap onto us and we fall to get away. The creatures follow us down. Fangs scrape against my arm plates, claws rake across my cuirass. Denya yells, but I can't help.

A demon steps on my sword and it's jerked from my hand. I don't try to retrieve it. Instead, I flail; throwing my fists left and right and kicking out with my good leg.

All I need is two seconds. I know exactly which pocket holds the holy flares.

My neck guard tears. A demon's clawed hand hooks into the tough leather. The creature rips its hand back, and I'm dragged away from Denya.

Anxiety spikes inside me. Did my skin break? Am I infected?

The demon jerks me again, harder. This time I'm pulled onto my side. Another swoops onto me, relentlessly trying to bite through my helmet. It steps onto my shoulder, and I feel a pop followed by a blinding pain.

I shift my hips, desperate to shake the demon off my shoulder, while throwing punches at the one still stuck in my neck guard. I feel the smooth part of its claw against my skin, dreading the sharp point.

A long, charcoal tongue rolls out of its mouth. Drips of saliva hang from the tip, and I turn my head, barely missing them. The creature leans closer, surveying me with one red-ringed eye.

We'll die if I can't get to my belt. I can't hear Denya anymore.

I abandon punching to tousle with the flap of the pocket holding a holy flare. I can't get it out. The demon caught in my neck guard clamps its teeth onto my shoulder plate. It pulls me out from under the other.

I cease fidgeting with the flap and ball my hands into fists, then bring them down with all my might. Glass shatters.

CHAPTER 20

Everything vanishes in a flash of white. Beyond the sudden, wintry world, voices yell and the sounds of blades whistle through the air. The weight of the demon that held me down lifts away.

"I can't see!" a woman shouts.

"To your left!" another answers.

Gray forms dance in the white clouds, colliding with other gray forms. Shapes fling out like tentacles. I try to blink the white away, but it still bleaches my vision.

The gray forms become thick, erratic shapes, like some kind of gargantuan spider. Two shadows break from one shape, darkening and darkening before I'm being grabbed and lifted to my feet. My shoulder and leg hurt too much to fight back, so I let myself be propped against the wall.

"Champion! We found you," a man's voice exclaims. "You two wait here. Don't move." The man's gray shape disappears.

All I can do is watch as wetness slaps across my armor several times. As the fog around me and in my head starts to thin, the man's words ring an alarm. *You two.*

"Denya? Are you there?" I grasp around in the fading whiteness, but there's only space. When a hand curls around mine, I nearly choke on relief.

"I'm here. I'm okay." Denya squeezes my hand. "Considering someone blinded me."

Somehow, I laugh. It shakes my nauseous stomach and pinches at my shoulder pain. I squeeze her hand back.

"What about you?" Denya asks.

"Still alive."

The vibrations of battle whittle down, letting the backdrop of the city's mayhem back in. As the distant screams, wagon wheels grinding into stone, and shattering glass returns, color blooms back into the world. The quiet lane of potted plants and vine-covered homes has irrevocably changed.

A dark mixture of demon and human blood winds beneath demon parts and fallen people – guards and citizens. Ten or so survivors walk between the bodies, arching to drive swords into skulls or stab through chests. One woman in a stained lavender dress looks down at a jagged scratch over her forearm. No one seems to notice when she lays quietly on the ground, raises a long knife over her sternum, and thrusts it down. A man in common clothing yanks a fire poker from the chest of a demon. Tears stream down his face, but he treads to another body, this one a guard, and stabs the poker down. Two in the group are older academy trainees still in their uniforms. More than half are citizens. They wear random pieces of borrowed armor and wield pitchforks, spears, and swords awkwardly.

It feels wrong, though I had tried to teach them myself. Only the Champion is meant to fight demons.

I rub the final effects of the holy flare from my eyes and step away from the wall, taking my hand from Denya's. My body shakes beneath my armor, and I'm grateful the plates hide it.

Finished with stabbing through the dead, the guards and citizens position themselves to face both ends of the lane as a captain comes to speak with us.

He gives me a small bow. “I’m Captain Tatum.”

I’ve never felt inclined to return a bow from a guard, but with my life still miraculously intact, it feels appropriate. As I lean slightly forward, the torn muscle by my shoulder blade flares with a vengeance. In response, I curl my arm into my chest and try to straighten, but I feel like a lightning-struck branch holding on for every ounce of life it has left.

Captain Tatum gives me a worrying look. I loathe this pity more than the pain, inspiring me to throw my shoulders back, wincing.

“How did you get these people to fight?” I ask, thinking of the citizens who refused to listen to me, and grew angry when I tried to protect them.

“Once the palace closed, and the academy was overrun, I focused on gathering as many guards as possible. At first, only a few hundred joined me; most barricaded themselves in their homes. In the last couple hours, I think it’s become clear hiding is not an option. I’ve since been organizing troops and dispersing them throughout the city. Mine happened to pass by this street and see demons scrounging to get to one spot. We assumed whoever was beneath them would be dead and came to clean up.” He looks me and Denya over. “I’m sorry to ask Champion. Have you been –”

“No,” I say.

“And the guard?”

“The escort’s name is Denya,” I correct him. She smirks at me, and a little blood returns to her face.

“Of course.” Captain Tatum bows to her. “We should keep moving. The demons spread quickly, and they’re getting stronger.” He calls to the troop, and they all turn in the opposite direction of the pink house.

“That isn’t the way we’re going,” I say.

"You won't fight with us, Champion?"

"We're grateful for your help, Captain, but I must find my family. They didn't make it to the palace." The longer we idle, the more I wither, the greater the chance my parents are already dead. Or worse.

"Then let us come with you," Captain Tatum responds.

I shake my head. "The city needs you and your troops to help stop the spread. If Fallon and Heir Abner can't close the Rive by the new day, there will be even more." I look up to the comet streaking across a sea of stars. It's made its way past the bright moon. There isn't much time left.

"The heirs mean to close the Rive? For good?" the captain asks, bewildered.

I need to think before I speak. Remember the abandonment I felt learning who the sibyl really is. It still festers in me, threatening to drag me down. Their devotion to her and Yulien may be the only thing keeping them on their feet.

"They're working with the sibyl to have it done." My eyes shift to Denya, but she doesn't expose the lie.

A toothy smile stretches Captain Tatum's battle-worn face. "That's good news. We'll continue to protect our people until it ends. Including your parents, Champion."

Pride chokes my good sense. I open my mouth to argue.

"We accept your help, Captain," Denya says quickly, averting my glare.

Captain Tatum smiles wider. "I'll admit, fighting at the Champion's side has long been a fantasy of mine. I've read so much about you. Studied you. There's a painting in my sitting room of your likeness that I've often looked to in times of unsurety."

I think of the large tapestry hanging on the palace doors and grimace. "We need to go in the direction of the main road, then to Rillowen Street."

"I know where it is," Captain Tatum answers. He turns to face the troop and states the new destination.

Denya hangs back with me as the group begins down the lane and I go to collect the sword. Only one of my arms is capable now.

"Just a little more time," I beg the Blessing.

We follow behind the troop.

Denya isn't fooling me in the way she starts to outmatch my stride, then deliberately draws back to give me a hair's lead. The troop even glances back at us often, making sure they don't move too far away.

"Just *walk,*" I grumble.

Denya frowns. "I'm not leaving you behind."

For a moment, I close my eyes. My feet continue, and I walk blindly, doing my best to block out the noise. In the darkness, I'm forced to focus on what I feel. My good arm is so tired it shivers in anticipation of drawing my sword. Burning spreads across the soles of my feet and races up my legs where the fire takes to my muscles like dry leaves. My temples pulse, and a pounding at the base of my skull has nagged me since leaving the palace.

Yet, a heavy stone of pride still sits on my chest.

"You chose to do this," I chide myself.

I open my eyes to see Denya squinting up at the temple we pass, searching intently for demons crawling over the belfry.

"Why did you return after all this time?" she asks.

There's no use in hiding from her anymore. "To get the Blessing again. It's fading."

"I gathered. And why haven't you returned before?"

My skin tightens beneath my armor as if it also tries to protect me. I've told her enough.

Denya continues despite my silence. "It must be strange to return to a life you haven't known for ten years. Every time I returned from the Edge, it shocked me how different the city felt. All these people shopping and dining, unknowing what it's like to see the Rive ripple to life. To witness pure evil." She turns her head towards me. "The city felt cheapened. Fabricated, almost."

I meet her gaze, not knowing what I want to say until I say it. "I left myself here when I went to the Edge. I didn't want to see her again."

"Hm. I did the same when I married my husband to secure my family's wealth. So, when I truly fell in love, I couldn't let it go."

I find myself wondering if Denya would like the wildberry bushes and lemon reeds. The brook whistling softly past the well. Maybe, if we survive, I'll show it to her. I wonder even further, if she understands what happened at the gate.

"I left you behind. I'm sorry. Something came over me."

She chuckles. "I don't hold it against you. You were scared. I was too. We were all frightened animals then, drunk on instinct. Might have shoved through a family or two myself."

Yes, she would love the wildberries.

The troop abruptly stops ahead of us. They push closer together, shouts coming from the front where Captain Tatum leads. I tilt the sword up, not knowing where to point it, until I hear moans coming from my right. A woman races from a building with two demons in tow. One creature wraps a long arm around her torso at the same time its teeth sink into her neck. She drops to her knees in the street, eyes glazed over.

Captain Tatum is driving his sword through the demon and

the woman beneath in seconds. Several others take care of the other one. Throughout, Denya angles herself in front of me while I stand and watch.

The battle is over quickly, and the captain urges us to keep going.

CHAPTER 21

This is not a mistake; you know what you're doing, the voice in Fallon's head repeats over and over. Fourteen guards march down the palace halls with him, including two tasked to watch over Wilcon – all that could be spared.

When he's able to wrangle the voice into shutting up, Fallon immediately dreads what waits for him in the tower. Some kind of creature the sibyl is "tinkering with," as Wilcon said.

He wishes Oly were here. Even without her full strength, her presence would inspire him to hold onto the courage he loses with every tick of the ornamental clock's hands on the throne room wall. It read three hours to midnight when they left the throne room.

Fallon rubs the green bowl nervously, wondering if he should have traded it for a weapon. But the look on Oly's face when she gave it to him was palpable. It means everything to her. So he'll protect it, as he promised.

He glances behind at Abner, their sword firmly in one hand. They walk near Wilcon, watching him from the corner of their eye.

Though Fallon was born in these halls, spent much of his life parading through them with a goblet in hand and a grin for every passerby, the palace now feels like a foreign land. Smears of shadow in the space between the lanterns spread like spilled ink. He used to love the way sconce flames sprinkled bright glints across the gold crown molding stretching overhead, on the delicate sweeps of color in the ancient paintings on the walls. He pines for the warmth that would flood his chest as he strolled along, head fuzzy with alcohol and a full stomach.

Tonight, it is cold and dark. Ashen. Death has found its way inside, blotting out the strong scent of vanilla sticks placed delicately into mounted flower arrangements beneath the sconces. Fallon's nostrils fill with stale, thick air, as if the palace has been left barren for weeks. He huffs to expel the acrid taste from his throat.

"What is it you're prepared to do, Heir Fallon?"

At first, Fallon assumes his thoughts returned to chastise him. Then he realizes it's Wilcon's voice slinking into his ears.

"What needs to be done," Fallon answers.

"You don't have the faintest clue what waits for us." Wilcon amplifies his voice, the words echoing through the hall like a haunting.

Fallon shoots a razor-sharp look over his shoulder. "Shut your mouth. That's an order."

The advisor laughs harshly. "Istral will destroy everything. Leizus is an ambitious, greedy sorceress who can't be reasoned with. You idiotic boy. Mentoring you as a future sovereign was a waste of time."

Fallon stops in his tracks and spins around. Abner already has the sharp point of their sword aimed at the advisor.

"That's enough," Abner says.

Wilcon stiffens, but his face remains without emotion. "Tonight we'll all die, and Niawa will follow."

"You agreed we could make a deal," Fallon challenges.

"I guess I've changed my mind. You should try to kill her. Or don't. It won't matter." The advisor smiles and it scares Fallon so much he looks at Abner for comfort, as he always has. His sibling returns a knowing look, wordlessly reminding Fallon they don't believe this plan, or him.

Fear quickly bleeds into ire. Fallon won't be anyone's puppet any longer.

"You've been colluding with the sibyl for twenty years. Why turn on her now?"

Wilcon's eyes rove over the ceiling, then trail down the white marble columns protruding from the walls flecked with green stone. "Leizus promised me she would spare the kingdom, but she never had any intention to do so. She wishes to *become* Istral, not just bring the god forth." He looks at Fallon. "And I won't be here to witness it."

There is yelling. The flash of blades. The green bowl rolls away. Fallon is slammed onto his back and staring up at Wilcon's face before he can comprehend how quickly the old man moves. Wilcon's hand tightens around Fallon's neck as his mind sprints between the dull pain radiating from his shoulder blades against the floor and his sudden desperation to breathe. He tries in vain to dig his fingers under Wilcon's, pull at the advisor's wrist, but the grip is like an iron shackle.

"Unhand him," a guard shouts. Fallon's vision blurs, but he can make out swords and spears pointed at Wilcon's back.

"Back away or I will crush his throat," Wilcon drawls.

"Do as he says," Abner demands.

The swords and spears disappear.

Fallon's feet go numb. Blood rushes to his head, leaving his arms ice cold. His eyes roll back as Wilcon hoists him up by his neck, his feet dangling above the ground.

"I'll release you, if you ensure I can leave unchallenged," Wilcon says.

Fallon can barely hear him through the pounds clogging his ears. He tries to kick, but his body won't respond. Wilcon takes a few steps back, taking Fallon with him.

Fallon's consciousness hangs by a thread. His vision goes black. Then returns. The corridor behind Wilcon is empty. Black again.

"Nod, Heir Fallon. For my freedom." Wilcon's face flashes in and out.

Fallon tries to nod, but his head is both too heavy and light at the same time. He blinks as many times as he can, praying Wilcon gets the message.

Then he hits the ground again.

Fallon's raw throat expands, drinking in as much air as it can. He chokes on the breaths, wheezing so violently his eyes water.

Abner is at Fallon's side, trying to lift him to sit, but he waves them away with weak arms. He stays on the cold floor, waiting for life to flow back through his limbs. After a while, he presses his hands into the ground and pushes his torso up.

Abner helps him to his feet as he holds his throat tenderly. Wilcon already flies down the hall, his green cloak flowing behind him.

"I'm –" Fallon stops, swallows a wad of spit and phlegm, then tries again. "I'm fine."

Abner also watches the advisor's darkening form. "Seems the sibyl gave him more than immortality. His own kind of Blessing."

"Should we go after him?" a captain asks.

Rather than speak, Fallon shakes his head. He finds the bowl feet away, thankfully unmarred, then turns in the direction of the sibyl's tower and begins to walk. The guard's footsteps start behind him. Fallon pushes himself to stay ahead as tears stream down his cheeks, crippling humiliation eating him alive. It wasn't until Wilcon's face hovered above his, a cold, bony hand squeezing the breath out of him, that Fallon truly felt the loss of his mentor. There was not one part of the advisor – Fallon wipes his nose roughly – that cared for or believed in him.

Sooner than he's ready, the short hall leading to the sibyl's tower sprawls ahead of him. At the opposite end, the black door looms.

Fallon pauses feet from the door, the guards and Abner stopping behind him. He could turn around now. Join his parents in their guard-bordered hovel, waiting for the tempest to pass, hoping there's something salvageable on the other side.

The window to his right looks out over Niawa. Under the moonlight, the emerald land is painted in sweeps of dim white. Fields of fat, healthy livestock roam the rolling hills. Glistening rivers slice through the landscape, feeding the ocean. This is the kingdom he knows. How it should be, always. Only the sibyl can give him that.

In his mind, the land shrivels to brown and gray. Livestock collapse onto their backs, plump flies buzzing around their milky eyes. The rivers are dry, cracked dirt. His people suffer, coughing into their hands, blood coating palms. He sits on the throne, the paint chipped, his clothing worn and dull. The Heads surround him, spouting report after report of calamity and sickness. They are a floundering, destitute kingdom.

He feels a weight on his shoulder, and Abner comes around to face him. Worry cracks so many small creases across their face Fallon can imagine what his sibling may look like when they're old.

"We don't have to do this," they say. There's none of the malice in their voice that saturated it in the throne room.

Fallon responds by takes the last remaining steps and wraps his hand around the black door's handle. It's freezing.

He pulls.

The door swings wide with a low whine, its heavy wood a burden on old hinges. Steep stairs curl upwards, the column illuminated by the same sconces found throughout the palace.

He ascends. Bent knee after bent knee, feet flattening atop the crude stone.

Fallon reaches the last step onto a small landing, facing a carved stone opening.

"God above..."

It's only the line of people behind him that would need to throw themselves out of his way that keeps Fallon from running.

A demon the size of a small house hangs suspended in the center of the tower. Below it, the sibyl's white staff stands upright on its own, a line of red mist floating between the two. The creature curls into itself, its mottled gray, pale, and purple back covered in dark, bulbous growths that pulsate. One long, thick arm dangles a hand with fingers the length of Fallon's entire arm. The other wraps over the demon's head.

Behind the monstrosity, on the other side of the tower, the sibyl stands perfectly still, speaking the strange language that saved Shavazme's life. Another line of red mist connected to the demon streams directly into her golden veil.

CHAPTER 22

I can hear the battles, but I only see the bodies packed around me. Two troops have joined ours, pushing myself and the injured into the center. Where they can make sure our uselessness doesn't get in the way.

Even Denya has gone to help clear demons from our path.

She yells from the front, announcing we have reached the main road. The troop, now forty or fifty strong, spreads out into the wider street. The portcullis is to our left and the ghostly remains of the parade route to our right.

I'm so close.

"...right back to hell!" someone shouts from the direction of the portcullis.

I know that voice. Denya calls after me as I break into a pitiful imitation of a run.

The group catches up almost immediately, and I'm too grateful to be scorned. I wouldn't be able to slay every demon crawling up the sides of the courier's cart and bunching up at its wheels.

Velma sits on the driver's bench, stabbing at the creatures with her spear. Her chair is toppled over on the ground.

Denya reaches the cart first and thrusts her sword through the back of a demon wearing a white tunic adorned with a dazzling print of dragonflies. An older man, whose twisted ankle kept him in the belly of the troop with me, bashes a nearly human demon over the head with a dough roller. I manage to slice through the leg of one and crush its skull – with four tired stomps – before all the moans cease.

"Dear!" Velma says with glee. She raises her spear, yellow-gray blood dripping down the staff and over her hands.

"What are you doing out here?" I ask, limping to her overturned chair. I flip it onto the wheels and roll it closer to her.

The courier hands me the spear before lowering herself from the bench into the chair. Then she takes it back and sets it across her lap.

"I came to free my horses from the stables, thinking the demons would come for them. Didn't figure out they have no interest in the animals until I was surrounded."

"You could have died," I say, concern welling inside me. I'm compelled to reach out and place my hand on Velma's shoulder. Nervously, I do.

The old woman clutches my fingers and smiles. "Think I was holding my own just fine. But I'm sure glad to see you" – she peeks around me to Denya – "and you."

"Likewise," Denya answers. "Let's get you to safety."

I look up the main road, demons already creeping into the street and blocking our way. The Blessing still lingers under my skin, trickling like the last drips of water from a stopped faucet. I have to get to my parents now.

Captain Tatum orders the troop to keep going. Once again, I'm enveloped by the group, this time with Velma, like the soft insides of a bread roll. In the wider street, I can now bitterly watch the demons being slain as my feet drag over the remains of the parade. Strips of colorful paper and single flowers on long stems. Candies and empty steins. I kick a stein by accident, and it barely skitters a few inches.

Denya yanks her sword from a demon's chest then comes to me. "Are we close?"

I look around, spotting an antiques shop ahead. The lane leading to the pink house is just beyond it. I picked through the shop's shelves many times when my parents' disappointed stares became too heavy. Or when mother was in a volatile mood. Its sign hangs from two polished chains, a frog carved into the wood. One window is shattered, and I take a quick peek inside. Blood coats the corner of a shelf. On the floor, a hand juts out from behind the shelf, holding a small knife. The fingers slowly curl around the blade, and I recognize a gold ring as the shopkeeper's.

I feel mournful. Enough to think of stepping into the shop and putting him out of his misery. The shopkeeper was always kind and would toss me a caramel from the jar on the counter. But I move past the building to a straight road only a little wider than an alley. Too narrow for carts. I had to haul groceries back myself. My parents were upset when I was late, and even more so if I forgot something. The humming sometimes made remembering the list difficult.

The end of the road opens into a circular dead-end. Overhanging trees with thick branches and leaves shaped like stars block my view, but I know the pink house is on the left side of the curve.

"Denya," I say quietly. "The sword."

She takes the blade from my hand and relief floods my tired arm. I lift the helmet and wipe at my sweat-slicked face with an even damper glove.

"Denya," I whisper again.

"Yes?" she matches my volume.

"Do I… look strong?" My bowels twist from indignity.

"You look like the Champion." Her face is stern. Not a speck of pity.

We enter the lane.

What waits at the end is a graveyard. It isn't clear who was victorious. There are as many demon bodies as guards and citizens, all stacked on each other. The surrounding houses are in disarray. Doors flung open, windows smashed.

The door of the pink house is shut, but the kitchen window's glass is jagged. Dark blue curtains snag on the shards, obscuring the inside. I try to control my breathing as I walk towards the house. Exhales catch in my throat every time. There isn't a sound. No crying or wailing. The house is a mausoleum, becoming more lifeless the closer I get.

I come upon a woman, half-hidden beneath a headless demon. She's on her stomach, a mess of wet, dark curls caked to her face.

"Mother?" I drop to my haunches and nudge the woman's shoulder until she rolls onto her back. It's not her.

Feet away, a man's chest rises and falls in an erratic pattern. His arm is unnaturally outstretched. A chunk of his thigh is missing. He moans, so faint it's almost unnoticeable. A guard catches it too, and he races over. He readies his sword over the man's heart.

"Wait!" I shout. My voice echoes, ascending into the sky.

I crawl to the man, over bodies, staring at a dark mole on his forearm, right above his wrist. The humming rises to shrieks and I clutch at my head, trying to stop waves of vibrations from thrashing about inside my skull.

A sob bursts from the depths of me.

Denya runs over, both swords reared up. She first looks at me, then down at my father, moaning and twitching on the ground. A sliver of pale skin peeks from beneath his brown scalp. His eyes are black pools. I know red rings will soon swim in them.

"My father," I push out.

I crawl closer, eyeing the sharp teeth pushing through his gums. Human ones tumble over his lips to make room.

"Don't get too close." Denya loops her arm around mine and tries to pull me away.

I jab at her with my elbow, not paying attention to which arm I jerk. The torn muscle in my back reacts in a jolt of pain. I pant through it, grabbing at my father's shirt. His broken arm flops as if he tries to grab me. The other doesn't move at all.

"Oly?"

I lift my head. Mother stands in the open doorway of the pink house.

From my periphery, father shoots up from the ground. I'm beneath him the next second, red rings peering down at me. Father's lower jaw unhinges, lengthening downward as he bares sharp teeth. He dips towards my neck.

I feel it then.

The wooden bowl carved with the two gods' final battle, filled with the Blessing, slips from the sibyl's hands. Every last drop soaking into the throne room carpet.

My power is gone. Leaving behind cracked bones, strained and torn muscle, skin bruised like rotted fruit.

I scream. So relentless, years of my life escape with the sound.

Two guards pull father off me. Denya lowers to my side, her arm around my shoulders. I hold onto her, heaving for air.

The guards hold father up by his elongating arms as he snaps his head from side to side.

This is my fault. I didn't come here first after the academy. Saving myself was all that mattered.

"I'm so sorry." I reach out to touch my father's hand. A strip of brown skin peels off his arm and splats on the ground.

Denya pushes my arm down.

"We have to kill him, Oly," she says in a tone I recognize. It's mine. Direct and pragmatic. I have used it to justify killing every demon that has crossed my path, no matter how human they still appear to be.

Father is dead. This creature would rip my throat out, given the chance.

I can't do it. I can't give the order.

The guards grow restless as the demon in my father thrashes in their hold. His strength rapidly evolves, and the guards can feel it. They struggle between tightening their grip and arching away from his jaws.

I can't say it.

I look from my father to Denya. She nods, then tells the guards to take care of it. But somewhere else. His body is carried away.

I force myself to study the back of my glove. The tough stitching is woven in a simple pattern. Up and down the back of my hand, tracing up my fingers. The pattern changes direction, angling slightly to follow the line of my thumb. I flip my hand to see if it continues on my palm. It doesn't. My palm is a thick, flat strip of leather with black thread.

The sound of a dragged body drifts off.

The moans quiet. Mother shrieks from the pink house.

I feel the empty space in front of me like a long drop off a cliff.

"He's gone," Denya says.

"It's gone," I respond.

"Yes, you won't see him – it – again."

"No, Denya. It's all gone."

Her expression softens when she finally understands. "Okay."

I press my good hand to the ground and try to push off it to stand. Unable to hold up my armored body, my wrist bends wrong, and I wobble. Denya's hands snake around my waist to help, but I pull away.

"Don't make me weaker," I snipe.

She ignores my demand.

Denya keeps an arm around my waist, holding me steady. Exhaustion forces me to surrender, and I lean into her. The troop watches us, including Velma, who waits at the opening. Worried, confused. Wondering why the Champion couldn't kill one demon. They followed me here because of my title. Who the sibyl made me. I regret their company with every ounce of my being.

"Keane," my mother wails. Her fingers stifle my father's name, pressing against her lips as if she fears the name leaving her mouth will further separate them. She takes one shaky step onto the top stair leading to the doorway. Then another. When she reaches me, her hand slides down her face to splay over her sternum.

"How could you let this happen?" she seethes.

No answer will satisfy her fury. She doesn't want the truth. She only wants to wring her hands around something warm and soft until it's as cold and hard as she feels.

"I came to find you and father," I say.

"Why did you take so long? Those demons came from nowhere. Your father ran outside when he saw guards to ask for help, and one bit him! Tore into his leg!" She coughs. "You should have protected us."

"Madam, we need to keep moving to the palace, where you will be safe," Denya says.

"Keane is dead because of you!" My mother takes a sharp step towards me, and I flinch.

Captain Tatum grabs mother's upper arm. The tangerine-colored fabric of her dress bunches beneath his fingers.

"I mourn your loss with you, but we can't stay here." He's nurturing, but his cadence is firm. He looks at Denya. "You say we can return to the palace?"

"There's a south side entrance we can try to get to," Denya answers.

The captain alerts the troop, and they start moving towards the mouth of the cul-de-sac. He forcibly guides mother to two guards and orders them to protect her at all costs. She argues as they push her along, spouting of the hell I've brought upon her. Damning my name between dry heaves.

Denya and I are left among the dead, facing the pink house.

I wonder if my bed is still beneath the window where I had moved it one restless night, just so I could fall asleep watching the stars. I wonder if my stories about animals and the lands beyond Niawa's border are still stacked in the orange-painted bookshelf.

"I wish I could see my room," I say.

Though I don't speak to her, Denya responds. "If we walked into my childhood bedroom, you'd find amateur paintings of Jackson Q'loren, the famed flutist, with his ruffled collar unbuttoned down to his navel."

The day weighs far too heavy to laugh or smile, but I understand what she attempts to do. For that, I pinch the green undershirt peeking out between Denya's arm plates at her elbow. Father used to pinch mother's elbow all the time, and she would giggle and slap his hand away.

"Where is he?" I ask, though I quickly regret it. Even so, I search the cul-de-sac with my eyes. Did they shove him into the bushes between two houses like broken furniture, or dump him through a window for someone else to discover if they return home? I don't believe Denya would have the guards be so callous, but there wasn't much time to do more.

"It's best you don't know. When this is over, he'll be properly buried. I'll see to it personally," she says.

"Thank you."

I crane my neck to find Yuli-en's Eye. There are only hours until the Rive wakes.

Denya must know my thoughts because she cocks her head towards the troop. I nod, agreeing that it's time.

She moves with me out of the dead-end street, and I limp along, fragile as the day I last called this place my home.

CHAPTER 23

At first, Fallon thinks the bulbous growths swell and contract, but he realizes it's the creature's back rising up and down as it slowly breathes.

Abner joins him on the landing. They raise their sword with a start as though the thing was charging at them. "What the hell is that?"

Fallon can't possibly fathom. Gulping down fits of air, he steps into the flat, round room. The tall ceiling steeps into a shadowed point, making the tower appear endless. The curved walls are the same crude gray stone as the staircase. Tapestries of Yuli-en hang between plain glass windows in a laughable display of worship. Clearly for the rare times his parents visited the tower. On the far wall is a brown wooden door, which Fallon imagines leads to a bedroom. Feet from the door, short steel shelves curve with the tower, holding an assortment of glass vials and jars filled with unnameable things, and what Fallon recognizes as demon teeth. The wooden bowl used to present the Blessing sits alone on a suspended shelf.

Glowing lights hang unattached in a perfect circle around the perimeter of the tower, just where the ceiling starts to slope. They don't allow anything in the room to hide in the dark.

Noting every inch between himself and the only way out, Fallon flattens his back against the wall and slowly moves around the room.

The guards spill in behind him, beside themselves with horror. Their weapons lower, even though the scene should incite furor. The sibyl has yet to acknowledge them. She is still, her golden veil masking whether her eyes track the intrusion.

Fallon, Abner, and the guards move further around the tower until they face the profile of the monster.

"Fallon…" Abner says with an alarming tone.

His foot taps against something hard. Had his eyes not been glued to the demon, he would have noticed the body on the ground.

General Jaits wears his full armor, the golden cape darkened with blood and wrapped around his torso. Exposed muscle stretches over his skull, tears in the pink flesh showing stained bone. His arm has been torn clean off, now a bloody stump. His sword lays beside him, clean as a shined dish, the separated arm still holding the hilt.

Fallon grapples at the wall, his ears ringing like a cathedral bell. He glares at the general's murderer, her arms hanging limp as red mist flows into her veil. Before he can find the strength to speak what he practiced while ascending the stairs, a shock of orange steals his nerve.

Small tufts of hair, the color of tangerines, stick out from between the monster's fingers wrapped around its head. A faint but repellent smell crinkles Fallon's nose: wet leaves covered in a sickly-sweet syrup.

"What have you done to Shavazme?" His bellow fills the tower, spiraling up to the shrouded point.

At first, the sibyl gives no answer. Then she sighs; small flurries of red mist puff from the veil. "I see Wilcon has betrayed me."

"Answer my question," Fallon demands in a shaky voice.

"I assume the advisor has told you who I am," the sibyl replies. Fallon then notices her entire body is slack, as though the beam of mist keeps her upright. "And what will soon come. Should we waste time with long stories?"

Beneath the monster, the white staff glows. The bursts of white light inside turn red, and the two beams of mist thicken in response.

"Is that Istral?" Fallon points at the monster.

"Not quite yet."

"We know what you did to the other sibyls, Leizus" Abner chimes in.

The sibyl tilts her head towards Abner. Just barely. Fallon notes the connection of mist may be delicate.

"And you've come to enact revenge for those cruel, insufferable fools? I would poison their food and slit their throats a thousand times over," she drawls.

Abner was right in their theory. When Fallon had imagined the sibyl's face in the past, his mind drew a beautiful, perfect woman. This time, she is badly scarred across her cheeks and forehead. One eye droops into an upside-down teardrop shape, the point dragged down by a blade. She cries as a robed sibyl carves up from her jaw, as others hold her still.

Fallon feels sorry for her. The way he has felt sorry – and somewhat responsible – for Oly. "Sacrifices," the sibyl called her Champions. As she had been to the sibyls. Did her family give her to the temples willingly? Or, like Oly's parents, did they rejoice as their child was taken away?

He is more vindicated in his plan. The sibyl is a human being, after all, who hurts. As Oly does. As he does. She will want to protect all the lives that have worshipped her. Abner is about to speak more, but Fallon throws his hand out, silencing them. He crosses half the distance between the wall and the sibyl. "We aren't here for the sibyls. I know what they did to you, and I'm sorry. All I care about is the safety of my people. The Day of Breath will end soon. What can be done to rid the kingdom of the parasites and protect us from the demons to come? I'm..." He jumbles his words. "I'm willing to make a deal."

"How easily you turn on Yuli-en. Allowing their shadow to return to the world for your own protection. Humans are impossibly weak," she says with disgust. "But I'm intrigued. What are you offering?"

Abner leans into his ear. "She is much too calm and speaking too freely. I think she's stalling to finish the spell; we need to act now."

As they speak, the beams of mist thicken even more, particles on the edges becoming erratic.

Fallon takes another step. He can't give up now. "Is Istral a merciless god? Can she be trusted to favor Niawa, your home for two decades?"

The sibyl laughs. "I have no home in this world."

Fallon squeezes the bowl until his fingers are sore. He had laid too much of his plan on the sibyl's humanity. "If you don't care about Niawa's fate, then what can I trade for our safety?"

"For your life, and all those you love, don't interrupt the spell," the sibyl states.

Fallon eyes the monster, picturing unspeakable things when it wakes. "And if I don't?"

"Istral will come. But you don't need to fear their wrath, as the god and I will be joined. This demon is a vessel born from the parasite, and soon it will carry our intertwined souls."

"You'll control Istral, then? And keep our lands from dying?" Fallon aches to look back at the guards, hoping he'll see approval. But he can't bring himself to take that chance.

Abner extends their sword. "She's lying, Fallon, and I can't let this happen."

"No!" Fallon yells. He blocks Abner's path to the sibyl and grabs their arms, dropping the bowl. His sibling's face contorts into anger as they try to twist out of Fallon's grasp. The heirs grapple over the sword, spinning in a circle as they push and pull against each other.

By the wall, the guards shuffle around in confusion.

The sibyl laughs again. Then she moans deep and loud.

Fallon and Abner freeze, their arms twisted together. They turn their heads in unison towards the monster. Red light seeps into the staff, filling every white space.

The sibyl's chest suddenly bucks out from her sternum with a loud crack, though her head remains upright. Fallon jolts at the sound and releases the sword. The beam of mist between the sibyl and the monster splits into another stream, connecting to the point of her broken chest.

"I will be a god," she gasps.

The arm curled over the monster's head falls. Its back rolls, legs stretching outward. Its head turns towards the heirs. Black eyes the size of serving platters stare at them, giant red rings glowing in the depths. Flaps of pale flesh move like silk around the eyes. Its mouth runs from one edge of its face to the other. Strips of Shavazme's pale skin stretch over its flat face, as though it wears the general's son in pieces of a horrible mask. His orange hair sprouts out at odd places: from the monster's cheeks, at random spots across its scalp, down the back of its neck.

Fallon's friend is truly dead. The sibyl killed him and the general with no remorse. More sacrifices for selfish gains. Wilcon believes in sacrifice. The sibyls did too. As did his parents, and all of Niawa, as they celebrated the Champions.

And Fallon. Until he met Oly. With scars across her face, her body weakening, she still wanted to be Blessed. Oly could have walked away, let a new Champion be called. She fights in the city's overrun streets now, the Champion until her last breath, because she believes in sacrifice the most.

All for a lie.

One thing Wilcon always said rings truer now than it ever has: Fallon is nothing like Abner. He is like the advisor. Willing to sacrifice more than he ever thought possible for power.

Fallon finally admits to himself that a small but brazen part of him wants this deal to secure the throne. That he would have finally earned it.

Greed allowed Leizus to plant her toxic roots in their kingdom. They must be cut out. Starting with his own soul.

The sibyl's groans deepen to an abnormal pitch. "She is near."

Several guards break and they dash to the staircase. Those who remain press against the wall, visibly shaking as the monster stretches and twists like the air surrounding it is mud.

Fallon picks up the bowl and holds it close, feeling Oly's strength from across the city. There's no time to explain what he means to do. He clears his head of any dissenting thoughts – of the longing for the throne still living deep inside him – and launches forward to rip the staff out from beneath the monster.

The sibyl howls.

The mist between the staff and the monster vanishes. Fallon stumbles backwards into Abner, clutching the glowing red staff.

The remaining beam between the sibyl and the monster becomes volatile, sparking like angry hornets. At the same time, the monster smashes onto the ground, cracking the stone floor. Fractures snake in all directions, one traveling between Fallon's feet to climb the wall behind him.

Screams erupt from the sibyl's veil. Her broken chest protrudes even further, bone tearing through the layers of green fabric. Her head flies violently backwards. The screams heighten as her arms twist, fingers snapping and breaking sideways. The monster slowly rises on all four of its thick arms and legs, its knees angled like a deer's. Massive hands stretch out, tipped with black claws. It levels its blocky head with the sibyl. She tries to turn away as its cavernous mouth opens, but the mist still holds her like a child controlling a doll.

Fallon clasps his hands over his ears just before the monster releases a roar that shakes the tower. It arches its head back on a wide neck and sends another to the ceiling.

Something forces its way out of the skin covering the demon's throat. First, what appears to be a large, glassy red orb, then another digs itself out beside it. Two slits appear beneath them. Then a mouth, bordered by slightly parted violet lips.

Fallon knows that face is Istral. The sibyl has succeeded.

"We have to get out of here," Abner yells. Most of the guards heed the warning and disappear down the stairwell. Only four remain to watch the sibyl rise from the ground. The mist holds her as she shrieks, her feet dangling and twitching.

Istral blots out her cries with another tower-trembling roar from the monster's mouth. Stone falls from the high walls. Fallon lunges at Abner, knocking their sword from their hand. Rocks bounce and roll over the ground where his twin just stood.

The bulbous growths over the monster's back split open, and tendrils the width of a forearm shimmy out. Viscous, dark red muck clots along the tendrils, leaving a trail of sludge as they crawl over Istral's back towards its head.

"Istral," the sibyl whimpers before the tendrils slash out to coil around her body. They yank her upwards and through the air until she slams onto its back.

Abner pulls on Fallon's arm, reminding him they should have run away by now, but he can't look away. The tendrils grow in number, all different widths and lengths. They weave over the sibyl like a quilt. She is quickly submerged under a sticky, living mound. One of her arms sticks out at a gruesome angle. Her head is half-covered, the golden veil still glimmering.

Istral turns sharply, facing Fallon and Abner. From the depths of its throat, more clotted tendrils slither out as the god's red eyes stare, unblinking, its purple lips silent.

Tendrils shoot towards Fallon. He shoves Abner away and throws himself to the side. The tendrils lick the wall before retracting back to the monster's open mouth, where they hover over its teeth in unnervingly smooth waves.

One guard raises his spear and plants his feet. He glances around at his brethren. They don't move. He charges at Istral alone. A tendril splits from the rest and laces around the spear, removing it with ease. He then draws a short sword from his belt and hacks at it, chopping through the tip. A roar sends the guard onto his rear. Before he can stand, tendrils wrap around his feet and drag him towards the monster's mouth. Teeth clamp down on his legs, spraying blood across the floor. Istral lets the guard's torso drop and spits out his legs, flinging them across the room where they crash into the archway.

More tendrils lash out at Fallon. He drops to his stomach, losing his grip on Oly's bowl and the staff. The items skitter in Istral's direction. Something stabs at his hip and he looks down. The General's severed arm is under him – still holding a sword.

"Move!" Abner yells.

Fallon rolls to the side, thinking tendrils are moments from catching him. But they wrap around the staff. It pulses with light like a beacon as it's brought to Istral. Red particles collect along the rod, twisting and funneling through the air until they connect with the demon god's eyes. The vessel she inhabits calms too, just as transfixed. Whatever connection the staff held with Istral still lives. The god desires the energy inside of it.

The staff's glow dims and Fallon catches slivers of white, as if the red light is being drained. He jumps to his feet, raising the general's sword high above his head and cleaves it through several tendrils.

Fallon groans as more tendrils appear to replace the ones squiggling on the ground.

"For Niawa!" a guard shouts. Her call rouses the other two that remain, and they start slashing and stabbing at Istral's stomach three or so feet above their heads. Abner joins Fallon in attacking the tendrils. They make the final cut that releases the staff. Fallon catches it awkwardly as he attempts to keep hold of the heavy sword.

The guards hardly damage Istral, only making shallow lacerations in its thick skin, but it's a needed distraction. He grabs the bowl, then Abner, and races towards the archway.

"Istral is drawn to the staff," Fallon pants.

"Destroy it," Abner responds.

Fallon nods, then faces the wall and rears the staff back. He stops. "I don't know what will happen. Breaking the spell changed everything. I could release the power inside."

Someone screams. Fallon turns just as three thick tendrils crush a guard as though she is made of paper. The last two slash at Istral with everything they have, but it's clear they're driven by unrelenting terror. They don't fight like Oly. She moved as though she knew she was going to win. These guards have accepted they won't leave this tower. For now, they'll do what they can.

Fallon looks at the staff, his thoughts racing. Then he nods. "I'm going to run."

"Absolutely not. We need to stay together," Abner says hastily, syllables mashing together.

"I'll lead Istral out of the palace. Further, if I can. Our family owes this kingdom a sacrifice."

"Yuli-en save us," Abner laments.

Fallon scoffs. "I think we're on our own, here."

Abner's fear-stricken gaze melts into hardness. "Then I'm going after Wilcon. If he knows how the Rive was opened, then he knows what closes it."

The twin's eyes hold each other for a long second. More words than Fallon can sift through hang between them. How could he begin to make amends after everything he's done? He hopes it isn't too late. He hopes he gets the chance to truly make things right.

Abner runs, leaving Fallon to face Istral. The last guard fights with every ounce of their strength and only succeeds in annoying the god. Fallon waits as long as he can, maybe a few minutes, to give Abner time to leave the tower. He releases the sword and presses the bowl to his chest. With the other hand, Fallon raises the staff over his head. He has never been more terrified in his life and already wishes Abner was still here. "Istral!"

The demon god stills, allowing the last guard's lifeless body to fall from its mouth. The tendrils flick in anticipation.

Fallon bolts down the staircase.

He hears calamity, destruction. Stone breaks, cracking against more stone. Dust rains over his head and down his back. Sharp pebbles trickle beneath his clothing, but he doesn't look back. He leaps down the steps, several at a time, even as the tower trembles. Never has he felt so appreciative for flat ground when he reaches the black door, still wide open.

He allows himself one glance upwards.

Istral's grotesque vessel smashes into the tower's column in a mad rush to get to him, moonlight slipping through the new holes. The demon god's red eyes gleam in the soft rays.

Fallon takes off down the hall. Halfway, a harrowing boom has him looking back once more. Istral rams through the stone around the door as if the rock is made of parchment. The black door falls, heavy iron against the tile floor, a halo of gray stone around it. The god bursts through a cloud of dust, its vessel roaring with triumph.

Fallon catches the red rings before breaking into a full sprint. The rings burn into his vision as if he stared at the sun. He chases them down the corridor until they grow faint.

CHAPTER 24

In the short time we were in the cul-de-sac, demons took over the main road. The people around me sway and shove and push against each other, trying to hold formation and fight.

"They're going to the palace!" someone shouts.

Against my body's needs, I jump twice to look over the surrounding heads. Demons stream from every side street. The ones who don't spot our group are heading straight up the road towards the white towers.

Everyone to my right lurches. Mother screams and tries to run but I grab her arm. Her glare barely has time to land before demons break through the outside ranks. Denya's arm wraps tighter around my waist as she stabs her sword through one's bloody, exposed ribs. She kicks it down, nearly taking us both with it. Our armored bodies make it difficult to keep me cinched to her.

Two more demons tear into the man with the rolling pin behind me. Another lunges at mother. A spiked spear tip bursts through its forehead, covering mother in yellow-gray-red blood.

Velma yanks her spear free. "You," she points to her. "Push this chair and you'll survive."

Mother hesitates, looking around for what I imagine is a more formidable protector. Her eyes never land on me. Everyone fights for their own life, our troop becoming fragmented across the road. With no other choice, Mother grabs the handles on either side of Velma's chair and pushes.

Ahead, Captain Tatum shouts. "Forward!"

As Denya and I stagger on, I see why we can't cut down a side street. There are none empty of demons, ahead nor behind. The palace attracts them in droves, as if they're being called. I can only conclude one reason. Istral has been summoned.

"We can't go the palace," I say to Denya.

She slashes wildly across a demon's neck. Once a young boy with messy brown hair and dark freckles. No time to crush his skull, we move on. "There's no other direction."

She's right. We're trapped. Fighting through another half mile only to reach a darker end. And there's nothing I can do but hold onto her body and slow her down.

Denya spins us to swing her elbow across a demon's face. Then back around to thrust her sword into another's stomach. She grunts with exhaustion as my axe lays pointless across my back.

"Leave me here," I insist. It's her best chance to live.

She doesn't hear me. Or chooses not to listen. Cheers rise up from ahead. The sound is so strange it makes my heart pound. Denya rises onto her toes to see. When she lowers back down, a smile dares to adorn her face.

A wave of silver, green, and gold crashes into the street. What must be thousands of guards and citizens fight through the demons clogging the side streets. Those who boarded up their windows and hid or tried to run. Guards who refused to help, immobilized by their own fear. They don't know that it's still not enough for what's coming.

But Denya lets out a howl of faith, even sheathing her sword to secure me. We quicken our pace to a slow run, soon catching up with Velma and mother. Demons lie dead around us, eyes solidly black. Red mist rises in thin strands like streamers. With the calvary as a distraction, we make it to the edge of the palace courtyard.

The circle is an impossible tangle of demons and humans. For every guard or citizen, there are three creatures hungry to spread their kind. Red blood spurts across silver armor. Voices are only just louder than a chorus of deep moans. Some demons have long outgrown their human shells, backs hulking, limbs stretched and sinewy.

Captain Tatum finds us at the precipice. He opens his mouth to speak, but a long-mutated demon springs from the mess of bodies and drags him into the war. A group of citizens jump into action, following the sounds of his armor scraping on the cobblestone.

I watch Denya's short-lived hope disappear. She looks nervously around until she points to a house at the junction of the road and the circle. "Shelter."

Velma immediately spins her chair around, yanking it from mother's hands and pushes towards the house. Denya is forced to hold me and steer my petrified mother along Velma's path.

Though the house is only thirty or so feet away, the battle already swallows us.

Bodies collide into ours, both demon and human. We try to skirt around them, dodging blades and swinging claws, only to nearly crash into another fight. I try to keep up, the strains in my legs locking my hips. Then my left knee buckles. Denya crumbles to the ground with me.

She jumps up first, then tries to help me.

I plant my hands into the cobblestone. "Leave me."

Denya scowls. "Shut up."

Someone grabs my injured arm and I whine in pain, tightening it to my side. I look up to see mother slip her arm under mine. With her help, I'm set back on my feet. Just in time for a demon spot us and come with its teeth bared. Denya unsheathes one of her swords, readying herself.

A broadsword spears through the demon's neck and it falls, head cracking at our feet. The guard behind it barely acknowledges us before turning swiftly towards another creature whose claws slash at her face. Denya and Mother haul me away before I can see if she survived.

Ahead, Velma pulls her spear from the chest of a demon, just outside the house. "Hurry like you want to live!"

Thunder claps overhead. I look to the sky, expecting droplets of rain. Another crack brings my attention to the palace. The emerald turret of the sibyl's tower breaks from the column and slides off. Thick clouds of dust billow up, cloaking the crumbling column as if to protect its dignity.

All heads, human and demon, turn towards the noise as if time stops.

"Have you done it, Fallon?" I ask the cloudy space where the tower used to be. My breath catches, waiting for the demons to fall and red mist to blot out the sky.

It doesn't happen.

The rift in time ends as quickly as it came. Unlike the guards and citizens, the demons are less transfixed by the falling tower. They take advantage of the distraction. All around us, silver helmets and human faces drown beneath pale bodies.

"Almost there. Don't give up." Denya tows me against my depleted will to the doorsteps.

She leaves me to slump onto mother. Her smaller form almost caves, but she manages to stay upright. Denya runs up the short steps to the door and turns the handle. It's unlocked. She pushes it open, then comes to help mother bring me into the house. Finally, she lifts Velma from her chair and carries her up the steps, setting her on a plush armchair. Velma's chair is brought in last before Denya shuts the door and I hear the lock click into place.

There's no sound other than Denya's heavy pants and the skirmish outside. The house is empty.

I sag into another armchair across from Velma. Red candles with long wicks flicker around the room, illuminating a couch, small tables, and bookshelves crammed into a large sitting room.

Mother leans against a bookshelf, her head just below a family portrait framed in stylishly patinaed metal. Denya paces. From the door to the back wall of the sitting room to a window facing the palace, then back to the door.

"I won't see the sun again," I voice.

Denya shoots me a dark look. She goes to the window and gently pushes the curtains aside. What she sees makes her look away quickly. "You don't know that."

"The sibyl's tower fell, and the demons are still here. Which means..." I realize Fallon may have been in the tower. He must be dead. I frown, grateful for the dim candlelight. Tears don't come, but my fingers dig painfully into the couch arms. I hardly knew the heir, with his sparkling eyes and bright smile – that pungent scent I remember from the Edge. But I feel myself mourning. Not just him, but the faint dream of a different end. One where he vanquishes the sibyl and closes the Rive. Without the portal, the Edge is just a cabin in a field. What could my life have been, living in the quiet until my body withered naturally. Perhaps Fallon would have visited from time to time. And Denya, too. We could have walked to the cliff edge, where the Rive once cleaved through the sky, and see nothing but the brilliant ocean.

"Oly?" Denya says from beyond my thoughts. She's lowered to one knee by the chair and takes off her helmet. "I'm going back out there."

"You'll die," I respond too quickly. Worry crawls around my stomach like ants as I push myself to sit up against the chair's back.

Denya chews on her lip. Then she says, "I have to help. I recognized so many faces fighting for Niawa. And… I'm the reason this all began." Guilt clouds her eyes. A lock of black hair falls from behind her ear, and she tucks it back.

"That's not true. The parasite found its way out of the Rive. We didn't know what could happen."

Denya nods, but I can tell she doesn't accept what I said. "This is my choice."

The sounds of war seep through the walls and the windows. We fall into quiet, listening to the truth they bring: Niawa will lose.

Denya pulls her helmet back on and stands. She holds out her hand to me. I look away at first, a swarm of uncomfortable, nagging feelings keeping my head turned. I hadn't even wanted her here, and now I wish I could keep her in the house. The humming brutalizes my insides, but I clasp her hand in mine. She firms her grip, and I squeeze weakly back.

"Alright, then," Denya says with a small laugh. She walks to the door and her hand rests on the lock. "It truly was an honor fighting with you, Champion. Liam would be so envious." The lock slides and she is about to turn the doorknob.

"Denya." I struggle to stand. She crosses back to me, ready to help. I stop her with a shake of my head while I lean on the arm of the chair. "Take my axe." I turn so my back faces her. Denya cautiously pulls the weapon from its straps.

"Heavy," she murmurs. She holds it unskillfully, trying to understand its weight.

"Hold it closer to the blades. And take this, too." I unbuckle the belt around my waist that holds my medicines and the magic spheres. "There's an ice bomb, two fire bombs, and one holy flare left."

Denya leans my axe against the chair to take the belt, her eyes widening. She loops it around her waist, then returns the axe to her hands. Watching her look between the weapon and the belt with unease, I wonder about giving her my armor. The thought is quickly hushed away. Without it, I'm no better than a newborn alone in the depths of the woods. I'm not ready to watch the last part of my title walk away on someone else's body.

"Thank you, Oly. I'll make good use of these," Denya says. She returns to the door and leaves, slamming it shut behind her.

I flop back into the chair, this time resting my elbows on my knees. Mother takes a few steps forward, stops, shuffles a few more over, then finally lowers in a third chair next to Velma. We don't speak while I strain to hear Denya's cries amidst the battle. It fills me with dread, but it's better than listening to mother sniffle and huff every few minutes.

"Keane always wanted a sitting area like this. Enough room for his books and trinkets from the market. There was always another miniature music instrument to collect. Now he's gone," she whimpers.

I tense, knowing more is coming.

"One of those *things* got into the house," mother continues. "I'd left the door ajar by accident. The closest weapon was a steel cooking pot. He used it to save me. Forced the demon into the street as it clawed at his arms and chest. Then you showed up, moments too late."

"I came as soon as I could," I lie.

She rubs her hands together in her lap. "Is it because you're injured that he died?"

"I'd like you to close your lips. You'd be dead or worse if Oly hadn't come at all," Velma gripes.

Mother flinches like the courier slapped her.

"Where are the sovereigns? The sibyl? Why aren't you fighting?" she spurts out, unable to contain herself.

I tap the ends of the chair arms, mulling over how much to reveal. Mother has never handled stressful news well. Hatred fights its way through my veins, towards the same heart that wanted to rescue her and father. She stares me down with my own dark-brown, almond-shaped eyes, a pinch growing above my own brown and pink lips at my silence.

"Dear, just say the word." Velma lifts her spear and points it towards mother. I know Velma isn't serious, but mother gasps and angles herself away.

A loud bang slams against the side of the house by the window. We all inhale sharply, waiting for the glass pane to shatter. A low moan sounds, then drifts off.

But soon the window will break. The door will burst. This isn't safety. This is the cabin at the Edge. Safety is an illusion, and the demons will come. What use is it to hold every shame and secret on my own anymore? Maybe I can die a little lighter. So, I tell them everything. From the first day I noticed my strength receding to hearing of the sibyl's deceit. When I finish, I sigh deeply. Nothing feels different. My muscles still ache over a hollow shell.

Mother wipes her puffy eyes on her sleeve, already crusted with grime. "You should have told the sovereigns about the Blessing sooner. How could you have waited so long?"

"I don't know," I admit.

"Maybe if you had, Keane–"

"I'm sorry!" I shout through the humming and the crumbling world outside. Mother's eyes flick nervously to the window. "I'm sorry I couldn't save him; I tried. I did everything I could. I didn't know this would happen. I –" My breath becomes shallow, the room beginning to spin. I press my hand to my chest, looking for my skin, but only finding armor.

"You still have these fits," mother mutters.

I had thrown my head back, hoping to open my throat, but now I snap it back down, anger burning in my eyes. Mother clutches her arms to her chest, as if protecting herself. She can see my rage, feel it making her smaller as she presses into the chair. The ghost of my power possesses me, and I welcome it like an old friend. I push to my feet and take two steps towards her.

Mother shudders while curling into herself.

"Oly, now, hold on..." Velma cautions.

I stop halfway. Mother is trembling, scared, wracked with fear. Expecting to be struck, or grabbed, or cursed at. She's never looked so feeble before. She looks like Hush.

The ghost leaves me. I imagine it rising like the red mist.

"I'm not going to belittle you. Or send you away. I wouldn't do that." The words I don't say still make themselves known by my glare: I wouldn't do what she's done to me.

Mother unfurls from herself, her nostrils flaring. "Keane and I thought we were helping by sending you to the academy.

We just wanted you to get stronger, and we didn't know how to do it ourselves."

"You made me weaker. Sometimes, it felt like you preferred me that way. I had no one at the academy. It wasn't until the Blessing that I ever felt like anything but a burden."

She stops looking me in the eye, and I see the guilt she refuses to express. "We didn't know."

"Yes. You did," I say, defiantly.

To my surprise, the humming pulls back like a tide, and I can breathe again. Velma awards me with a proud smile and a wink.

"My chair," she suddenly says. "I heard something." I leave mother to her sulking and wheel Velma's chair towards her.

We go to the window and she pulls back the curtains. "The palace doors are opening."

The tapestry of my face slowly splits apart. When the opening is wide enough, Fallon sprints through and down the front steps. He pauses on the last few, just above the battle, holding something in his hands that resembles a red stick. And my bowl.

My heart flutters. "He's alive."

Fallon looks from the battle on the other side of the black gates and back to the palace doors several times. Guards finish pushing open the doors then scatter, some going inside the palace, but most race down the steps. I can't imagine what scares them so much they head towards the fight.

I don't have to wonder long.

A monstrosity crashes through the doorway. Bigger than a Gargantuan, with the flat face of a Burrower. Its arms and legs are tall and thick, roped with muscles. Gray, pale, and violet skin covers it in patches, as if it were cobbled together from several horrors. From what I can see of the monster's back, a dark shell covers it. Pale stretched skin sticks to its face among tufts of bright orange hair, like a mask.

Protruding from the demon's broad throat, another face stares blankly ahead with eyes as red as fresh blood.

CHAPTER 25

Istral is here.

I try to keep the shudder up my back from showing, but Velma still reaches out to grab my arm. The god opens its mouth wide and roars, dark tendrils protruding from its gullet. A wave of helmets turn in the battle, bodies freeze mid-swing.

"Oly, what is that?" Velma asks.

Mother joins us at the window and screams. She runs back to her chair, choking on air.

"Istral. The sibyl succeeded," I respond in a monotone voice. I've gone numb. From fear, or acceptance of my death, I'm not sure. I search the palace steps for the red flash in Fallon's hands, hoping it reappears, but he's lost among guards surrounding the black gates. The gates are pushed open into the battle, clearing a small space. Fallon runs into it, holding the red thing above his head. Guards quickly rally around him, keeping demons away. That won't last long.

I press my forehead to the glass, trying not to fog it. Fallon moves further into the fray as Istral stomps after him, but the god is hindered by the battle at its feet. The tendrils begin to toss bodies aside with ease, demon and human alike.

I can't watch anymore. Unable to help. Barely able to stand.

Letting the drapes fall into place, I leave the window and return to the chair. Mother shivers at the far side of the sitting room while Velma keeps watch.

Seconds later she cheers. "Atta girl!"

My body protests sharply with how fast I return to the window.

Istral towers over the war. Its tendrils thrash at a brave group of guards bunched at its feet. One slices long gashes across the god's legs with a double-headed axe. I lay my forearms on the window as if it could get me closer to Denya. She fights impressively, wielding my axe as I told her. Istral roars as Denya drives my weapon into another leg. I smile even as my fists squeeze the blood from my fingers.

"Watch out!" I yell. Two tendrils snake up behind Denya and wrap around her waist. They hoist her up as she struggles, my axe falling to the ground. She's brought dangerously close to the god's open mouth.

A flash of blue bursts out. When it dissipates, I recognize the cloud of twinkling dust hovering over the Istral's head. An ice bomb. The god's left eye is entirely frozen over. It screeches, lifting one thick arm to claw at the ruined flesh, raking strips of skin clean off. What's left is a dark, bloody pit missing a red ring, and half of the pale mask hanging in peels.

My chest swells with pride – and distress so twisting it makes me sick.

Another tendril sneaks up to wrap around Denya's torso. Then another. She keeps flailing, but only her head and feet move.

"No," I exhale.

Denya's head and torso disappear down Istral's throat. Long, sharp teeth spear through her armor. She stops moving.

Velma shrouds a cry with her veined hands.

Sound becomes dull pulses in my ears. The battle is a blur of shapes that slow as my sight tapers to a needle point.

When the god's mouth opens again, the upper half of Denya's body falls out. The tendrils release her legs. She disappears among the mass below.

Istral's rampage heightens. It doesn't stop to reflect on whose life it took.

I totter backwards until my legs hit the chair. My sternum has split open and all the warmth in my body flees from the rupture. Denya's face blights my vision. Determined, when she pledged herself to help me. Proud, when I handed her my axe. Kind, when she gave me comfort in front of the pink house.

I thought I knew pain. Better than anyone born before me and anyone who would come after. I never even scratched the surface.

I wipe the tears from my cheeks so harshly my skin burns as I stomp across the sitting space. Nothing I need is in here. There's another connecting room, so I go there. It's a kitchen. Exactly where the knives should be.

Mother races in after me. "What's happening?"

I set my sights on drawers beneath the marble countertop. The first I pull so hard the drawer flies out. Spoons and forks clatter against the floor. The second drawer nearly receives the same fate, but at the last second, I find them. Two cooking knives with short, wooden handles and broad metal blades with keen edges.

"Where are you going?" Mother follows me back to the sitting room. She grabs my arm.

I spin around and she backs away.

Velma moves in front of the doorway, blocking me. Her eyes shimmer with wetness. "I know I can't stop you, but Denya wouldn't want you to do this. She wanted you safe."

Denya is dead. Fallon may be next. Niawa will follow. I won't spend the last hours of my life watching Istral slaughter everyone in her path. When I die, I'll bring that abomination with me.

"If this is my last fight, then let it be against a god," I say. Velma sighs, then rolls out of the way. I open the door.

"Hush, *please*," mother pleads.

I turn my head, the battle raging before me and mother's glassy eyes pinned on the exposed bloodshed. "I hate that name."

I shut the door and walk down the steps.

A demon to my left stalks towards me with ravenous hunger.

CHAPTER 26

Abner knows exactly where Wilcon is. The old man's arrogance has always been his flaw. He fancies himself the only one paying attention. As Wilcon watched the royal family, weaving his lies and pulling strings, Abner watched him. The most precious of the advisor's riches aren't kept in the palace's coffers, but in his quarters. His obsession with power would not allow him to leave that behind.

Abner walks the painfully familiar path to Wilcon's wing of the palace, one they took nearly every day before the advisor turned on them. Even back then, they knew it was deliberate. A message. Ask no more questions or suffer grave consequences.

Once, the advisor saw Abner's inwardness as an asset. He assured them introspection was more important than a flashy demeanor. Fallon had always been treated like light itself, but with Wilcon, Abner was soil. They needed that.

Wilcon's tactic of spinning insecurity into genius worked on both twins. Pushing them until they were at each other's throat to make him proud. As Abner turns into a long corridor cutting from the west wing of the palace to the east, they admit they never truly shook the need to make Wilcon proud. But Abner has had years to cage their dependency and tame it into submission. They glance down at their sword. Fallon would not be able to do what's necessary and live with himself.

The long corridor leads Abner to an ascending staircase. Halfway up, the floor trembles, following a loud boom. They leap up the steps to the nearest window. Large plumes of dust cloak the outside world. The tower has fallen. Abner takes a minute to pray Fallon has made it out alive, then continues with only that truth in mind.

Abner soon reaches a short corridor with tall, vaulted ceilings. Paintings hang on both sides, leading to a set of white-painted doors flung wide open. They eye the artwork as they hurry. Depictions of Yuli-en in the sky overlooking Niawa, the god's face beaming with pride; the royal family's crest in thread; a painting of Perrin the Dawn. Hilarious. Wilcon truly sold his devotion like the dramatic lead of a play. He draped himself in righteousness so brilliant it blinded anyone who dared to look closer.

Abner hardens their bearings before stepping into Wilcon's expansive welcoming room. Large, velvet couches of emerald and off-white fill most of the space, with cherry wood tables placed in front of each. Moonlight from the many windows shines over the floors and melts into the upholstery.

After long hours of schooling with tutors, the real lessons began here. Wilcon would share the fraught histories between nations. Gossip that toppled empires. Shady dealings that built others. He taught Abner how people truly think, how to persuade them, and the costs of power. Most importantly, he made sure Abner knew they could only rely on him to navigate those troubling waters.

Several halls run from the welcome area, and Abner takes the one leading to Wilcon's study. His recordings and documents are there, but so is his private safe. Jewels, gold bars, coins, notes, proof of landownership, everything he would need to disappear into the night.

Scuffling, like a rodent sifting through debris, grows louder as Abner approaches. Wilcon's curved back faces the open door. He hunches over the wrought-iron chest in the corner. When Abner steps out of the hallway into the well-lit room, he straightens. Abner brings the sword into both hands and points the end at the advisor.

Wilcon turns around. The two stare each other down for what feels an eternity.

Always be the first to speak. Command the room, drive the conversation, he once taught Abner.

"So Leizus failed," Wilcon says.

"To control Istral, yes. But the god has been released," they respond.

"You must feel vindicated, Heir Abner. Knowing the delusions in your notebook are not delusions after all." He sneers. Necklaces and bangles – rose pearl, ruby bracelets, onyx chokers encrusted in diamond and silver – hang from his brown-spotted fingers. At his feet is a black leather bag.

"Quite."

"Ah." Wilcon drops the jewelry into the bag. He glances at a bronze clock sitting on a desk to his right, and Abner does the same. Two hours left until midnight. "It amounts to nothing. We may all die. Had you kept your mouth shut, this could have been a different day. I was right to pivot my interest to your brother."

Wilcon returns his attention to the safe. He thinks he's landed a devastating blow, bested Abner into a shameful retreat.

When facing your allies, and especially your enemies, never show your hurt. Acknowledge faults, nod your head at suggested improvements, but never let them know blood can be drawn.

Abner steps forward, extending their blade. "Do I look like Fallon to you? Jabs at my ego won't work. I don't care where you go, or what you do, but you *will* tell me how to close the Rive."

Wilcon once again faces Abner with a quirked eyebrow. The corners of his mouth fall slightly. He presses the tips of his fingers together. A display that means he's got more threats to make.

"As you've seen, I'm not as frail as I appear. It would be too easy to snap your neck where you stand," he states.

Abner's nerves rattle, but they're equally pleased the advisor resorts to intimidation. He's nervous.

They bring the blade to eye level and twist it. "You are not leaving this room without giving me what I came for."

Wilcon's frown deepens. His gaze trails about the study, seeming to catch here and there but never lingering for long. Abner wonders if he thinks of what he's lost aligning himself with the sorceress.

"Do you want to see the walls of this palace, your home, dirtied and covered in unkempt weeds that break through cracks in the marble? Blood stained into the whites of the tile? The throne room chairs toppled over and scarred?" Abner presses. "If the Rive opens, demons will lay waste to this world. Not even your Blessed strength will spare you."

Wilcon's fingers whiten at the tips. His expression hardens, but Abner can see the fissures in his armor. They realize he doesn't care about this kingdom, or its people. This coward only fears death.

"The sibyl can no longer protect you. Istral took her." Abner takes a step forward. "Demons will come into your quarters, find you among your trinkets," another step, "and rip your head from your shoulders."

Wilcon's hands fall to his side. His face betrays a ferment of emotions, each one as fleeting as the last. Finally, he rests on fatigue, revealing himself a worn old man.

"Leizus' greed has ruined everything. Drawing out Istral

would have taken many more years if that primordial demon hadn't come. I tried to convince her otherwise. Tried to tell her no one can control a god."

"And what of *your* greed? You allowed this, helped it along, for your own selfish needs." Abner refuses to let the advisor think he holds no blame. "Was an elongated life worth countless Champions, and the awakening of Istral?"

Wilcon's eyes sharpen. "Yes. Niawa would collapse without me."

Abner is saddened to find they don't disagree. They think back to the throne room, when the sovereigns were faced with the demons and the sibyl's true nature. Their heart broke watching their parents waver because Wilcon couldn't tell them what to do and how to think.

"You will never poison my family again," Abner growls. "Tell me how to close the Rive."

Wilcon tilts his chin up. "I won't spend the rest of my days becoming weaker until I'm forgotten bones in a dungeon cell."

"Suit yourself."

Abner thrusts their sword at his neck, close enough to shock but not puncture his skin. With speed they had forgotten to account for, Wilcon grabs the steel with his bare hands. Abner grunts as they are spun to the side. The advisor's strength is overwhelming, turning Abner with the sword, nearly knocking them off balance.

Blood stains the cream carpet below. Wilcon's hands tremble, sending vibrations down the blade. He may be strong, but he still experiences pain.

Abner lets go of the hilt with one hand and lands a punch into the advisor's stomach. Wilcon bends forward, his grip loosening on the blade. Not wasting the opportunity, Abner slides the blade away, then thrusts it into Wilcon's gut halfway to the hilt.

The old man gurgles, eyes so wide the whites overpower his inky irises. His blood-soaked hands come up to the embedded blade, but he can't grasp it. Abner steps back, shaking with him. He had left them no choice.

Wilcon drops to his knees, the pointed end of the blade screeching against the safe. His gaze brims with fury. Dark blood spreads from the wound, soaking the front of his emerald robe.

Abner crouches so they are eye level. With a composure he had learned from mimicking Wilcon's famous calm, they say, "Assuming your Blessing gave you the same healing abilities as the Champions, you're toeing a very thin line between life and death."

Wilcon coughs foamy pink blood over his lips.

"If you don't help me, I'll spend what little time I have left twisting this blade over and over until demons devour us both. You will not die in comfort and peace. You will die in unimaginable agony."

Wilcon falls onto his side. He tries to grab the hilt, but Abner gets to it first. They make good on their promise and twist the blade. His scream pulsates through the room, but Abner holds steady, even as a wave of nausea threatens to subdue them.

"Tell me what to do, and I will leave with my sword, allowing you to heal. You can run away with your tail between your legs, never to be heard from again."

They squeeze the hilt enough that Wilcon feels it. He clenches in anticipation. Then, his blood-coated lips part.

"In the safe," he croaks. "Scroll."

Carefully, Abner reaches over Wilcon into the safe. What's left inside are stacks of pouches they imagine hold coins and bundles of notes. They move the pouches around, searching for parchment, never taking their other hand off the sword. Their fingers brush over what feels like rolled up paper, and

Abner pulls out thin parchment held with a strip of cracked leather. The paper is as yellowed and browned as the oldest tomes in the libraries.

They show it to Wilcon. He nods, grinding his head into the carpet with misery.

For good measure, and because their questions are not yet over, Abner twists the blade again before using both hands to open the scroll.

It unfurls to reveal small and faint writing. Abner recognizes a drawing at the top as the insignia of the Veins of Istral, the same one burned into the floor at the Southern Temples.

"What does this mean?" they demand. The language is ancient. A bastardized dialect of Yuli-en's tongue, only distinguishable by minor changes in symbols and consonants. Abner is only vaguely versed in the language, so the changes strain their understanding.

"Recite," Wilcon says weakly.

Abner flicks their eyes up to the clock, then back to the scroll.

"I can't read this. Not entirely." They shoot to their feet and cross to Wilcon's desk, quickly uncorking an ink bottle that splashes black liquid over the wood. Then they dab a pen in the bottle and bring the scroll and pen back to Wilcon. "Transcribe it."

Wilcon attempts to grab onto the hilt once more. Abner reaches for it too, and his hand drops immediately.

"No, no," the advisor huffs. He licks his lips, then begins.

The transcription comes much slower than Abner likes, but eventually they arrive at the last word. The clock tells them twenty minutes have been lost. It'll take Abner just as long to reach the palace's front entrance. Wilcon curls within a pool of his blood as Abner's pumps hot and fast into their temples. There's no time to make sure he hasn't misled them.

Abner lays the scroll down to dry and looks upon the revered advisor to two generations of sovereigns. Their once-treasured mentor. He doesn't deserve it, but Abner is not a murderer. Or a liar. They pull the sword from Wilcon's gut. He cries out, eyelids fluttering.

"Am I right in thinking this will also stop the infestation?"

Wilcon nods weakly. "Demons cannot… exist in this world… without the Rive. Their lives are… linked."

The ink on the scroll is not entirely dry, but it's good enough. Abner rolls it back up and stands.

Words evade them, but they want the advisor to know the irreparable hurt he has caused to their family, their kingdom – to them. They want Wilcon to *feel* it.

Your enemies don't care for your feelings, Heir Abner. They don't speak that language. They want to conquer you, and they will leverage your hopes to do it. Do not expose your neck to the blade, Wilcon once instructed.

Abner tucks the scroll into their pocket, retrieves the sword, and leaves.

CHAPTER 27

My damn shoulder won't let my arm rise higher than parallel to the ground. I discover this too late when the demon's teeth latch onto a pauldron from the front. If I had a longer weapon, I could stab its head from a lower angle. But I have two kitchen knives, and my body refuses to cooperate with my mind. Every movement is stopped short by a flash of sharp pain. If not for my armor, I would already be shredded to pieces. The demon lays its weight on me and my legs surrender. I let it follow me to the ground. In the last second, I bring a knife to my chest, blade out. The demon lands on it with a thud. Warm blood leaks over my cuirass as the creature's life fades into the air.

After shoving it off, I climb to my feet, huffing like I sprinted across the Edge. I can't count on every demon to stab itself in the heart.

"Low strikes. Only fight the more human ones."

Three long strides, and I break into the war.

Too many sounds. Too many limbs flying in all directions. Blades and claws swinging, clashing. A pale, snarling face launches at me, but in a flash, a citizen rams herself into it. I push on, leading with my shoulders.

Blood spurts across my face, coloring the world red. I wipe it away frantically to be met by two red rings. I slash at the demon's gut, leaving a gash it barely reacts to. Its teeth come for my neck, and I throw my arm up to block. It tosses its head to the right, spinning me off balance. My cheek grinds into globs of wet, dark liquid on the ground. I flip onto my back and kick out my legs, catching the demon in the chest. But my knees twinge, and my legs bend.

It lowers, a long drop of spit hanging from its fangs.

I let the drool get far too close to my helmet before remembering Captain Tatum, his guards, and the citizens swinging household items like swords. I don't need to do this alone. "Help!"

The demon lurches backwards. Two guards hold its shoulders while another's arms are around its waist. A fourth plunges his halberd into its chest. He slides his weapon back out then extends his hand to me.

"Champion," he says with a weary voice, his tabard soaked in blood.

"I need to get to Ist – the big one." They may still fight for the sibyl; I can't shake their hope now.

He looks towards Istral slowly making its way across the circle. It swings its head from side to side, still searching for whatever it's after. From the way it tore after him, I've got a sneaking suspicion it seeks Fallon.

The guard frowns. This morning, he wouldn't have questioned me. Would have fallen on his own blade before denying me. Now I'm a distraction, another thing to protect when his own life could be taken in the blink of an eye.

He looks me over: my hunched form and shaking legs, the two cooking knives. But he makes the order. "Border the Champion. We're taking her to the beast."

Guards rush to lock me into a claustrophobic hold. A few citizens who heard the call join as well, ready to clear a path. The box of armored bodies begins to move. I remember the procession leading me to the courier's cart ten years ago. I was sure then, as I am now: I'm being escorted to my death.

Dead bodies impede our way, more human than demon. I step over torsos bitten in two, legs crushed and broken. The border of guards is forced to nudge or kick the bodies aside like debris.

Istral soon rises above my head, veins running in bulging lines over its thick arms and legs.

A lump grows in my throat seeing the face embedded in its neck more clearly. The ruby eyes stare at nothing. Its slightly parted lips emit no sound. It's the monster's eyes that truly see everything, and one was destroyed by Denya. She brilliantly left a blind spot by its right leg.

The guards open around me like a doorway to hell.

"Thank you," I say. They dive back into the fight, the time for pleasantries long over.

Guards and citizens dart around Istral's legs, ducking under its tall stomach and dodging the tendrils. I don't have time to warn a woman only donning a helmet and breastplate is crumpled under Istral's hand.

Limping, I make it to the blind spot. The flesh of Istral's leg has been slashed to ribbons, but the muscle and bone look far too strong for normal steel. These knives may as well be pillows.

"Shit."

I look past Istral to its trail of demise. A small field of silver, green, and gold. Dresses and soft-looking pants. Patterned blouses. I traipse through the graveyard, scouring for my uniquely designed belt, or my axe. I spot the bulbous pouches of my belt far too quickly.

It's still looped around the lower half of Denya's body, her upper half lying feet away. Her helm has been knocked off, allowing her face to thoughtlessly behold the sky. My axe peeks out beneath her head.

"I'll make this right, I promise," I whisper, placing the knives on the ground, then wrench the belt down her legs. The leather is soaked through with her blood. I fumble buckling it to my waist, and even more when I move her aside to free my axe.

Denya's head turns towards me.

Startled, I reach for her face, my fingers hovering above her skin. She doesn't blink, but her cheek is still warm and pink. I lean closer, waiting, hoping, for another sign of life.

Denya bucks up, her bare forehead knocking into my helmet. I yelp and back up on all fours. Her upper half continues to rise, until she falls flat on her face. A demon emerges from beneath her, pushing itself off the ground.

Rage captures me swiftly, towing a profound sadness. It eats away at the humming like acid, leaving behind a rotten chasm. I had truly hoped.

I grab one of the kitchen knives and slam the blade through its neck. The creature's head rolls away.

Trying to steady my heart, I grab at my axe and pull it close. Denya remains face down in the muck. Her black braid lays across her back, frayed and sticky. She is dead. And I have work to do.

Using my axe as an aid, I rise. Each step is painstaking as I race back to Istral, dragging my axe with both hands. Swinging it with precision will decimate my exhausted arms, so I'll have to use every part of me. I come upon Istral's back leg. Focusing, I plant my feet, tighten my fingers around the staff's end, and throw my body in a circle. The blades fly through the air until slicing through my target.

Istral lets out its most piercing roar. The deep gash reveals gray muscle before a torrent of yellow-gray blood obscures it. Through a wave of dizziness, I catch the blackened side of the monster's face arching to look back. Knowing the tendrils will soon come to investigate what it can't see, I spin again, slashing into the same spot. This time I hit something hard, like bone. The leg bends, and Istral tilts.

Several guards who were hopelessly hacking at its arms run towards me.

"Tendrils," one yells. They scatter, but another doesn't move fast enough and is thrown clear across the battle.

I prepare myself to spin again, but Istral lifts its injured leg. Before it comes down, I roll away. By the time I'm standing again, my body weeping, Istral's remaining red ring faces me.

Tendrils shoot forth. Instincts that don't know any better ignite, and I raise the axe, but my shoulder disagrees. I watch helplessly as they come. Then they stop, inches away. Guards strike at the injured leg furiously, splitting the wound further.

I don't wait for Istral to react. I dash to the arm on the same side as its blind spot, and spin into another slash. Before the head rush vanishes, I twirl again, the circle courtyard a blur of death and despair. A third spin is not immediately in me, and I sway forward and back, waiting for clarity to return.

Gravity gives out, and I'm looking at the sky. Then the palace behind me, upside down. I crank my head up. Tendrils wrap around my waist, with more slinking over my legs. My neck tires and I hang it back down to watch the battle move farther away as the tendrils lift me higher.

My axe starts slipping from my hands, so I hold it to my chest.

Blood rushes to my head, pulsing in my ears.

Suddenly, the ground races towards me at an odd angle, as if Istral also fights gravity. The god roars again. Though it makes me ill, I angle my head to look below. More guards and citizens hack at the deep wounds. Istral sinks, its clawed hands carving into the ground to keep it steady.

If it falls while I'm in its grasp, I'll surely land on my skull. I try to wriggle my hips, but I'm held tight. I slacken, too tired to keep my torso stiff and focus on keeping my axe tight against me as the god's head swings to and fro, its attention torn between me and the attacks.

My head grows fuzzier. Vomit collects in the base of my throat. I cough, trying to clear it. Istral roars, and a burst of hot air whistles between my armor plates. Moisture beads over my face and shoulders. God above, it's pulling me into its mouth. I attempt to curl my torso towards my feet, but flexing my stomach only riles the nausea.

Rows of teeth slide right over my head. The fangs clamp down on my stomach and a scream rakes its way out of me. My armor crunches and cracks.

I stare up at the roof of the monster's mouth, locked in a humid cave. The teeth come down again. Bile sprays from the corners of my mouth. My armor dents into sharp points. I can't tell if it's blood or sweat that makes my stomach feel wet.

A musty stench irritates my eyes, but I keep them open, searching the roof, unsure what I'm looking for. Until I find it.

Soft muscle glistens and pulses.

Every demon has a brain. And every brain is in its head, above the roof of its mouth. I pray Istral is no different.

"Champion!" I hear the title called from outside. Istral roars and angles to the side, the fight below buying me time. When the god quiets, my ears ring horribly, sound becomes muffled.

Istral clamps down on me again. Immense pressure spreads across my waist, squeezing air from my lungs. A crack runs up the center of my cuirass. Another races across my shoulder.

Wheezing, I flip my axe over on my chest and hold it just under the blades. My forearms shake madly as I push it against the spongy texture above. Muscle gives way easily and blood gushes down like a waterfall. I shut my eyes tightly, but warm liquid still seeps beneath my eyelids.

Breathing becomes impossible. Bile still leaks between the gaps in my teeth.

Istral's screams rattle my head. The tendrils around me pull, trying to fling me from its mouth, but I hold onto the axe. I let my hands slip down the staff so I can push it further. It carves through more muscle until halfway submerged. Then I lift my torso and thrust with all my might. There is hardly any left, but I don't need much.

Blinding pain swells from my stomach and my lower back. I'm pinned in place by the demon's gouging teeth.

Life starts to flit away from me and I'm too tired to grasp it.

Istral's roars weaken into screeches as I drop to my back, letting go of my axe.

Everything goes dark.

Denya, Fallon, Velma, and I eat wildberries with stovetop bread. The sun is shining. Fresh grass grows between the bones and armor from the war. Everything is soft green. Fallon plants another kiss on my cheek. Denya smiles.

The pressure releases and I spiral back out into the world.

CHAPTER 28

Warm, stale air on my tongue. Everything is wet and sticky. What can I see? Gray stone. I lay on my side in a pool of demon blood.

Red stains my exposed undershirt. My cuirass is gone. And my helmet. In a strange twist of fate, it was the demon-teeth armor that saved me from Istral. Its teeth only left shallow puncture wounds.

Boots pound in my direction before I'm being hauled up. Demon blood drips to the ground around my feet. If it weren't for the arms holding me upright, I'd collapse among the slop. Guards and citizens surround me. Smiling. Their lips all move at once.

"You killed it!"

"Thank you, Champion."

Clanging in my ears and a slight blur over my eyes begin to fade. I'm thrust back into the war. Killing Istral didn't stop the carnage. Behind me, the demon god is nothing more than a massive lump. Torrents of red mist flow from its back. Chunks of my broken cuirass lay around its head.

"I need a chest plate," I say, feeling far too naked.

A guard nods. She only has to look for a few seconds before spotting a fallen armored body. Quickly, she unbuckles the two halves of the cuirass, as if the dead person wasn't just fighting at her side moments ago. She helps fasten it to my body. It's too tight and presses on my torn stomach.

The guards don't linger. We've already caught the attention of several demons. One is a child. It claws pathetically at a citizen with remnants of decorative paint from the parade still on their face. The guard hesitates before stabbing it through the heart.

I need a weapon. My hands yearn for the axe, as they always do, but there's no time to search. The fighting will never end. My life will never be a calm day in the rolling fields at the Edge. Every demon I've killed has meant nothing. The creatures are endless, multiplying rapidly. So, I will keep fighting as I'm meant to, until I can't anymore.

A long halberd catches my eyes and I lumber a few feet away to pick it up.

With one nearly useless arm wrapped around my stomach, I jab the light weapon into a demon. Another shoves past it and I swipe the halberd across its neck. More come. And come. I'm forced past Istral towards the palace where I join what seems to be the last line of defense. Tired guards and depleted citizens, shoulder-to-shoulder between the two halves of the fallen black gates.

This is a good place as any to die.

CHAPTER 29

Fallon can't see Oly anymore. One moment, she was lodged between Istral's fangs, her legs dangling out. His voice had gone hoarse from screaming her name and urging the procession of guards around him to help her. Then Istral toppled over and Oly was gone. Along with the red glow in the sibyl's staff.

He wouldn't believe the demon god's vessel was truly dead otherwise. Fallon still throws the hollow staff to the ground and slams his boot onto it – just in case. It cracks in half, small slivers shimmering in the blood and muck like glass. It was much stronger with the demon essence caught inside. He had jabbed it into the heads of several creatures who somehow got through his protection.

"Spear," Fallon yells to no one in particular. He only holds Oly's bowl now. A guard replaces the staff with a spear before turning back into a battle. "Towards the palace!"

It shocks Fallon how easily he overcomes the angst of using the spear. Though it takes several messy tries, he becomes very reflexive and accurate in shoving the spear's blade between the guards and right into a demon's heart.

The chaos had deterred Fallon from luring Istral out of the city like he planned – he'd barely made it across the courtyard circle – so it doesn't take him and his guards long to fight their way back. When he reaches Istral, Fallon searches in vain for

Oly, his eyes desperate for glimpses of demon teeth armor, the axe, anything to hint she survived. The battles around Istral are vicious and numerous. Too much is happening to pick out any detail. Heavy-hearted, he passes the demon god laid on its side, one eye an empty black pool, the other demolished. The face in its neck has disappeared.

They reach the black gates, where demons savagely push against guards and citizens with their backs to the place steps.

He sees her.

Helmetless. Wearing a guard's chest plate and half her Champion's armor. Demon blood cakes over her skin. She wraps one arm around her waist and the other works tirelessly to stab at the oncoming demons.

Fallon opens his mouth to direct his guards to bring her into their midst, when movement at the palace doors catches his attention.

From the lit entryway, Abner steps into the opening. They hold something in their hand. When their eyes find him, they raise the item high above their head and wave it. A scroll.

"They did it," Fallon proclaims. He looks back at Oly, then back to Abner. There isn't time. With a tight throat, he yells, "Push through!"

In unison, his procession rams into the mass of demons growing at the black gates. With surprise on their side, they hack through, leaving dismembered limbs and severed heads in their wake. For a split second, almost too quick to grasp, Fallon locks eyes with Oly. Her brows turn up in recognition, then she's lost in the savage mess. Fallon is thrust past the line of defense into the oddly open space at the base of the steps. It feels immediately wrong to be here. Like the mirage of an oasis in the desert. His procession joins the fight without his order and he lets them. More guards race down the steps from inside the palace to join the fight.

Abner calls to him with urgency, reminding Fallon every second is precious. Shaken from his stupor, he bounds up the steps.

The moment Fallon reaches Abner, they bring the scroll up between them. They unfurl it to reveal faded symbols surrounded by fresh ones scribbled hastily on the edges, the ink slightly smeared. They look to Fallon like drawings of little trees with branches twirling and bending in all directions.

"Do you recognize this?" Abner points to the insignia at the top.

Fallon shakes his head.

Abner's usual annoyance in him flashes across their face. "It's the seal of the Veins of Istral. Remember? From the parcel? The writing below is a chant to funnel demon essence from their world into ours. The essence pushes against the barrier until it makes a tear."

"The Rive," Fallon says.

"This is the chant that both opens and closes it."

Fatigue clutches onto Fallon's shoulders and climbs to press on his temples. "Do you really think we can use magic like the sibyl?"

Abner nods, but their tight lips give away strong doubt. "Let's find out. But we'll need more than our voices. We need a chorus."

The heirs look into the entryway and throne room beyond, still crowded with citizens. The ones able to see outside are paralyzed with fear.

Fallon shares Abner's doubt. These people, separated from their loved ones and unknowingly abandoned by the sibyl are Niawa's last hope. This morning, he was as devout as any of them. Blind in his faith to the sibyl and the rules of magic. Not even Abner could ever convince him that kind of power was inside him, that he could wield it. He's still not convinced.

Abner walks first into the entryway, and Fallon releases a hot, ragged breath before following. The citizens shuffle aside, making a tight lane for the heirs to pass through to the throne room.

Fallon feels the anger in their stares. He sinks into every wrong turn the day has taken, and how many times he was the one to choose that path.

Abner stops at the cusp of the throne room. "Right here. So we can be heard by all."

They both look at the clock above the doorway. Nineteen minutes left.

When Fallon looks back down, Abner is handing the scroll out to him. He shakes his head and takes a step back. Before reading the parcel, he would have taken it without hesitation. Before hearing Wilcon and the sibyl speak about Niawa's future as if the kingdom was a chessboard. Before interrupting the sibyl's spell. Before traveling to the Edge and meeting Oly.

"We need a true leader now. You've risked everything to liberate Niawa."

Abner tenses. "I can't. They need to be assured. Rallied."

"Who better to convince them? You opened my mind, after all."

Abner looks around anxiously.

The sovereigns push through the crowd then.

"Thank the heavens," their mother pulls her children into her chest, weeping profusely. Their father wraps his arms around them all.

Fallon holds onto his parents for one moment longer than he should, fearing this may be their last night together, before breaking the embrace.

"Abner has something important to do," he says.

"What do you mean?" Sovereign Gerves starts.

"Just listen."

Fallon clasps Abner's shoulder, then moves away with their parents, giving Abner a small space.

"Where is the sibyl?" a woman nearby shouts.

Other voices layer over hers.

"What was that giant demon?"

"Tell us what is happening!"

Abner stays silent for far too long, the minutes ticking away. Twelve left.

They look at Fallon. "I'm wasting time. You have to do this."

His head clouds with worry, but Fallon firms his expression. "We can spare ten seconds to count backwards."

The corners of Abner's lips twitch into a near smile. They close their eyes despite the surrounding anger. All the while, Fallon whispers the numbers loud enough for Abner to hear.

At 'one', Abner opens their eyes. They stand taller, eyes clearer.

They take a deep breath. "Quiet!" Abner shouts with a volume Fallon didn't know they were capable of.

Silence rolls in a wave through the throne room and entryway. Outside, the war rages on through the distant clash of metal and low moans.

"I have never been so scared in my life," Abner begins. "Demons in our homes, wearing the skin of our loved ones. Your leaders," they place a hand on their stomach, "squabbling while ignoring your pleas for answers. The truth is, we didn't have them. All we knew was that demons roamed our streets on a day meant for solace. We, regretfully, weren't prepared.

"But we have answers now." They hold up the scroll, letting it roll down to its full length. "This is the key to closing the Rive

– not for one day, but for good. And it will stop the parasite from spreading. To do this, I need your help, and your faith." Abner turns the side of the scroll with writing to face them. "I will recite the words, and you must repeat them."

The citizens burst into a frenzy, lobbing more questions at Abner. A man tries to grab at the scroll, but another holds him back, begging him to calm down.

"Please, listen to me!" Abner yells above the unrest.

"The sibyl's tower has fallen, *where is she?"*

The uproar worsens, more demanding the sorceress show herself. Others questioning why the Champion left.

Fallon's stomach plummets. Niawa hasn't known strife in so long. Its people have given their troubles to the sky, believing Yuli-en and the sibyl will take care of them. Now, their beliefs have been shattered, and they don't know where to place their trust.

"We'll do none of your magic unless you call the sibyl!" The man who tried to grab the scroll steps inches from Abner's face. Fallon's twin doesn't flinch, but they look to the clock.

Fallon looks as well. Eight minutes.

Abner tries again and again to take control, their attempts becoming more fruitless. When the sovereigns join in to suppress the voices, it only incites more furor, the last of Fallon's hope ceases to exist.

Shrieks explode from the entryway. Fallon twists around to citizens stampeding into the throne room. Those who aren't able to get in, scatter left and right towards the connecting halls.

Fallon hears the moans before the entryway is nearly cleared of people.

Demons come towards the throne room, streaming from outside.

Oly is among them. Her bare head hangs low, arms dangling, knees bent awkwardly. When she lifts her head, revealing one black eye, Fallon's heart stops.

She opens her mouth and releases a drawn-out moan.

Fallon takes a step towards her, unsure what he's prepared to do, when a guard collides with her. They grapple on the ground, Oly holding the blade of their sword from embedding into her chest.

Abner turns their back on the demons to face a glacier of citizens watching the Champion change before their eyes. "Listen to me," they shout. "Your friends and family fight for their lives with the guards. They need you to fight with them."

Fallon moves to stand between Abner and Oly. Even as a demon, the Champion is ruthless. She stalks towards him, leaving bloody footsteps painted from the guard she killed.

"After all the Champions have done for us, you'll let her die? Like *this*? The sibyl is not coming. Niawa stands alone. We are all we have. I know in my soul that's enough," Abner says.

Fallon glances over his shoulder. Expressions shift among the citizens. Realization dawning. He recognizes the change as his own rebirth. Scared witless, but unable to ignore the new thoughts burrowing into their heads.

He looks back to Oly, whose teeth bury into a woman's arm. Abner begins to recite words he's never heard before. Fallon repeats the first line. The language is thick on his tongue, with an elegance reminiscent of ancient days. But it's only his voice that mimics Abner's.

Abner recites the same line frantically and once again, only Fallon repeats. Then more voices join, ones he knows. The sovereigns shout the line at the top of their lungs. The throne room suddenly fills with the chant. Abner continues with the next line.

Fallon's recitation tapers off. Oly is feet away, flanked by more demons. She raises a clawed arm that thins so rapidly her armor plates slide off. Red rings float in both of her eyes.

She lunges past him at Abner. Fallon doesn't think. He drops the spear and the bowl and throws himself into her, sending them both barreling across the floor.

The chanting continues.

Fallon hears his parents shout his name as he pushes against Oly's chest, straining to keep her back on the floor.

His arms give out and an inconceivable pain explodes from his neck. Oly's fangs sink deep into his skin. Another demon latches onto his leg and he screams.

Fallon surrenders. Even if he could somehow wriggle away, he's now infected. He lets his arms flatten on the cold marble, his body burning from the inside out.

The citizens follow Abner's commanding voice. Line after line.

Everything goes dark.

CHAPTER 30

Hot, bitter liquid ignites small sparks along my tongue. Like licking a coin. All children try it at least once. I grin at the memory, causing the liquid to trail from my lips.

Another memory comes, of agony so searing as I plummeted into endless shadow. I'm propelled into opening my eyes, starving for light, scared of returning to that place.

Tall beams rise high above me, carved with florals and fruits, painted a soft white. It takes a moment to recognize the ceiling of the palace entryway. Once I do, the day returns swiftly. Guards at the palace doors fighting desperately to keep demons from entering. I fought with them as best I could. Until…Red rings at my right. Claws gouging into my neck.

It happened so fast. Dizziness. Confusion. Heat spreading through my body. Then I was plunged into darkness, as if I had died. Except I never left. I was stuck. Between nothing and nothing.

There's a heavy weight on me. It spasms. I arch my neck to see. Thick black curls brush against my cheek.

"Heir Fallon is over here!" someone shouts.

Guards surround me. My head is spinning, and the stomps of their boots are too loud.

"Look at the Champion's mouth, and the heir's neck…" A guard points down, horror evident even through their helmet.

I push through the fuzziness to grasp the dark curls and lift. Fallon's eyes are shut, lips covered in white spit, his skin lifeless and dull. Blood smears over his face. I follow the spatter of red to his neck where several puncture wounds ooze a steady flow of fresh blood.

The metallic taste in my mouth is suddenly so potent that bile surges up my throat.

"Move him." The guards reach down and pull at his arms. "Gently," I warn.

When they've slid him off me and laid him on his back, all the pain in my body returns like an avalanche. I groan as I roll up to sit.

"Fallon?" I whisper to his still form.

He doesn't respond, but I catch the slightest rise and fall of his chest. I pat at my waist, feeling for my belt. I pull out the tin of starmoss and pop off the lid. Stiff all over, I lean to slather the ointment over Fallon's neck wounds.

As it dries, I lay my cheek on the floor, my face across from his. The marble is cool against my skin, and I sigh from the small relief. At first, I think I imagine the twitch beneath his eyelids. Then they blink open.

"Oly?" he says weakly. His eyelids lower, and they don't open again.

I push myself up, ready to call for healers, but they already crash around us, leather bags flying open.

"There's starmoss on the wound," one healer says, inspecting Fallon's neck.

"Are there any others?" another asks.

"We'll need to take him to the medical wing to see."

"Is he dead?" I ask.

A healer feels the other side of Fallon's neck. "Heartbeat is slow, but still strong." He jumps to his feet to help two other healers bring a gurney closer. They carefully lift Fallon, then lay him on the cushioned top. Just as they start to wheel him away, Heir Abner bursts from the throne room. They come straight to Fallon, rubbing at their cheeks anxiously.

"Is he…?" they heave.

"No, Heir Abner. We're taking him to the medical wing, but he should be okay." The speaking healer jerks their head towards me. "The Champion's starmoss may have saved him."

I watch them take Fallon across a crowded entryway until he's gone. One healer stays behind. She crouches over her bag and takes out a metal canteen and a strip of linen, which she douses with water from the canteen before bringing it to my face.

I recoil, so she places the linen and canteen next to me. She returns to the bag to fish out a small mirror and holds it up.

Drying blood covers my mouth and colors my throat. Red streaks run down from my eyes, as if I cried bloody tears. The healer holds out the wet rag again, nervously, and this time I take it. It smells like mint and eucalyptus.

"I can take it from here," Heir Abner says. The healer nods and scurries away, leaving the items behind.

"Everyone who was infected by the demons has those tears," they say as I drag the rag around my lips first. "When the Rive closed, the demons that were still alive changed back into humans. Their teeth blunted, color came back into their skin. Those red rings dissolved."

I think for a moment. "It must be the demon's essence. It had nowhere to return to."

Heir Abner waits for me to wipe all the red from my face. My skin is raw and sensitive when I finish. I take a swig of the eucalyptus water, swish it around my teeth, and spit onto the floor until the taste of Fallon's blood is gone.

"It's really over," the heir seems to say to themself. Then they address me: "Can you stand?"

I nod, and Heir Abner helps me up, with effort, as my legs shake like tall grass in the wind.

I look around the nearly destroyed entryway. Heir Abner explains that the marble jutting out from the floor is from Istral chasing Fallon. Craters in the wall showed where the god slammed its body in its haste. People stream in and out of the palace's open doors, blood-soaked and tired. Guards collapse against the walls, heads tilted to the ceiling, their weapons beside them. Healers offer them water and food before running off to tend to someone else. Names are called over the noise, voices aching to hear someone yell back. Faces marked with demon essence look frantically around, tears doing their best to wash the streaks away.

"Fallon sacrificed himself to save our people. To save me," Heir Abner says. "He," they smirk, "tackled you."

"That was idiotic."

The heir looks at their hand. "Many of us were driven to points of madness we'll never be able to take back." Dried, human blood crusts over their palm. Brown stains splash across their gold jacket. They sigh. "But today is a fresh start."

I wrap my arms around myself. Yes, the day is new. The world is new. Though I truly believed I wouldn't be alive to experience it, here I stand.

"I was so sure we'd failed," Heir Abner says. "After the chant, nothing changed. Then the sounds of battle lessened, and we heard confusion coming from outside the palace. I've never felt so terrified, thinking I'd only see more carnage, or Istral risen again. I had started to accept our world would fray at the edges and violently unravel with each passing day. But I saw joy. And sadness. A guard had just sent his spear through the chest of a fellow guard, only for them to die human on their staff. It'll take Niawa generations to heal."

I have nothing to impart on them. No words of encouragement or hope for the years to come. It feels too easy. Simple. Just lay down my armor and never look towards the sky for demons again? I don't believe it.

"I'm going to visit my brother. You're welcome to come."

There's something I need to do first. "I'll find my way there."

They dip their chin. "Thank you, Champion." Then they go.

I start towards the doors, keeping my gaze lowered, worried I'll be stopped. But no one notices me. Everyone is adrift in their own shock and rejoicing. At the threshold of the doorway, against the wall like swept away dirt, I see soft green. There are light cracks around the bowl's surface, but it remains intact. I bring it with me outside.

The moon above is a pale saucer, surrounded by countless twinkling stars over faint verdant brushes. It must still be the early morning. Only a couple hours since midnight. Healers race past as I descend the steps, lanterns bobbing from their hands like light bugs.

I limp into the circle, carefully stepping between the prongs of the fallen black gate, past people sobbing in each other's arms, past red-teared citizens curling into themselves on the ground, trying to make sense of what happened. I understand. The place between nothing and nothing still haunts me. I move cautiously by, ensuring I'm not another jolt to their sensitive minds.

Across the circle, I spot mother being escorted towards the palace by guards. Velma is with her, scowling as mother rants about something I can't hear, hands flying wildly about. I'm glad to see they're alive. Despite my relief, I keep quiet. We'll speak eventually.

Bodies that won't return to humanity cover the ground around the Istral as if they're the cobbled street itself. I wander through them, searching, taking care not to step on any limbs. It proves difficult. Fingers crunch under my boots. I accidentally kick an armored torso. After a while, sadness begins to weigh me down.

My search takes me to the god's massive body. Its back faces me, covered in a strange dark shell. The closer I get, I see the shell is its tendrils woven over and over. Gold flashes in a small gap. I'm struck with a sudden burst of humming. The sibyl's veil. Below it, a still hand pokes out, gloved in green leather.

I set my bowl down and inch closer.

The hand flicks and I jolt. When it doesn't move again, I lean in.

A small ripple moves through the veil, like a breath. Sweat drips down my back as I slowly pry the tendrils away from her face. By the time I've uncovered the sibyl's entire head, the fluid coating the tendrils saturates my gloves. I pause before touching the veil. She's still a sibyl, so looking upon her face is an affront to Yuli-en. But so is demon worshipping. The thin metal bunches between my fingers like silk as I lift it.

Her brown skin is marred. Badly healed scars spread across her forehead, from cheek to ear, from the corner of her mouth to her jaw, the skin around them raised and dark. Beyond the scars, her face is plain, ordinary. I hover my fingers over a pale line across my own cheek in a nearly identical place to hers. She's just a woman like any other. I feel disappointed.

The sibyl's eyes wrench open. My heart leaps into my throat, but I don't jump back. Warm hazel eyes peer at me.

Her lips move, forming shapes, but I can't hear what she says. I bring my ear closer.

"Kill me."

I rear my head back, bewildered.

Her eyes flutter closed, then crank back open. "Kill. Me."

I should. For all the damage she's brought. Killing Denya. Maybe it's more fitting she goes slowly, trapped in her own failing.

Loyalty thrums in my sternum. I still marvel at this mighty being, whose mysterious power was the foundation of an entire kingdom. We were taught to worship her, give her our trust without question. Most of all, we were taught to believe we would be dead and god-forsaken without her.

I believed every word. I may have admired her above all. She created me.

"Please," the sibyl begs.

A question pricks at the back of my mind. It first appeared when I heard who the sibyl really is. Knowing the answer terrifies me. Would it be so terrible to live out the rest of my life in ignorance?

Yes, it would.

Leaning close again, I whisper into her ear, for fear the wind may carry my words away. "I'll do what you wish, if you answer this question. Was I destined to be the Champion?"

"No Champion was," she answers. "You were all chosen… at random."

I look over her face, hoping to see malice. Praying she only spoke that lie as revenge for stopping Istral. But there's no anger. Only a chasmal sadness. There can only be truth in such melancholy.

Numbness grows from my skull down to the tips of my fingers and toes. I am not the Champion. No one is. Just a girl chosen from a list. Even so, the last ten years were real. The demons were real, and I survived them.

For showing me what strength is when I couldn't fathom it, I'll give her one kindness.

The veil conceals her face as I slide my hands down. I wrap them around her throat. Tears warm my eyes as I feel her muscles tighten. Her windpipe closing. She gags, and I squeeze harder. Her head twitches. Once. Twice. Then no more.

I retrieve my bowl and walk away. Denya needs me now.

My search continues through the dead. Each one without green eyes and black, braided hair makes my footsteps feel heavier.

"Are you gone forever, Denya?" I ask the graveyard.

It listens, perhaps taking pity on me, and I spot a tangled mat of black hair beneath a pile of bodies. I lower to my knees and set my bowl aside before sliding the bodies off each other with sore arms. The last one is more demon than man, their sternum caved in entirely. I flip the creature over, freeing Denya's bloodless face. Her eyes are half open, a slit of white beneath translucent lids.

In a small, unencumbered space of ground next to her, I sit. My legs shake unagreeably, and I land hard on my backside.

"Heaven above," I whine, slumping over at my waist. The movement strains my shoulder, and I spring back upwards – which feels just as tender. I throw my head back, gulping in the stale air, waiting for the worst of the aches to subside. I'll be waiting an eternity.

Denya seems to watch me from beneath her eyelids as I look around until finding a small knife among the many discarded weapons. I arch over to fist a handful of her tabard, lifting as much of it from her chest as I can. With clumsy motions, I slice at the cloth until a large piece cuts clean. Then I fold it neatly and place it on the ground.

Her body will soon be cleared away and burned with the others. I won't let her be forgotten.

Though Heir Abner was sure the fighting has stopped, the humming won't. It radiates as though the dead demons around me will rise up at any moment. Feeling uneasy, I bring my knees to my chest.

Across the circle, people find survivors to heal them or collapse into their arms. The night hides their faces in shadow, but I still sense their reprieve.

I'm envious. Their hands are free of weapons. Guards remove their armor with surety. They believe this is finally over.

"How can they all be so certain?" I ask Denya.

My plates are heavy and dented. They press against my skin uncomfortably. But it still feels necessary. Even the small knife in my hands feels like an extension of me. I think about my cabin, and what it will be like to turn my back on the windows. Take a long, fully nude bath.

I want to know what it's like to feel safe.

Slowly, I uncurl my fingers from the blade and let it drop. Immediately, I want to pick it back up, but I fight the urge. Then I loosen the clasps of my ripped neck guard and allow it to slip down my back. Refreshing, cool air trickles over my skin. Next, I unbuckle the chest plates. One by one, I remove every piece of armor until the last plate hits the ground.

Another breeze sneaks beneath my undershirt, sending a chill up my spine. Closing my eyes, I listen for the wind until it's all I can hear.

In my head, long, dark logs stack around me, making up walls and a ceiling. A wooden bed appears in the corner. A large window displays a vast green field. In the distance, where there once stood a massive dark rock rippling with anger, there's only sky.

My arms loosen as I pick out details of the sea beyond the cliffs; the scent of briny air, pale jade foam washing up against the sand. I watch myself leave my cabin and walk across the field. My movements are light, unencumbered by battered muscles. When I reach the center of the Edge, I lie flat on my back.

At the Edge and in Niawa, I straighten out my legs and let my arms hang.

Taking a breath so deep, my lungs seem to fill for the first time.

CHAPTER 31

When Fallon stirs awake, it takes some time to recognize he's in a private room in the medical wing. The same one where he last saw Shavazme alive. Healers bustle in and out with trays of bloody rags and clean fabric, apologizing each time they bump into Abner, who stands by the bed. Fallon smiles, watching them struggle to both stay by his bedside and keep out of the way.

"Are we free?" Fallon pushes out through a tender throat.

Abner releases a very uncharacteristic yelp, which makes Fallon chuckle.

"Yes. The Rive is gone," they say.

Healers descend upon Fallon before he can react. One props up his torso with an extra pillow while another holds a large pair of razor-sharp scissors. Fallon shakes his head at the tool. He's had enough of blades. A wound in his neck opposes the movement, and he winces. The healer ignores him and snips at the bandages around his neck. A trickle of warm blood dribbles into his collar bone.

"Small tear in the stitches," she mumbles. She brings a needle and thread from a tray another healer holds. Fallon tries to fidget away.

"Stop moving around," Abner reprimands.

Fallon glares, but it doesn't stop the needle from pricking

his tender skin. As the healer works, poking and tightening, he digs his nails into his palms.

"That should do it. If you are still as a log." She places the needle and thread back on the tray.

As new hands smear salve over Fallon's neck and wrap fresh bandages, he stares out the window, counting bluebells on their tall stalks in the garden outside. Eight, with two new buds ready to bloom. He calms, knowing the sun will rise and they'll have a chance to grow.

The healers finish and step back. Fallon is inspected by the one who sewed his neck. She nods approvingly.

"Now, rest. Calming tea will be brought to you and Heir Abner shortly." She hurries the healers out the door, closing it behind her.

Abner drags a chair by the window to the bedside. Fallon lays his hand out, palm up, and his sibling wraps both of their hands around it.

"Are you alright?" the heirs ask in unison.

Abner speaks again first. "You saved my life."

Fallon wants to shake his head but remembers his bandages. "No, Abner, you saved mine. Everyone's. You got the citizens to fight for themselves despite everything."

Abner smirks. "I'm just happy my pronunciation of demon-worshipping spells was correct."

"Wilcon would have been seething watching you command the room like that."

Abner's expression darkens and they release Fallon's hand to tuck theirs between their knees.

The door opens and a healer enters. He sets down two steaming cups on saucers. Abner takes a saucer and sets it on their lap. The other is laid on Fallon's. When they're left alone again, Abner takes a sip. Their lips purse with disgust. "Valerian and lemon."

"Where is our revered advisor, anyway?" Fallon asks, eyeing the blood stains across Abner's clothing.

"I surmise that traitor gathered as many riches as he could and oozed out through a back entrance. If a demon didn't get him, rapid aging without the sibyl's magic will. Or," Abner's voice lowers along with their cup, "he died in his study."

Tea splashes across Fallon's legs when he jolts upwards. "Did you...?" he asks while dabbing at the hot blotches with his blanket.

Abner places their saucer and cup on the table. They squeeze their hands together so tightly in their lap their fingertips blush beneath the skin.

"I might have. The threat of death was the only way he'd tell me where the scroll was and transcribe the language." They speak plainly as if reading a report to the Heads. "I knew he'd heal eventually, but I used his pain to my advantage."

Fallon can't hide his alarm. Abner has always been a deep well, the bottom of which even Fallon has never known. But violence is not something he believed lived in those depths. He watches Abner fight their shame to appear unbothered – and lose.

The Day of Breath illuminated his depths just the same. He's always seen himself as shallow, transparent. An enigma to no one, least of all himself. But an insatiable hunger for glory and prestige lurked within, and Wilcon fed it like a starved beast in a cage. Fallon wouldn't have had the guts to do what Abner did.

"You did what you had to, nothing more or less," Fallon states.

Abner clearly isn't absolved of their guilt, but they nod sharply.

The heirs let silence fall naturally. Abner clearly thinking about Wilcon, and Fallon ruminating on everything he has driven himself to do since their presentations at the east rotunda. A day ago, he had attempted to steal the throne, and even more recent, deceived Abner with his plan to make a deal. In the sibyl's tower, Fallon had hoped he would get a chance to apologize. He clears his throat.

"I really believed I was doing the right thing. For Niawa. And, for myself. I thought… if I could save Niawa and secure our future… I could change my fate, too. But you were right about everything. Stealing the throne by going to the Edge. The preposterous belief I could make some kind of treaty with a corrupt sorceress. All of it."

"What was so wrong with your fate, Fallon?" Abner responds.

Fallon thinks. All that comes are echoes of Wilcon's praises. Now endlessly hollow when they were once the solid ground he stood on. Without the advisor's cold stare pressuring Fallon to heed his words, let them fester inside, the belief he *must* become sovereign to live an important life becomes an echo too. Faded, but not gone. A future in Abner's shadow still lingers like an early morning fog. "I just wanted to be more." He makes himself hold Abner's gaze. "Do you forgive me?"

"Without question," Abner says.

Fallon smiles. "Thank the god." He finally takes a sip of the tea. Steam rolls from the faintly green liquid, leaving small beads on his chin. He quickly sets it back down. "That's disgusting."

Abner smiles back. "Should we talk about tackling the Champion – a *demon* Champion, at that? Might be one of the bravest things I've ever seen."

Fallon's cheeks warm, and he tilts his head bashfully, the tenderness reminding him how that decision turned out. He pats at the bandages to make sure they haven't budged. "How is Oly? Do you know if she's coming?"

"She's fine. Well, as fine as she can be. Told me there was something she needed to do and then she'll visit later."

Fallon can hardly recall waking up in the entryway. But he remembers Oly's dark eyes looking into his, her face crinkled in worry, blood coating her mouth. The kingdom no longer has use for her title, but he still feels the familiar comfort of knowing she's somewhere in Niawa.

"Figures," Fallon sighs. "I meet a nice, lovely girl and she rips my neck open."

Abner chokes on their sudden laughter. It's a hideous laugh, unperturbed by formality or apprehension. It's immediately contagious.

"Some would call that divine will. Perhaps for the time you used Emperor Kalzhing's sacred tapestry to wipe her son's rouge off your lips," Abner says between laughing fits.

"No, no, it was for my nude midnight dip in the rainbow fish pond mother had waited three seasons to be built."

"Couldn't be. It's for convincing Shavazme to swallow a handful of bronze coins on his fifteenth birthday."

Fallon's cheeks grow sore from laughter, remembering Shavazme's green-tinted face after swallowing the last coin. He watches Abner act in a way he hasn't seen in many years. They laugh through their guilt about Wilcon. Through harboring suspicion of the sibyl on their own for years. Through watching their brother set his ambition above Niawa. It wasn't Abner's meddling that truly threatened Wilcon, but their selflessness. The citizens will grow stronger under Abner, self-reliant and curious. They'll question the greater good, undermining everything Wilcon and the sibyl designed.

Niawa needs a leader that will walk with them through the ashes of the past. It was never meant to be him.

As Abner's laughter fades, Fallon's cuts short. He crosses his arms over his stomach and sets his face into a stern expression.

"Congratulations."

His twin looks at him curiously. "For what?"

"For earning the honor of becoming Niawa's next sovereign." Abner goes rigid in their chair. The laughter already feels like a distant memory as apprehension takes hold of them. "I mean it. Your rule will mend many bridges that our family has destroyed in our ignorance. And I will proudly stand by your side."

Abner softens, and they lean forward to grab Fallon's hand again. "I can't express how glad I am to hear that. Because I'm going to need you. You'll be an exceptional advisor."

Fallon tries to smile, but every muscle in his face feels too heavy. He can only squeeze Abner's hand as his most coveted dream becomes their certain future.

CHAPTER 32

Everything is the same but the wood.

Emerald Pine is nothing like Edge Forest. The Emerald's trees are thinner and lighter, colored with a red tint. They have a strong citrus scent that lingers even after the wood is chopped, cut, trimmed, and built into a cabin.

Fallon doesn't believe me when I say I still feel the citrus tang in my nostrils, even two seasons after the new cabin was built. He says, "…trees just smell like trees…" with that child-like grin. But he doesn't know how the wood from Edge Forest bled shadows at night, filling the air with a strong musk. When I would snuff the lantern embers out, the walls, ceilings, and floors of my old cabin were nearly black. Now I still see the bright sheen of the Emerald's wood reflected off the lanterns hanging outside my window.

"Whatever she needs," Fallon had instructed the builders.

I told them where to form shelves for clothing and medical supplies, where my bed would go, my washing room, my stove, and to leave a large space for a table and one chair. One story, not two, as I was told I could have. I asked for a trap door in the floor with a brass-ring handle where I store a salt meat locker and other possessions; hooks in the wall to hang my armor on – only one suit remains rather than several plates; and a large window facing my bed so I can watch the world outside.

I do this now, swallowing a spoonful of pickled beets, steamed vegetables, cooked meat, and grains simmered in cream. The flavors are delicious and fresh. Another difference from the Edge. Fallon was horrified when he visited me after my first week here and discovered I was eating stale bread left in a gift basket at my door. He sends a nice man named Harlin from the palace kitchen every week with fresh groceries.

I can see when Harlin is coming through the window. The new cabin sits at the base of a small hill that obscures much of the city. Visitors emerge as a small black shape at the top of the hill, growing in size and detail down a kept dirt road until they reach the short stone wall surrounding the cabin.

I press my back harder against the headboard, sighing as the pressure massages my muscles. They still ache sometimes, like a long-forgotten thought that suddenly drifts to the forefront of my mind. Bruises have faded into my brown skin, tears and cuts formed into pale scars. I wore a sling while my shoulder healed. That barely pains at all anymore. I no longer wince when I reach for something. It took five seasons to stop limping.

Something tickles my neck and I nearly drop my breakfast. I tuck the curly lock of hair behind my ear, though it will inevitably pop out again. Another change I've had to grow accustomed to.

"Like a baby learning to walk," I groan to Denya.

Her tabard hangs on the wall next to the door, where the sibyl's tapestry hung in my old cabin. Fallon had it framed and set behind glass so it wouldn't unravel.

I voice how she would respond: "So much has happened Oly, be patient with yourself. You're returning to a life you've forgotten. Now, take your tablets."

The glass bottle with my tablets is on the table beside the bed. I shake one into my palm. It goes down easy, coating my throat with strong herbs and pastes.

Fallon should be coming over the hill any minute now. I glance at the empty space above my door, remembering his frustration when I refused a clock. I wake when I wake, and I don't like the constant ticking of the hands. Besides, the sun still tells me what I need to know.

"Come when the sun is at its highest, but not before the sky is fully bright," I explained when he last visited.

He gave me another one of those grins, then left for a gathering of the Heads. I was invited to attend, as I always am, but I have no interest in politics. My new duties as a captain overseeing training at the academy will begin soon, and I'll be much too occupied.

The humming buzzes over my skin at the thought of hundreds of eager eyes awaiting my instructions. I think I'm looking forward it. Since the Day of Breath ended, I've felt purposeless. My demon-teeth armor hangs like a decoration, my axe displayed beside it, shiny and unused.

"I miss it," I admit what burns inside me every day. "I don't know how to be here, sitting on this bed with the hill to stare at. Cooking meals and going into town for clothing and other frivolous things."

A light shape appears at the top of the hill. It moves down the slope until I can make out a horse-drawn carriage. The same one that took me through that horrendous parade. I glance at a gown draped over the back of the chair by the table. Judging by the distance of the carriage, I have a small bit of time until Fallon is at my door. He'll be bothered if I'm not ready.

I tilt my head back and shovel down the rest of the food. Coughing through the bits caught in my throat I hop up, then fling my shirt off and drop my pants to my ankles. My boots are thick and won't come out of the pant legs easily. After much hopping and yanking, my legs are freed. I slip the dress from the chair, then pause.

The window calls to me. Keeping my back to it still feels wrong. There's no demon portal to watch, no creatures shrieking across the field. Still, the hairs on my neck stand on end.

"Put on the gown."

The dress slips over my head easily. The color is magnificent, and identical to my bowl. Soft silk makes up the long sleeves, and the skirt hangs just above my ankles. Branches bearing fruit stitch across the cotton bodice.

Fallon is nearly halfway here. He hangs from the carriage window, waving like a lunatic. In the time it takes him to reach the short wall around my cabin, I've traded my daily boots for a pair of clean white ones with a slight heel that Abner gifted to me.

I run my hands up and down the gown, savoring the smooth material and twisting my feet this way and that to study the boots until a knock makes me jump. My eyes dart to my axe.

After collecting myself, I open the door. Fallon greets me in a long emerald jacket with sharp shoulders and black pants. He clasps his cheeks with his hands, gaze wandering from the white boots and up the dress to my blushing face.

"Champion. I am truly without words," he marvels.

"I'm not the Champion," I remind him. Though, the part of me that flinches at sounds and struggles to turn my back on the large window still clings to my old title, hoping he'll never stop saying it.

"I know, I know." He smirks.

Behind him, Velma calls out from the royal carriage's driver bench. "Hello, dear!" I give her a wave.

Fallon should now escort me to the carriage, but he lingers in the doorway, staring. I realize he waits for an invitation.

"We should be on our way." I inch over to take up more space.

Having others in the cabin is grating and uncomfortable. For ten years, the escorts would only drop off my items, then leave. After the new cabin was constructed, Fallon often stopped by to check on me. The humming wouldn't lower until he left. He soon caught on and began waiting in the small garden outside for little chats or before trips into town.

"I'd like to come in for a moment, if that's okay… We won't be long, I promise!" he adds when my nose wrinkles.

"Okay," I concede. I walk backwards until I'm standing in the middle of the small space.

Fallon follows me in. His shoulder turns slightly, as if he's going to shut the door, but decides not to. I relax a bit.

"May I?" he asks, holding his arms out.

A wide smile pushes my cheeks up. I step into his arms, and they wrap around me while I rest my head on his shoulder. His embrace is lighter than usual.

"I don't want to flatten your beautiful dress," he says.

I nod against his shoulder, taking a big inhale. I had confessed I liked the perfume he wore when he came to the Edge, and his face crumbled with sadness. He told me it was Shavazme's.

"What did you like about it? I thought it was retched," he asked.

"It smelled like the earth, but not like flowers. More like mud after a storm, stuck with decomposing leaves and rotted wood. But sweet," I replied.

He laughed. "I'll see what I can do."

For weeks after, he brought samples of perfumes and we would smell them together. The goal was to find a scent reminiscent of Shavazme's that wouldn't make Fallon gag. We're still working on it.

"Almost there. Needs a little more mud," I murmur.

Fallon pulls back so I can see his exasperation. "I really thought I had it this time. I can actually stand to wear this one."

I shrug. "Not quite there for me."

"The chemist will be glad to hear. He's made a small fortune from these experiments."

We're caught smiling at each other, what feels like so many unspoken words filling the cabin from wall to wall. We have many of these moments. I'm usually the first to break them. "You have something to say?"

"Uhm, yes." Fallon places his hands on his hips and rocks back and forth on his heels. It's strange to see him so visibly nervous. "See, I would have brought this up sooner, but I wanted to give you time to adjust."

He raises and lowers his arm, gesturing at my body. "You seem to be looking quite well." His arm whips back to his hip. "*Doing* quite well."

"I'm trying my best," I answer honestly.

Concern replaces his nervousness. "Can I do anything to help?"

"No, it'll take some time, is all. Being in this cabin, even with the different wood and scent, makes things easier. I'm not sure I would have stayed otherwise. Mother sporadically visiting doesn't help."

"She still hasn't let go of the idea to move the statue of you at the academy to the market center."

I frown. "Don't you dare."

"You've made your feelings on that very clear." His hands rise in defense. "Although, if an unsanctioned one goes up in the dead of night, don't come bursting into my quarters with your axe."

I shudder at the thought of browsing through the merchant's rows, my own eyes peering down at me.

"How is Abner? I've heard great things about their rule even in this short time."

Fallon lays a hand on his stomach. He does this when talking about Abner as the sovereign. As though he's holding something from spilling out.

"They're a sensational leader, as I knew they'd be. Their plans to keep our lands as healthy as possible without the sibyl's magic are brilliant. Every day, they meet with the Heads to discuss irrigation, dams, ways to purify water, extending our reach for trade – it's humbling to see their passion for guiding us into a new era. I couldn't have done it."

"That's not true," I say quickly. "I saw your bravery on the Day of Breath. Don't look down on that. Abner is grateful to have you as their advisor."

Fallon rubs their jaw thoughtfully. "Thank you for the reminder. I'm where I need to be. Where my skills are best served. I guess I've helped Abner host many visiting royals and ease tensions created by our family. They're always reminding me how important these relationships are to our success." He hums. "This is all very daunting, isn't it?"

He speaks of his role, but also my new life. It's been difficult to hide my anxiety from him.

"There are days when I prefer the threat of demons," I say.

"Now you must shake hands and fend off adoration while trying to shop. And pay taxes. It's clear which one is worse."

My eyes narrow. "You won't let me pay taxes." When Fallon smirks at me again, I roll them. "Always making jokes."

"Humor is how I got the sultan in the north to forget it was me who unchained his pet lizard dragon when I was ten and tried to ride it through the palace corridors, but it broke out of a window and escaped into town. Four hours it took to wrangle it." He makes a face like he just remembered something important. "Anyhow, we've gotten off track."

Through the open doorway, I catch Velma pulling her spear out of a compartment beside her. She begins to wipe the sharp tip with a rag, a content look on her face.

"After Abner and Princess Sonia of Kanan's wedding today, they plan to go on a trip to celebrate their union. The original idea was to go south to the Malikye Isles. But I convinced them to head west to the Pearl Desert – where the elephants live."

Excitement shoots through me, though my mind scolds the feeling back down. I assure myself this only means Abner is going to see elephants.

"How nice," I utter.

"Well, things are stable enough right now that Abner feels comfortable leaving General Erald and the Heads in charge for a few weeks while I accompany them. Though, watching my twin and Sonia stare lovingly into each other's eyes while I gag sounds appealing, I thought it would be better to bring a friend along. Perhaps a friend who likes elephants."

When it dawns on me what Fallon is saying, I gasp into my hands. This is not a reaction either of us expect, and Fallon's eyes widen while embarrassment raises my shoulders.

"I'll take that as a yes," he says.

My excitement is short-lived. I'll be so far from my cabin. I look to the suit of armor and axe on the wall. Though I haven't needed them, knowing they're close by, being able to run my fingers over the opaque ridges of my helmet has kept me sane. I'm not sure I'm ready.

"Can I bring my bowl?" I ask feebly.

"I assumed you would," Fallon replies. The bowl sits on the table behind me. He winks at it as though it's a friend.

The humming intensifies, but I speak over it. "Okay, yes, I'd like to try."

Fallon claps. "Wonderful. It's a bit much for a first courting, but I am known for my extravagancies."

"What–" I begin, the word *courting* ringing in my ears as they grow hot. Fallon loops his arm through mine and starts guiding me out the door.

The sky spreads clear and blue overhead, faint whisps of white clouds in the far distance. Halfway through the garden, Fallon pulls us off the path towards a corner with a small pond nestled between a bush of wildberries. Tall lemongrass reeds grow beside it. He snaps two yellow stalks free and hands one to me. My mouth waters in anticipation of the tartness. I'll save it for the ride into the city.

We leave the garden and walk towards the carriage. Velma smiles at me as she slides her weapon back into its compartment. She tightens the reins, and the horses flick their white and brown heads.

Fallon opens the carriage door. He holds out his hand, and I place mine in his. Before I can take a step up, he presses his lips lightly against my skin.

"Champion," he bows his head.

Butterflies take flight in my stomach as I climb into the carriage and take a seat.

Fallon sits beside me rather than across. He has yet to let go of my hand. The horses trot up the hill, pulling the carriage along as we stare out the window together.

At the crest, a Niawa reborn sprawls out across the land.

ACKNOWLEDGMENTS

This book would not be shit without my writer's group, so I'll thank them first. Thank you to Sonia, Maya, Vivian, Angie, Jeremy, and Devin for reading countless versions of this book and many other manuscripts. I grew a thick skin to criticism and learned to accept praise because of you all and I wouldn't have had the courage to go to New York where I met my agent without your support.

Thank you to my agent Amy for your belief in my book and your immense excitement that keeps me energized. Thank you to the Angry Robot team, and especially Des for helping get this book in the best shape and chatting with me about British teen movies and shows.

Finally, a very special thank you to an angel on earth: Chelsea. My best friend, my soulmate, the person who truly knows me the best. Magic is real.

Photo © Veronica Lescallette

Darby Cox is a self-described giant dork who loves to write about complex and flawed characters in fantasy and speculative settings. She has lived in over seven countries and states, including Alaska, Sicily, and Guam, and attributes her love of storytelling to all the cultures she has grown up around. When she isn't escaping into a book or writing, Darby is out in nature or working in independent music and nonprofits as a marketer. She currently lives in Philly with her dog Milez but dreams every day of moving to the coast of Ireland and opening up a coffee shop/bookstore.